"With a resourceful and cunning heroine, a compelling and nuanced romance, and a truly fascinating system of magic, *Ever the Hunted* ensnared me from the very first pages. Absolutely marvelous." —SARAH J. MAAS, #1 *NEW YORK TIMES* BEST-SELLING AUTHOR

"Britta's fierce tale of love lost and family found, combined with the lush setting and intriguing worldbuilding, make for an unforgettable read." —ALLY CONDIE, #1 *NEW YORK TIMES* BEST-SELLING AUTHOR OF THE MATCHED TRILOGY

"A fascinating world, intriguing characters, and an adventure with plenty of thrilling twists and turns will keep readers turning pages long into the night." —C. J. REDWINE, *NEW YORK TIMES* BEST-SELLING AUTHOR OF *THE SHADOW QUEEN*

"Erin Summerill showcases stellar worldbuilding in her debut novel, *Ever the Hunted*. She uses artful prose to tell a captivating story that is emotionally engaging and hard to put down. I can't wait to read the sequel!" —CHARLIE N. HOLMBERG, AUTHOR OF THE PAPER MAGICIAN SERIES

EVER THE FEARED · EVER THE WICKED

EVER *The* BRAVE

· ERIN SUMMERILL ·

HOUGHTON MIFFLIN HARCOURT
BOSTON NEW YORK

All rights reserved. For information about permission to reproduce
selections from this book, write to trade.permissions@hmhco.com or to
Permissions, Houghton Mifflin Harcourt Publishing Company,
3 Park Avenue, 19th Floor, New York, New York 10016.

hmhco.com

The text was set in ITC Legacy Serif Std.
Map illustration © 2017 by Jennifer Thermes
Design by Lisa Vega

Library of Congress Cataloging-in-Publication Data is available.

ISBN: 978-0-544-66446-3 hardcover
ISBN: 978-1-328-49795-6 paperback

Printed in the United States of America

DOC 10 9 8 7 6 5 4 3 2 1

4500735562

To Mark,
my husband, my heart, my true half—
You taught me that friendship
is the best start to any epic romance.

Kolontia
Isles of PLOVIA
SHAERDAN KINGDOM
DRY PLAINS
PADRIN
Jacinda's Well
Lockdell
Meridian
Alyze
FENNI
CELIZE
Meet-Up with Lord Conklin Girls
Small Town
Lord Conklin
Enat's Home
Rasimere Crossing
GREAT CANYON
AKARIA

CHAPTER

1

COHEN

A MINUTE SPENT IN A SHAERDANIAN TAVERN is a minute too long. I motion for Finn to fall behind as the creaky door slams closed, leaving us in the loud, crowded, lantern-lit room. We garner a few glances, but most turn back to their cups. Only a one-eyed cat perched atop an ale barrel keeps my younger brother and me in its sights. I don't mind the surly types who hang around these places, the wenches with their skirts tied up and colorful shifts showing, and the bawdy songman accompanied by a guitar-plucking fellow. All are rightly pissed—eyes blurry, smiles toothy, and voices gratingly bright. It's the smell that gets me every time. The rain in Shaerdan makes scents stronger. Makes taverns a pungent mix of moldy floor planks, vinegar, and fermented despair.

I hold my breath and slide a folded piece of parchment into the pocket on my belt. Finn watches me. He's seen me pull it out more than a few times in the last month. Probably noticed the action has increased the farther we've traveled from Malam.

He knows not to mention it.

Finn and I walk through the tavern and sit at the bar. After the long night and half day of riding, it's good to rest. If I dropped my forehead into my hands, I'd be asleep in a blink. Tempting if we weren't so close to the end of the hunt. And if we weren't still on Shaerdan soil, where being identified as a Malamian will get you gutted. A vision of a pale blond, freckled girl with a smile that has to be earned spurs me on, pierces me with longing.

A card game plays out on the nearest table, Shaerdanian silvers piled high enough to entice hungry onlookers. Pushing away the fatigue, I sit taller. Force my hands to relax, one resting over my left trouser pocket full of coins. My other hand is splayed on the bar. I fight to look the part in this tavern. Mistakes cannot happen today, not when we're so close to finding Lord Jamis's mistress.

The barkeep is a big man, no taller than me, but thicker through the gut like he's packing a barrel of ale. Busy talking to patrons, he gives no heed to Finn or me. Typical tavern kinsmen. They love their gossip as much as a Malamian market-goer.

I scowl in the man's direction and rap my knuckles on the tacky surface of the bar.

"Coming, coming," the barkeep grumbles. He moves in front of me, arms resting on the bar between us. His eyes, yellowed whites surrounding black irises, take in my little brother and me. "What'll ya have?"

This town, Rasimere Crossing, in the remote southern plains of Shaerdan, isn't one I've been to before. Since both countries backed down from the war, tension is mountain high. Harder to navigate too. Hardly a contact in Shaerdan will speak to me without drawing a sword. Yesterday, a barkeep up north confirmed that Lord Jamis's mistress, Phelia, was only a half day ahead of us and headed here. Within days after Jamis's arrest, the high lord had squawked about the Spiriter's identity. Course, it took a bit of Omar's torture to get it out of him.

It's not uncommon for noblemen at court to have mistresses. The women keep to themselves. For this reason, I doubt anyone would've thought her a threat. Especially since association with a high nobleman comes with some protection. Still, it's not a mistake that I, or the few men who know the harm the Spiriter inflicted, will make again.

As soon as she was identified, King Aodren sent me after her. I've followed Phelia's trail across Malam and into the dangers of Shaerdan. And now, finally, Siron's speed has bought us enough time to cross paths.

The bloody hunt's had me noosed for a month. That's a month longer than I've wanted to be gone from Brentyn and Britta. And damn if I haven't felt off the entire time we've been apart. Like distance has set me adrift.

Today the hunt ends.

Most barkeeps won't suffer a man who'll fill a chair and not pay to fill a cup or four. Even so, I've no time for primer drinks. "We're looking for our mother, who came south to find work." In a Shaerdanian lilt, I go on with the fib, explaining that we're soldiers returning from the war—or almost war since it ended a little over a month ago, before it officially began. "Light brown hair, blue eyes, about this tall. Goes by the name Phelia." I hold my hand up, providing the description that the castle attendants gave me. "Seen anyone like that?"

The man pushes his tongue into the side of his cheek and then slides it over half-blackened teeth. "Aye. Perhaps."

"I'm all ears."

"Yeah. Might've seen someone matching that description earlier."

"How long ago?" Finn cuts in. I shoot him a look. His Shaerdanian accent wouldn't fool a deaf goat. Told him as much in the last town.

The barkeep doesn't seem to notice. He plunks a couple mugs on the counter. "Before we get too chatty, let me get you fellas a drink."

It's a fight to keep the easy smile on my face, knowing he likely holds information about Phelia. My hand shifts to my belt, to cover the parchment hidden in the leather. The motion usually centers me.

"Or, if you're aiming to take off sooner . . ." The man taps a glass on the counter. "You can pay for a drink and leave with some answers."

Right. Should've thrown money at him in the first place. I withdraw some coins, dropping them to plink on the wood. "Good enough?"

"Cohen." Finn's sharp whisper snags my attention. He reaches for the coins.

The man's fist slams Finn's hand flat against the bar.

My brother yelps.

Confused, I shove my chair back and lean into the barkeep's face. "Get your hand off my brother."

The music stops. Every eye in the tavern cuts to us. A few men rise to their feet.

"No Shaerdanian would pay with Malam coins," the barkeep says.

My jaw ticks, insides seizing like Siron's kicked me in the gut.

Bloody seeds.

"You think I'm one of those scrants?" I spit, leaning heavily into a Shaerdanian accent that sounds loud but flat in the silent room.

Finn's eyes volley around the tavern and back to his trapped hand. The kid hides his panic as well as a tabby cat in a wolf den.

"Your brother looks like he's about to toss his last meal. Doesn't seem soldierly to me." He grips Finn's fingers, ripping away my brother's hand to pick up the damning coins.

Three prayers Finn doesn't open his mouth.

"Must've forgot those were in my pocket." I lean back in my chair. Shrug. "Needed some Malamian silvers at the border. Nothing to spoil a man's drink over."

Boots scratch the plank floor. Men step closer.

The barkeep cocks his head. "A fortnight back, two teenage girls went missing. Upset a lot of kinsmen 'round here. A town over, a girl was taken just a week ago. Her pa saw the men who did it. Tried to fight them and lost his life. Poor man's wife caught sight of the raiders as they were shoving her girl in a carriage. Heard 'em speak. Said they sounded Malamian. Now, why would a few ball-less scrants from Malam want our girls? Maybe they're itching to rekindle the war they almost started. What do you know of that, traveler?"

"No more than tavern hearsay." During my travels I've caught a few stories similar to this man's. Daughters taken at night. Some snatched during the day. No women, just girls. It's enough to raise concerns, but that's something to focus on after I've got Phelia manacled.

"Now, I can see you're a smart man," I tell the barkeep.

"You don't really think my brother and me have something to do with that. Coins don't mean anything. Collector's items."

"Your brother's awfully silent."

"He's shy. You scare the piss out of him."

A shadow shifts over my left shoulder. A giant of a man glares down at us. "Yeah, speak, boy."

"Leave him out of this." My unspoken warning is clear.

Another person moves behind Finn, blocking the path to the door. "Maybe we've caught us two of their spies. Maybe we pry loose answers about where they been hiding our girls." His bush of a beard barely moves when he talks, the comment sliding from the slits of his lips like snakes from under a briar. He must not really think we're the kidnappers, or he'd have gutted us already. Still, I eye his hand as it moves to the dagger tucked into his belt. "Explain yourself, boy."

In Finn's fourteen years, I figure I've seen every one of my brother's expressions. The wide tooth-and-gum smile he flashes when he catches a river trout. How tight-knit his brows get when he's frustrated or angry. The somber set of his eyes before we part for months on end. None of those expressions match the look he's giving me now. Panic and fear and something more. Something like disappointment.

I put a hand on Finn's shoulder, squeezing. Reassuring. "He's a boy. One who needs to get back to tending fields. Not sit around in taverns. Time to go, Finn."

"You aren't leaving so soon" comes from the Goliath behind me.

"It's the truth." Finn misses the accent target by a league.

"He's from Malam!" the barkeep yells.

Bloody seeds!

Someone reaches for Finn, but my brother skitters out of his seat. I slam an elbow into the man behind me before he can grab Finn. "Get out of here," I rasp.

My brother jerks away, maneuvering for the door before more kinsmen come at me. Four to one aren't bad odds, considering the barkeep is blocked by the counter.

The bearded man charges. I jump back, grab my stool, and shove it into his gut. Angling for the door, I slam a shoulder against another fellow. Fend off a punch. Take a fist square to the chin. *Bludger.*

I block a hit, bob out of reach from someone coming at my side, and narrowly avoid a crashing stool. Cheers erupt over the fight. A few voices shout to end it. Or end me. The tavern is chaos.

I manage to push someone onto the playing table. Cards scatter. Money falls to the floor. The diversion leaves one mountain of a man between the exit and me. He's easily a half-head taller and a half-body bigger. The zing of his drawn sword has me cursing.

The man swings. I grasp a stool, thrusting it between us to catch his blade before it takes off my limb. My arms rattle from wrists to elbows. I use all my strength to twist the stool and shove, a move that sends the man off-balance and gives me the opening I need to flee the tavern.

Finn's across the street, headed for an alley. I scramble after him, my breath running hard. The tavern thugs chase us around town, but they're drunk and we're sober. We wind through shops and hide in shadows until we've lost any followers.

On the northern outskirts of Rasimere Crossing, an old barn sits unused. We settle against the wall that faces the forest and catch our breath.

Sweat slides down Finn's temples. "Cannot believe that."

"I nearly got you killed." I'm so angry, it comes out choppy. I promised Ma and myself I'd keep him safe. Piss of a job I've done.

"Nah, you made me leave before it got to the good part."

I rub my thumb over the scar that starts beneath my cheekbone and hides in my short beard. "The good part?"

"I didn't get any punches in, but still . . ."

"Shouldn't have been in a situation for you to throw punches."

"My first tavern fight," he says, awed.

"Don't be a fool."

He grins, teeth and gums shining under the sun.

Footsteps clap against the ground around the corner. I grab my dagger as a girl holding a sword steps into sight. There's something familiar about her raven hair and tan face. Irritated that she was able to sneak up on us, I gesture with the point of my blade. "Stop there and state your business."

Her lips twitch. "Nice to see you too, Cohen."

My frown sets. I rack my brain. Who's this girl?

She lets out a short, squeaky laugh that sounds like it's being pressed through a windbag. "You don't remember who I am? We met once . . ." She trails off, as if hoping I'll pick up the scent. "In Celize."

"I meet a lot of people."

Her grin fades. "At Enat's home."

A memory surfaces of a log home outside of Celize. My scowl shifts into surprise. "The Archtraitor's daughter. Lirra, right?"

Her father is infamous for openly opposing the Purge Proclamation—a decree that eliminated most Channelers in Malam—and defecting to Shaerdan after his wife and small child were killed because of his outspoken defiance.

Lirra cinches up straighter than an arrow. "Don't call him the Archtraitor. Around here, he's just Millner Barrett."

"No offense intended."

She eyeballs my dagger. "Lower your blade, hunter. I know where you can find the woman you're hunting."

CHAPTER 2

BRITTA

B RITTAAAA!" GILLIAN DARTS AWAY FROM THE window, her midnight-black brows arcing up toward her perfectly combed hairline. Her small hands snake around my arm without care for the dagger that I'm sharpening, and she yanks me toward the window. "Riders are coming this way. They're carrying the royal flag."

I pry her fingers off, pushing down the anxiety that her comment raises. In the month since she was assigned as my nurse by King Aodren, to live in my home and care for me, she's never gleaned that I don't share her excitement for court visitors. "Careful. I could've gutted you."

She lets out a huffy laugh. "Hardly. Or should I say, it wouldn't happen by accident."

A snort bursts from me. For a royal handmaid, raised to be refined and proper in all matters, Gillian has some sass beneath her sophistication.

"Your dagger is plenty sharp. Put it away and go make yourself presentable. What if the king is with them?" She wrinkles her nose at my old trousers—Papa's old trousers—that hang on my hips beneath a faded beige tunic that once was a rich brown.

My blade zings over the whetstone, and I give her an *I don't care* look. But I do. I wish he'd stop coming to visit and drawing attention to me. Every time he's around, I become prey to town gossip. It takes only one person to accuse me of being a Channeler.

"You are . . . argh . . . belligerent." She throws her hands in the air. Then, regaining herself, her fingers float over her hair, moving an invisible strand back into place, even though every piece is tugged and taut into stiff exactness. She's mastered the raven-haired helmet. The girl is a couple of years older than Cohen, but damn if she doesn't act like a stuffy old woman sometimes.

I slump into the wooden chair, feigning disinterest. "If someone's trespassing on my land, they can take me as I am." It's all I can do to ignore the way the approaching visitor pulls at my insides, making me feel like a bear woken early from hibernation, cranky and drawn to exit my cave. I dig my fingers into the wood.

Seeds and stars, why won't he leave me alone?

"By the gods, Britta. I cannot fathom why anyone would

want to pay you a visit. Please, just this once, can you show a shred of decorum?" Her worried gaze shifts from me to the window, where the afternoon sun is starting to sag in the horizon.

In the last month, Gillian and I have spent nearly every waking moment together, and we've learned each other well. The only time we're apart is while I'm hunting, since Gillian refuses to hunt. *Ladies do not hunt,* she said last week. I assured her ladies do, in fact, hunt. My weekly fowl catches were proof. Gillian rolled her eyes. Said she meant noble ladies of the court. Obviously, coifed noblewomen didn't catch their own food.

My father was noble, but I'm half Shaerdanian — about as good as garbage in Malam. So, seeing as I have as much claim to nobility as Gillian's fat heifer that's been hogging my stable, what "ladies" do has no bearing on me. Her response to this explanation was a long-suffering sigh.

A small vibration unsettles the floor beneath my boots in time to the *clip-clop* of horses growing louder.

Gillian's tawny skin pales to a shade closer to mine. Her wide, ebony eyes dart from the door to the window to me. "What if it's the king? Will you greet him like that?"

Knowing it *is* the king makes me feel guilty. It makes me think I should take her advice. It also makes me resist moving from my chair, clench my dagger harder, and curse his name under my breath. I wish I didn't know it was him at all. Or that he'd realize he's putting me at risk every time he comes around. Mostly, I wish I wasn't keeping this secret from everyone.

Especially Cohen.

Over the last month, King Aodren has visited three times. Each time filled me with certainty that the strange bond that shackles us together—drawing me toward him when he's near—was forged when I saved his life. The link I once shared with Cohen, which ended when the king's connection formed, was different. It was one-sided. And because it was so subtle, I'm certain Cohen wasn't aware of it. We never spoke of it since I didn't understand it. But there's no ignoring the king's connection. It's so much stronger.

Which is why his persistence in visiting is worrisome. Each time King Aodren comes around, I fear someone will notice the way we're tuned into each other and call me out as a Channeler. Aodren may be the king, but I doubt he'd stop an entire mob of Channeler haters if they set their sights on me.

Three distinct raps rattle the cottage door.

"Sit up. Look sharp." Gillian's plea is a hurried whisper. She goes to answer.

Her hands shake as if the king himself might be on the threshold. Ridiculous. That man's hand is so weighted in jewels, servants have to knock for him.

The rusty hinges on the door cry when it opens, letting in the late fall chill. The king's steward stands on the threshold. "A delivery for Miss Flannery."

Gillian peeps past the steward. Her gaze sinks to the floor, followed by the rest of her body, skirts piling on wood planks in a deep curtsy. "Y-Your Highness."

The steward retreats and is replaced by a lean servant in a royal gray-and-maroon wool coat. He carries a box past me into the cottage's bedroom. Someone murmurs from outside, and Gillian rises and follows the servant.

I consider staying in my seat, except the pull toward the king has grown to an itch that has me white-knuckling the chair. The link to Cohen never felt so aggravatingly strong.

With a growl, I stalk to the door.

The steward stands beside a gray horse, the royal flag propped in a leather holder on the saddle. Next to him, the king sits on a wheat-colored steed.

Unlike the other three times he has come to my cottage, flanked by a half-dozen royal guards, he's with only two men today. I figure the added protection is no longer needed now that he isn't the slender, sickly man I saved a month ago. His shoulders and legs look broader, sturdier, stronger. His fair skin has a touch of golden coloring, which must've been earned under the sun. It makes the silvery scar on his neck, a gift from my blade, stand out even more.

Gillian reappears at my side. Her nails dig into my arm. She drops into another curtsy, dragging me down alongside her. "Your presence honors us greatly, Your Highness. Britta is so pleased you've chosen to visit her humble cottage." Her face is so low that she speaks to the steppingstones. Her words run cold through my veins, my Spiriter senses picking out the lie.

The truth—for example, if I actually *had* been honored by the bludger's presence—would've warmed me.

"You may stand." King Aodren's voice grates, a hint of a rough edge beneath fine breeding. "I'm here to speak to Britta privately."

I rise, bristling at the way his voice softened around my name. When will he leave me alone?

His golden hair, combed smooth despite the two leagues he rode from the castle to my land, rivals Gillian's helmet head. No dirt specks his polished sable boots. When I found him in his chamber, unconscious and pulse weak from being controlled by a Spiriter, he seemed more human, more inviting, than now. Sort of wish I was facing that man again. I clench my fists, irked by every stitch of his noble perfection as he dismounts and leaves his men's side. And irked even more by the urge to reach out and touch his hair. Just to see if it really is as smooth as it looks.

The king strides to my door and brushes past me. Gillian shoots me a saucer-eyed plea as she exits the cottage, and I harrumph under my breath, digging my toe into the moss that's sprouted through the cracks in the cottage's stone floor. Even the way he enters my home, authority punctuating each step, irritates.

"Welcome," I mutter, slamming the door on the king's men and Gillian.

He says nothing, only scans the main room of my cottage. Wooden chairs, threadbare curtains, mats made of rushes by the fireplace and table—not much to view. His gaze moves on, pausing at the blades and whetstone on my table before stopping at the open bedroom door. Papa's old, ratty quilt is covered with dresses. *Dresses?*

Five fine silk dresses.

Unsuitable for hunting, tracking, or normal life.

My eyebrows squish together. Last time he brought a fancy cloak and a gold necklace. He's lost his seeds. When would I use any of these things?

"A gift," he says, as if reading my mind. "For the Royal Winter Feast Ball."

I went to the Winter Feast celebration when I was fifteen, sixteen, and seventeen on Papa's request. Papa said we had an obligation to attend once I was of age. So, he paraded me around the lamp-lit streets of Brentyn, where boughs of holly and sage rested on tables and pigs sizzled over fires. Townspeople chatted in groups and danced in the square. Luckily, most ignored me. The few who didn't dampened the merriment of the evening with their insults that were forgotten until now.

No way do I want to go again, let alone to the pompous Winter Feast Ball at the castle itself.

King Aodren's jade eyes jump to mine, and I realize I spoke my protest aloud.

"I . . . uh, pardon me." I rub my clammy palms on my trousers. This man could order my execution if he wanted— unlikely, but still. "Five dresses are, um, excessive."

"To give you a choice."

I frown.

"At the Royal Winter Feast Ball. Where you'll be presented to the court as nobility."

Warmth oozes from my belly to my toes — confirming that he speaks the truth. I clutch my queasy stomach. Nobility? He's definitely lost his mind.

Does he even realize how that would look?

Ever since my father's death, all I've wanted is to live my simple life outside the public eye in Papa's cottage with Cohen.

But Cohen is gone. He made no offer of marriage before he left. A painfully brief kiss and an *I'll catch her* was all I got. Now I'm stuck with a king who won't leave me alone and my Spiriter ability burning like wildfire through me, driving me mad with want to use it.

I hate being near the king, feeling the connection pull me to him with invisible claws. First, because I don't know how to break it. And second, because Cohen doesn't know about my bond with the king. Knowing nothing much gets past Cohen and that I'll have to explain the strange link douses me with anxiety.

I cross the room to the table, putting myself in arm's reach of my dagger. Right now, I need its stability. "Your gesture is . . ." — I fumble for the right words — ". . . unnecessary. I'm not noble, and I've no lofty goals. The Winter Feast Ball isn't for me."

"Your father was a noble. You've inherited his land. You deserve the privileges that come along with it."

My laugh sounds salted and dry. "If by 'privilege,' you mean the acceptance of the nobility, no thank you."

"I was told people in town have made you feel unwelcome." He sounds uncertain. "And I . . . well, I've seen some things. After the declaration, you would be treated differently."

"No." I stand stiff, not sure if I'm more annoyed by his admission that he's seen others' cruelty toward me, or by his preposterous idea that would only serve to draw more of their ire. More attention that could get me killed.

His face slackens for a beat before hardening. He's not used to people telling him no. I don't know what else to say to make him understand that I've no interest in mingling with the flocked and feathered of Malam, so I remain quiet.

"You saved my life. And in return . . ." His voice is subdued, cadence measured. "I insist on improving yours. Also, the gowns are a gift, not just a token of my gratitude, but to wish you a merry birthday."

How did he know? I pluck my dagger off the table and flex my fingers around the handle.

"I know I'm a day late, but I chose not to come yesterday so I wouldn't disturb your celebration with Miss Tierney."

I will strangle Gillian. We made sweet cakes and rode into the woods to ring in my eighteenth birthday. When I stayed out, she must've sent a missive to the castle. I wish I could throw the dresses and the king out the door. The only thing I want is for Cohen to return home. That would be a much better birthday gift.

King Aodren turns away and enters my bedroom, where he touches a green gown. It's almost the exact shade of the lake's reflection of the pines.

"Whichever one catches your fancy, wear it to the ball two weeks from today." A command, not a question.

A scowl is all I can muster. "I don't know the first thing about attending a ball."

Can he not see my favorite accessory is a dagger? I'd rather tromp naked through a forest full of bears and mountain cats than get gussied up for a royal ball.

"Surely, you could spare a night." His lips curl into a subtle, almost imploring smile. As if he's giving me a choice.

Something hard and heavy forms in the pit of my stomach.

"If you're worried about the dancing, I could teach you."

"I'm worried about my life." I glare at him.

"I would never let any harm come to you."

Right. I drop my dagger on the table with a clunk, cut to the door, and yank it open.

"You'll come, though?" He says it like a question, but it isn't. Not when he's who he is and I'm who I am. I glance back at my dagger on the table and consider throwing it right through the heart of the dresses. He might understand that message better.

"Fine," I say, with teeth gritted, leaving a sour taste on my tongue and a dull ache behind my eyes.

He gives a tight nod and leaves.

My fingernails chew my palms as the king and his men ride away into the Ever Woods.

Gillian sweeps in, face beaming. I want to shake her shoulders and erase that smile. I slam the door.

"You look murderous." Gillian spins around, her skirts swishing against the stone.

"I am."

A blink. "You don't like the dresses?"

"Really? You've been living with me for a month."

"Right. So they're not your usual choice, but there's a variety. Something different from brown trousers."

"They're for the Royal Winter Feast Ball. He wants to sprinkle royal dust on me and make me noble."

Gillian presses her hands to her cheeks and pretends to swoon.

"Stop it," I snap.

She flounces into the bedroom and lifts a rose dress from the bed. That grin. *Seeds.* She's as mad as the king.

The pull to the king, still taut in my chest, halves my attention from her squealing prattle. I press my palm to my sternum. I'd give anything to be free of him. To be able to live in peace on Papa's land. But I don't know how to break the bond.

If Enat were still alive — the thought flattens me — *she'd know what to do.* She'd tell me how to free myself from King Aodren.

He's been gone for five minutes, and I can still pick out his location in the Ever Woods.

I pound my fist on the door. I have to figure out a way to rid myself of the bond. *I have to.*

Gillian jerks to a stop. "It's not the end of the world."

I start to respond, but an answering rush of something strange and shuddery slips under the surface of my skin. I lurch, cradling my suddenly clammy hand, eyeing Gillian, then the door with growing alarm. Unease spreads from the top of my head to my heels, a drop of poison fanning through a jar of ale.

I've felt this way before.

"What is it?" Gillian's fists crinkle a rose-colored gown.

Breath suddenly short, I yank the door open and stare deep into the Evers. The breeze's icy fingers caress my face. There's nothing to see, but something is very wrong.

"The king."

CHAPTER

3

COHEN

"GO ON, TELL US," FINN BLURTS.

I shoot Finn a look. He tucks his lips in and leans back against the barn.

Scratching my scar, I give the girl a once-over. She's Britta's age, give or take a year. Though she's a tad shorter than Britt, her shoulders square in the same confident, seasoned way. She's been trained to fight. Her grip on the sword's hilt, loose but sure, is a sign she knows how to wield the weapon. This girl makes the ache of missing my girl swell.

Finn whispers something awestruck about this girl being the Archtraitor's daughter. I ignore him and turn back to Lirra. "How can we trust you?"

Her smile creeps up. "You got any other options?" Her Shaerdanian accent makes the words sound like a song.

"We could leave."

"And go where? Word's probably spread to the coast about you two. Any Shaerdanian who figures out where you're from will bludgeon you before they talk to you."

"I've friends."

"Not here." She sheathes her sword.

I crack my knuckles against my dagger. That's the truth.

"What do you propose? You give me information. Then what?"

Finn pops up at my side before she answers. "I'm Cohen's brother." He thrusts out his hand.

"Finn," I warn.

After their handshake, he gives me a sheepish smile. He deserves a chewing out for letting his guard down so easily. I bite my tongue for now. It'll come after we ditch her.

"Last I saw you was in Celize. What are you doing this far south?" I ask.

Her gaze slants down and to the left. "Looking for you."

I don't need to have Britta's Spiriter ability to know she's hiding something. "That so?"

She shrugs.

There's no time for this. I'm bloody tired of games. If I have to knock on every door in Rasimere Crossing and fight every kinsman who thinks I'm a spy or a kidnapper, I'll do it. "Give your pa my regards. Let's go, Finn." I walk along the shadowed edge of the barn, eyeing the patch of forest for Siron.

"Where are you going?" the Archtraitor's daughter calls after me.

Finn rushes to my side, throwing a glance over his shoulder, confusion wrinkling his forehead. "Cohen, what if she can help?"

"Then she'd be helping. Not pestering."

Lirra scrambles around us and thrusts out her hand to touch the barn slats, barricading me.

"I'm looking for someone, as well. Two weeks ago, my friend Orli was taken. I've been trying to figure out where."

"By whom?"

"Obviously, I don't know. Thus, our conversation." Her hand flicks between us.

This girl's got the prickles of a cactus.

"Perhaps she left. Wanted to go somewhere else."

"Girls just don't go missing."

"Seems like they do lately."

Her nose scrunches up. "Are you always this difficult? I know you've heard the rumors." When my brows shoot up, she smirks. "I could teach you a thing or two about stealth."

Finn laughs, and I glare at him before turning the same look on Lirra.

"Three girls in this county alone have been taken. Word is, a nobleman from Malam is to blame. Even if the rumor's twisted a little, every man and woman in Shaerdan is going to be looking out for Malamians."

She's got a point.

Lirra crosses her arms and drops her shoulder against the wall. Some of the sun-crusted green paint chips off the barn onto her orange dress. "Thing is, I want to find my friend, and if your king was wise, he'd want to find out if the rumors have merit. Wouldn't take much more to fan the embers of the almost war. Far as I can see, things between Shaerdan and Malam are still smoking."

"The king doesn't put much weight on rumors," I tell her. Mostly I say it because I don't want to consider spending any more time away from Brentyn, even though there's no forgetting that I serve the crown. I've sworn an oath to uphold the king's command and the good of Malam.

But a rumor isn't just cause to launch another manhunt. The thing with rumors is they run as straight and true as creeping weeds.

"Anything else?" I ask.

Lirra dusts the barn scrapings off her shoulder. "Aye. Orli didn't return from doing her barn chores. By the evening, her family started to worry. She just disappeared."

"That's if someone actually took Orli." I cross my arms.

"Your skepticism is obnoxious." She stares hard at the barn before turning back to me.

"Your pa in town?"

That small flicker of a frown quirks her lips before it's replaced by a shrug. "Pa's not much of a traveler."

Lirra's avoidance kicks my irritation up three notches.

"Neither's our ma," Finn adds, which is true. But not needed right now.

"You've come all this way from Celize on your own." I slap Finn's hand away from picking at the peeling paint. He gives me a wounded look. "Why do you need my help now?"

"I suspect Orli's been taken to Malam. It's illegal for me to cross the border. If I make it past your border guards, I would then have to worry about someone in Malam tagging me as a Shaerdanian. If that happens, I might as well sign my death certificate. So I propose a trade." She scoots back and flicks a bug off her skirt fold. "I'll tell you where Phelia is, then you keep me safe in Malam until we've found Orli."

"That all?" She wants a bodyguard and tracker for the price of a location? Horse dung.

She nods.

I laugh and her eyes narrow.

"I'm taking Phelia to Malam as soon as I catch her. Got no time to babysit a Shaerdanian girl."

"If you don't find Phelia soon, she'll be on the move again. You'll be back to the chase. You've been through enough towns over the last few weeks to be noticed. Soon enough you're going to walk into a trap. Maybe very soon."

Her tone says more than her words. Says that she knows

something real and dangerous. I realize I've clamped my hand over my belt. I slide my grip to my dagger. "And what sort of trap might that be?"

She props her hands on her hips. "A group of kinsmen wait in the next town over. Phelia's been slowly leading you there."

"How do you know this? Your father?"

A nod.

Fair enough. The Archtraitor of Malam has a powerful underground of informants.

A wide river snakes across the plains east of Rasimere Crossing. Sighing, I let my gaze rest on the horizon past the water's curves, wishing the Malamian Mountains that lead to Britta's home were in sight.

"Cohen, the thing is, I need your help." Lirra edges closer. "I can track better than my pa. I can read a person in a blink and know half their life story. But I've never been into Malam. I wouldn't know my way. And I'd more than likely get caught."

I look at her boot moving around in the dirt and recognize the gesture as unease. "What does your father think of you going into Malam after Orli?"

Her mouth tightens. "He doesn't know. Orli's in danger. I couldn't sit around and wait. I'm good at finding out information. All I need is a little muscle on my side."

Finn clears his throat and puffs up his chest.

I shove his shoulder and Lirra cracks a smile.

Taking the Archtraitor's daughter into Malam could spell trouble for me later. I don't like the idea much, but I admire her courage and drive. I let out a breath. "You really think she's in Malam?"

She nods at the distant hills.

Finn snorts. "No Malamian man would kidnap Shaerdanian girls and take them into Malam. It's too risky to get them across the border. Besides, we got pretty-enough girls of our own."

"They're not taking them to make them their wives." She rolls her eyes.

"Why, then?"

I don't hush Finn because I'm curious too.

"Every single girl who's been taken is some sort of Channeler. They're stealing them to use their gifts."

Her words take a beat to sink in. "Magic is outlawed in Malam." A woman accused of being a Channeler is thrown in the pillory or the dungeon, before eventually being burned. The trail of thoughts puts a rock in my gut.

"Why else would they gather large numbers together?"

"You think the person taking all the girls is making some sort of magical army? To fight against what?" I try not to look at her like she's scattered her sense in the wind. I fail.

"That's what I'm trying to figure out. We answer that, and we'll find Orli."

Finn moves into the barn's shade. His jaw is hung wide open like he's auditioning to be a bug catcher. I elbow him and turn back to face her. "Did you come to this theory on your own?"

She shakes her head. "My pa did."

"Because an informant told him?"

"Because he once had the same idea. After he crossed into Shaerdan to hide from the king's guard, he thought about forming a Channeler army in retaliation. Malam has more weapons, more soldiers, and strongholds that are difficult to penetrate. But they have no defense against a magical attack."

I imagine the need for vengeance Millner must've felt after the murder of his wife and child. Don't know what I'd do if I lost Britta.

If the girls are linked to a greater threat, it's my duty to the crown to look into it.

Still, something doesn't add up. "Why would they be taking Shaerdanian girls into Malam?" I ask. "Wouldn't they keep them and fortify their army here?"

She shakes her head. "That's what we need to find out. You're right. It doesn't make sense, but no matter, if the kidnapping of Shaerdanian girls continues, it may be the push Judge Auberdeen needs to send both our kingdoms back to war."

Her words ring true in a way that sends a chill deep into my bones.

"You have a deal." I thrust out my hand. "You help me. I'll find your girl and the rest of the girls. And I'll figure out what threat Malam is truly facing."

BRITTA

BOW IN HAND, I SPRINT TO THE STABLE AND saddle up Snowfire. She's older than the moon, but she's all I've got. If King Aodren had brought a horse instead of dresses, I wouldn't have kicked him out so fast.

For once, I don't loathe our connection.

Hooves flying over frosted brushes and dirt, Snowfire darts through the Evers in the direction I sense the king. I urge her to pick up the pace the deeper we go into the woods. We wind along the trail at the base of Mount Avemoir, one of the highest peaks in the pine-covered range. As we start to climb, I can sense Snowfire's struggle and exhaustion, and it worries me.

No, it angers me.

I don't want to lose my only horse because His Royal Travesty foolishly walked into danger. I hold that thought, following the man's link, until a half league later, his draw intensifies, the invisible rope cinching between us. The pines here grow tall and proud like soldiers lined up to fight. The harsh slant of afternoon light cuts between trunks, glinting off frosted branches. Snowfire slows to a walk. I squint, scrutinizing every detail for clues.

A fallen log, the frost-covered leaves strewn across the underbrush, the narrow glade between trees — the surrounding forest shows no signs of others.

Frustration beats through me because I cannot see him, though I can tell he's close.

"King Aodren?"

The question ricochets around the stagnant forest, lifting the hairs on my arms. I slam my mouth shut. I might as well paint a target on my chest and wait in the nearest glade.

I quietly slide off Snowfire. *Focus is a weapon as much as your bow.* Papa's words beat through me. I add caution to my movements.

Arrow nocked.

Steps soft.

Ahead of me, something moves in the thick knot of underbrush — the breeze blows a black flap of material forward and back, forward and back. The pull in the direction of the material is all I need to know. It drives me from hiding.

I rush forward to find that the caught cloth is an arm span away from the arrogant man who stood in my house thirty minutes ago. Unconscious, Aodren is slumped on his side, the tautness of our bond confirming he's alive. He could be mistaken for a man taking a nap if not for the biting cold or his collapsed stewards a dozen paces farther.

I cross to the other men, hands jittery, steps wary. The icy space between the trees crackles underfoot.

The first man has both of his hands resting around his neck as though he was signaling he could not breathe. His brown eyes are glass, staring at nothing. He was at my home less than a half hour past, delivering gowns for the king's feast. Bile burns my throat as I scurry backwards, gasping to catch my breath. My heart rages a violent beating in my ribs. *Mercy.* What's happened here?

I force myself to kneel down beside the second man. Though his eyes aren't open, I know—I know before I've even touched him that he's passed.

As the hunter's daughter, death has been my companion my entire life.

This man's passing feels like a patch of cold water in a summer-warmed lake. One hand white-knuckling my bow, and the other pressed to my mouth, I quickly look both men over, searching for signs of death. Only, there are no visible wounds. No marks of struggle other than the first man's hands around his neck. And yet, under his fingers, I see no bruising to indicate he was choked to death.

It's as if they both lay down and died.

Survival instincts kick propriety on its arse. I race to the king's side and quickly run my hands over his shoulders and neck, down his chest and along his thighs, checking for wounds. The buzz of his life force resonates beneath my hands and through me. I've never been more thankful for our ever-present connection, a confirmation he's alive. Even so, I put my bow on the ground and hold my hand near his nostrils until a warm breath puffs across my fingers. Just to be sure.

A sword and a saber are belted at his waist. He must not have had time to draw either. Other than the cloak, his clothes are neat and clean. His leather gloves show no sign of struggle. No blood spots the material of his pants. So how did Aodren survive? Why was he left alive?

All the unknowing rings through me like a storm-warning bell. *Flee this place,* it cries. *Run away. Danger.*

"King Aodren, wake up." I tug his shoulder, urgency making my motions rough.

He doesn't respond.

My pulse thunders, uncertainty spiraling into panic. *What do I do?*

I stand, pulling an arrow to the bowstring.

Enat taught me to listen to the pulse of life in the woods around me. If I can hone in on human energy, I might be able to determine the proximity of the threat.

I start by quieting my thoughts. I try to tune into the constant low thrum of life. Slowly, I let my awareness of the nearby woods take in more. I hear my breath, the quickened *ba bam, ba bam* in my chest, and the *whoosh whoosh whoosh* of the life running through the trees and plants. If I weren't so panicked, I'd be awed by this Spiriter gift of mine.

My vision starts to dim. Needle points prick my arms until my muscles grow heavy like I've been lugging water buckets for hours. My breathing echoes loudly through my ears. The beginnings of exhaustion drag through me, and I know it's time to stop. Enat warned me about spending too much energy. It could be fatal.

Right then, something more vibrant than the forest's thrum, like notes of a viol rising over a cittern, catches my attention. The blend of energies must be more than one person. Judging by the way I managed to pick up on them, they cannot be far from here.

Time to run.

Two clicks of my tongue, and Snowfire is at my side. King Aodren dwarfs me by a head and a half and seventy-plus pounds, so moving him won't be simple. I place my bow on the ground to free my hands. Rushing around the glade, I find a sturdy log. I drag it near Snowfire and use the rope from the saddlebag to truss up the king like big game. I weave the remainder over a thick tree limb and around the log, then put all my weight against it, rolling it to tighten the rope and hoist the king off the ground and onto Snowfire. Muscles shake and breath snags in and out of my lungs as I fight to maneuver him so he's lying across the saddle.

It's not a pretty process. If the man wasn't bruised before, he certainly is now. I feel bad about that, but since I'm trying to save his life, I'm sure he'll understand.

Bow in hand, I hoist myself up behind the king and reach for the reins.

Snowfire's ears flick forward.

My gaze follows the movement, arrowing in on the mountainside, where fifty strides uphill, a woman steps into sight. Her black cloak lifts from a sudden gust. The corner, raggedly torn, flaps at her side. She walks toward us, steps so soft that her passage is noiseless. She reminds me of a winter wolf, icy grayish-blue eyes beneath silvery slashes for brows, ivory skin, and light brown hair with moonlight streaks.

And though she seems leached of color and life, darkness radiates from her like hunger.

I stifle a shiver. Willing my fingers to be still, I lift my bow, pointing my arrow at the woman's heart. "S-stop there."

Her chin drops a fraction and, surprisingly, she obeys.

"Who are you?" My voice bobs. I grimace.

King Aodren lets out a low groan. I straighten on the back edge of the saddle, an intense wave of protectiveness rolling through me. "Did you kill these men?"

Her hands, long fingers marked with black paintlike swirls, grasp the edges of her cloak. "Hello, Britta."

Every part of me turns on edge at the familiarity in her tone.

Lots of people from the royal city of Brentyn know me. After all, my father was the king's bounty hunter and my mother a despised Shaerdanian. My name is usually followed by a curse, not curiosity. This woman speaks like she knows me, but watches me like she doesn't.

A wintry blast of air tunnels through the woods, flinging the woman's cloak over her shoulder.

I gasp at the sight of her neck, the ivory skin covered in the same markings on her hands, obsidian veins that curl and twist. Men in the king's guard have the symbol of the royal stag inked onto their skin like a cattle brand. But her snaking marks are different. They follow no pattern.

"I've wanted to meet you for quite some time." Her voice, a mixture of scratches and soprano notes, stops my study.

"Me?" The question tumbles out. It takes a moment to realize that when she spoke I felt nothing. No warmth in my belly for truth, no chill for a lie. That nothingness hits me like a discordant note. My mind rings with the sharpness of it, along with the familiarity of having felt the same way once before.

Snowfire paws the dirt, pacing back restlessly.

I—I know who this woman is.

Enat once explained that while I could sense the truth when others speak, my gift didn't work on Channelers like myself. I cannot feel truth or lie from Spiriters unless they will it.

"You—You're her." I lock my elbow, bow arm straight. The woman doesn't cower.

She stands taller. I flex my fists against the sudden reminder of a childhood bully. Like the other kids, he taunted me often. After the insults were slung, he didn't leave. He'd wait and observe like he was studying a cricket he'd captured in a jar.

She watches me that same way now, her pale eyes provoking.

My arrow could end her in an instant. She consorted with Lord Jamis to overthrow King Aodren. She bound the king in Channeler magic to play him like a puppet.

She's the reason that not so long ago I was in a glade similar to this one, holding my grandmother as her last breaths rattled through her body.

Regret is a dye, blackening my heart and head, spreading hatred and blame.

This woman's death would be justified.

But even as I think that, no matter how much darkness has tainted my insides, I know that punishment isn't mine to deliver. After I killed Tomas, the guard who took Enat's life, I vowed not to hastily take another human life. And yet, right now it's hard to remember why.

Arms jerk to lower the point of my arrow a fraction, aiming for her thigh instead. "You're Phelia," I say, wanting her to understand that I know exactly who she is.

"I am." Her eerie, scarred voice grows louder. "Only, you've stolen my surprise. I wanted to first introduce myself as your mother."

What?

I stare at her, horror-struck. She cannot be my mother.

Not her. In the thousands of times I've dreamt of the woman who gave me birth, I imaged an open-armed woman who radiated warmth and love. Not this. Never this. She's lying. It's a manipulation tactic.

Snowfire pads back, huffing and snorting. I've dug my knees into her sides. I don't have it in me to calm her. Or even to find words to react.

The gift is passed through the maternal line. Enat's words kick through me.

I start to shake my head, threaten that I'll shoot, but I halt when the woman's hands lift and stir the air as though she's moving them through water.

An invisible force pushes past me, around me, through me, and draws every hair on my body to stand. I gasp, unable to stop the quaking in my arms and legs brought on by the wave of energy—her energy. Unlike Enat's strong steady buzz, this woman's life force is frighteningly powerful. Fierce and free.

Snowfire whinnies. I hold tight to King Aodren to keep him from falling in case Snowfire lurches.

"My name is Rozen. And, Britta, you are my daughter." Her voice shocks me still with the power of a mountain cat's menacing growl. This time, because she's somehow allowed it, the warmth of her words, like hot oil, burns through my stomach and boils beneath my skin, searing me with the truth.

Terrible, terrible truth.

CHAPTER

5

COHEN

Lirra blinks twice as if she's taken aback by my change of mind. She grasps my hand. "Phelia's at the oilery in town. Her parents own it."

I yank two new tunics out of my satchel, tossing one at Finn before we reach the main part of town. We change so we don't look the same as when we high-tailed it out of the tavern. A poor disguise, but I'm too eager to get to Phelia to come up with something better.

We hug the shadows of an alley by the main road. Skipping from one narrow way to another, we go unnoticed past a church in the heart of the town. Statuettes of four different gods watch us from each corner of the roof. At the end of the road is the tavern and the oilery.

I study the distance and count the people nearby. Near us, birds fly into the church's rafters, cooing as they nestle down. Doves.

At fifteen, Britta's fingers were slender. I couldn't rip my eyes away when she touched my arm. Couldn't shake the image of the mountain cat. Or how unnatural she looked a speck away from death. When she spoke, "I care about you," I burned with shame.

I'd come to say goodbye, to tell her I was going to Shaerdan to hunt—

". . . I have feelings for you. I want to be with you."

"Britt." I pulled her in, my heart a winter-storm. I didn't deserve her. Definitely didn't deserve the life she nearly lost to save mine. But gods, she was soft. Her hair, her skin, her lips. She always had a way of scrambling my thoughts. The words I should've said were gone. Instead, I said, "Tomorrow, wait for me. I'll come back."

After she left, Saul's warning returned to mind.

If Britta's Channeling ability was discovered, she'd be killed. The healers had asked too many questions. The longer I was in Brentyn, the more she was in danger. I would never allow harm to come to her.

I hated myself for leaving. I rode all night. No matter how fast Siron galloped, there was no outrunning the guilt. Shouldn't have told her I'd be back. She deserved a goodbye, but I was too weak to give it. She'd hate me. Hell, I hated myself.

The gray morning filled with squawks and coos. As I passed under the branches that overhung the road, birds darted away. Except one, a grayish puff. When I rode beneath it, the bird flew ahead, finding another branch from which to watch me. Its presence galled, like a market square pigeon begging for scraps.

"Get out of here." I pulled Siron to a stop.

It didn't spook.

"Haw! Go!"

It cooed. Bloody bird.

"Get!"

Don't know what about the fowl rubbed me the wrong way, but I yanked my dagger from my belt and hurled it. A cry of rage tore from my lips. A cry I'd been holding down since leaving Britta. The dagger found its mark. A startled chirp broke the forest calm, and the feathered ball tumbled into the dust.

I slid off Siron, hands jittering. The bird was too small to bother plucking to eat. What a waste. What a stupid thing to do.

Blood sullied the white feathers around my dagger. I crouched down, yanked my blade from the bird, and stared at the mess. The dagger, ridiculously huge against the pigeon's tiny body, had impaled the bird through the breast. Overkill.

No, not a pigeon. This bird was smaller. Rarer.

Guilt, like rats, crawled down my throat and left a trail of acid. I picked up a red-stained feather. My throat closed.

I'd killed a dove.

I rest my hand against my belt, over the pocket that holds the folded parchment where I've been carrying a snowy gray feather going on two years.

The clank of metal on stone alerts me to a group of drunks milling outside. I curse under my breath, recognizing two from earlier.

I gesture for Finn and Lirra to pick up their stride. But when we step out of a nook to cross the street, I lock eyes with the huge bearded man from the fight. Dammit. He's far down the road, but recognition is clear on his face. "Hey, it's those Malamian scrants!"

I grab Finn by the upper arm and yank him into the church's doorway. Lirra scrambles after us. Our steps clatter against the tiled stones laid under pews, which are lined up like soldiers. The yawning ceiling juts up in a spade-shaped arch, echoing in a way that makes me shrink. I gesture for Lirra and Finn to tread softly. We move through the shadows toward a burning lantern that rests at the head of the room on top of a stone altar.

No matter whether you're in Malam or Shaerdan, the clergymen always keep one lit.

We take a doorway left of the altar. It leads to an empty clergyman's office, complete with brocade robes in a closet.

I grab one for myself and thrust a second at Finn. His shoulders hike up, kissing his ears, and his face lines with anxiety. Ma's voice is probably ringing in his head about reverence and respect, but there isn't time to worry about that. No showing anyone respect if you're dead.

Outside, in the main part of the church, a door bangs open and someone yells. Footsteps clunk on the stones.

"Don't think about it. Put it on." I tug the robe over my tunic and sword.

Finn shakes his head.

A clatter of movement and voices spread through the church.

"Listen to your brother. There's no other way out." Lirra pulls out her sword and points it at the door.

Finn's mouth guppies, his fingers clenching the material. He pulls the robe over his head till the material pools around his lanky form.

Nobody's going to believe his disguise.

Swearing under my breath, I draw the hood over my head and slice the air with my hand, motioning for Finn and Lirra to stay silent and still. Then I step out of the office.

The door snicks shut and the church goes quiet. The eyes of the four men among the pews turn to me. Their fingers twitch on their hilts.

"Kinsmen, have ye come to make penance?" My voice sinks lower than usual, a baritone that echoes from the walls.

The man closest to the altar speaks. "Where's Clergyman Nevin?"

"Saying prayers."

"He's usually alone."

My chin is down, but I look up from beneath my brows, seeing the resolution in his glassy eyes falter. If these men weren't so drunk, this plan wouldn't work.

"I've come from Celize to meet with him," I say.

"I thought two men came in here. Seen anyone?" The man fidgets with his sword.

"No. There's been no other commotion than yours."

I wait, watching him wrestle with what to say next, relieved when he motions for the other men to leave. They're almost out the door when the man turns back.

"You say you're from Celize?"

"Aye."

"My sister lives there. Must be one of your congregation."

I pause. "Perhaps. We are lucky to have the gods' gift of ocean beauty. The way the waves strike the cliff just outside the cloisters is truly the music of the divine." I hold my breath and wait for his reaction. I nearly smirk thinking of the last time I was there. Britta was tucked against my side.

His face relaxes. "Aye, she says the same. G'day, Your Grace."

They leave. I don't move until their footsteps fade. A scurrying mouse could be heard in the church. I don't know when the real clergyman will return. But I know a group of three would draw more attention than a single man.

So, with a quick glance of apology at the closed office door, I turn toward the exit and head out alone.

Keeping my head hidden in the hood, I cross the road. There aren't many people outside other than the few men lingering near the church. I wave in their general direction. They must not be believers, because they shuffle away until they're out of sight. I hurry to the oilery's door.

A cloud of humidity and perfume drifts through the entire

shop. Herbs coated in some sort of lard and pressed between plates of glass rest on containers that catch the aromatic drippings. This oilery is larger than most. It has stables out back and clotheslines hanging from a second-story window.

After discarding the robe and shoving it in a basket, I wind through the maze of distillery tables, barrels, and shelves of flutes filled with yellow, green, brown, and gold oils until reaching a desk where a man and woman work side by side.

At first glance, the dark-haired man reminds me of Saul —it's the patient expression he wears as he watches the much-younger woman. Their features are similar enough. She must be his daughter.

Upon noticing me, the woman's shoulders go rigid and she grabs the satchel at her feet.

"Rori?" A quizzical look comes from the man.

"Nothing, Pa, just something to add to the oil press." Her gaze shifts to me, and a mask of indifference slides over her panic. "Did you need something?"

"I'm looking for someone, a woman named Phelia." I run my finger through the dust coating an oil crock. I watch the woman's reaction. She's jumpier than a smuggler at the border.

"There's no one by that name around here." The man's chair creaks as he leans back.

"Certain?" I dust my hands off on my pants. "Someone told me she came in here."

The man shakes his head. "I'm sorry to say only my daughter —"

"Pa." She stands, maneuvering so his view is blocked. "You've been given wrong information. If you don't need oils, please leave."

"Rori, don't speak to customers that way." The man rises and walks around the table to his daughter's side.

She doesn't match Phelia's description. Despite what she says, the dust and worn marks covering her boots tell a different story. A story of travel. Based on that, her jumpiness, and Lirra's tip, I'd wager this is the woman I've been following or the woman who will lead me to Phelia.

"No harm done." I step back, looking around the shop. "I'll be on my way."

Rori nods, her posture relaxing. I turn and wind my way back to the door.

When I return to the church, Lirra's a hissing rattler.

"Leave me again and our deal is off." She cuts through the gardens, spitting out something about ruining me.

Finn trails behind. "Where'd you go?"

After checking that the road's clear, I point to the far end where carts creak past the oilery. "To the oiler."

Lirra spins around, plowing into me. "What game are you playing, hunter? Why would you leave us at the church? Are you trying to get out of our deal?"

"Settle down. No one's reneging. I already told you I'd help find your friend and the girls. My word is good."

She blasts me with a squinty-eyed scowl. "That had better be the case."

We run from the shade to a shadowed space between buildings, and after confirming once more that the tavern kinsmen are nowhere in sight, on to the oilery. Finn and Lirra go inside while I head for the stables, hoping their presence will spook the oiler's daughter into running. She has to be on edge after my visit. Gut instinct tells me she'll run straight for the stables when they show up in her pa's shop. Right to where I'll be waiting.

It isn't long before boot steps rustle against the hay-littered floor. I wait behind a tired colt, guessing it's the oiler's daughter's based on the crust of dried, foamy sweat on the animal's haunches. He's the only horse here that appears recently ridden. Gets me angry she didn't take care of her animal. Girl shouldn't own a horse if she cannot take care of one.

The young woman approaches and slings her saddlebag over the animal's flanks, barely missing my chest.

"Where are we headed next, Phelia?" I catch the edge of the burlap and swipe my hand inside to grab whatever she's carrying.

She yelps and yanks the bag off the horse. "That's not my name."

"Maybe so, but half of Shaerdan thinks you're her. And you're going to tell me why."

She pinches her lips together.

My sliver of patience snaps in half.

I thrust a pouch of herbs in her face, and she blinks. "No? Then perhaps your father can tell me about this. Not many carry a Channeler mix. Only ever knew one other woman to do that. A Spiriter. Used the herbs for healing teas and other charms."

I move to her side, dagger in hand, swinging the small bag. Last time I saw something like it was on Enat's hip. The old woman carried one everywhere. She used the herbs to make sleeping draughts, healing aids, and wards to protect her home. "An explanation. Now."

She staggers. But there's no escape — something that seems to dawn on her a moment later when her hands start trembling. "I — I don't know her. She crossed my path near Padrin and somehow knew I needed money. All I had to do was make a tea every morning on my trip home. Her requirements were to go quickly, avoid you, and lead you to Sima."

"What's that?"

"The next town over."

The town with the trap. "What does the tea do?" I glare. Her explanation of the herbs makes as much sense as a donkey in a mare race.

"It's a charm. When people look at me, they see her."

I didn't know charms could work that way, but there's more to Channeler magic than I'll ever understand. Of course Phelia, a Spiriter — the most powerful type of Channeler —

would know how to use her magic this way. But why wouldn't she just disappear? Why keep me on the hunt for a month, chasing a mirage?

"Where'd she go?" The desperation in my words sounds like a growl.

"S-s-she didn't say." The girl cowers, wringing her hands. "But I, ah, watched her leave. She took the northern road that cuts through the Bloodwood Forest back to Malam."

Her words spiral inside with jagged edges. Suspicions run under my skin. Why would Phelia return to Malam? A couple of reasons come to mind—to help her lover, Lord Jamis, escape the dungeon or to take back control of the king.

I kick a hay bale to shake my frustration.

Doesn't work.

One thing is for certain. I'm going home.

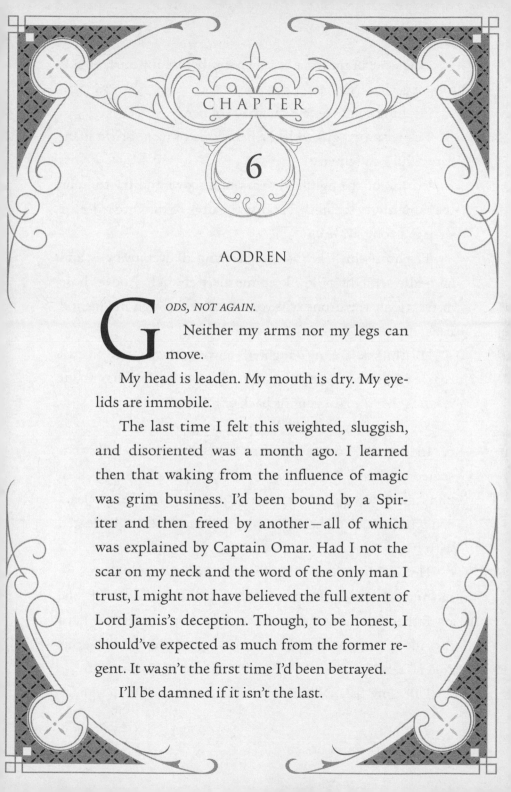

CHAPTER 6

AODREN

GODS, NOT AGAIN. Neither my arms nor my legs can move.

My head is leaden. My mouth is dry. My eyelids are immobile.

The last time I felt this weighted, sluggish, and disoriented was a month ago. I learned then that waking from the influence of magic was grim business. I'd been bound by a Spiriter and then freed by another — all of which was explained by Captain Omar. Had I not the scar on my neck and the word of the only man I trust, I might not have believed the full extent of Lord Jamis's deception. Though, to be honest, I should've expected as much from the former regent. It wasn't the first time I'd been betrayed.

I'll be damned if it isn't the last.

I rack my brain for a last memory before my current suf-focating, sluggish state.

Nothing comes except an image of her.

The wisp of a girl with the backbone of iron. Britta Flan-nery, Saul's daughter.

I think of the fight she wears in a scowl and try to hone the same angry strength, because the urge to dip into a deeper sleep is strong. *Wake up.*

The horse smell, achiness registering all over my body, and an oddly scratchy pillow keep me alert enough. Above those distractions, the drone of a voice breaks through my mental haze.

"Britta, you are my daughter," a woman says, her voice all coarse edges and shards of granite. Something familiar about it raises the fine hairs on the back of my neck.

My attempt at talking shapes into a groan.

In response, warm pressure lands on my back. Is that someone's hand? My eyelids crack open, finally. It's work to blink away the grit, but after a dozen tries, my vision clears enough to make out horse hooves and squashed shrubs dusted with frost.

Hooves? I squint and try to turn my head, only there's no moving. My head feels heavier than the ostentatious throne my father commissioned while he was alive. Something hard digs into my stomach and chest, cutting my ability to breathe. And it feels like two bony knees are shoved against my ribs.

I flex my fists, willing my arms to move, but they're secured to my sides in a way that feels different from the sluggish effect of magic. Have I been bound? I want to yell like an Akarian warrior, but all I can manage is a grunt.

"I could end your life with the release of my arrow." The words are clear and spoken by a voice I recognize. Britta Flannery. It comes from above me. She must be the one touching my back. I relax a bit under her hand.

"You could, but you won't. You know by now I'm not here to cause you harm." The terrible voice rings with disquieting familiarity. "If I wanted that, you'd be dead already."

"Like them?"

No response.

"What about him?"

"He's my way of getting you here. You look like you don't approve. I left him alive, for now."

"You're not going to kill him." The pressure on my shoulder blade increases.

The blood rushing to my head is dizzying. I try again to lift my chin, move my legs, anything to change positions and see how I've come to be face-down over a horse.

"Wouldn't his death be to your benefit?" the woman says, and I instantly find it imperative to break free of whatever's holding me in place. "The bond you have with him must've been an adjustment for you. Such a taxing price for giving away your energy. Don't you want to be free of him?"

"You don't know me." Britta's words are sharper then the dagger she carries. I imagine her face is pulled into the same menacing scowl she's thrown my way many times. "Don't speak as though you do."

"I wanted to meet you. See for myself the girl who broke my bind. Did Enat tell you how at eighteen you fully come into your ability? Merry birthday, my child."

A scoff or a gasp and then the hand on my back leaves, taking its warmth. I stretch my neck, but all I can make out is the broken brush around the horse's legs. My position makes it too difficult to take in anything beyond the ground beneath me.

"No farther." Britta's command has me momentarily pausing my struggle to loosen the ties on my wrist.

"Aren't you the least bit curious? No one in all of Malam is like you. No one but me. I brought you here today to join me. It's my gift to you. You can come with me, to be with other Channelers."

"And if I don't?"

"You don't want to be on the losing side, Britta. Why stay loyal to a man who hunts our kind? He's weak. Look how easily his men fell before him. Aodren doesn't deserve your allegiance any more than he deserves to rule this country. Come with me and I'll teach you. I'll give you your independence from him. I'll show you how strong Channelers truly are. Don't you want to know all you're capable of?"

Silence.

Flashes of memory break through—

A maid in my bedchamber, saying she'd come to collect

a chamber pot and seeming startled because she hadn't expected me.

The same woman standing over my bed beside Jamis. Her voice in my head. Her words coming out of my mouth.

A veiled woman on the path today, seeking help, claiming her carriage had overturned just around the bend.

Her face, showing through the veil as she stepped closer. Recognition slamming into me.

Britta's talking with the Spiriter!

I groan and fight harder against the restraints. She said she was Britta's mother. But that cannot be. I've known Britta's father—and by extension, Britta—her whole life. Her mother died when she was born. The woman is either manipulating Britta or she's returned from the dead. Either way, I wonder if Britta knows the Spiriter isn't alone. I remember that much now.

I wiggle some more.

Whoever tied me up did a bloody good job.

Phelia was backed by a group of at least six young women, none of whom were armed. I didn't think them a threat when my men dismounted their horses. It wasn't until Phelia touched the girl closest to her and an unnatural blast of wind, like a swift jab to the jaw, knocked me off my horse. Britta's tough, but can she take on a half-dozen Channelers?

Compelled to protect her, needed strength surges through me. "No," I manage.

"Shhh." The warmth of her touch returns to my back.

"No," I try again. She needs to know we have to get out of here. "Uhng . . . trap. A t-trap."

Britta curses. A *ffffffp* sounds just above my head, like an arrow has been shot. A gasp. Then an *oomph*. Have we been shot? I rock right and left over the blasted horse trying to speak her name. All that comes out is "Brrrrit."

My arms are being tugged and yanked. A knife grinds across the rope binding my wrists. Then my arms are free, and she rolls my body until I can feel the point of her knees in my back. I feel the movement of a horse beneath us. I see the treetops, the gray sky, and her face. She's a messy painting in shades of pearl and the barest hint of gold, scattered with freckles. I fight to stop my head from lolling.

"Can you sit up?"

I stare at her, a blur of pale skin and blue, blue eyes.

"Sit up." Her expression could frighten the barbarians from the south. Who am I to argue with this girl?

"I-I'm trying." It's an embarrassing, wobbly struggle, trees and shrubs spinning past my vision, but with her tugging at my coat, I manage an upright position on her horse. She thrusts the reins in my hand and commands me to ride.

But where are my guards? Have they already escaped? "My men?"

An arrow scrapes my shoulder, zipping on to a tree, but not before slicing my shirt. My shoulder burns. Britta curses like a royal guard.

"Faster," she shouts, and turns, her elbow digging into my back, as she raises her bow and shoots an arrow.

"Where are my men?" My dry throat turns each word into a bark that barely carries over the horse's gallop.

The warmth of her breath returns to my cheek. Her voice is in my ear. "I-I'm sorry. They didn't make it."

Shock snaps through me. They're dead? Nicolas and Einer are dead?

Gods.

I grip the leather straps as best I can and—heart thundering in my chest, shoulder stinging—command the horse to flee the glade. My focus, thin as commoner threads, barely manages the trees blurring past, the shouts echoing from pursuers, and the guilt knotting my stomach.

As king, the death toll in my name never ends.

It never ends.

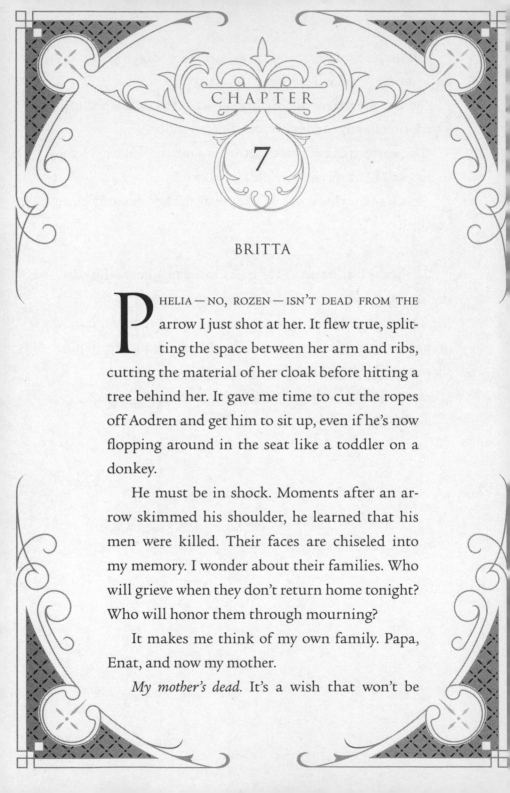

CHAPTER

7

BRITTA

PHELIA — NO, ROZEN — ISN'T DEAD FROM THE arrow I just shot at her. It flew true, splitting the space between her arm and ribs, cutting the material of her cloak before hitting a tree behind her. It gave me time to cut the ropes off Aodren and get him to sit up, even if he's now flopping around in the seat like a toddler on a donkey.

He must be in shock. Moments after an arrow skimmed his shoulder, he learned that his men were killed. Their faces are chiseled into my memory. I wonder about their families. Who will grieve when they don't return home tonight? Who will honor them through mourning?

It makes me think of my own family. Papa, Enat, and now my mother.

My mother's dead. It's a wish that won't be

silenced in the roar of Snowfire's gallop. The blast of truth in her words has marked me permanently. Part of me leapt at the feel of truth, reached for it in a hungry, anxious way a starved beggar might scramble for food scraps. What I wouldn't give to know my mother.

Just not *her*. Never her.

The mix of desire and dread makes me feel like my insides are trying to gnaw their way out of my skin. Gods, the sight of her alone turns my stomach. What are the black marks from? Could it be a sign that she works black magic? Her eyes were soulless. If she truly is my mother, how much am I like her? I fight the urge to glance down at my arms to ensure no obsidian veins are crawling across my skin. A tremor winds up my spine at the thought . . . all the thoughts . . . too many thoughts shoving around inside, banging shoulders, throwing fists, breaking walls.

She's not my mother, not my mother, I repeat like a mantra as I bounce over the back of the saddle. My mother passed away when I was a baby, a fact confirmed by my father and then my grandmother. My mother was kind and loving. My mother would never align with a snake's spawn — Lord Jamis. My mother would've returned for me.

And yet, I know her claim is true. Hang the truthful heat of her words.

I cannot think straight. What I should be focusing on is the woman's ulterior motives. Why, after eighteen years, would she return now?

"Britta!"

An arrow slices through my side vision. It hits the tree to my right. The fleeting sight of another rider, a man, isn't enough to provide information about whom the Spiriter is working with.

Bludger. I heel Snowfire to go faster.

Aodren groans—a good sign. He's still awake. Another arrow narrowly misses my ear, but cuts close enough that the little hairs on the side of my face tingle. I duck and simultaneously shove the king forward. He goes down with an *oomph,* falling against Snowfire's neck. The trees add a minor layer of protection as we dart away. But it still seems like we're mice, trying to outrun a cat in a field of grass. I yell at Snowfire to sprint faster. I pray her energy will last.

My shooting hand grips Aodren's waist, keeping him down for a beat before I draw another arrow and, leaning into him for support, aim behind us. The king mumbles, only it's unintelligible, getting lost in the chase.

I see a couple of riders in the trees, but they're not visible long enough to get off a solid shot. Eventually the sound of galloping diminishes. I no longer glimpse others. But I stay ready, weapon up, keeping an eye over my shoulder until we reach the royal hunting grounds where the king's men catch prey to stock the castle. I figure we've lost them, or they've fallen back for whatever reason. Still, my nerves are in stitches.

The king groans a few times. At one point it comes out like "Your ma?"

Sounds muddled, but I'm pretty certain he's asking if Phelia is my mother. I was hoping he hadn't heard that part of the conversation. I'm not sure what to say or how to defend myself. I need time to process what I just learned.

Instead of trying to explain, I urge the horse onward, pretending I don't understand.

The farther we travel, the more his head bobs, until he's slouched, leaning against me, and emitting light snores. Placing my bow on the saddle holder, I keep one arm around Aodren. I relax a little, grateful l don't have to talk. If Phelia's chilling confession isn't plaguing me, it's what Aodren will do with the news. It's difficult to focus on the gravel road ahead or the trees as they thin out the closer we get to Castle Neart.

I rub my forearm across my eyes.

Aodren's head flops to the side, weighing his body down to the right. I nearly lose my grip. Since I cannot have him breaking his neck on royal grounds, I hold him firmly to me, allowing his head to tip against my shoulder.

I check his head for lumps to perhaps uncover how he was knocked out. His silky hair glides over my fingers, surprising me with its softness. Despite the events of the day, a smile cracks across my mouth at how easily his fair perfection messes up. After a moment or two, it's clear he doesn't have a head injury, so I pull my fingers away, but not before running them through his strands of gold once more. For good measure.

An hour later Snowfire's steps echo off the wood beams and stone supports of the bridge that arcs over the steep valley surrounding the stone beast, Castle Neart. A slight touch of fear gets me to nudge the king in the side. Once I came here unconscious. The time before that, I was shackled. Last thing I want is for the castle guards to think I've harmed the country's leader and done away with his men.

I'm tempted to withdraw my bow from the saddle holder. "Hey, wake up."

Aodren moans and mutters garbled nothings.

I tug away the rest of the cut rope that's been hanging on his legs.

Aodren's sleepy jade eyes turn to me. He lets out a behemoth of a yawn. "Thanks. It . . . was chafing . . . me."

I stare at him for a minute, not sure what I was expecting from His Royal Highness. "You doing all right?" I ask, after a beat.

He squints, golden brows lowering. "Yes . . . thanks to . . . your help." It's a scratched crackle of a sound. He clears his throat. And his expression turns more somber. "You . . . you said my men didn't make it."

"I'm sorry."

Perhaps it's the tired haze mixing with a frown, but the seeming sadness and vulnerability looking back at me softens my attitude toward the man. "I should've died . . . died with them."

"No," I say, and then stop, unsure where to go from here.

"Regardless. It . . . appears I'm in your debt . . . again."

Now that he's found his tongue, I'm surprised by his candidness. His reaction makes me see Aodren in a different light. He's not the detached ruler I always believed him to be. I don't know what I was expecting; perhaps that he'd ask again if Phelia is my mother. But I'm grateful he didn't. I've always thought him presumptuous and pompous. I like this King Aodren more than the king who usually visits my home.

I dip my chin, not sure what to say. *Anytime* seems like the natural response, only I don't really want to sign up for that, and considering it's a bit lighthearted for the situation, I settle for "You're welcome."

The royal guards tend to strike first, question later. Two men approach Snowfire as we stop at the outer gate. I fear what conclusion they've formed upon noticing their king, sans guards, riding with me. My heart shifts into a rickety state.

"I have King Aodren," I blurt, though it must be obvious. Times like these I could crack myself over the head. When the king doesn't open his mouth, I consider doing the same to him.

Say something. I poke him in the spine, and he speaks, thank the gods.

"Open . . . the . . . gate."

The two guards, like scared dogs, cower into bows before scurrying to the guardhouse and yelling into the courtyard at their fellows. Not a moment later, the metal teeth of the gate screech upward from the bridge's end.

How can I explain that King Aodren was attacked in the forest by a Spiriter without giving myself away? The guards will question the death of the king's men who didn't return. I doubt anyone besides Cohen, Captain Omar, Leif, Gillian, and me know what happened in the king's quarters that day over a month ago. If I want a chance at living a peaceful life on Papa's land, that's a secret that'll have to follow me to passing.

Other than the guard holding his sword ready, they've made no threat on my person. Still, I watch them carefully as the guards escort us beneath the spiked metal gate to the outer keep.

The yard smells of smoke and manure. Two men emerge from the stables. At the sight of the broad-shouldered red-headed bear of a guard, relief cracks the tension weighing on me since the glade.

"Britta." Leif rushes to my side. "You've been riding?"

With the king? can be heard in his tone. He knows I'd never visit Castle Neart of my own volition. Nor spend time alone with the country's ruler.

I shrug, having no answer to give in front of present company.

A groom lays down braided thrushes for the king to dismount onto. I slide off Snowfire's other side into the stable dirt.

Leif approaches me while others swarm Aodren. I wonder if it's always this way for him, men at his heels to do his bidding. I scrunch up my face. Seems that way.

Leif takes my bow from Snowfire's holder and gives it to me. "Tell me what happened." Coming from him, it doesn't seem so much like a command from one of the king's guard as it does a nudge from a good friend. He escorts Snowfire and me into a stall at the back where the stable is empty.

"He was attacked in the Evers." My voice drops to a whisper. "I found him unconscious."

"What about his men? Where were they?"

"Both dead."

Leif's shock turns his ruddy complexion pale. "Have you informed the gate guards? Anyone?"

I shake my head.

"Captain Omar needs to know right away." He starts to leave but must see the distaste on my face. "I thought you were past that."

I straighten my quiver and hold my bow to my chest. "Would you like to see the scars on my back?"

Leif has the decency to wince. He softly chucks my shoulder with his fist. "I'll do all the talking. Yeah?" He signals a groom, who comes in with brushes and a towel for my sweating horse.

I mutter an agreement and reluctantly fall into step with him, trailing the guards and Aodren.

Leif veers closer, lowering his voice. "They're going to ask how you came to be alone with the king. It's better to have the captain on your side for this."

I chew my lip, because though Leif has visited me nearly every day, I still haven't confessed the connection that was forged between the king and me. I cannot tell anyone until I've told Cohen. There's also the matter of telling Leif and Captain Omar that the Spiriter who conspired with Lord Jamis is nearby. She isn't alone. And she claims to be my mother.

Unlike the few times I've been here before, the inner court is empty of lords and ladies. The guards must be pleased about this, seeing as the moment they got Aodren off the horse, they formed a cocoon around him. The guards can relax their circle.

Inside the inner gate, Leif informs the others that he's taking me to be questioned by the captain of the guard. Leif and I take the hall leading away from the inner court, while the king and his men travel beneath the arcading.

The farther we walk from Aodren, the more his tug diminishes. It's still there, but not as insistent as we pass the dungeon and take the stairs to the lower yard. With the chaos in the woods, I hadn't noticed it till now. Even so, it's nice to be free of the connection.

A span of emerald lawn runs from the stairs and the guards' quarters, hugging the base of the castle to a low rock wall that edges the cliff. Here, the castle is free of the battering northeastern winds that tear through the Evers in the winter. Here, it almost could be spring for how the winter sun warms the side of the castle. It's tempting to throw my head back and breathe in the sunshine, but I follow Leif to the guards' quarters, where he stops at a door and knocks twice.

A whispery breeze manages to wind around the castle and whip strands of blond into my mouth. I rest my bow against my leg and weave my wayward hair into a braid. Just as I finish, the door swings open, handle grasped by Captain Omar. I pick up my bow, fingers flexing around the curved wood.

Don't sneer. Do not sneer.

Severe scowl and a sleek graying beard give the captain of the king's guard the look of a hawk. Hungry, ruthless predator. His gaze flicks over me, landing on my bow, before turning to Leif.

"News?" The man's mouth pinches.

Leif explains my arrival, telling the captain the basics —King Aodren was attacked; I found him in the woods, protected him, and returned him to the castle. The tightening muscles around the older man's eyes tell me he's preparing to fire question after question at me.

"What happened? Who attacked him? What of his men?"

"One at a time." It takes effort not to glower, considering the bitter taste in my mouth whenever he's nearby. I reiterate what Leif said and end with "I don't know how he was knocked unconscious or how his men were killed. I looked for injuries . . . There wasn't a lot of time. But I know the person responsible was Phelia."

Captain Omar's hand clenches the sword fixed to his waist. "Phelia's in Shaerdan."

As if he could dismiss my information that easily. *Apparently not* is what I want to say. "She confirmed who she was to me."

"Mother of stars, Britta." Leif pushes off the wall. "Why didn't you say something?"

"I just did."

"Yeah, you should've led with 'the Spiriter killed the king's men and knocked King Aodren unconscious.'"

"Is he under her control again?" Omar demands.

The king didn't say much of anything on the way to the castle, but I would know if the Spiriter had bound him again. I would feel it. As of this moment, our connection is still intact. Still as infuriating as ever. "No."

"Leif, you send word to Cohen. I will inform the men's families and send guards out to retrieve their bodies." His eyes drop, but not before I see a flash of something. Pain, perhaps regret. Captain Omar paces out of the doorway and back, turning to me. "Is there anything else?"

I know he means to take care of any questions people might ask. To control — as much as he can — what people say about the king, as I'm the last person anyone would expect to share a horse with royalty. And though I care little for Captain

Omar, in this moment, I'm grateful for him. He's the one who managed the story of what happened behind the king's closed door a little over a month ago, making sure people know only what he wants them to know. What won't reflect badly on the king.

And what's good for the king, in this case, is good for me. No one has accused me of being a Channeler. No one knows the true cause for Jamis's arrest or his dismissal from nobility. No one knows that the king was controlled by a Spiriter. For all his faults, Captain Omar is a loyal man. He would never allow information to leak if it might make the king look frail. I should confess what Phelia, or Rozen—if she truly is my mother—said, but disbelief and bile keep me from talking.

After Captain Omar dismisses us, Leif leads me up the stone stairs and through the web of hallways to the gate in the inner wall.

A guard steps into our path. "Miss Flannery, your presence has been requested."

I yank my bow up. Leif holds his hand out, as if he's settling a horse. Even so, the intrusion unnerves me. Makes me think of how easily Phelia got to the king today. How easily she could get to us anywhere.

The guard repeats himself, adding that the request is on King Aodren's behalf.

I saved the man's life and safely deposited him back at his castle. What more does he want?

I hand over my bow—no weapons are allowed in the king's presence. Leif remains at my side as I follow the guard through the marbled halls that lead to the king's quarters. The pull to the king grows with each step closer to his polished doors.

I swore I'd never enter the king's private quarters again. Yet my boots dirty the lush carpet in his study, adjacent to the room where we both nearly lost our lives. I've gone this far; I don't need to enter the king's private sleeping quarters.

Leif gives me a questioning look when I refuse to go farther. I shrug and act as though my body isn't crying to edge closer.

The guard who escorted us here along with the two who are stationed by the entrance to the king's quarters cluster near the door.

"Leave us." Aodren walks out of his bedroom. He's wearing clean clothes, a change from what he had on in the woods. I glance to his shoulder, where the arrow scraped him. He moves it stiffly as he crosses the study to sit in a chair so large I cannot stop myself from guessing the number of trees cut down to make such a pretentious seat. Three? Four?

His royal head tips to the side, eyeing Leif after the guards exit.

"He can stay," I blurt before thinking to censor myself.

Surprise flickers through Aodren's eyes, turning them a brighter shade of ivy. They're more alert than when we came to the castle less than an hour earlier.

"My apologies, Your Highness." Leif bends at the waist, holding a hand over his heart. "I'll be outside the door if you need anything."

My glare swings to Leif, but the traitor has already turned his back on me. I curse under my breath, and Leif's neck reddens as he slips out the door.

"He's your friend."

I spin around. Doesn't sound like a question, but I nod anyway.

"Do you trust him?" All the scratchiness from earlier is gone.

"Yes."

Aodren's chin moves in the smallest acknowledgment and then his gaze drops, allowing me an opportunity to study him. Gold lashes contrast the dark smudges under his eyes. Earlier, he showed a bit of kindness. Something I never would've imagined from a king. It makes me wonder who Aodren really is. His shoulders aren't as rigidly square as I imagine the shoulders of royalty should be. In a way, he reminds me of a lone wolf, a survivor, though managing poorly on his own.

His fingers run over the chair's arms, dipping into the carved wood and gliding out. "How many others have your trust?"

I frown, puzzled by the path the conversation's taking. "I . . . I don't know."

"Truly? There cannot be many—"

"Is that an insult? I did just save your life." I lean my weight onto my right leg, needing the pressure of my dagger against my ankle.

"No . . . I . . ." His face goes tomato red. "I didn't mean any offense." He presses his lips shut. "Forgive me. I'm grateful for what you did today. I know there was nothing to be done for my men. But without you, I'd likely be dead."

The cadence of his speech is choppy, as if he's inexperienced at giving apologies. Which is probably true, considering he's the king. It makes me appreciate the truthful warmth and rarity of his words.

"Three," I admit. "There are only three who have my trust."

"And they are?"

I shake my head.

He pauses, perhaps taken aback by my refusal. Even his hands stop tracing the carved wood. "Fair enough. We have that in common."

A question starts to form on my lips.

"We do not trust many." He's careful in the way he delivers each word. "I wanted you to know that you are one of the few on my list."

I blink, warmth crawling from my belly to my toes to the top of my head. I'm not sure whether to be flattered or to call him a fool.

"You have saved me twice now. I trust you with my life. But not just that—I also want you to trust me, Britta. I heard what the Spiriter said to you. You are her daughter."

I was wondering when he might bring that up. "It—it seems so."

He draws in a slow breath. "Did she say why she's after me? What her plans are?"

I shake my head. "Only that she used you to lure me there."

Understanding dawns, widening his green eyes. He clears his throat. "Our connection?"

My nod is met with his frown.

"How long will we be this way?" He stands, stepping away from the ostentatious chair, coming closer to me.

"I wish I knew."

His feet stop. "She offered to teach you." There's a hint of a question. Does he think I'm tempted?

"I want nothing to do with her. She's a murderer."

"I'm sorry. Today's meeting must've been a shock for you."

"That's an understatement."

A smile cracks his stoic face. He runs his hands one at a time along the sleeve of his overcoat. "We cannot choose our parents, can we? Only who we become." It seems like the strangest thing for the king of Malam to say to me, and yet it's the most comforting thing he could say.

"I offer you a suite in the castle, to stay in as long as you'd like, for your own safety. However, I don't expect you to accept. I know you are partial to your land. If you choose to return to your cottage, I'd like to assign guards to you. Considering Phelia is nearby, you'll need to stay vigilant."

"Rozen," I correct. And when he squints, I explain, "Her real name is Rozen."

His mouth shifts into a small O of understanding. "I'll pass that information along to Omar."

Anxiety spikes through me. "You won't tell him she's my mother, will you?"

"I was planning on it, but if you don't want me to, I suppose I can keep that information for now. Regardless of what she's to be called, she's wanted for murder now. Captain Omar won't stop until he catches her. Though, he'll likely have to know sooner than later."

"Just for now."

"For now, Britta."

The soft pause he gives my name tongue-ties me and pushes me into the ineptitude I've always felt while trying to pilot a conversation. "Um, no thank you for the room at the castle or the guard. I'm capable of taking care of myself. I'd rather not have men posted around my cottage. If that's all, I should get—"

"I insist on the guards. At least until we know the woods nearby your home are safe."

"You can have men search the woods and watch my land from the border. That should be enough."

Brows raised, he steps back to rest a hand on the edge of the ornate wood. "Not many people would come in here and negotiate with me. But your request, though not my preference, is reasonable. I'll talk to my men."

What do I say to that? I don't want to press my luck, so I remain silent.

"We'll meet again in two weeks' time?"

Two weeks?

Bludger. The king's Royal Winter Feast Ball.

"Right, the ball."

He grins, momentarily stunning me with a flash of genuine happiness. It's disarming, causing me to nearly walk into the door. I mutter goodbye and, with a small awkward wave, leave before he can say anything more, or before I can make a fool of myself.

Leif falls into step with me once I'm out of the room. He walks with me down a spiral staircase, through the east corridor, past the Great Hall, under the arcading, and through the gate. In the outer yard, billows of steam puff from the blacksmith's shop like smoke from a dragon's nose. Our steps part the hot cloud, giving us a brief break from the chill in the air.

Leif waves at the smith and then nudges me toward the stables. "What happened? You haven't said a word."

"Just thinking about today." And what the king said about trusting me. King Aodren's frankness makes me think that perhaps my dislike of the man is a bit unfair. It's not his fault we're connected to each other.

"I promised Cohen I'd watch out for you," Leif says. "I'm not doing a very good job of it."

"Cohen knows I can manage on my own. Focus on being a friend. All right?"

A sweet smile lifts Leif's freckles for a moment before his expression sinks. "Wonder what Cohen'll think when he finds out she's here. That she's killed two men and went after you."

He'll be angrier than a bull elk in rut with no cow in sight. Even so, and despite what happened in the woods, I cannot help being pleased. Cohen will be headed back to Malam.

Leif whistles to a stablehand and orders Snowfire and another horse to be readied for travel. I retrieve my bow from where the guard placed it in the weapons hold. After I attach it to Snowfire's saddle, I turn to Leif. "I can find the way home. You don't have to come."

"Safety first." He leans closer. "Phelia is somewhere out there in the Evers. She's after something. Until we know what, you're not safe."

Me. She's after me. I think of her offer. Join her, learn from her.

Would Leif think less of me if he knew Phelia is my mother? Would Cohen? Aodren's reaction wasn't what I expected.

I want nothing to do with Phelia, and she knows it.

When we meet again, it'll be the day I capture her.

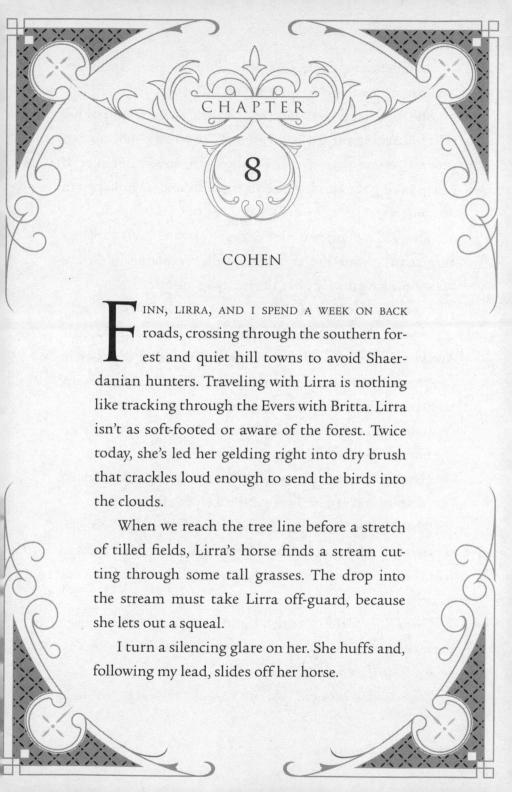

CHAPTER

8

COHEN

FINN, LIRRA, AND I SPEND A WEEK ON BACK roads, crossing through the southern forest and quiet hill towns to avoid Shaerdanian hunters. Traveling with Lirra is nothing like tracking through the Evers with Britta. Lirra isn't as soft-footed or aware of the forest. Twice today, she's led her gelding right into dry brush that crackles loud enough to send the birds into the clouds.

When we reach the tree line before a stretch of tilled fields, Lirra's horse finds a stream cutting through some tall grasses. The drop into the stream must take Lirra off-guard, because she lets out a squeal.

I turn a silencing glare on her. She huffs and, following my lead, slides off her horse.

"Thought you could teach me about stealth," I whisper. "Are you trying to get us noticed? Or killed?"

She runs her fingers through her hair and straightens her skirt, smacking off flecks of mud. "The woods are your territory. Give me a town, and I'll show you stealth. Besides, if you're asking if I can kill you in three seconds, I'm happy to demonstrate."

This girl has more coarse edges under her pretty appearance than anyone I've ever met. Well, except maybe Britta. Makes me long for my girl's sharp, sweet mouth.

"Yeah, yeah, show me later." I move behind a tree to take in the town ahead. It's smaller than others we passed through. And by small, I mean blink too long and we would've passed it.

"There's at least ten people out and about," Lirra pipes up, pointing to the few houses closest to the town center.

Ignoring Lirra's response, I turn back to Finn. "Stay with the horses. We won't be long."

His pinched face makes it clear he isn't pleased, but I don't care about his pleasure. I care about keeping him safe.

The smaller Shaerdanian towns usually have an inn that serves as a bed, breakfast, and brew house. On foot, we head past the homes to the one building with a faded wood sign out front: HOGS HEAD TAVERN.

Lirra nods at the two-story building. "There?" Her crooked expression matches the inn. Beneath a thatched roof, the plaster walls have a cockeyed lean.

"Looks safe enough." I snort. "Doubt the place will hold

up against someone slamming a door. Considering how we left the tavern in Rasimere Crossing, our stop here might raze the building."

We enter the inn and cross through a sitting room to sidle up to a bar. The wooden counter runs the length of the room, separating the brew house from a few dining tables and scattered chairs.

A sweaty, red-faced woman tops off jars from a keg of ale, and then turns to face us. "Haven't seen you two around 'ere." Her gaze skips back and forth between us, narrowing. "Where ya from?"

Wasn't expecting a cold reception this far south. Puts me on-guard.

Lirra curls into my side and exhales a squealy sigh like she just won a prize cobbler at the fair. I stare at her.

"Hullo. We're from Celize. Just had our nuptials." She lays her head against my arm.

The woman's face brightens so fast, I would've thought Channeler magic was used.

"That so? Newlyweds! Lovely. Come in. Do ya need a room?"

I shake myself out of being momentarily stunned. "No, we don't."

Lirra shoots me a look before she starts rubbing my arm like I'm some damn pet cat. "Don't mind him. He's always gruff. That's what I love about him. We thought we'd stop in for a drink before we head east."

"Oh? You're going such a long way for a wedding trip."

"We're headed to my aunt's house. She lives near the border."

The woman sets two cloudy glasses on the counter and fills them with tea-stained water. "Be careful and watch out for travelers. Probably don't need to tell you that." She winks at me. "You look like a strong buck. You can take care of yourself."

"That's me." I pinch Lirra's side. "Me and this gal. Gotta keep her out of trouble."

A cough flies out of Lirra's mouth. She quickly covers it with a worry-filled "Oh no! You haven't heard of any dangers ahead, have you?" A seamless maneuver. So innocent and wide-eyed, I'd think she was harmless if I didn't know her better. Lirra may not be the expert hunter and tracker Britta is, but she has a set of skills that are just as lethal. There's a viper behind those big blue eyes.

"The Channelers Guild has called a meeting in Gilson," the woman starts, but when the door swings open, screeching on its hinges, she smacks her lips together. "Finished with the woodpile?" She turns to the bearded fellow in the doorway. Against a shoulder he carries a mammoth of an ax with a head as large as a man's. Wood chips dust the tunic where his belly presses the material outward.

"Who're these lot?" The woodsman wraps his hand around the handle of the ax.

"They're newlyweds, Amil. Nothing to get excited over." Her smile wobbles a bit, and her hand, which has flattened on the bar, loses its color.

I straighten, instinctively pulling Lirra closer.

"Don't tell me not to get excited. They look like strangers. We don't do business with strangers. Not these days."

"They're harm—"

"Shut yer hole. Stop interrupting." His coarse words turn the atmosphere wintry.

"I—I didn't mean to. I'm sorry, Amil." She turns a flustered smile on us, but her arm jitters, belying the fact that he's treated her this way before, and she's afraid of what else he might have in store.

My hands are fists before I can even process my reaction. I should teach him a lesson for not properly caring for this woman. When my father was alive, he never treated my ma with anything less than adoration and respect. It sickens me that any man would lay a hand on his wife.

Lirra must notice the tension in my arm because she slides her hand over mine and tries to work my fingers open. Once she does that, she slips her palm against mine. It feels all wrong, wider than Britt's and clammier. But it's enough to keep me from reacting in a way that'll draw the attention of the rest of the town.

"We don't mean any harm." Lirra's voice is a smooth, lulling song. "We've been traveling so much, in a rush to get to my aunt's home so I can introduce my new husband. And I was tired." She lets out a long sigh, sagging against me. "This guy of mine doesn't seem to need any rest."

The woodsman huffs a bit of a chuckle, and it makes me want to punch him all over again. Of course he'd think she was implying something about the marriage bed.

"We can be on our way, though, if you're busy . . ." Lirra leaves the comment on a questioning note.

The man stares at the two of us. I want to lay him flat for how he treated his wife and what he's probably thinking of Lirra, but I remain by her side.

"Well, cheers to you," he says, gaze still scrutinizing.

"Oh, yes!" His bartending wife lets out a little whoop, and then raises the cup she just poured and taps it three times on the bar.

Lirra yanks on my arm. It's right as I'm looking down at her, meeting her slightly panicked expression, when I realize what I'm missing. The three taps of a glass is part of the nuptial celebration. Each time someone in the wedding party hits their cup thrice against the table, the bride and groom kiss.

Lirra's blue eyes plead silently.

I drop my chin. Before I can think twice, Lirra's lips are pressed to mine. They're warm. Full. And when they open, extending the kiss, I go along with the charade, tasting spring water and guilt.

Our act must be convincing enough, because the woman claps, and then the man grunts approvingly.

We move away from each other, and though I want to look anywhere but at her, I keep my eyes on her and a fake smile plastered on my lips.

I break eye contact and turn back to the woodsman. "We do have to get back on the road. Only, your wife was kind enough to warn us about danger ahead. Have you heard or seen anything?"

"Actually, yeah. I just came in 'cause I saw smoke out north of here. With all the ravines that way, it's a fool's journey. Nobody's traveling through the woods unless they're hiding out."

Lirra's little squeak keeps me from speaking out. "We heard a little bit about girls being taken, but not much. I'm sure you know more than us."

The man drops his ax at the door and comes closer. It doesn't take much more coaxing from Lirra, the innocent, naive newlywed, to make him talk.

He reiterates all the rumors we've already heard but adds something more. "Judge Auberdeen's offering fifteen hundred silver coins for the capture of the kidnappers. I figure I'm about to be a rich man."

I watch him slug back a glass of ale, spill a second one on his wife's countertop, and then snap at her to get him dinner. The man's disgusting. He's also wrong. If anyone's going to catch the men in the north woods, it'll be me.

Lirra cinches up tight to me. "Come on, love, we should go before dark."

I straighten my spine, fighting the urge to wriggle out of

her grip, and nod. I give my thanks to the barwoman and her poor excuse for a husband. Then we exit the inn and head for the woods.

Finn has the horses watered when we return. I start to explain what happened at the inn, when Finn cuts me off. "Explain later. There's no time."

He points to the space between the trees where we have a clear view of the inn. The woodsman we just spoke with has saddled up his horse and is galloping toward the east side of town. He must be gathering his men. Together they won't have the stealth to sneak up on anyone in the woods. If the smoke he spoke about belongs to the kidnappers' camp, we'll have only one chance to sneak up on them. Finn, Lirra, and I have to reach the smoke before the woodsman does.

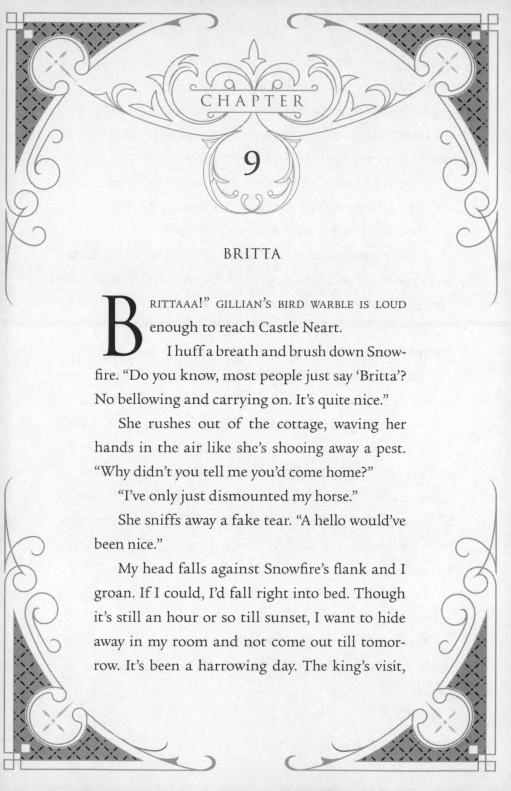

CHAPTER

9

BRITTA

"B RITTAAA!" GILLIAN'S BIRD WARBLE IS LOUD
enough to reach Castle Neart.

I huff a breath and brush down Snow-
fire. "Do you know, most people just say 'Britta'?
No bellowing and carrying on. It's quite nice."

She rushes out of the cottage, waving her
hands in the air like she's shooing away a pest.
"Why didn't you tell me you'd come home?"

"I've only just dismounted my horse."

She sniffs away a fake tear. "A hello would've
been nice."

My head falls against Snowfire's flank and I
groan. If I could, I'd fall right into bed. Though
it's still an hour or so till sunset, I want to hide
away in my room and not come out till tomorrow. It's been a harrowing day. The king's visit,

Phelia's attack, and the visit to Castle Neart have worn my sanity as thin as my old hunting trousers.

My frustration is drowned out by her laugh. "You're so dramatic. The kind Captain Omar sent a missive, which of course I opened." Gillian flits around Snowfire.

I start to argue with her over the merits of Captain Omar, and then realize she just disclosed she opened my letter.

"Gillian, was the missive for me? Or you?"

"You're ridiculous. All my letters go to the castle. Before you invited me to live with you, I lived in the servants' quarters. So of course the missive isn't for me."

"You mean before the king commanded you to live with me."

"Details, details." She flicks her hand in the air between us and laughs as she pulls a folded piece of parchment from her pocket. "Captain Omar has assigned two guards to patrol the land around your cottage, and another two to search the woods. He's kindly asked that you report to him if there are any more disturbances. And he shared his gratitude for seeing the king home." Her hand presses against her chest. "You rode with the king to the castle? What happened? Why didn't you tell me?"

I snatch the letter from her hands. "And you say I'm being ridiculous. I've only just returned home."

Leif steps out of the cottage and waves at me. I glance around, shocked because I thought I'd ditched him at the castle.

"There's a shorter route through town. Captain Omar asked me to deliver the message, but you'd already left."

"That's the only reason?"

Leif's face reddens. "The king asked me to ensure you returned home safely. And I'm assigned to see that your property remains free of trespassers."

Figures. Between Cohen and the king and Captain Omar, it's shocking I'm allowed to use the privy without someone holding my hand. Though, when I glance at the wall of trees along my property, the accompanying bout of unease is lessened knowing Leif and the other guards are nearby.

I turn to put my tack away. Frost crunches the field underfoot from the stable to my cottage. The air nips at my exposed skin, making me wish for a thicker coat.

Gillian's hands go to her hips when she catches up to me. "I heard you trussed the king to the back of your horse like some sort of deer you'd shot in the woods."

I roll my eyes at her and trudge to the door. She follows behind with Leif, entering the cozy warmth of the cottage.

A sigh slips out of me as I plunk down in Papa's old chair, its familiar curves hugging my body, wood worn smooth from years of use. When I close my eyes, I can practically imagine Papa's here with me — reading beside the fire, cleaning his daggers, showing me how to skin and gut prey. Papa taught me to shoot an arrow, ride a horse, and anticipate danger. Like the years of wear on his chair, his lessons have shaped me into who I am.

This thought I hold on to like a lifeline. Papa made me who I am. I am his daughter. Not Phelia's.

I see her face again. The black veins curling over her skin. *I wanted to first introduce myself as your mother.*

Did Papa know she was alive? I hate to even think it, but considering all the secrets Papa kept, I'd be a fool not to suspect. Where has Phelia been my entire life? How is she alive when everyone thought she was dead? And why return now?

I've lived so much of my life not knowing who I really am that now I cannot settle for not having answers.

Across the room, Gillian lowers herself into a seat, her movements giving new meaning to the word "genteel" as she picks up her needlepoint. I smile at her, my frilly friend, remembering her last comment about putting the king on my horse. "First of all, I wouldn't truss an animal to the back of Snowfire. I'd gut and quarter the beast in the woods. Entrails make too much mess."

She makes a delicate gagging sound. "Ladies of the court do not talk about entrails."

Court. The Winter Feast. The king's voice: *At the Royal Winter Feast Ball. Where you'll be presented to the court as nobility.* My hands are fists and I've forgotten all other worries.

"This is something you'll have to learn once the king presents you to court . . ." She's still talking. Nobody talks more than Gillian. "Nobility has a refined way of—"

"No" comes out like a groan. Do we have to have this conversation tonight?

Leif, who hasn't taken a seat, shuffles awkwardly near the doorway that looks a little too small for his wide frame. "I should go meet up with the other guards and set up our patrol times."

I stare out the window at the woods, Phelia and her words and her strange dark markings sitting heavily on my mind.

"We'll find her," Leif says, though that's not truly my worry.

"I trust you." I turn back to face him.

He echoes my somber smile before nodding to Gillian. "Good day, Miss Tierney."

Two bright spots of color touch Gillian's cheeks.

Her mouth opens and closes. Leif usually achieves a maximum of three words in my handmaid's presence. I haven't noticed Gillian's interest in my friend before. It's somewhat of a shock—I'd have thought Gillian and all her fanciful ideas would be more interested in a stuffy lord or a haughty guard. Not Leif, who is as gentle as he is large.

If only Leif could appear at a moment's notice. The snap of my fingers and my handmaid would go silent. That would be magic worth using regardless of the risk of being caught. I chuckle at my own thought, and Gillian's eyes cut to me until I hide my mouth behind a fist.

"Please, call me Gillian." She curtsies to Leif.

He repeats her name in a murmured tone. As soon as he steps out the door, she whips a deadly glare in my direction and hisses, "Not a word."

My laughter doesn't stop for quite some time.

You don't need a lot of friends, just a good one, Papa had said at a time I felt the crush of loneliness. I thought he meant Cohen. But in the time since Enat was killed, while Cohen's been away, Gillian has been my rock. A pretty painted rock, but someone to lean on nonetheless.

I would've never handpicked her as a friend. But we've shared more laughter in the last month than I've had most of my life.

When she exits the room, my humor fades. What will she think of me when she finds out Phelia is my mother?

Gillian. Leif. Cohen. I remember the time before them, when I almost starved after Papa's death. Now I have three people to depend on.

When they know the truth, will I be alone again?

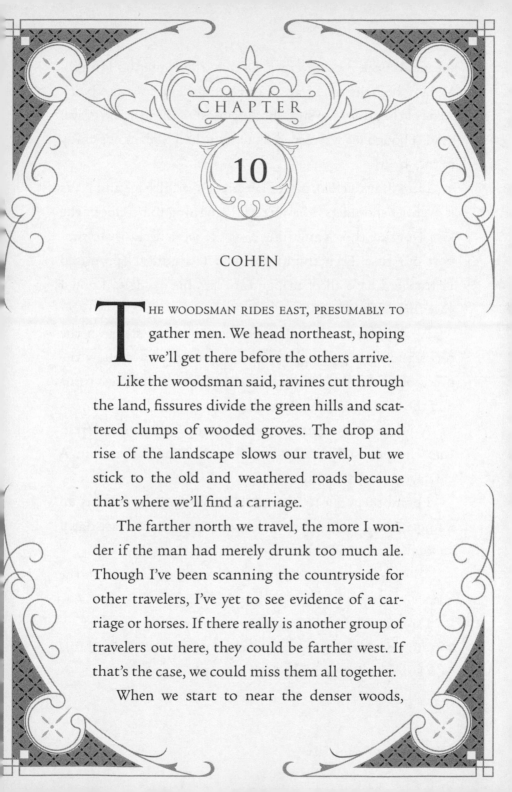

CHAPTER

10

COHEN

T HE WOODSMAN RIDES EAST, PRESUMABLY TO gather men. We head northeast, hoping we'll get there before the others arrive.

Like the woodsman said, ravines cut through the land, fissures divide the green hills and scattered clumps of wooded groves. The drop and rise of the landscape slows our travel, but we stick to the old and weathered roads because that's where we'll find a carriage.

The farther north we travel, the more I wonder if the man had merely drunk too much ale. Though I've been scanning the countryside for other travelers, I've yet to see evidence of a carriage or horses. If there really is another group of travelers out here, they could be farther west. If that's the case, we could miss them all together.

When we start to near the denser woods,

the small back road diverges. Despite the winter building in Malam, here the trees have enough limbs and leaves to block some of the afternoon sun, shading most of the dirt and gravel road. Though it's warmer in Shaerdan than Malam, it's chilly in the shade.

Lirra drags a cloak out of her horse's saddlebags and pulls it over her shoulders. I haven't said anything to her about the kiss. Not sure there's anything to say. It was a necessity to support our ruse. Even thinking this, I feel guilty. I promised Britta she'd have all of me, and it tears me inside to know I gave that one kiss away.

We hit another hill. The horses slow their steps on the rocks and roots jutting out of the ground as we follow the overgrown road east. When we come off a rise, the forest thins and the road looks more formed.

A quarter league past the ravine, I stop Siron at some fresh ruts where the soil's been softened by the Shaerdanian rain. A carriage passed this way recently.

I point them out to Finn and his eyes widen. He holds up a finger, indicating these tracks were made in the last day. I shoot him a look of approval.

"Why isn't anyone talking?" Lirra's voice is a shock in the silence.

I spin around and turn a frown on her.

"You don't talk when you're close to your prey," Finn fills in, a lesson he learned from me years ago.

Lirra nods like she understands, but then keeps talking. "How close are they?"

"Close enough you shouldn't talk," I cut in.

She huffs out a breath. "How do you know it's them?"

"I don't," I tell her. "But we'll find out soon enough."

She nods and sits straighter, her expression sharpening, like she's preparing herself for a fight. I hope it doesn't come to that. Though it might.

Lirra and Finn follow me for another quarter league, before I signal for them to stop. The tracks are fresh here, and judging by the steaming pile of horse manure, our quarry is close. We'd be best to go on foot so the sound of the horses doesn't alert them to us.

Finn is quick to gear up, pulling a quiver over his shoulder and holding his bow. Then he pats the dagger at his waist and the one strapped to his ankle. I grimace watching him, wishing I'd said no when he asked to learn to be a bounty hunter. It's too dangerous for my little brother. When I look at him, I don't see the man he's becoming, but the toddler I once saved from our pecking chickens. The gangly boy who cried on my shoulder when our pa died.

"Follow," I mouth, gesturing to the woods that line the road. "But keep at a distance."

Finn and Lirra run behind me as I dart through the trees, staying parallel to the road. I run for a quarter league before I pick up the *eeek eeek* of their carriage's wheels and the *clop* of their horses' hooves. I cut slightly east, continuing until I lope alongside them, but far enough away, hidden by the trunks and ferns and underbrush, that they won't notice me.

Two riders on horseback flank a carriage with no visible markings to show ownership. It's driven by a third man. Though I cannot tell how many people are inside the compartment, I can count a number of weapons on the three men. Arrows, bows, daggers, and long swords—these men are armed for a fight.

Behind the group, the sun dips, bathing the forest in a dusky haze. The carriage slows to a stop.

The men on horseback quickly move to the carriage door and dismount. Their motions seem practiced, like they've done this a few times before. The door opens, and a fourth man emerges.

My eyes nearly bulge out of my head. I've seen this man before.

I squint, trying to make sure the haze isn't messing with my sight. Even though he's not garbed in the clothing of a nobleman, there's no doubt. It's Lord Conklin, a Malamian with a fiefdom around the border town of Fennit.

Could it be another Spiriter identity trick? Like how Rori was able to fool anyone she passed in Shaerdan, so they thought she was Phelia?

"What's the plan?" Finn moves beside me, his voice a speck over a whisper.

I shake my head, baffled. I need answers. "See the older man." I point him out to Lirra and Finn. "Whatever happens, keep him alive."

Lirra raises her brows.

"He's a lord in Malam."

"No way," Finn blurts, and then smacks his hand over his mouth when he realizes he didn't whisper.

The men are too busy pissing on the fronds around the thick tree trunks to notice us.

"Should we move in closer to see if there are any girls with them?" Finn asks.

Before I can answer, a female voice from inside the carriage cries, "Please let us go!"

Lirra meets my eye, hand on her blade. I notice she doesn't carry a bow and arrow like Britta. If it were this easy for me to find them, I've no doubt that woodsman fool and the townsmen he's managed to gather will be upon us in no time.

One of the guards yanks the door open, reaches in, and withdraws a young black-haired girl. I stare at her, my heartbeat banging in my chest with a fierce need to protect her. She cannot be older than thirteen, my sister's age.

I watch as he jerks her around like a cloth doll. Bloody seeds, I want to kill him now. I could loose an arrow and drop him in an instant. When he backhands her and another two young faces, dirty, tear-stained, and colorless, peer out the door, I cannot watch any longer.

I lift my bow and loose an arrow. It hits him between the ribs. The man drops, and the girl falls to the side, her knees crashing into the dirt.

Only now I have the attention of the other men. A sick sack of a man has a girl in front of him, using her as a shield. Another has a sword drawn, and he's hunkered down by the carriage. A third fellow has his bow up, arrow aimed at Finn. Right as I notice this, the man releases the arrow and it sails straight at my brother.

Panic rips through my chest. I yell Finn's name. *Move, Finn.*

He leaps to the side. Thank the gods. I rush to him and shield us behind a tree. He winces. Red stains the left side of his tunic, a bloody blossom that grows with each beat of his heart.

"Finn," I bark. "You all right?" My voice is too harsh. I thought it missed, but he's bleeding. Gods, why is he bleeding?

"Must've grazed me."

He lifts his tunic for me to see a scrape along his ribs. If he hadn't moved, that arrow would've pierced him through the heart instead of taking a chunk of skin from his side. Blood drips steadily from the slice. It'll have to be cleaned. Stitched.

I clench his tunic in a fist and let it drop. He could've just died. My kid brother.

"Stay back," I tell him.

"What? No, I'm coming with you."

I connect gazes with Lirra, who's also hunkered behind a tree, and give her a signal before turning back to Finn. "Keep pressure on the wound. And stay low. I want you to keep out of this. Hear me?"

He shakes his head, but there's no time to listen to his argument. I'm sure he's disappointed, but this isn't another learning opportunity. His life is on the line. I need to keep him safe.

Readying an arrow, I motion to Lirra and dart around the tree, headed for the next one that'll give good coverage and bring me closer to Lord Conklin and his group of traitors.

Two arrows fly right past my head. The guy's a quick shot, but my movements are too erratic for him to keep up.

I shoot one back at him. It misses, but it takes his attention away from Lirra, giving her a chance to get a dozen paces closer to them than I am currently. She's half the distance to the carriage. A dozen more paces and she'll be upon them.

Providing another distraction, I shoot two arrows into the side of the carriage, knowing it won't go through the panel. The girls inside start screaming. The man using the black-haired girl as a shield edges back toward the carriage, while Lord Conklin stays out of sight behind the horses. My third arrow is aimed at the archer, but again it misses because his eye is trained on my movement.

He doesn't see Lirra sneak up until her blade is thrust between his ribs. Lirra pulls her blade out, swipes it on the fallen man's tunic, and turns toward the remaining men. I stare at her, shocked by the ease of her brutality. Fighting and survival are a part of my job. Though Britta was trained alongside me, it was always hard for her to stomach death. Even while hunting, she'd offer a prayer of thanks to any prey she took down, always mindful and grateful for the life around her. But Lirra, she's killed men before. The effortlessness in her movements proves as much. Maybe that's what it takes to be the Arch-traitor's daughter.

Since the remaining two men aren't armed with a bow, I move in. Lirra's switched blades to a long sword, holding it out at the man hiding behind the young girl. "Let the girls go, and I'll spare your life."

The man spits on the ground.

Thunder rocks the forest. It's the sound of at least a half-dozen horses. The man hears it and shoves the girl forward before he darts behind the carriage. The girl stumbles over her feet and crashes into Lirra. Both girls trip back.

The man jumps into the seat and the carriage takes off. Lord Conklin must've entered the carriage on the other side, because he's nowhere in sight. I watch them splatter mud as they drive away quicker than any of us can follow without our horses. I want to spit a slew of curses. How many more girls were in that carriage? What is Lord Conklin going to do with them?

Bloody seeds and stars.

Now it's just me, Lirra, the young girl, and the pounding of hooves drawing closer.

"We have to get out of here," I yell, rushing back to Finn's side. With Finn down, I don't want a standoff against half a dozen Shaerdanian men — even if they're a local ragtag group of men. They'll be able to see through Finn's awful Shaerdanian lilt before he finishes saying his first word. We're dead men if we stay here.

"What about her?" Lirra has her arm around the girl's shoulders.

I glance back at the trees where birds are taking flight. "Bring her. Hurry."

Lirra rushes the girl forward, and the four of us dash northward. I whistle for the horses and pray to every god that hasn't forsaken me that the Shaerdanians won't follow our tracks. That they'll keep on the carriage trail leading east. We're two Malamian men with two Shaerdanian girls. No matter what the girls say on our behalf, no kinsman with his blood up would believe their story.

Finn winces with each jostle from the horse, and the young girl silently sobs as we stay on a due east course, hoping like hell we're riding toward freedom.

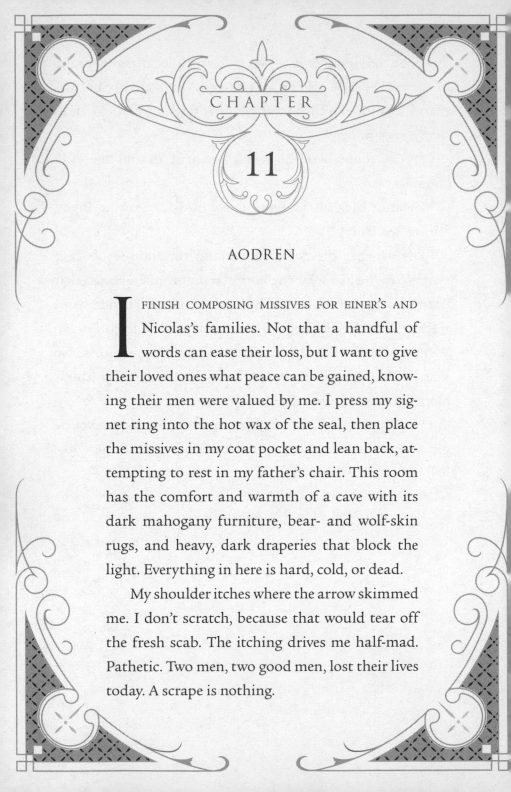

CHAPTER

11

AODREN

I FINISH COMPOSING MISSIVES FOR EINER'S AND Nicolas's families. Not that a handful of words can ease their loss, but I want to give their loved ones what peace can be gained, knowing their men were valued by me. I press my signet ring into the hot wax of the seal, then place the missives in my coat pocket and lean back, attempting to rest in my father's chair. This room has the comfort and warmth of a cave with its dark mahogany furniture, bear- and wolf-skin rugs, and heavy, dark draperies that block the light. Everything in here is hard, cold, or dead.

My shoulder itches where the arrow skimmed me. I don't scratch, because that would tear off the fresh scab. The itching drives me half-mad. Pathetic. Two men, two good men, lost their lives today. A scrape is nothing.

I push the chair back and stand.

I can still sense Britta through our strange connection. She's a faded echo. When I first realized the bond Britta forged when she healed me, it was bewildering. I was off-kilter when she was around, lonely when she was gone. Now, my reaction is more controlled. But one thing remains constant: the draw to Britta grows daily.

I leave my quarters—a rarity these days during daylight hours. Since Jamis's deception, I've found myself distrusting of others and wanting to avoid them altogether, only attending meetings when necessary. I walk toward Britta's pull. It leads me down the stairs, through the halls, and down another staircase like a dog on a leash. Halfway through Neart's guts, the connection disappears completely.

What am I doing?

Britta's left the castle. The guard, Leif, should already be headed for her home. And I've two letters that need to be delivered to grieving families.

Even so, I consider having a horse saddled up so I personally can verify she's made it back to her cottage safely. Only, the rumors circulating about my temporary madness keep me en route to Captain Omar instead. Tongues will wag enough when I announce Britta's ascension to nobility at the ball. It wouldn't be prudent to encourage more damning tales.

As always, the guards who trail me everywhere are paces away. I cross under the arcading around the inner court and think of Britta's hesitation to attend the Winter Feast. My smile quirks at the memory of her scowl. She may not want to be noble, but she deserves it. She saved my life. Twice, now.

The image of her in a silk gown that matches her brilliant blue eyes is a welcome distraction today. Britta's blond hair swept off her slender neck, exposing even more of her freckles . . . It plays in my mind, and something like longing curls through me.

It seems Britta Flannery is more potent and destructive than the local ale. Every time we talk, whether she's doling out bladed words or scrutinizing looks, I leave our conversation wanting more. Always more from her.

I've been mildly curious about the bounty hunter's daughter for most of my life. Now that we're bound, my inquisitiveness is insatiable.

The guards shadow me as I walk down the stairs. The stone path leads to the open training yard, where a dozen or so men cross swords with one another beneath a cloudless sky. Winter's claws are in the air. It's evident by the puffs of steam that billow from the men's mouths and noses as they lunge, duck, and hit blades.

Omar's growl blares over the men, shouts of drill changes coming one after another.

I wait on the edge of the lawn, rolling my neck and shoulders, working out some stiffness. The ache might've come from being tied up on Britta's horse or the night sparring sessions I've had with Captain Omar. In the last month, we've spent the late evenings working on rebuilding the strength I lost, and adding muscle and agility.

Though it didn't help much today. I grit my teeth.

Omar notices me. He breaks from the formation and takes long strides in my direction. The man is nothing if not a rigid observer of custom. Fist to his chest, he drops to a knee until I ask him to rise. This is something I've repeatedly told him isn't necessary. I think of Omar as a grumpy uncle. Then again, I once looked to Jamis as a father.

Judging others is not my strong suit, but I do trust Omar. He's proven himself many times over. Just as I trust Britta.

I cut a sideways glance at the men beside me. Both fall back, providing the pretense of privacy. "Do you have a plan in motion?"

"Men are assigned to scour the woods beyond Britta's land and set traps. We'll find Phelia. I've sent a missive for the bounty hunter to return."

Cohen Mackay. Though I trust the man with my life and he's served Malam diligently, the mention of his return slides like a sliver into my conscience.

"He's in Shaerdan?" I verify.

"Last he reported, that was the case."

Depending on where he is in Shaerdan, he could be one to two weeks of travel time away. Knowing Cohen and his Akarian horse, I wouldn't be surprised if he arrives here six days after he receives Omar's missive.

"We've also assigned guards to Britta's cottage." Omar pauses with a judgmental sour face. "Those guards are in addition to the ones combing the forest for Phelia and her co-conspirators," he says, as if I don't already know this.

Omar is likely wondering why Britta would need the added protection. Considering she shot arrow after arrow while riding halfway out of the saddle as her horse galloped full speed between trees, there's no doubt in my mind that she can defend herself. If even a quarter of my soldiers possessed Britta's courage and fortitude, Malam would be unstoppable.

"She was attacked today," I say. "Two men were murdered. It's better to be safe."

"Very well."

"You don't seem pleased. What is that look, Omar?"

"I feel as though I should warn you that courting Britta Flannery could have . . . consequences. After all, she's practically engaged."

"Is she?" My teeth click together. "I wasn't aware Cohen Mackay had offered her marriage."

Omar's eyes narrow. For a moment I wonder if he'll actually air his grievances about Miss Flannery. It's no secret that he dislikes her. "He hasn't. That doesn't mean he isn't planning—"

"Her engagement or future engagement is little matter to her safety now. I want her protected, and you'll see to it. If I need market gossip, I'll ride into Brentyn."

Omar's mouth twitches, but he doesn't say anything more.

The problem is, now that he's said something, the idea that Britta Flannery is soon to be engaged sits like a damp blanket on my thoughts. Irritation flares inside my chest. Britta and I are connected intimately. We have a relationship. Granted, a tenuous one. Even so, I find I want to pursue it, regardless of Cohen Mackay's return.

Before I move to leave, I draw the missives from my pocket. "Deliver these today. Also, please see that both families' debts are covered."

"Einer's widow will be grateful. But Nicolas wasn't married. He lived with his parents. Last I heard, their debts were overwhelming. It isn't the responsibility of the kingdom to pay off his parents' debts." Omar's rigid sense of justice is another reason I've only ever seen him as an uncle and not a fatherly figure.

I fix him with a stare. "Those men are dead. For me, money is hardly equal to a life."

I think of the years Lord Jamis ruled as regent, how he ignored the poor and needy. The conversations in which I pleaded with him to allot more money for the homeless and hungry went ignored. Harsh winters passed, and townspeople froze to death while Lord Jamis sat in my father's throne room, preaching about survival and strength. *The weak are a weight upon us. If they are not strong enough to see to their own survival, why should I?*

Britta Flannery has given me a second chance. There are times for justice, but I have been shown mercy. I will give my people the same.

Omar's displeasure could start an early winter. "I would caution you not to pay it all. Nicolas's family's debts are indeed excessive."

"You're right. They are sizable." I glance at the side of the castle, to the stone fortress that rises upward, hard and impenetrable. I think of the years I did nothing, the suffering of the Purge Proclamation, the way Jamis ground commoners under his boot to make sure all trade and business with Shaerdan ceased except for his own, the manipulations Jamis used to pit noblemen against noblemen. "But so are mine."

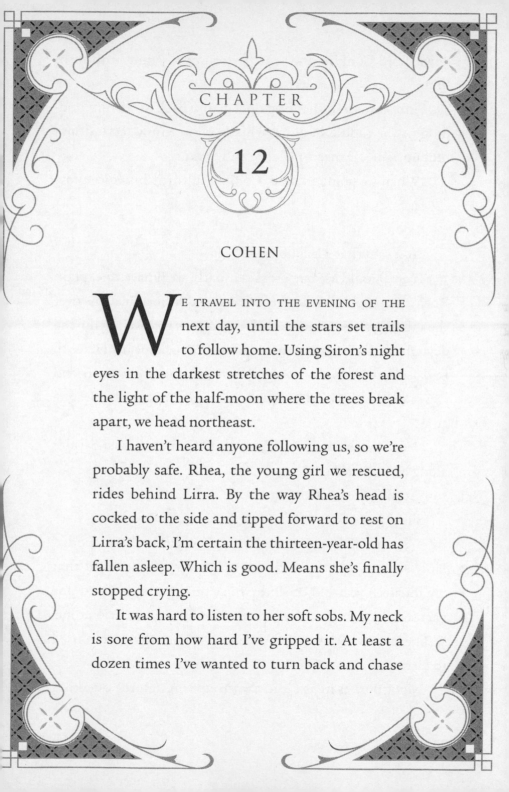

CHAPTER

12

COHEN

WE TRAVEL INTO THE EVENING OF THE
next day, until the stars set trails
to follow home. Using Siron's night
eyes in the darkest stretches of the forest and
the light of the half-moon where the trees break
apart, we head northeast.

I haven't heard anyone following us, so we're
probably safe. Rhea, the young girl we rescued,
rides behind Lirra. By the way Rhea's head is
cocked to the side and tipped forward to rest on
Lirra's back, I'm certain the thirteen-year-old has
fallen asleep. Which is good. Means she's finally
stopped crying.

It was hard to listen to her soft sobs. My neck
is sore from how hard I've gripped it. At least a
dozen times I've wanted to turn back and chase

down Lord Conklin and tear the son of a scrant limb from limb.

Finn seems to be holding up. I glance back to see him nodding in the saddle. A quick whistle between my teeth draws him upright. He meets my gaze and groans.

"When we going to stop, Co?" Sleep turns his voice gravelly.

"Soon."

"You said that a league back."

True. Should anyone cross our path, we'll have to explain Rhea's presence. The number of men and women in arms over the missing girls has increased. Enough that traveling during daylight with this girl is an added risk. Which means I have to find a safe place for her tonight. And then hopefully my friend can take Rhea home. The town's no more than another league away.

"How much longer?" This comes from Lirra, who rides along my right side.

"At this rate, half an hour."

She groans.

"You can make it. You're the toughest girl in these woods." Finn's sleepy voice reminds me of my father's. It's odd that my fourteen-year-old brother, who's nine parts goofy to one part serious, inherited my father's calm-in-any-situation tone. Well, except for when a girl is nearby. He must've gotten used to Lirra.

Night pushes in as I lead the group through the outskirts

of a small town that sits in the woods on the border of the drylands. Following my memory, I lead us to a well hidden in a grove of trees. A few hundred paces away, golden lamplight bleeds from a small cottage.

Britta and I met Jacinda when we were on the run from the guards, searching for Britta's father's murderer. We stumbled across Jacinda's well and later found out that Jacinda's Channeling gift made it so the water in the well was Beannach. Blessed water.

I stop at the well first. I pull up a bucket and tell Finn to dismount.

"Drink this."

He approaches the well and takes the bucket, gulping back a big swallow without question. He's such a good kid. The blood on his tunic is just another black shadow right now. Seeing it as he brings the bucket to his mouth turns my stomach. This water will help him some. I wish it would completely heal him, but I don't think it has the full healing power that Britta's Channeler gift possesses.

"What are you doing? If you're going to steal, you should do a perimeter check first." Lirra's whisper cuts through the night, scrutiny whittling her words to fine points.

"Belongs to my friend. Try some." I help her and her groggy young riding companion off their horse.

Rhea sits at the edge of the well next to Finn while Lirra takes a sip.

Lirra's blue eyes rise to mine. "This water's been gifted."

She twists around, taking in the house. "Are you certain it's all right to be here?"

"Like I said, it's my friend's place." I finish drinking my fill before setting out a second bucket for the horses.

"Feel better?" I place my hand on Finn's back.

He nods and drinks again. Finn comments on the sweetness of the water to Lirra, a point he punctuates with a belch. Fourteen years old. I sigh. At his age, I'd just moved to Brentyn to apprentice with Saul. Britta was all elbows, knees, and attitude.

I tell Finn and Lirra to wait for me, and then I head to the door.

Jacinda's home, a mushroom-shaped cottage, blends into the reddish tree bark and tall shrubs. Someone traveling by might easily miss it. A smart choice for her husband to have made before he passed. The boards crossing one another to bar her windows don't match the rest of the home's construction. They've been tacked on recently, I'd say, by the fresh look of the wood. No rust stains the nails.

I knock and wait until she calls through the door. "Who's there?"

"Jacinda, it's me. Cohen."

The door swings open. An arm encircles me before I have a chance to step back. The stout raven-haired woman clutches me in a chokehold even though a little voice cries out, "Momma, squeezing me."

When I pull back, I see a miniature version of Jacinda, hair darker than the shadows, propped on her hip.

"Sorry, Lou." Jacinda hugs her daughter once and then sets her on the ground where she remains beside her mother, hugging flame-colored skirts. "My youngest forgets she's not a baby. She doesn't need to be carried everywhere."

I kneel down, coming face-to-face with the little girl. "Hi, Lou, I'm Cohen."

A shy smile winks at me before Lou shoves her face into her mother's skirt.

"How old are you?" I try again.

She holds up a hand with all five fingers extended. Then she holds up her other hand with one more finger.

"I'm six too," I tell her, and she frowns at me. "Well, six plus fourteen."

"You're old."

I chuckle, but in truth, some days I feel old, bone-tired old. I think back to when Finn was this girl's age, and I get itchy inside at the thought of taking him into any more danger.

"Did you find her?" Jacinda steps to the side and stretches out her arm, welcoming me in.

"Not quite. I found a girl from Rasimere Crossing who was taking Channeler herbs to change her appearance."

Jacinda carries Lou inside and tucks her into bed by her sisters, and then she follows me outside. She wrings her hands and shoves them in her pocket. "That's old magic. Charms can be created only when two or more different Channelers combine their efforts. I don't know much about it, other than it's risky. And in most cases, the Channelers Guild outlawed making charms a long time ago. It's been at least fifteen years."

That's interesting. A woman at an Elementiary gave Britta a charm in Celize. We used it to gain entry to Enat's home. "Why would they outlaw it? I thought all Channeler magic was allowed in Shaerdan. And what is the Channelers Guild?"

"One question at a time. The Guild was formed by the elders in the Channeler society. Years ago, they appointed women who possessed the strongest strains of magic. Because they have the most skill, they've been tasked with creating lessons for each division of Channeling."

"Like at an Elementiary?"

"Who taught you about those?"

"Britta stumbled into one in Celize."

"What's taught at an Elementiary is overseen by the Guild."

Makes sense. "And they make laws as well?"

She lifts her skirt to step over a fallen log. I slow my pace as she looks to the moon and back to me. "When needed, they make laws around our magic. They set precedence and a code by which all Channelers live. The chief judge is keen on all Channelers following these rules. It's for our protection as much as it is for others."

In all the time I've traveled through Shaerdan, I haven't had many interactions with women who have outright identified themselves as Channelers. Seems like Channelers in

Shaerdan don't advertise their ability. Makes me wonder if it's a cultural way of existing or a defense mechanism.

I push a branch out of our path, glancing ahead to the well where Lirra, Finn, and Rhea sit. The horses mill around the well behind them, drinking. Siron's ears flick and he lifts his nose to the air as we approach, but drops it back to the bucket a moment later.

"There must be some that break the Guild's law," I say, picking up the conversation.

"Rarely. The first and foremost rule of Channeler magic is that it can be used only for good. We never use our abilities to harm. Which is why most charms have been outlawed." Jacinda continues, "They fall into the gray area of that rule. A charm could be created by a Channeler with the intent to do good. But someone else could use it for harm. Because there's a lack of control when it comes to charms, most are prohibited by the Channelers Guild's law."

Interesting. Could've sworn Enat had no reservations against using charms.

"What happens if someone breaks the law?"

"They get turned over to the chief judge and his council, where you're tried before a court of your peers."

Lirra's voice breaks into our conversation. "Hello there."

Jacinda turns to Lirra. Beyond her, Finn and Rhea sit at the well's edge. "Who do we have here?"

"Sorry." I gesture to each one. "Lirra, my kid brother, Finn, and Rhea."

Jacinda takes in the group and turns to me with one raised black brow. "Intriguing travel party you have here in the middle of the night. They look dead on their feet. Come on inside and let me get you a place to sleep."

Finn's eyes bounce to mine, pleading and big like a puppy's. Exhaustion shows in the slope of his shoulders and curve of his scrawny back.

"Go on," I tell him.

His face flushes with relief as he leans forward to stand, elbows and knees bending like a scarecrow's in an autumn wind.

"Thank you, Jacinda," I tell her.

She guides us down the path to her home. "You're welcome anytime."

Jacinda ushers us inside and lights a candle. The flame flicks to life, spreading weak golden light in the small room. From there she leads us down a small hall to a larger room, where a fire crackles in the hearth and a massive snowy dog curls up on the wood-planked floor.

Jacinda takes out blankets from a chest and sets them on the ground. The dog lifts its chin, surveying the action as Finn and Rhea curl up on the ground.

The kids and the dog are asleep moments later. One snore out of the animal and Jacinda spins to me, hands on hips, fingers tapping against the fiery material. "Cohen, did you want to live another night? Do you know who this girl is?"

I step back, shocked by the ferocity of her whisper. "Who?"

"This is Seeva Soliel's daughter. Seeva is the leader of the Guild."

"By Guild do you mean the Channelers Guild you've been talking about?"

Her chin rises up and slams back down in a definite nod.

Bludger. "So you're saying if anyone catches me with her, I'll be killed first, questioned later?"

She gives me a worried look. "Exactly."

13

AODREN

NEAR THE INNER GATE, A THIRD-STORY room the size of a closet has loophole slits that look down on the outer yard. The room can be accessed only from the parapet. I discovered the spot at the age of seven, after Jamis turned me away from the lords' meeting and tasked me with reading a particularly dreary tome in the castle library. Boredom goaded me to explore.

To ensure no one sees me, I scurry along the battlement in a half-crouched position. Though it's been a few years since I've come here, my muscles remember the balance needed to cross the sections on the parapet where the stones have crumbled.

A wool banner rests against one of the keep's

south towers, hiding the entrance into the room. I shove aside the heavy material and duck into the small opening.

Archers once used this nook for defense. In the centuries since it was built, more strategic defensive locations have been added to the castle, and this room has been forgotten. When I was younger, I watched people through the loophole slits.

The earthy smell of the room dredges up memories. I rest my head against the smooth, chilled stone.

The first time I noticed Saul Flannery, I was in this very room. He was rushing across the yard to help a stablehand with a foaling horse. Unlike other birthing horses, this one's movements were jerky and frantic. It paced and kicked, eyes rolling to whites. Despite the danger, Saul reached for the animal and assisted until the newborn horse had been foaled. The mare died from complications. The foal had been injured during birth and the stablehand thought it would die also. But Saul stayed with the vulnerable animal for days, and when it was stronger, he took the animal home.

Saul was kind and caring and, most important, always courageous in the face of danger. My father was not a good man. A terror of a king, he let his superstitions lead to mass execution of his people. When he passed, his conspiracies bled to his nobles and onto the country. After yesterday, it sickens me to admit that I understand my father's choices a little bit better. I don't agree, but I understand his fear.

Unlike my father, however, I won't let fear control me. During my reign, the people of Malam will see the abolishment of the Purge. If it's the last thing I do, I'll bring about a change that clears the haze of hate and fear clouding the vision of the citizens of Malam.

The peepholes give me a view of the road and woods beyond the castle where a brisk breeze pushes through the tops of the trees and whistles through the cracks in the tower. A couple of carts crunch over the gravel approaching the bridge. I watch them, wondering when I'll see Britta again.

I saw Britta Flannery for the first time four years ago. The bounty hunter's shadow took cautious steps into my Winter Feast celebration. Grim mouth, wary blue eyes, and the scowl she wore like chainmail fascinated me.

The luxuries of the castle and opulent décor of the celebration didn't seem to draw her attention. I wanted to know more about the strange girl. I still do. Back then, it didn't take much prodding to discover who she was. Or that, despite the noble status her father held, Britta was an outcast.

In that aspect, we were similar. I grew up a ghost in my own castle. No one spoke to me for fear of offending the future king, the son of the tyrant. No one met my eye. No one held my trust, other than the two men who raised me.

Now that one of them has betrayed me, I feel like I'm navigating through the woods in the dark.

As king, I have to weigh each decision, anticipate how it'll affect the kingdom. If I could be more like Britta, shrewd, self-assured, strong . . .

My leadership has given little for the people of Malam to trust. Before I took over from Jamis, who'd become regent after my father's death, I stood aside while he demanded that the Purge Proclamation be upheld, that every Channeler in Malam be hunted down. After I became king, I allowed my high lord to deceive and manipulate me.

I scrub my palms against my face.

"Get the healer."

The shout echoes up from the courtyard, followed by a clatter of metal. I press my face to the stone, seeking the source of the noise. One of the elite guards, Leif O'Floinn, passes an unconscious girl to another man before dismounting his horse. Once on the ground, he takes the girl back into his arms and says something I cannot hear. Then the stablehand ushers the horse away as Leif rushes toward the inner gate, a flopping autumn-haired teenage girl in his arms.

I push aside the tapestry and rush along the parapet. I leap down the stairs two at a time, reaching the main level of the castle as a couple of servant girls go rushing past. They squeak at the sight of me, mutter an apology with their eyes to the stone floor, and scuttle away. I follow, heading toward the castle's healer, picking up pieces of their conversation.

"Said he found her in the woods . . ."

". . . scars on her wrist . . ."

". . . breathing, but her eyes won't open."

I hurry past them, scaring them once more, and turn down the hallway to the healer's room.

"What happened?" I approach Leif and Omar, who are standing beside a bed.

Omar turns, the angry slashes of his brows lifting in surprise. "Your Highness, the situation hasn't yet been assessed. I'll come report once I know what's going on." He glares at Leif. "And why Leif thought it was a good idea to bring an unknown girl into your castle."

"She's dying." Leif's reddened face is drawn tighter than I've ever seen. "Where else would ya have me take her?"

"She could be a trap. Or at the very least, a threat." Omar spins back to face the younger guard.

"A threat? Open yer eyes. She's a wee gal. She cannot be more than thirteen."

"I can see that, but have you forgotten what happened yesterday?" Omar's jaw flexes.

Nona, the healer, rushes into the room from an adjoining door, carrying a bowl of water and white towels. A man follows behind, a local healer named Hagan that I've not seen since the week I spent in the castle healer's care.

"Omar." I cut into their ongoing argument. "Let the healers do their work before we determine whether she's a threat."

I can tell Omar isn't pleased by the way his lips tense and whiten. Empathy isn't his strength. But I suppose it makes him an excellent captain of the guard. He questions Leif about the girl and where she was found.

"I'd just rotated shifts with the guards at the base of

Mount Avemoir. The girl came stumbling through the trees. I saw her collapse. Before she lost consciousness, she asked for help."

"For what?" Omar says at the same time I ask, "From whom?"

Leif shakes his head. "Don't know. Said 'help' a couple of times between short breaths. Then her eyes closed, and they haven't opened since."

Nona and Hagan move around us, examining the girl. Her skin is tawny, but it lacks the usual warmth from someone with a similar tone. The gray pallor makes her look frighteningly close to death.

Nona tells Hagan to make a brew before she turns back to the girl and lifts her lids. Unfocused orbs of silvery-blue gaze at nothing. Breath stutters out of the girl's pale lips.

Nona's mouth pinches. "Come on, girl. Don't leave us," she whispers.

Hagan returns with a small cup of brew, but sets it to the side of the bed when Nona points out the girl's wrists. Hagan emits a small gasp.

"What is it?" Omar crowds the healers.

Nona turns the girl's arm to show two burned circles with four small dots on the inside of her wrist. The puffy, red skin makes it appear as if someone's branded her with an iron.

I start to repeat Omar's question when a fragment of a memory returns.

· · ·

"Did it work?" Jamis walked over to Phelia and pushed the length of her hair off her shoulder. He lowered his head, his lips touching the spot where the fabric of her dress met her neck.

She drew in a slow breath and stared out the window of my private quarters, eyes calculating, hard, and icy. "Must we always meet in here?"

"He's a puppet." Jamis waves his hand in my direction. My body is a lump under the blankets of my bed. "And if he wasn't, you could inflict enough damage to erase his thoughts, couldn't you?"

Phelia lifts one shoulder.

"Now tell me, have you figured it out?"

"Not quite. The girl died too quickly."

"Were you able to use any of it?"

"I lit a candle." Phelia crosses her arms.

Jamis approaches and rests his hands on her shoulders, squeezing.

Phelia steps away.

"What happened?"

"She died too fast. There wasn't time."

Jamis scowls. "That's what happened to the last girl. How will I explain another death?"

Phelia spins around and whips out her arm, pulling the draping sleeve of her dress up. Black marks crawl over her skin. Semicircles, points, snaking lines. "The rune wasn't right. Stop thinking about the inconvenience. This is a breakthrough. I've almost figured out how to keep the girls alive long enough."

Jamis smiles. "That's what I want to hear. But tell me, love, how many more times will you try? You've completely disfigured yourself."

I rub my temples. I've seen the girl's mark before, in my bedroom chamber. My gaze flicks from the rune on the girl's arm to Hagan, whose shrewd gaze holds understanding.

"Come on, girl," Nona pleads, swiping the medicinal brew on the young patient's lips. The girl doesn't respond. Her breaths seem to labor a little harder. Nona whispers the same encouragement once more as the rest of us around the bed hold our breaths.

One more rise and fall of her chest holds our attention. And then nothing more.

Even the muscles in her face slacken.

We wait. A couple of minutes pass, perhaps more. We're all under the young girl's spell, hoping for a change that isn't going to happen. Eventually, Nona moves. She drops her chin to her chest and places a hand over the girl's eyes, murmuring a prayer of passing.

I don't know what to do or say.

Omar walks to the foot of the bed. His beard does little to hide the deep set of his frown. "A shame. Damn shame." The argument he had with Leif moments earlier is forgotten. "Does that mark mean something to either of you?"

Nona exchanges glances with Hagan before the man says, "It's a rune. Channelers used to use them to strengthen their power."

"Is that what killed her?" Leif cuts in, struggle apparent on his features.

Admittedly, I'm equally shaken. Perhaps I'm just better at hiding my reaction.

"I don't know," Hagan says. By the way his eyes meet mine, I know he's not being honest with Omar and Leif.

We discuss the girl further. None of us have a clue as to who her family might be. So in addition to adding guards in the woods, Omar assigns Leif to question the locals about a missing girl.

"No one speaks a word of this," Omar cautions everyone in the room.

I nod in agreement. It's better to keep word of this young girl's death tightly wrapped until we know for certain who she is and how she died. For now, the healer will have to come up with a passable excuse to spread among the talkative servant girls.

Once Omar and Leif leave, I stay behind to have a word with Hagan.

He steps into the adjoining healing room with me while Nona tends to the girl, preparing her for burial.

"What more do you know?" I close the door so Hagan and I are alone.

The man crosses the room and picks up a metal tool, something that's probably used in surgery. He rolls it in his fingers. "I do not want to cause trouble or have trouble turned around on me."

I nod. "Go on. Whatever you have to say, I'll keep a secret."

He stares at me for a moment, as if sizing me up. "When

I tended to you last month, I could tell you were overcoming more than simple sickness. That scar on your neck"—he points at me with the metal instrument—"has the look of a Spiriter's healing."

Perhaps I'm sometimes good at hiding my reaction. Now is not one of those times. "How do you know this?"

"Because I know Channeler magic. Been around it my whole life. My mother was one."

"And have you kept my secret, then?"

"I have. I'm a man who can be trusted."

I weigh his words. If he wanted me overthrown, he would've already spread word that a Channeler healed me. "Go on."

"That rune on the girl's arm is old magic. Dark magic. It's a gifting rune. It allows one Channeler to lend her power to another."

I think of the memory, unease like ice crippling my veins.

"Mind you, I've never seen it in action. And by the way the girl's skin was infected, I'd say it didn't work. But you should know I've heard word of Channeler girls going missing in Shaerdan. If this girl's one of theirs . . . well, it doesn't look good for Malam."

No, it doesn't.

I ask Hagan a few more questions, and he tells me the rumors he's heard about Channeler girls being taken. I think of the girls I saw in the woods yesterday and the body of the amber-haired girl resting in the other room.

Since Lord Jamis was arrested, I expected Phelia to run.

What more is Phelia up to? Could she truly be trying to use the Channelers as weapons?

I'll not break Hagan's trust, but Omar needs to be alerted right away.

Phelia is more of a threat than any of us knew.

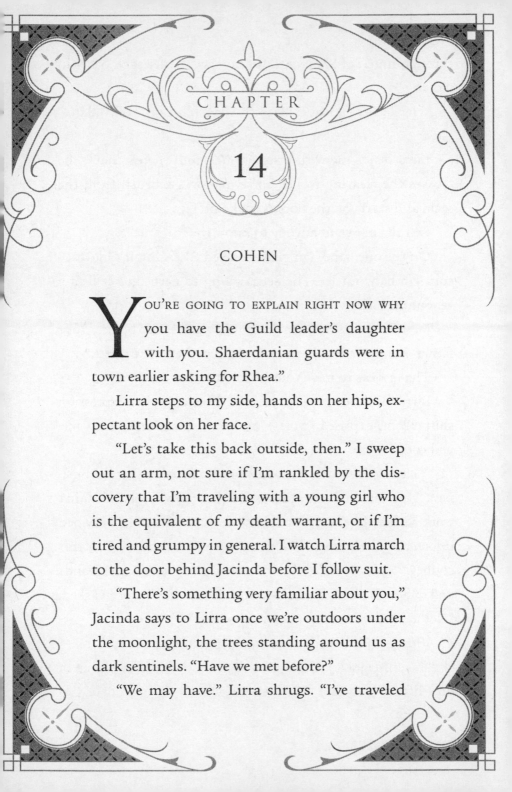

CHAPTER

14

COHEN

You're going to explain right now why you have the Guild leader's daughter with you. Shaerdanian guards were in town earlier asking for Rhea."

Lirra steps to my side, hands on her hips, expectant look on her face.

"Let's take this back outside, then." I sweep out an arm, not sure if I'm rankled by the discovery that I'm traveling with a young girl who is the equivalent of my death warrant, or if I'm tired and grumpy in general. I watch Lirra march to the door behind Jacinda before I follow suit.

"There's something very familiar about you," Jacinda says to Lirra once we're outdoors under the moonlight, the trees standing around us as dark sentinels. "Have we met before?"

"We may have." Lirra shrugs. "I've traveled

through much of Shaerdan. Perhaps we've met each other in passing."

"Her father's Millner Barrett, the Archtraitor of Malam," I add.

Lirra blasts me with a scowl. "Yes, and there's that." She crosses the clearing to her horse, removes a brush from the sack, and starts on the horse's back and legs.

Did she not want anyone to know that?

On the one hand, I'm glad we saved Rhea, but it's like capturing a baby rattler. The act is going to earn us a hell of a venomous bite.

Jacinda smiles at Lirra. "Right. We have met before. Your father and my late husband worked together a few times."

That's news to me. "Your husband was a rebel?"

Lirra blinks owl eyes at Jacinda. I watch as her expression shifts from surprise to worry. "You won't mention you saw me, will you?"

"Getting in touch with Millner was my husband's business. Not mine," Jacinda reassures her. "My husband didn't work with Millner very often but, yes, when asked he provided information. He knew practically everyone who lives in this county." Sadness sinks the corners of her mouth. She stands and moves to Finn's horse, helping without having been asked. "Not a day goes by that I don't miss him."

"Sorry. Didn't mean to bring up anything painful."

"It's all right." Jacinda pats the horse's back. A plume of dust lifts into the air. "Now tell me, what's going on here, Cohen? You're a Malamian man traveling with two Channeler girls. One of whom most of the country is looking for. And the other whose father is infamous and probably not keen on finding out his daughter is with you. Have you a death wish?"

Lirra chuckles, but ducks her head when I look in her direction.

"Lirra's choices are her own since she insisted on coming along. Now Rhea, that's different. Didn't realize who she was." My thumb grazes my scar before shoving my hand into my hair. Siron walks to my side and nuzzles my hand. I rub his nose and ears, then spend the next twenty minutes explaining how Lirra joined my traveling party, and then how we saved Rhea. Jacinda's eyes are two round moons when I tell her about Lord Conklin.

"You did the right thing." Jacinda brushes the horse's mane. "You shouldn't be faulted for helping her. It'll be too dangerous for you to drop her off in town, so you should leave Rhea with me, and I'll send word that I have her."

"You'd take care of her for me?"

"You know I'm in your debt. Besides, the girl is scared and needs a warm, safe place to sleep. I'll keep her here till they come." Not sure if it's the moonlight's gray kiss, or if Jacinda's eyes are getting misty.

"You know you've already paid us back tenfold," I tell her, but she shakes her head, not accepting that she's done more for Britta and me than we could ever repay.

"Who do you think Lord Conklin is working with?" Jacinda's hands pause, caught in the tangled mess of black horse hair. "There have been too many girls taken for one man and his group of muscle to be running around all of Shaerdan." She glances back toward her home where the boarded windows keep the light in. "Two girls, twin sisters, from this town were taken three weeks ago. They vanished in the middle of the night."

"That's terrible." Lirra puts the brush in the saddlebag.

"The Kelstion family woke to find both their girls missing, a window left open, and prints in the soil. Men from town followed them until they were lost in the river."

"Feels like no girls are safe." Lirra shivers and wraps her arms around her ribs.

"That explains the boarded windows." I step away from Siron and give him a pat so he leaves to drink some more well water.

"Aye. It's hard to know how to protect yourself when you don't know who or what you're facing. But I go to bed each night determined to fight for my family," Jacinda says. The sadness lining her words hits me in a way I'm not expecting.

I think of when I found Britta in the king's chambers, heartbeats from death. The piercing anxiety and the helplessness. Don't ever want to be faced with that again.

I tuck the thought away, knowing right now I have to figure out what's happening to the Channeler girls. Even if my duty to the king didn't already demand it, I cannot forget what I saw today. The fear shaking through Rhea's body. The worry in Jacinda's eyes.

Lord Conklin's not working alone.

I rub the back of my neck, wishing the tension in my shoulders would go away. Doubt that'll happen till Finn is patched up and home safe, and I'm back beside Britta.

"You think there's a connection between Phelia and the missing girls?" Lirra dusts off her skirt, which has seen better days. Tears and stains define the struggles of the last couple of days.

"Aye. It's a possibility," I say. I walk away from Finn's horse.

Jacinda crosses the clearing to a mammoth limb that drags on the ground. The tree resembles a man pushing himself up after a fight. Jacinda sits on his knobby shoulder. "Not many women would blatantly disobey the Guild's laws. If you're found guilty, it's a death sentence."

Steep punishment. "I thought Channelers were revered in Shaerdan."

"They are, but they still need laws to govern themselves."

Makes sense. "I've used a charm before," I admit, grimacing as I explain the charm needed to gain access to Enat's home.

"Could be she petitioned the Guild for it. But does Enat using old and perhaps illegal magic surprise you?"

Nope. Sounds like something the spry old woman would do. Except . . . "Why would she caution Britta not to use her gift for dark magic if she was using charms?"

"It's not the same sort of magic," Jacinda explains.

"There's a difference," Lirra cuts in. "The main classification for dark magic is that it siphons energy from another. It's all about the Channeler's intent to do ill. Whereas a charm could be created by a Channeler to be used for a good purpose, but someone with nefarious purposes could get their hands on it and twist it to their own ends. See the difference?"

"Nefarious?" I smirk.

Lirra throws a stick at me, and I suddenly feel like I'm teasing my sister, Imogen. "It's called reading. Try it, you stupid mule."

"I know what the word means."

"Remind me to give you an apple."

Jacinda claps her hands. "You two are worse than my kids. Stop fighting. It's time to get to bed."

I sleep better than I have in days beside the warmth of Jacinda's fire. There's nothing like a soft pillow and a blanket after a long day of riding.

In the morning, Siron's stomps wake me. His snort and shuffle sound from outside the cottage. It's a sound he makes only when he's alarmed.

I throw off the blanket. On instinct, I wrap my fingers around the hilt of my sword and lunge for the door. Outside, my gaze ricochets around the clearing.

An older man, his hair as gray as Captain Omar's, stands

a dozen paces away from Siron, holding the reins of his dusty brown horse.

A man I've met before. Duff Baron. Courier. Underground informant.

"You're a hard fellow to find." He approaches me.

"I try to keep it that way."

"My asking around probably won't help your cause much. You should know that there are Shaerdanian soldiers in the area. They're looking for you."

Bludger. I glance to the house where Finn and Lirra are still sleeping. Scratch that. Lirra's standing at the door, wide eyes on the two of us.

"Is that what you came to tell me?" I cross my arms.

"Duff, is that you?"

Of course Lirra knows him. I fight not to roll my eyes.

His face breaks out into a fatherly grin. "Lirra Barrett." He tips his chin up at her before remembering I'm here. "You two traveling together?"

"For a bit," she says, not adding anything more.

"Does your father know? That the safest thing for you?"

"Probably not," I say. "But she won't leave me alone."

She flares her nostrils. But she's quick to explain why I'm her travel buddy, making up something about needing a guide near the border. The longer I know Lirra, the clearer it becomes that she's got more silver on her tongue than exists in all the coffers of Malam. The girl could talk a horse right out from under a man by convincing him he's riding a badger.

"Then you'd best take this missive addressed to the bounty hunter and be on your way." Duff holds out a rolled-up piece of parchment. "Guards are searching the town. I'd hate to see you get caught up in his trouble."

Lirra walks forward to take the scroll, but I grab it before she can get her little hands on my letter.

"Thank you, Duff. I'll keep an eye out. Don't worry about me." She turns wide eyes on the older man like she's perfectly innocent.

I huff out a breath and roll open the scroll.

> *Phelia attacked the king and B. Return.*
> — *Omar*

I stare at the words. Read them three more times.

Attacked? How? When? Where?

If there was ever a time I wanted to school Omar on communication, it's now. The lack of information slams me with anxiety. I reach for my belt, running my hand over the hidden feather.

Phelia's in Brentyn. She's hurt Britta.

Dammit.

I punch the tree to release the fury crashing through me. Doesn't help, but it does crack a couple of knuckles. I'm useless this far from Brentyn.

"Get Finn," I bark at Lirra, causing her to jump. "We're leaving now."

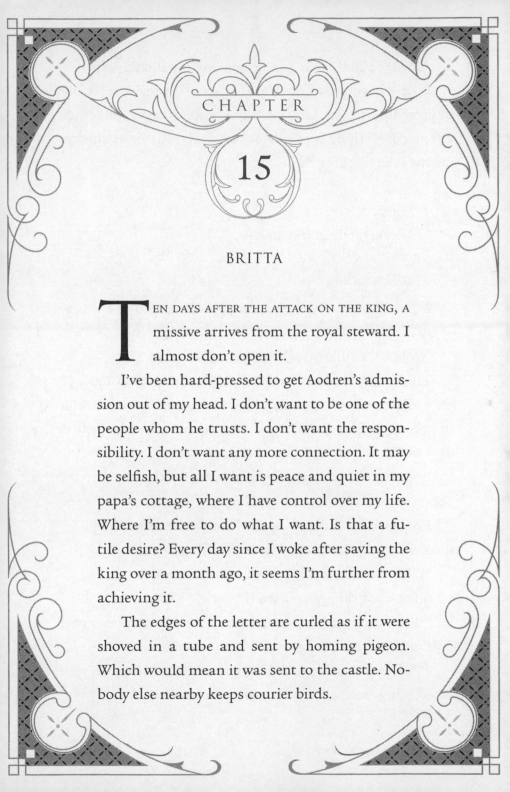

CHAPTER

15

BRITTA

TEN DAYS AFTER THE ATTACK ON THE KING, A missive arrives from the royal steward. I almost don't open it.

I've been hard-pressed to get Aodren's admission out of my head. I don't want to be one of the people whom he trusts. I don't want the responsibility. I don't want any more connection. It may be selfish, but all I want is peace and quiet in my papa's cottage, where I have control over my life. Where I'm free to do what I want. Is that a futile desire? Every day since I woke after saving the king over a month ago, it seems I'm further from achieving it.

The edges of the letter are curled as if it were shoved in a tube and sent by homing pigeon. Which would mean it was sent to the castle. Nobody else nearby keeps courier birds.

"It's not a snake." Gillian hovers over my shoulder.

I turn, hiding the note from her view. Is this what it's like to grow up in a house of siblings? People always underfoot. Overhead. Nothing is private or personal. My fingers slip under the seal, cracking the wax.

> *Dove,*
> *Meet me at the clearing at noon.*
> —*C*

My heart turns into a hummingbird trapped in the cage of my ribs.

"Cohen?" Gillian's eagle eye misses nothing.

Thrilled that he's hours away, I cannot speak. I move to the wall where my bow and quiver rest because I won't be able to sit in this cottage and wait. Time is always better spent in the woods.

Boots laced and dagger bedded by my ankle, I stalk to the door.

Fists plop on Gillian's hips. "What did he write? Where are you going?" She trails me. "Say something, Britta."

"I'll be back later. I'm headed to the clearing."

She growls through pursed lips.

"Was that sound befitting a lady?" I slide my quiver over my shoulder with a smirk.

"Not two weeks ago, the king was attacked. Two men were killed. The woods aren't safe. Must you go out?"

A hit of guilt gets me between the lungs. I've not shared the secret about my mother with anyone other than Aodren. I've wanted to talk about Phelia, but shame and residual shock keep me from opening up to Gillian.

"I'll be fine," I tell her. Leif and his men have spent the last ten days scouring the Evers for any sign of Phelia and her accomplices. They've found nothing. The clearing, on the king's land, is safer than where the king was attacked. "I'll bag a goose for supper while I'm gone."

"We have enough meat for the rest of the week. And that's not an answer to my questions."

"Winter's coming." I open the door. Echoing one of Papa's many lessons, I add, "The best defense is being prepared."

Her hands wrap in her skirts, wrinkling the dusty blue fabric. "Don't just run out. I—I suppose I could come with you. It'll be safer if we go together." It ends on a questioning high note. Her upturned nose and the tight clench her hands have on her dress spell out how much she'd dislike tagging along. Gillian would be content if the world were covered in gravel roads and stone buildings, swept free of all dirt.

"I'll be well. Promise." I tap my bow on the ground.

Her look of relief amuses me as she wraps her arms around me in a tight squeeze of a hug. We are so different.

There's an undercurrent of energy in the Evers. In all life. Enat taught me to recognize it. But something about healing Aodren has awakened my awareness, making it impossible to ignore the forest's thrum. The tune sticks with me while

Snowfire carries me to the base of the narrow canyon that leads to Papa's old training spot.

Nobody crosses my path as I ride to the clearing that sits on the edge of a frozen lake. Here, the quaky trees are little more than skeletons this time of year, leaves hanging from limbs like tattered rags.

I rub Snowfire's neck while I wait. The sun moves behind thick, overcast clouds. When the light lowers in the sky, edging further past noon, Cohen still hasn't come.

Needing a distraction, I slide an arrow out of my quiver. Steadied to the bowstring, I aim at a cluster of dead leaves on a quaky tree and shoot. My arrow snaps a branch that's no thicker than a raven's claw. The leaves sail to the frosty ground.

I scan the shadows between pine trunks. With an ear tipped toward the gray sky, I listen for anything beyond the rustle of wind.

Few birds remain in the trees now that winter has settled over the Malam Mountains, and those great black predators who have lingered don't seem to be on alert against anyone besides me.

I'm alone.

Don't you want to know all you're capable of? Phelia's question taunts me. It's wound through my thoughts a dozen times since the attack in the woods.

Enat's lessons on our trip from Shaerdan to Malam taught me the basics. I'm not sure about much else when it comes to

Channeler magic. There's no one in Malam who can teach me because there are no Channelers here, let alone rare Spiriters. Only Phelia.

I shudder, wanting to pry her words out of my head.

No way would I ever go to Phelia to learn. Not ever.

I pick up the broken branch and then walk to find my arrow. The three leaves on the branch look like dead mice curled around the stick. Resting my bow against a boulder, I focus on the gray veins that stretch over the browned velvety leaves, honing in on the branch. A week more and they'd be brittle enough to crumble between my fingers. As they are, I might be able to bring them back. Under the branch's white skin a *hmm hmm hmm* registers. Barely there, barely moving, barely enough to recognize as life.

I imagine my energy is a dance of bright blue color zipping through me to the beat of my heart.

What I'm doing is illegal. It likely will always be in Malam. Knowing that should be enough to make me stop.

Like Enat taught me, I push some of that sapphire energy from my elbow, past my hand, and into the branch. It's much easier this time. If I didn't know better, I'd say I was stronger now. Phelia said something about turning eighteen. Could my birthday have changed the way I sense energy around me?

Tingles spider walk up and down my forearm. My pulse throbs in my hand as I push a little more. A little more. A little more.

The first leaf uncurls, its teardrop shape returning.

The second leaf opens, exposing veins of amber that crawl from the stem outward.

The third leaf flames to life like a spit-shined gold coin.

Awe and relief course over me, warming me like an August sun at high noon. I sink down, place the branch in my lap, and pump my hand in and out of a fist to encourage more blood flow. An ache blossoms between my elbow and fingertips, sleepy tingles like mites crawling under my skin.

Wind chills the forest. The bite of the season is dulled by the drowsiness spreading through my body. I wish I could sustain the leaf's vibrancy, but to keep this branch alive, I'd have to push life into it every few days.

Ravens flap out of the nearby trees.

At their sudden departure, adrenaline shoots through me. I shake my limbs awake and on instinct dart behind a trunk. The rough bark's ridges press into my back.

The guards are patrolling the woods around Mount Avemoir. No one would be near this clearing.

Except Cohen . . . but it could also be Phelia . . . Rozen . . .

To be safe, I slide the hood of my cloak back for better visibility. I slip the branch into my pocket and nock an arrow.

Footsteps crunch.

I twist to the left and . . .

Cohen moves at the far end of the clearing, slipping between the evergreens, his broad shoulders bunching beneath a mossy-brown coat. The rough elegance of his movement. The precision. The predatory grace. I forget what I'm doing and just stare, transfixed by the sight of him. My heart thumps and jumps beneath my breastbone.

Cohen. I lower my bow and return the arrow to the quiver.

His head snaps up; recognition alights in his features even though we're far enough apart that he couldn't have heard me. For a split second, hope kicks through me that nothing has changed between us. That I still have the ability to know when he's near or in danger even at times I'm unable to see him.

Only, that's not the case. Unlike Aodren, my bond with Cohen was one-sided. Cohen could never sense my nearness. Since he didn't know we shared a connection, he doesn't even realize it was severed. I've no clue why Aodren can sense our link. All I know is the strange invisible thread that used to connect Cohen and me was broken when I healed the king.

Now I no longer have a heightened awareness of Cohen. I could no more say Cohen was at my door than I could guess if it was Gillian.

"Should've figured you'd beat me here." Snowflakes scatter over his knit cap. He's a vision with an easy grin, assessing hazel eyes, and a small headshake that obliterates my thoughts.

"Been waiting ages. Thought I'd have to set up camp." Exaggerating stiff muscles, I clomp across the clearing until all that separates us is a game trail beaten between the naked gray shrubs. Frosty cloven prints dimple the path, immortalized until spring's thaw.

Cohen glances at the orb of light fighting to break through

the gray wall of clouds. Half his mouth hitches up, crinkling his month-old scruff. He never shaves when he's hunting. "Camping sounds fun."

I hide my smile. "Your letter said to be here at noon. That was a couple of hours ago. I thought you wouldn't show."

"Got here close enough."

His tired eyes tell me that, in order to return on time, he must've slept little, ridden Siron hard, and hunted tirelessly. Of course, he doesn't say any of this. Instead, he crowds my space, towering over me. "You must be chilled. Let me warm you. Make up for the long wait."

I laugh, unable to keep a straight face.

His eyes target my lips, and a thrill shoots up from my toes. I wonder if he'll kiss me. But no, his arms enfold me, stealing my thoughts as he draws me into a hug that leaves no room for shyness. "Come 'ere, Dove. Missed you."

Seeds and stars, it's nice to have him back. His beard tickles my neck. Cohen's body lends heat better than a fire raging in an iron stove.

"Missed you too," I echo his words, though he cannot hear me since my lips are muffled by his brown overcoat. Cohen isn't required to wear the official maroon-and-gray layers the king's guard does, even though he's the king's bounty hunter. It's a blessing. Enat died only six weeks ago at the hand of a royal guard, and Papa three months before her.

"Your hair looks different." Cohen's tenor rumbles against my cheek.

I lean back to look up at him. "Gillian" is all I say as he continues to study the crisscrossing braids atop my head.

His attention lasts entirely too long, so I jab him in the ribs. "Don't act as though you've never seen a woman wear braids. Gillian was bored. She sits at my cottage all day."

Cohen moves his head side to side. "Shame they're so pretty, Britt."

"Oh?"

"They're gonna get messed up."

"What—"

His gloved hand slips around my cheek to the back of my head, and the other brands my hip. My breath catches as his lips mark my temple, my forehead, my cheek. Before his kiss touches my mouth, he pauses in silent question. The week after I woke from healing the king, Cohen was nothing if not cautious and considerate.

My answer is immediate. It always will be with Cohen.

I rise on my tiptoes, pressing my mouth against his, coaxing his movement over mine. He leans back to bite the tip of his glove to rip it off his hand before his fingers return to the base of my head, tilting my face to a better angle. His kiss is slow and cherishing, heated and sweet, a *hello* and *so damn glad to be back with you*.

My body hums against his like the string of a bow after the arrow's been freed. His kiss shifts, growing more urgent. His fingers wind havoc through my hair, making good on his promise. I'm lost to him, my worries obliterated by his touch.

Here, in his arms, I feel safe and loved. I grasp at the broad muscle beneath his shoulder blade, urging him closer even though a sheet of parchment couldn't fit between us.

His groan is on my lips. His grasp migrates down my sides and under my cloak and the edge of my tunic until his palms find my ribs and sear me with want. Stars, could anything be better than the touch of his calloused fingers against my ribs?

A *crunch* sounds from my pocket.

I break away, breath as ragged as my thoughts, my face tingling from the scratch of his beard. Our inhalations and exhalations and banging heartbeats drown out the wintry world.

I slip my hand into my cloak pocket, registering what made the sound a scant second before withdrawing my little branch. The stick, broken into two pieces, hangs with one of the leaves now in a sad, crumpled state.

"What's this?" Cohen's voice is harsher than seems right from kiss-swollen lips.

"Nothing." I frown at the quickly browning leaf, frustrated with myself for wanting to hide my actions and irritated with Cohen for giving me reason to be frustrated. I'm not going to feel ashamed for wanting to learn about something that was hidden from me most of my life.

"Where's Siron?" I switch subjects.

"I sent him on. His prints can be tracked in the frost too easily." He nods to Snowfire. "Perhaps you should've done the same." Then his fingers brush over the leaf. His voice drops. "Are you trying to distract me, Dove?"

I put three steps between us and cross my arms. "How else am I to learn if I don't practice? There's no one left to teach me."

"It's too dangerous to practice, even out here. I went to the castle before coming here. Omar informed me of the attack. Said he put guards in the woods."

His comment bleeds through me with warmth and a slight chill at the end. Truth mixed with a little untruth. My guffaw is short. "Their patrol isn't nearby. And nobody else would come here besides us. No one would risk hunting on royal lands."

"Still . . . I don't—I don't want to think what would happen if you were caught."

I cross my arms. It's a terrifying thought. Even so, it's my choice to make. "No one's going to catch me. You forget we were trained by the same man. I'm just as capable of hiding my tracks as you."

Cohen shoves off his cap and pushes a hand into his matted sable waves. "I'm not saying you're unable. Only it's dangerous. Your life is at stake."

"I won't get caught."

"I wish you'd consider letting this go. At least for now."

Let it go? I stare at him, frustrated with the turn in our reunion. "Would you *let go* of the one thing that connects you to your family? Papa's gone. Enat's gone." Speaking their names dampens my chest like the dark wet of Castle Neart's dungeon. "This is all I have left. Being a Channeler is who I am, even if I didn't know it till two months ago."

He rubs his neck. Pauses. "I don't want you to give it up."

Another lukewarm half-truth. I huff out a breath of annoyance.

"All right. I do want you to take a break. For now. Until there's less danger. I'm worried about you. People take notice of you, Britt. I hate to think what would happen if you were accused."

It's not a pleasant thought. Still, it frustrates me that Cohen doesn't understand how much it means to me to learn about my Channeling ability.

He reaches for my wrist, gently wrapping his hand around mine, and bringing my fingers to his lips. He drops a soft kiss on them. "I'm sorry, Britt. I don't want to argue."

Allowing our fingers to weave together, I stand beside him. We fall into silence and stare out over the glassy lake, half the water flattened and dulled by a layer of ice. Geese waddle around the hardened end, honking and quacking to one another.

"Come on, let's bag a few geese. Then head back before it's too late." Cohen grabs his gloves off the ground.

We walk along the hardened rutted shoreline and onto the narrow path through the pines. The wind lifts and twirls the snow around our boots, dusting the ground with winter. My thoughts swirl with the flurries. When I think of my peaceful cottage, Cohen is there with me. But I never imagined I'd have to live my life pretending I'm something I'm not. I want Cohen to love me and accept me as I am. Despite the danger.

I don't want to forget everything Enat taught me. I value my Channeler heritage as much as I value the time I spent with my grandmother.

When we near the far edge of the lake, Cohen points at the reeds — *take a vantage point here* is what he's saying.

I do, spreading the reeds to make squatting room, just like we've done a hundred times before.

Stalking silently away, he finds a place to hunker down in the scrub oaks. I pull three arrows from my quiver, lifting one to the bowstring and holding the remaining arrows ready to nock with my free fingers of my right hand. Cheeks puffed, I blow air past my curled tongue to intimidate a soft goose's honk. Cohen hears my sign, telling him I'm ready for him to call the birds. Once he does, the leader will fly in his direction, and hopefully his fellows will follow.

Cohen turns to the geese, sucks in a chest full of air, and lets out his signature goose call. A honk-cackle combination that always makes me snicker. If Cohen weren't so good at calling them, we wouldn't eat goose so often.

Here, in these woods, we work seamlessly together.

Here, we're good.

When we're apart — Cohen traveling across Malam and Shaerdan, and me trying to avoid most of Brentyn — everything gets too complicated. I wish there were some way to simplify, to align our goals, just like we do here.

The leader of the gaggle takes to the sky, and the others fall into formation. The geese pass over me. Once I have a clear shot, I aim for an animal's neck and let loose. My arrow plucks the bird right out of the air. My second and third arrows manage to impale birds near the back of the formation as the remaining geese escape over the treetops, unaware of the fallen few.

I glance across the clearing to Cohen, who's scratching his scar. He points up at the limbs over his head where his arrow protrudes from a dead branch. He shrugs and turns away. But before he does, I catch the frown that carves a canyon between his brows.

I don't want him to feel bad for having missed his goose, so I don't mention anything as I move to my first kill. I say a silent prayer of thanks and well-meaning as the fowl's energy fades. Once the words are spoken, the goose seems to accept death, its frenzied energy slowing to a calm, weak beat until its body stills.

My arrows have no bends or breaks, so I snatch them from the three geese, clean the tips, and tuck them back into my quiver. When the birds are strung together, Cohen slings them over the saddle as I put my bow in the holder.

"Well done, Britt," he says.

"Same to you."

His small shrug tells me he doesn't believe me, so I add, "It took both our efforts. Don't forget that."

He squeezes my hand. "I won't."

Together, we head down the mountain, walking with Snowfire in tow.

"Will you tell me what happened with Phelia?" Cohen asks. "When I got the news, I rode back to Malam as fast as I could."

I touch his beard. "Is that why you look like you haven't slept in days?"

"Didn't want to sleep anywhere but in your cottage."

Even though the thought of him being nearby at night thrills me, I remind him, "Gillian practically had an episode of fits when you last slept there."

"We were in separate rooms." He pulls me close. "Not nearly close enough."

"Tell that to Gillian."

He ducks and pecks my cheek with a quick kiss.

I start with my discovery of the king and his men in the clearing. I don't say how I knew the king was in danger. It's not that I want to lie; it's that the words don't come. They're locked away with worry. I'll explain my connection to Aodren later. Instead, I tell how I loaded the king onto Snowfire before the Spiriter showed up.

"Wasted a month searching for her." He huffs out a wintry breath.

"Was it Omar's missive that let you know she wasn't in Shaerdan?"

"I figured it out just before I got word. Came across a girl who was working for Phelia. She'd been employed to lay a false trail." He goes on to explain the charm Phelia used. Then he shocks me with news about Channeler girls being taken, and how he saved one from Lord Conklin.

I swallow over a dry throat. "One more thing." Pushing out the words feels dangerous, like I'm yanking on the thread that holds me together. "Phelia's real name is Rozen. She's my mother."

He stops.

Blinks.

Blinks again. "What?" His bafflement would be comical if it didn't make me ill.

"She did something . . . I could sense her energy and feel the truth."

"You're certain?"

I nod.

Cohen scrubs his face with his hands, running his fingers along his scar. "Unbelievable. Phelia is Rozen? Your mother is Lord Jamis's mistress?"

I hadn't thought of it that way. Now I might lose the contents of my stomach.

"Who else knows?"

"Only you and the king, who heard most of the conversation. I told Captain Omar everything except the bit about Phelia being my mother."

"You should tell him, Britt."

My fingers are icy and tingling by the time we reach the edge of the Evers where the hills flatten into snow-dusted fields broken up by dirt roads. In the middle of the valley, Brentyn is a spider lording over her web.

I stare off to the east, where Castle Neart is visible in the tree-topped mountainside. "Knowing Phelia's my mother won't give the captain any more reason to find her." If anything, admitting she's my mother will draw more of the captain's judgment.

"Yes, but it might help him figure out her end goal."

Perhaps. But I already know one thing she wants. "She asked me to go with her," I admit, "and said she'd teach me about Channeling."

Cohen stills.

I can see the war behind his eyes, the way he wants to protect me, yet doesn't want to overstep his bounds.

"Not that I'd consider her request," I say before he responds. "But I need time. Let me make sense of this. I thought my mother died."

"Far as I'm concerned, she is dead. That woman might've given birth to you, but she's no mother."

The brisk air raises bumps on my arms. Somewhere nearby, a crow caws.

"I agree. I just don't want the captain to know. Not yet."

Neither of us says anything more. The road home takes us past a few cottages that huddle like weary travelers beside the wall of Ever Woods.

I think of how Phelia's a part of me, how we share the same blood, and how I must be capable of the same darkness. And it's hard not to wonder if Cohen, in his silence, is thinking the same.

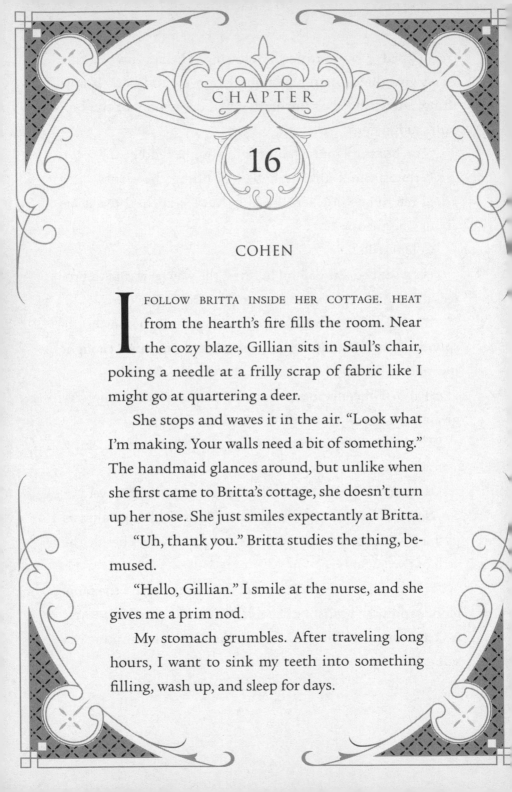

CHAPTER

16

COHEN

I FOLLOW BRITTA INSIDE HER COTTAGE. HEAT from the hearth's fire fills the room. Near the cozy blaze, Gillian sits in Saul's chair, poking a needle at a frilly scrap of fabric like I might go at quartering a deer.

She stops and waves it in the air. "Look what I'm making. Your walls need a bit of something." The handmaid glances around, but unlike when she first came to Britta's cottage, she doesn't turn up her nose. She just smiles expectantly at Britta.

"Uh, thank you." Britta studies the thing, bemused.

"Hello, Gillian." I smile at the nurse, and she gives me a prim nod.

My stomach grumbles. After traveling long hours, I want to sink my teeth into something filling, wash up, and sleep for days.

My eyes catch on Britta's cloak as she hangs it beside the door. It's new. For the first time I remember that her old one was stained by Enat's blood. Makes me ache for Britta and the losses she's suffered. "I'm glad you got a new coat, Dove."

Britta blushes my favorite shade of rose. "Oh, I . . . yeah."

"The king gave it to her," Gillian says.

"The king?" I'm not sure why Gillian's comment doesn't sit right.

Britt takes one look at my face and clarifies that the king noticed her cloak was ruined, so he replaced it.

"Nice of him," I mutter.

"You should see what he gave her for her birthday." Gillian sets her stitching down and moves to the bedroom door. *Her birthday?*

"Stop, Gillian," Britta snaps.

And realization hits me hard. Britta turned eighteen a little over a week ago. I was so focused on getting home that I overlooked the day. "Gods, I'm the king of bludgers. I forgot, Dove. I—I'm sorry."

"You've been hunting." She shrugs like it's not a big deal.

But it is. "Bloody seeds, Britt. What am I good for if I cannot remember your birthday?"

"You're not a bludger. At least, not at the moment." She nudges my shoulder, attempting to soften my own disappointment. Only makes it worse. "Besides, you're good for catching dinner. I think I'll keep you around."

"I had time to work on my stitches since you shot out of

here like there was a golden stag in the forest." Gillian holds her handiwork to the light once more. "I'm nearly finished."

Britta drops her head back and laughs. I'm mesmerized by the sound. I get distracted by the smooth column of her neck. I want my mouth on her, just there. "A golden stag would weigh more than Snowfire. How would I get it home?"

The nurse stabs a needle into the material. "It's a figure of speech."

"What kind of entrails does a golden—?"

"Clearly, you're missing the point."

The sight of Britta's grin breaks my remaining disappointment at having missed her birthday. I like to see that she's friends with her nurse. Six weeks ago, Britta and the maid got on like oil and water.

While they talk, I slip out of the cottage to fetch a bucket of water. I return and pour the water into a cast-iron pot. Once it's in the embers, I stoke the fire and wait for the water to boil.

I overlooked Gillian's presence here in my haste to meet Britta in the woods. Seems my plans for a private reunion are foiled. Wish I'd taken more time with her in the practice clearing. Since I became an official bounty hunter for King Aodren nearly a year and a half ago, our only moments alone were as fugitives.

I've loved Britta since she was fourteen years old. Loved that she could hold her head up, shoulders back, and face each day despite how townspeople in Brentyn taunted her. There's no other woman who possesses her strength and resilience.

I've had time to know, without a doubt, she's the woman I want by my side. And if she'll have me, she's the woman I want to spend my life with. Now that we're not running from guards or stopping a war, we can focus on the future.

The entire way back from Shaerdan, I planned out what I wanted to say to Britta. Except, no matter what I hoped for tonight, it's not happening. That's not a conversation to be had while Gillian's around.

So I tuck away my disappointment and save my words for another day.

When the water's boiling, I drop in a goose, giving its skin time to loosen. When the stink of wet down fills the cottage, I thrust my knife in the goose and, with the help of a long spoon, lift it from the pot. The bird's wet splat on the table draws the girls' attention. But I keep to my business, putting another goose in the water before returning to the table to pluck out the first bird's feathers.

Next thing I know, Gillian's standing beside me, two bowls of pottage in her hands. "You're not going to do that nasty business here?"

I drop a feather in the basket beside the table because obviously I'm doing this here.

She sets the bowls down. "How Britta doesn't swoon at your gentlemanly ways is beyond me."

"A struggle, certainly." I wink at her.

Britta steps between us and rests her hand on the table. "Don't let him get under your skin, Gillian."

Smiling, Gillian shakes her head. I cover Britta's fingers with mine. I'd do anything to make this girl happy, even if it means plucking geese in the cold. "Want me to take it outside?"

"Do you think the table's large enough for all of us?" Britta looks imploringly at her handmaid as she hands me a bowl of pottage.

Gillian mutters something under her breath that I don't catch because I'm still goose plucking in between taking bites of supper.

At first I think it's another playful jab until Britta's fists clench.

"What was that?" I ask.

"I only said this sort of thing wouldn't be a problem if Britta had accepted the king's offer." Gillian's gaze glosses with longing. Whatever the king offered must've been as tempting as a crown of rubies.

"Offer?" My hand stills on the goose.

"Nothing," Britta says at the same time Gillian reverently murmurs, "King Aodren invited her to live at the castle."

My face feels stretched thin for how far my brows shoot up. "Is—is that what you want?"

"It was nothing." Britta glares at Gillian and drops into the seat nearest me. "He offered after . . . after what happened in the woods. It was a safety measure."

Right. I pluck and pluck. Feathers float to the floor, filling in around my feet like blood-stained snow.

When I glance up, the crinkled skin around Britta's eyes tells me there's more.

It's impossible to keep the frown off my face. "Anything else happen with the king?"

Britta pushes her food to the side. "Before Aodren—"

"Aodren?" My hand tightens around the damn goose's neck.

"Before King Aodren was in the woods, he stopped here. To bring the dresses. And he invited me to—"

"Dresses," Gillian echoes with a squeal. She crosses to the bedroom door, pushes it open, and points at the heap of color filling the chair beside the bed. Then she lets out one more *eeek*.

"Dresses," I mutter to myself.

I've been away six weeks, and now Britta's calling the king by his given name and he's delivering dresses. I push the goose aside. Though I was hungry as a bear waking from hibernation, the few bites of pottage I've eaten in between plucking turns to stones in my stomach.

Nothing about the king giving gifts to Britta sits right with me. Still, I manage a tight smile. "Won't make good hunting wear, but you'll look pretty. Then again, you look good in just about anything."

She rolls her eyes. "It was just his way of saying thank you. It's nothing, really."

He's a fool. Britta couldn't care less about gowns.

Gillian flounces back to the table. "They're for the king's

Winter Feast Ball, where she'll be presented as nobility." The handmaid's singsong gushy words strike like an ax right to my core. I don't understand the man's intentions toward Britta. Realizing he's got some agenda makes me feel off-kilter.

The glare Britta shoots Gillian's way sends the maid for the door. "Looks like we'll need another bucket of water."

The door shuts, and for a moment neither Britta nor I speak.

I'm dazed, like someone just punched me. Britta bites her lip, making them blossom red against her snowy skin. Seeds, she's beautiful. "Aod—King Aodren said Papa was nobility. That I should be given the same title."

"That what you want?"

"I—I told him I'd go."

Sounds ridiculous coming from the girl who wanted nothing to do with anyone in Malam, let alone noble lords and ladies. I finish plucking the goose bare. Feathers fill the basket. Cover the floor. I move onto the next bird, drag it from the boiling bath with a long spoon, and throw the third in the water.

I don't want to ask if there's more, but I'm a jealous runaway horse, plowing straight for a cliff: "How many gifts is he going to give you?"

She glares at me. "He can afford a hundred cloaks. A thousand dresses. A few gifts mean little to him, just a way of thanking me. How can I say no? He's the king."

I snatch the third goose from the bath. Return it to the

table. Drop the fowl with a *thwack,* splattering hot, stinking water. One hand pins the goose down; the other pulls and plucks, pulls and plucks.

The warmth of her grip on my wrist breaks my thoughts.

"The bird's already dead, Cohen." Her soft voice jars my riled mood, putting the room in clearer focus. Feathers and the pink residue of diluted blood coat my hands.

I drag in a slow breath. I promised her honesty after she forgave me for keeping secrets from her in Shaerdan. Resolved to it, I speak my mind: "Just seems like he wants something from you."

Her chin jerks up, a scoff parting her lips and hurt shading her voice. "You think the king would only show me kindness to get something in return?"

"That's not what I—"

Her blue eyes narrow. "Because *obviously* I have nothing else worthy to give. What else could he possibly want from someone like me?" The hurt turns harsh. "Someone with no family, no friends, no money. No skill, other than hunting?"

I growl at the plaster above. "Dammit. No, I don't think that."

She stirs her soup vigorously.

I shove away from the table and walk to the cleaning water to dip my hands. Once they're free of grime, I squat beside her chair. "Come on, Dove. You're smart, kind, true. Beautiful, bloody capable with a bow, and tougher than any girl I've ever met. You have much to offer."

Her gaze stays down, targeting her lap.

"All I'm saying is the king showed his thanks when he overlooked you being a Channeler. You saved his life, and he spared yours."

Her grip tightens around the curve of the bowl.

I should stop. Work on the birds and keep my mouth shut. Only, I think of King Aodren showering my girl with gifts, and it hits me hard between the ribs. It's a pretty trap for a girl who's grown up with nothing. Gillian's already fallen for the idea.

Saul told me that being a Channeler, more specifically, a Spiriter, attracts two different types of people: those who'll want to hurt her, and those who'll want to use her.

I run my fingers up and down my scar, remembering all that she did for me. All she's capable of doing. Anyone with knowledge of her gift might be tempted to take advantage of her.

I draw in a deep breath and look straight into her wintry blue eyes. "Ever consider he wants to use you for your ability?"

Britta curses under her breath and mutters something about me having lost my seeds. Thing is, she's still got all his gifts around her home. If they were nothing, she'd have gotten rid of them.

Britta thinks the man wants friendship. But I think he wants something more than friendship, or he wants something only a Channeler with her capability can offer.

Either way, both options put me on edge.

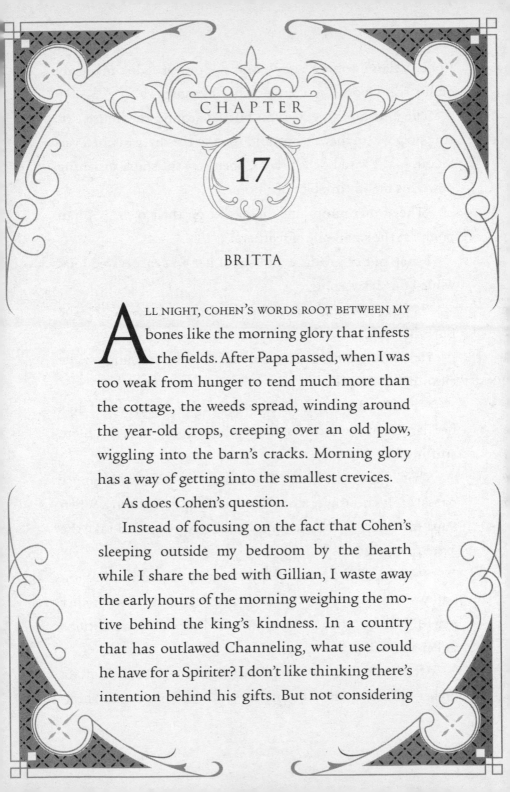

CHAPTER

17

BRITTA

ALL NIGHT, COHEN'S WORDS ROOT BETWEEN MY bones like the morning glory that infests the fields. After Papa passed, when I was too weak from hunger to tend much more than the cottage, the weeds spread, winding around the year-old crops, creeping over an old plow, wiggling into the barn's cracks. Morning glory has a way of getting into the smallest crevices.

As does Cohen's question.

Instead of focusing on the fact that Cohen's sleeping outside my bedroom by the hearth while I share the bed with Gillian, I waste away the early hours of the morning weighing the motive behind the king's kindness. In a country that has outlawed Channeling, what use could he have for a Spiriter? I don't like thinking there's intention behind his gifts. But not considering

Cohen's claim would be naive of me. If only it didn't make my ability seem more like a curse than a blessing.

The next morning, Gillian bustles around the house, setting pots where they belong and tossing the dirty kitchen water out in the yard by the privy. Cohen is in the stable brushing down his moody ink-blot of a horse.

"They won't jump into the basket on their own." Gillian points at the small pile of feathers.

I snap out of my daze and shoot her an exasperated look while I finish sweeping.

"Is that your new morning greeting? An eye roll?" She fluffs her hair.

Her teasing breaks my bad mood. I huff out a laugh while cleaning up the pile.

When I'm done, Gillian takes the basket from me and dips her hand into the feathers. "The pillows could use a bit more stuffing."

That's putting it nicely. The pillows are practically empty oat sacks. It's been ages since I kept feathers for bedding. When Papa was alive, we'd use the quills for arrows or we'd take the extra to market.

"Perhaps it'll help you sleep better." Her lips curve in sympathy. My tossing must've kept her up last night. Despite her playful picking, she's never complained about the conditions in Papa's cottage.

After gathering the few pillows from the cottage, she sits on her favorite chair — the one Papa carved from an old chestnut tree. I find it impossible to dislike Gillian. I doubt she's ever met a person who didn't become her friend.

"Need any help?" I ask.

"No, thank you." Her fingers work at unpicking the seams on my pillow. She glances up, her head tipped. "Perhaps Cohen needs help in the stable."

The door swings open, cutting me short.

Cohen's brown mess of hair hangs over his forehead. Using his forearm, he pushes it back. "I just got word from the castle. Captain Omar's requesting a meeting. The man doesn't like to be kept waiting."

An understatement. Captain Omar's about as patient as a pig in labor.

Cohen hesitates, then asks, "You want to come? You can meet Finn. And Lirra."

Gillian's eyes whittle to points. "Who's Lirra?"

Cohen shrugs. "Just a girl I met in Shaerdan. She helped me track the woman I thought was Phelia."

Gillian pauses before entering the bedroom. "You brought a girl home from Shaerdan?"

I sit straighter than an arrow, taking this in from the very man who was acting like a jealous fool the night before. Anger flashes through me.

"You rushed home from Shaerdan, and yet had time to pick up a girl?" I work out my confusion and irritation aloud.

"Yeah." Cohen moves to the table and crouches to pick up a few stray feathers. He acts like he's said nothing of consequence. "Lirra helped me discover Phelia's ruse, and I agreed to help her find someone. Her friend is one of the Shaerdanian girls who've gone missing."

Mention of the girls cools my temper, and I feel silly for having been irked in the first place. I also feel guilty. After all, I'm the one who is still keeping secrets.

Surprise replaces Gillian's confusion. "Have there been that many?"

He gives a solemn nod, and then puts the extra feathers in the pillow pile.

I can tell he's more troubled than he's letting on. Cohen rubs the back of his neck until his skin brightens. "Would it be possible for Lirra to stay here?"

Surprised by his question, I step back and knock into a small table. "Here?" My voice is a squeak. It's not that I don't want to help Cohen, but my space is a commodity I've fought hard for. And there's not much here to share. Not with Gillian living with me. Although, now that she's been at my cottage for over a month, I cannot imagine how quiet and lonesome it would be without her. Of course, I won't tell her this. Wouldn't want to inflate her raven bouffant any more.

"She cannot stay at the guards' quarters for long. It would just be until I can locate her friend and then return her safely over the border." Cohen's voice lowers. He glances over his shoulder at the bedroom door where Gillian's disappeared. "Lirra's the Archtraitor's daughter. You met her at Enat's home."

Oh. The memory brings a smile and then the sharp pain of grief.

"I don't want Omar to find out who she is," Cohen is saying. I blink, coming fully back to the present. "He'd throw her in the dungeon without a second thought. I'd take her on the road with me, but it puts her at risk of getting caught. She'd be killed if that happened."

So why'd he bring her to Malam? I ask him as much and he says, "Because she's stubborn, and won't leave till she finds her friend. The girl's so stubborn that she insisted I make arrangements for her to stay in my empty quarters so she could follow up on servant gossip about a girl who was found in the woods. Doesn't matter that she'll be poking around under Captain Omar's nose."

"Seeds, she's definitely going to get thrown in the dungeon."

Cohen huffs. "Here's hoping she hasn't been already. That's why I need to get her out of Neart after I meet with Omar."

"Who's going to throw whom into the dungeon?" Gillian reenters the room.

"A little privacy, please." I break out a pleading look.

"Can that be had in a one-bedroom cottage?" Gillian inspects her nails and then flicks her hand in the air. "I think not."

Cohen chuckles.

I sigh. "Yeah, I'll make room for her here."

"Thank you, Dove," he says, his tenor soft and sweet. His

fingers hook mine, and he tugs me to him. "Come to the castle with me."

My choice is made. The six weeks of separation was torture. Yesterday's reunion had too many rough edges to be satisfying.

I hurry into the room to hide my trousers under a skirt and tuck my tunic into my waistband. Gillian's comb smooths my hair, and I braid it into a plaited length. After cleaning my hands and face in the washbasin, I tuck my dagger into my boot and belt one of Cohen's old rapiers at my waist. I wave goodbye to Gillian.

Cohen stands beside Siron, hand on the horse's withers. "Ride together?"

I consider it for a moment, but shake my head. To get to the castle, we'll have to ride through Brentyn. Cohen cannot help but draw attention from adoring townspeople because he's the king's bounty hunter. Especially the female population. It's been years since we rode together in Brentyn. I'm ashamed to admit, I'm still self-conscious about the fact that Cohen could be with anyone.

I look at the castle's sword-like spires that protrude from the tops of the evergreens. Maroon flags stain the tips of each gray peak. Castle Neart is supposed to be the heart of the Malam Mountains. Today, though, it seems to have taken on a darker aura, like each spire is a giant sword impaling a great green beast.

We garner a dozen glances and half a town's worth of hushed gossip as we ride through the royal city.

I'm a landowner, unlike most of the townspeople clogging the market. I've a right to be here as much as they. I repeat this to myself as we pass the church and the pillory, where, yet again, a woman is manacled to a cross of cedar and shame. I fight the temptation to sink low in the saddle and let my shoulders slump forward. Holding my head high, I own the road all the way to Castle Neart.

The outer yard of the castle is bustling with servants. At the sight of Cohen, a stablehand scurries across the yard to retrieve our horses. All throughout Malam, Cohen is regarded as a hero. Once his name was cleared, the townspeople rallied around him. Once more their beloved bounty hunter.

I'm relieved. Having never felt the country's judgment before, it must've been hard for Cohen.

Once our horses are stabled, I follow Cohen through the inner keep and down the stone stairwell to the guards' quarters. We've barely stepped onto the training yard when a vision of Cohen at fourteen comes barreling toward us.

I stumble back, happily surprised at the welcoming reception. "Well, hello."

"Finn," Cohen barks. The rest of his words are lost to the arms flying around me, snaking me in a headlock. Or a hug. I cannot tell.

"Get off her." Cohen yanks me free.

I take in the boy with big fawn eyes and a sloppy grin.

"I'm Finn." He lifts up on his toes and then settles into his heels. "You're Britta, Cohen's girl."

My brows shoot to my hairline and I laugh. Cohen sputters out a cough. The scene draws Captain Omar's attention away from the guard he's sparring with. The captain sheathes his sword and stalks across the yard to greet Cohen.

"You're thinner than I thought you'd be," Finn says, snagging my focus from the men.

Cohen stops talking to the captain to swat the back of his brother's head. "Not how you start a conversation with a lady."

Color like a ripened peach overtakes Finns cheeks. He ducks away from his brother, stepping closer to me and dropping his voice. "I'm not saying it's bad. I just thought, by how Cohen described you, ya might look more like those guys." He throws his thumb over his shoulder in the direction of the sparring guards, strapping and muscle-bound. Sweat dampens their tunics. Metal clashes. Their faces contort as they grunt and parry blows. "But you're decently pretty."

I laugh, liking the straightforward ring of his compliment.

I shift my weight. "How exactly does he describe me?"

"Tough and full of grit. Like Leif, but in a skirt. Well, maybe not a skirt. But a Leif-like girl, though a little more sure-footed."

Well, then. I grin. "I wouldn't go that far."

"But he also worries about you because he's gone for you."

Now I'm the one blushing.

Finn shoves his hands into his pockets and shrugs. "Guess I should've waited to meet you before making a judgment."

Cohen, who's been watching our exchange, wraps his arm around Finn's neck and tugs the younger boy closer. "Did you and Lirra stay out of trouble?"

Finn points toward the row of doors that line the side of the castle, where a handful of guards surround the dark-haired girl I recognize from Enat's home.

Captain Omar ignores me as he starts up a conversation with Cohen about the attack in the woods. I listen in as the man explains they've had no luck finding Phelia or the people she's working with.

Captain Omar taps his fingers on the hilt of his sword. "There's been another development." His eyes shift to me and Finn.

"Go on." Cohen crosses his arms.

The captain's mouth twists before he whispers, "A teenage girl was found in the woods." This must be the gossip Cohen heard from the castle servants. Omar goes on to explain that Leif rushed an injured girl to the castle. The healer tried to save her, but she died before they could find out what the marks on her arm meant or whom she was running from.

Cohen's shock mirrors my own. I hope for Lirra's sake it wasn't her friend.

Cohen runs his finger along his scar. "Her family hasn't been located?"

"No. We think she might be from Shaerdan."

"And you don't know what led to her death?"

Another shake of Omar's head.

A curse sounds under Cohen's breath. "Near the border, after I met up with Lirra, I came across Lord Conklin. He had a few men with him and some girls who weren't there of their own will."

The only time I've seen shock register on Omar's face like now was when he discovered Lord Jamis had killed my father.

Omar lets out a heavy breath. "What happened to him?"

I wonder why Cohen didn't mention this to the captain yesterday. But my body flushes a little when I think of yesterday's reunion. Cohen relays the story of how they killed a couple of Conklin's men, but saved a young girl before the lord got away with the rest of the girls.

"Do you know whom he was working with?"

"No. Whoever it is clearly wants Malam and Shaerdan to go to war."

Omar takes a moment, hand gripping the hilt of his sword. "I'll report the information to the king. For now, stay vigilant, return here tomorrow. You can have one more night away from the guards' quarters."

Cohen starts to argue, but the captain jumps back in. "It is unseemly for you to stay at Britta's cottage, whether or not you care. At least Miss Tierney is there as a chaperone."

Cohen steps forward, hands in fists. "Don't say another word."

Omar straightens his coat. "Only a warning, Cohen. Rumors are hard to stop once started. Right now, with unrest in the country, you don't want to draw negative attention to yourself." Omar's eyes flick dismissively to me. "Or others."

"I'll be back tonight after I see the women to the cottage," Cohen bites out.

When Captain Omar leaves, I can tell in the pinched lines around Cohen's mouth that he's angry. I hate that he isn't going to stay another night. But this is better for him. I know what it's like to live under others' scrutiny. I don't want to be the person who brings Cohen down.

Lirra says goodbye to the guards and crosses the yard.

Cohen shakes off the conversation with Omar and introduces me to Lirra as if we've never met. The sadness that blows through me at the sight of her makes it impossible to not remember our first meeting at Enat's log home.

"Find anything out?" Cohen's voice drops to a whisper.

"It wasn't Orli." Lirra's shoulders sag.

"But that's good news, right?"

"I saw her body, and I think I know how she was killed." Lirra's glance darts around the field, but we huddle closer, keeping her words secret. "I'm afraid Orli might face the same fate."

"Which is?" Cohen steals the words right out of my mouth.

"Her power was stolen."

"Is that possible?" I blurt, and then realize it wasn't a whisper. I ask once more, quieter.

Lirra nods. "Aye. It's Spiriter dark magic, but it's possible. A Channeler cannot live if all their ability is stolen by a Spiriter."

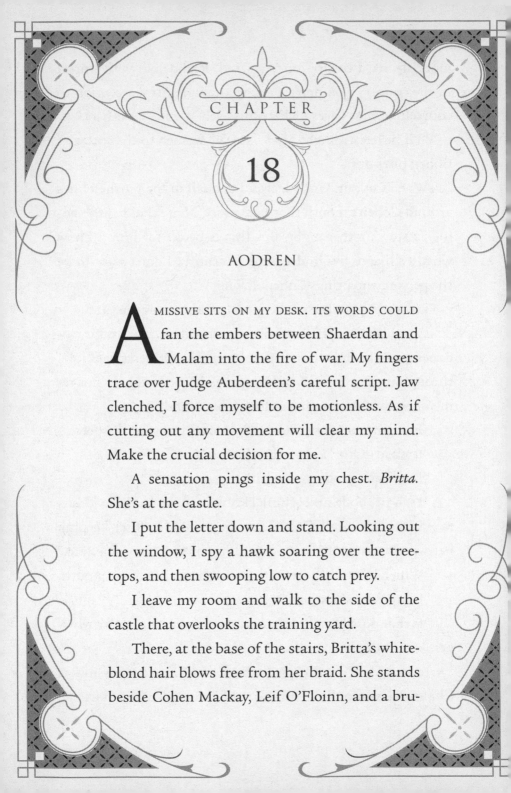

CHAPTER

18

AODREN

A MISSIVE SITS ON MY DESK. ITS WORDS COULD fan the embers between Shaerdan and Malam into the fire of war. My fingers trace over Judge Auberdeen's careful script. Jaw clenched, I force myself to be motionless. As if cutting out any movement will clear my mind. Make the crucial decision for me.

A sensation pings inside my chest. *Britta*. She's at the castle.

I put the letter down and stand. Looking out the window, I spy a hawk soaring over the tree-tops, and then swooping low to catch prey.

I leave my room and walk to the side of the castle that overlooks the training yard.

There, at the base of the stairs, Britta's white-blond hair blows free from her braid. She stands beside Cohen Mackay, Leif O'Floinn, and a brunette girl I don't recognize. I watch until they leave, and then I make my way down to talk with Captain Omar.

"Was that Cohen I saw leaving the castle?"

"Yes, sir."

"When did he return?"

"Yesterday. He arrived with his brother and a friend."

The way he says the last bit makes me wonder what it is about the friend that Omar dislikes. "Did you talk to him about the girl who was found in the woods?"

A nod. "And other news as well. We'll need to discuss it in the privacy of your study."

"All right. Where is he headed now?"

"He left to escort the friend to Miss Flannery's home."

My frown catches Omar's notice.

I ignore the pucker of judgment around the captain's mouth as I return to the knowledge that Cohen had the privilege of spending the evening with her. The thought comforts me about as much as a week of grueling training with Omar.

The awareness I have of Britta leaves me thinking about her far more than I should. Mostly, it leaves me wanting more than I should. Captain Omar's frown is a minor comparison to how my circle of advisers will react should I tell them of my interest in Britta Flannery. I'm expected to marry the daughter of a lord from higher nobility. The problem is, I've met them all, and none hold my interest like Britta Flannery.

Of course, as it stands, Miss Flannery's interest in me is about as great as her interest in every gift I've given her—

which is to say, not at all. I'm driven to find something she'll like, and I begin to contemplate the ridiculous. Perhaps a bale of hay, or a cooking pot, or rope for trussing up the next man she finds unconscious in the woods.

I massage my temples, glad the headaches following the attack have finally subsided, and lonesome as I feel Britta move farther from the castle.

The guards do not look our way as Captain Omar accompanies me out of the yard. That's the way it is with most people in the castle. Nobody dares meet my eyes. It is a custom born of respect that leaves me feeling like I'm in solitary confinement.

Britta Flannery sees me. That's something I don't want to lose.

Once inside my study, I lift the letter off my desk and pass it to Omar. As he reads, lines appear around his eyes and mouth, tightening.

"We need to clear ourselves of blame." I turn to the window that faces west, toward Shaerdan. My blood is thick and cold in my veins, like winter creeping beneath my skin.

The letter includes the names and villages of thirty kidnapped girls, all Channelers. Names of witnesses who claim to have seen men in Malamian dress or heard Malamian accents on dates coinciding with the abductions are listed on the parchment. Including the four girls the kinsmen had recovered when they arrested Lord Conklin, a Malamian noble, heading for the border with them.

Omar moves into my peripheral vision and coughs. "Cohen Mackay reported the involvement of Lord Conklin."

Omar has my rapt attention as he recounts Cohen's run-in with the lord. A girl was saved, but Conklin got away with the rest. I tap the desk. "Besides kidnapping girls, what was Lord Conklin doing in Shaerdan?"

"I don't know, Your Grace."

I flex my jaw. The stress in this office suffocates me. I wish Omar would address me as Aodren, like he did when I was a child. Only Britta dares call me by name.

"What do you know of Conklin? Does he have proclivities I should be aware of?" I resist a shudder at the idea. It wouldn't be the first time an older man had kidnapped young girls for despicable reasons.

Omar hums darkly to himself. "He has a sizable fief east of Lord Fennitson's land, he turns in a sizable tax payment every year, and he's always been a supporter of the crown. As for other interests, I cannot say."

"The crown no longer desires his support." I pause, mulling over what I know. "Phelia is a part of all of this. I'm sure of it. Was Cohen able to identify who else Conklin was working with?"

Omar answers to the negative. He crunches the offending paper in his meaty fist. "It pains me to admit that I've heard nothing among the nobles."

"It isn't likely that Conklin is the only co-conspirator."

"No, but he could've been working with other Malamians," Omar says. "This could be a way of carrying out the Purge Proclamation. Perhaps he wants to rid Shaerdan of Channelers in order to keep them from slipping into Malam." In all the Channeler trials held by my inner circle, I've not seen a trace of emotion on the man's face. Though lack of sentiment is not uncommon for the captain, it makes me wonder if he fears the Channelers. Or is he secretly a sympathizer who hides behind an iron mask?

I lean on the side of my desk, ill at the mention of the Proclamation. It'll forever be a dark stain on Malam.

"Have we not killed enough of our own women? Must we kill Shaerdan's women as well?" There's no masking my bitterness. The Proclamation passed in the first place only because I was a child, too young to rule, and the men my father had left to govern the country in the interim were fools. To pass such a contemptuous, ludicrous law was extremism in its most uneducated form. Their actions have caused a division in Malam that, I fear, is irreparable.

When Lord Jamis was king regent and my adviser, I spoke with him many times about abolishing the Purge Proclamation. Back then, he said he agreed with me. Then again, the man sought to control me and usurp my crown. Clearly, he's a liar.

I press my hands flat against the desk, using the support to think through the issue. I think of what Hagan told me in the healer's room. I've no doubts that Phelia is behind this, gathering girls to use as weapons. But knowing this doesn't give me a clue as to where to find the girls, or what Phelia's end goal is.

"I don't think this has to do with carrying out the Purge," I tell Omar. "Phelia herself is a Channeler. Why would she want to have all the others killed?"

Omar stares at the crumpled letter. "Even if she's not doing the killing, the rumors of Channeler girls being brought to Malam has already spread. Soon enough we'll have Purge zealots to deal with."

Neighbor turning on neighbor would be the final blow needed to tumble this kingdom. I fear that, in trying to repair the broken country my father left me, I will be the man who destroys it.

Something else occurs to me, leaches the blood from my face. "Britta Flannery isn't in danger, is she?" Zealots rising. Another Purge. Women burning at the stake.

I look to him, not caring about the disapproval writ across his face. He must always have Britta's secret locked tight, her best wishes at the core of his actions.

His mouth tightens. "No, Your Grace."

I compose myself. "See that it remains so."

He nods and flattens out the creases on the paper. "And Lord Conklin?"

"The man was caught kidnapping five girls. He murdered one of their brothers when the boy attempted to stop him. Let Judge Auberdeen do with him as he sees fit."

"They'll execute him." Omar watches me much like he

used to when he taught me to meticulously pick apart the potential threat of a person. Build, facial expression, weapons exposed outside of clothes, and bulges in attire that might be hidden weapons. In the event I was ever unguarded, Omar wanted me to be prepared to defend myself. "This will be your first . . ."

He doesn't need to finish his sentence. In the year I've been king instead of a ward beneath the regent, I never ruled in favor of an execution. Then again, I was subdued by a Spiriter for much of that time.

I take the missive from him and flatten it on my desk. "So be it."

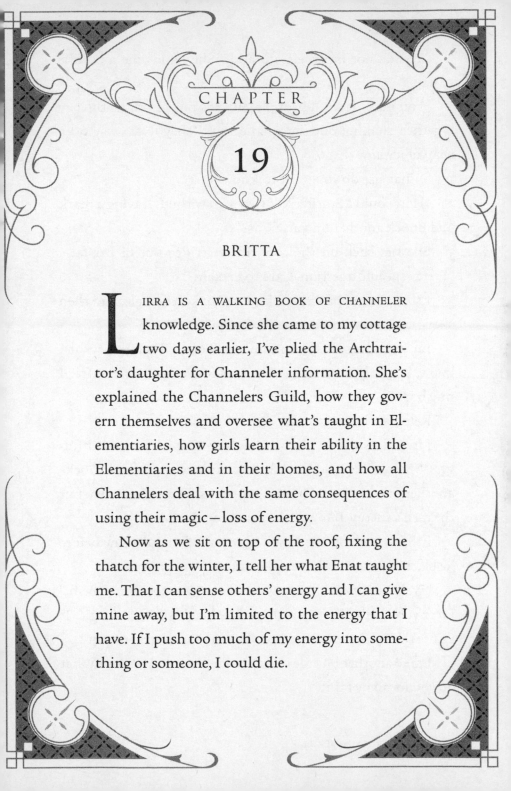

BRITTA

LIRRA IS A WALKING BOOK OF CHANNELER knowledge. Since she came to my cottage two days earlier, I've plied the Archtraitor's daughter for Channeler information. She's explained the Channelers Guild, how they govern themselves and oversee what's taught in Elementiaries, how girls learn their ability in the Elementiaries and in their homes, and how all Channelers deal with the same consequences of using their magic—loss of energy.

Now as we sit on top of the roof, fixing the thatch for the winter, I tell her what Enat taught me. That I can sense others' energy and I can give mine away, but I'm limited to the energy that I have. If I push too much of my energy into something or someone, I could die.

"There's not much else to add." She hands me a bundle of hay.

"You make it sound simple. But it's not." I bunch the hay together, shaking out the smaller bits. They float away on a snap of icy air.

"What else do you want to know?"

"How could a Spiriter kill two men without leaving a mark and knock another unconscious?"

She sits back on the roof. Blows fringe out of her face. "Pretty specific question. Care to explain?"

I shrug, wind hay into a knot to make a wangle, and then shove it into the hole on the roof.

Lirra studies me for a moment. "Fine. I'll tell you what I know, but only for a trade. You explain your question after I finish. Yes?"

Reluctantly, I nod.

Lirra plays with a piece of hay, running it around her fingers. "This is like a riddle. A Spiriter kills two men and knocks another unconscious. Hmm, I suppose she could've drawn out the men's energy. But was she touching the men?"

I think back on the king's account of what he saw before he blacked out, and shake my head to the negative.

"Well, that would only work if she was touching them." Lirra rubs her chin. "Also that's the blackest of all magic. It taints the Spiriter. So that's probably not what you meant."

I take another bundle of hay from Lirra and pause. "What do you mean by taint?"

"That kind of dark magic stains a Spiriter's mind. When a Spiriter pulls the energy from another, effectively killing the person, that person's last intent comes with the energy. It gets into the Spiriter's mind and sticks."

My face must be utter confusion.

"Think of it this way, if a Spiriter steals the energy of someone who, in their final moments before death, was intent on quartering a pig, then the Spiriter would want to find a pig and butcher it."

A laugh bursts out of me. "That's ludicrous."

Lirra shrugs. She takes the hay from me, whips it into a wangle, and jams it into the thatching. "Aye, but it's the truth."

"How do you know?"

"I worked at an Elementiary. I had access to ancient tomes. And my aunt is one of the Guild."

I blink at Lirra, stunned for a moment, though the warmth of her truth eases my shock.

"It's not something I wave around on a flag. But I trust you'll keep it to yourself."

"You trust me?" I squeak.

"As much as you probably trust me. Besides, you're keeping some intense secrets, so I've leverage over you in case you ever want to start sharing too much information."

Lirra's savvy and clever in a way that amazes me. I like her confidence and ease around others. But there's an edge to her words. "You're not very trusting."

She laughs. "Neither are you." Lirra shakes out a bundle

of straw, letting the pieces fall between us. "Trust is an interesting thing. You don't trust people because they've never accepted you. They've never shown you any kindness. Am I right?"

I shrug, bristle a little, even if she's right.

She continues, "I know too many of the secrets my father's garnered. I don't trust anyone because I know they're liars."

A laugh bursts out of me at her candidness. "Not everyone lies."

"Really? You with your ability to discern the truth are going to sit there and tell me not everyone lies." She harrumphs. "I don't have to be a Spiriter to know even you are full of secrets. And secrets lead to lies."

True. Cohen comes to mind. Though he's been back a few days, I've still not figured out how to tell him I'm connected to the king. If I could find a way to quickly sever the bond, I could move on and Cohen would be none the wiser. And yet, even thinking as much fills me with guilt. If the situation were reversed, I'd want to know the truth.

I sigh and push another wangle into the roof. "Yes, many people have secrets. Not everyone tells massive, life-altering lies. Just small lies. Inn—" I stop myself from saying the word *innocent,* because are there really any innocent lies?

"A lie is a lie. You have to know that people see what they want you to see."

Being the Archtraitor's daughter has jaded Lirra, that's for sure. In all things there's good and bad and in between. I think of my own life and the secrets that have been kept from me, as well as the ones I'm keeping.

I fight with whether or not I should tell her who my mother is. I don't always want to be the girl who doesn't trust anyone. Besides, her father is the Archtraitor of Malam. She'll understand why I don't want anyone to know.

I let go of my reservations and explain everything that happened in the woods the day I found the king.

When I finish, she gapes at me. "Whoa. Phelia is your mother." She rubs her forehead. "Your question makes more sense now."

"Good, because I have more. Would taking someone's energy also physically mark a person?"

Lirra tips her head to the side. Her dark brown braid slides off her shoulder. "I've never personally met anyone who fits this description, but the tomes mentioned something about darkening a Spiriter's skin along with their insight."

Interesting. "What do you think Phelia is doing with the girls?"

A gust of wind rolls over us. "I—I don't know." Lirra frowns and then stares up at the sky. "You said Phelia touched a girl, and then Aodren couldn't breathe?" Dread slackens her expression as I recall the memory Aodren shared with me. "Let me try something, all right?"

"Yeah, go on."

Lirra frees her hands, putting some hay under her legs so it doesn't blow away. Then she extends her palms toward my face. A sudden burst of wind weaves through my hair, drawing it toward her.

My lungs tighten. I try to draw a breath, but there's no oxygen.

I gasp at nothing, my eyes drying out. My head spins.

Just as quickly as the air left, it returns, coolness breaking across my face. I gasp and snag breath after breath. When I manage to get ahold of myself, I whack Lirra in the shoulder with my fist. "Could've warned me that you were going to try and kill me."

She rubs her arm and sags against the roof, seeming much more tired than before her demonstration. "It would've ruined the surprise."

"How did you do that? Take the air away?"

She yawns and her hands tremble in her lap. "Sorry, that took a lot of energy. It's not easy. I drew the air toward me, creating a vacuum, leaving nothing left for you to breathe."

"Do you need to rest?" I point at her jittery limbs.

"I won't argue if you say it's time to go inside and see if Gillian's done preparing supper."

"All right, let's go." I take the remaining hay and put it back in the basket, then carry it to the ladder. I go first, and then watch as Lirra follows, making sure she doesn't misstep.

Lirra trudges to the stable, tailing me as I put away the tools and remaining hay.

I walk over to Snowfire and rub her nose. "But Phelia is a Spiriter, not an air Channeler."

Lirra pinches some feed hay off the ground and holds it out to her horse, Traitor. Clever name. I inwardly snort every time we're near her gelding.

"Go back to the basics," Lirra says. "Spiriters can give energy or take energy. Phelia took energy from the other Channeler."

Lirra rubs her horse's jaw. She looks over her shoulder at me. "Other Channelers can only manipulate their specific energy. I'll only ever be able to push the wind around. Whereas you have the ability to take and give energy."

"But if I took another Channeler's power, that would be dark magic."

"Well, yes."

"And even if I did, I didn't think a Spiriter could then use another's power."

"That's what the runes are for." She reminds me of the mark she saw on the deceased girl in the castle. Using the stable floor, Lirra squats and draws the rune in the dust. "This particular rune is used to transfer energy to a Channeler and allow that Channeler brief control of the ability."

"So Phelia could use this rune on any Channeler to steal her ability?"

Lirra scratches out the mark on the stable floor. "That's the thing that doesn't make sense. The rune is supposed to work when both Channelers are giving their power freely. Not that I've seen it happen. Runes are banned by the Guild. But I doubt any of the kidnapped girls are going to willingly give their power to Phelia."

"How is she taking their power and using it, then?"

Lirra shakes her head. "It could be as easy as a combination of runes. I just don't know them all."

"That look you're wearing." Lirra points at me. "That's how I feel inside when I think about what Phelia might be doing to Orli."

"I'm sorry she hasn't been found yet."

"Yeah, well, if Cohen doesn't turn up something by the feast tomorrow . . ." She doesn't finish. Not that she needs to. I know she'll leave. She's been talking about it since she arrived. Mostly she needed Cohen's help to cross the border. Now that she's here, she can search for her friend in Malam herself. Her Malamian is flawless. I'd expect nothing less from the Archtraitor's daughter.

Unlike me, Lirra is a chameleon. I envy her that, especially with tomorrow's feast looming over my head.

The next day, I wish I were still patching the roof.

Instead I'm preparing to go to the Winter Feast.

Even my old trousers and tunic would be preferable to the fancy undergarments I'm wearing. The thin, fine linen chemise is an itchy torture chamber. The constricting boning around the midsection and the neckline that threatens to expose my breasts are only two of a hundred reasons for throttling my maid and former friend.

Gillian threw a fit after discovering I was going to wear the shift Enat gave me, arguing it was too boxy and baggy to be worn beneath one of the king's dresses. I accepted Gillian's new underclothes only because I had finally realized that the shift used to belong to Phelia.

It took only half a second in this contraption to regret my decision. "What was she thinking?"

Lirra flips a length of muddy-brown hair out of her eyes and looks up from where she's seated cross-legged on the floor.

"Or maybe I should say, what was I thinking?" I amend.

Lirra picks at a speck of nothing on her knee. "Considering the giver, it could've been worse."

"Doubtful." I groan.

"They could use a little more color. But in truth, they're gorgeous. If it were me, I'd wear —"

Gillian pops her head through the open bedroom door. "It wouldn't be you in a hundred years, so that's neither here nor there."

Lirra scoffs. "Only because I'm not angling for an invite."

I clear my throat. "There was no angling."

"The comment wasn't intended for you," Lirra says with a flat look at Gillian.

Gillian stands in the center of the door frame looking like an adorably ornery canary in her frilly, feathered yellow dress. "You sound petty in the most unattractive way, Lirra."

The Archtraitor's daughter scowls.

Gillian points to the rainbow pile of silk gowns. "We don't have much time before the carriage arrives."

Lirra pushes off the floor. "In Shaerdan, women ride their

own horses. And buy their own material for clothes." She gasps in mockery. "Imagine that."

"Snip it." Gillian's gaze slices to Lirra with the ferocity of a mother bear. "The king knows Britta doesn't own a carriage and riding Snowfire to the castle would dirty her skirts. King Aodren offered out of kindness. We couldn't turn him down." Gillian points to the door. "Go feed the horses since they're your company for the night."

I watch Lirra's face redden under her tree-bark tan and wait for words to explode from her. For as jolly as her father is, Lirra is equal parts unruly and taciturn. Surprisingly, she doesn't argue. She stomps out of the room, shouldering Gillian aside as she passes through the doorway.

"After I fetch a bucket of water, I'll be back to do your hair." Gillian slides her hand over the coiled and curled concoction on her own head and looks pointedly at the dresses.

I nod, though it's a fight not to roll my eyes until she leaves the room.

I scratch my shoulder where lace trim rubs it and debate between the pink and green dress. And then I nearly cackle, because what am I doing? I feel as though I'm drowning in silk. How did I become a girl whose biggest problem is choosing between ball gowns?

If anything, I should be grateful for this distraction. It's better than thinking about the alternative, thinking what it means to be Phelia's daughter. The same blood. The same Channeling gift. *The same propensity for darkness?*

The door opens, emitting a screech like a field cat in heat. I jump and spin around.

"Britta, I— What . . . what are you wearing?" Cohen's voice, gravel mucking up his rich tenor, instantly erases my thoughts . . . most of them.

"What are you doing here?" My legs lock. My arms cross over my breasts. Though the shift isn't exactly see-through, it leaves little to the imagination, and I fear Cohen will find reality lacking. I was frighteningly thin this past winter. I've put on some weight, but not curves like Gillian has.

"I—I have to pick a dress." I jut my chin at the colorful pile.

Cohen steps closer. Hazel eyes dip to my arms, and then the shift's scooped neckline. He reaches out and runs a finger along the old faint scar above my left breast.

I shiver. "Scrape from the woods."

He pulls his hand back and rubs his chin, fingers grazing his scar. "I . . . uh, I should leave."

I quirk my head to the side, noticing his new coat. It matches the uniforms of the royal guard, except his has an arrowhead emblem beside Malam's stag. Similar to the coat my father had, the sight fills me with pride.

"You look so . . . it's a nice uniform . . ." I shake my head, wondering why Cohen's wearing one now when he never wore one before.

"It's for the king's Winter Feast Ball. I have to head back to the castle to report, but I wanted to stop here first."

My cheeks color, but I'm pleased. "Have you come to escort me to the castle?" I'm delighted that he's our carriage driver.

Cohen clears his throat. "No. I just had to see you."

"You've seen me nearly every day this week."

"That's not enough." The rough texture of his voice shoots fire-tipped arrows through me.

He approaches slowly, reaches for me. His hands grasp my arms, calluses gliding over my skin from elbows up to shoulders. Goose bumps rise in their wake and I shiver. He runs his nose down my cheek, until his lips find the sensitive stretch of skin in the hollow of my neck. He plants a kiss and then taking soft steps with his lips, moves back up around my jaw.

A moan slides out of me.

I fall into him, wanting to wrap myself in his arms. Our bodies line up, his muscular frame undisguised by his coat and the thin fabric of my chemise. When his lips find mine, coaxing them open, I fear the linen I'm wearing is seconds away from igniting. Though I've never been drunk on ale or wine, I imagine this is what it's like. A heady mix of longing curls low in my gut.

I deepen the kiss, winding my arms around his wide shoulders, embracing him in my cottage, where I dream we'll live out our lives —

Cohen rips himself away. He takes a big breath and shuffles back until his spine hits the door frame.

"Why'd you stop?"

"Gods, Dove, you get me wound so tight." He shoves a

hand through his hair. "Your skin's so soft. And I... We shouldn't... n-not yet... I mean, I shouldn't let us get so..."

I laugh a little, feeling shy and still dizzy from his nearness. "So like that?"

"Yeah."

But why, if it's what I want too? I was kissing him just as much as he was kissing me.

I snatch a dress off the bed and hold it in front of me, as if I'm checking the size instead of hiding myself and my embarrassment.

He walks back over, his fingers lifting my chin. "Don't duck your chin. There's nothing to be embarrassed over." He can read me so well. "It's not that I don't want to. I was taught some things are saved for marriage."

Escaping his grip, I tip my head to the side. "So, kissing is meant for marriage?"

He rocks back on his heels. "Well, no. But beyond kissing... that's for after you marry." The way he says *you* carries weight in a way that makes me want to bury myself beneath the entire pile of dresses. What does he mean by *you*?

I'm sure I'm overreacting, what with the stress of picking a dress and getting ready to attend the king's Winter Feast Ball. Still, I echo, "After *I* marry?"

He nods. The small movement feeds the fear that he doesn't see the same future.

Cohen turns over one of the dresses; a scowl pushes its way over his relaxed smile. "Fancy lot this is."

I lift my fingers to my lips, hiding my frustration.

He lets go of the material. "Why so many?"

We've already had this conversation. I know this is going to lead to accusations of the king wanting to use me for my powers.

Ignoring the edge in Cohen's gaze, I hold the dress to myself and grip Cohen's arm with my free hand. "He pardoned you and gave you back your position. In a sense, he's given me you. His gifts cannot be all that bad."

His face softens. Warmth fills his hazel eyes, turning them more golden. "Brought you something . . . I figured since you had to go tonight, it would be more your style." His smile fades slightly at the mountain of dresses looming beside me. He steps out of the room and returns a moment later with a brown package.

"What is it?" I touch the twine wrapped around the package.

"Open it and find out."

Gingerly, I tug the string and peel the paper back. The wrapping falls away to reveal a simple pale blue gown. My fingers flutter over the scooped neckline and cinched waist. The unexpectedness of it takes me aback. I cannot fathom why Cohen would ever purchase me a dress.

"You had this made?" I cannot help the squeak of astonishment in my voice.

"The tailor had it already. Just needed sizing." He studies

my expression and then adds, "Gillian helped with your measurements."

I find his actions sweet. Cohen does not often ask for help.

"It reminded me of the one you wore in Shaerdan."

He's right. It's simple like the gown Enat gave me. Emotion burns in the back of my eyes. "Cohen," I whisper.

"I know it's not fancy like the king's dresses." His words carry an edge. He touches the arm of the gown. "Gillian wanted lace edges. But I thought it'd suit you perfectly as is. Same shade as your eyes."

I duck my head to hide the smile eating my face.

"Wish I had more to give, Britt."

"You've given me enough." I close the gift box and wrap my arms around Cohen's waist. Stepping closer, the need to eliminate the space between us is as essential as feeling the familiar edges of Papa's blade pressed against my ankle.

It takes him a second to respond. I wonder if he's still looking at the king's gifts. Then he cups my jaw and drops his forehead to mine. Our breaths mingle.

The silence aches for more to be said.

But I've never been good with words. Especially not when a conversation seems as precarious as navigating through an overgrown field full of rabbit traps.

Instead of talking, I hold on to Cohen for as long as he'll let me.

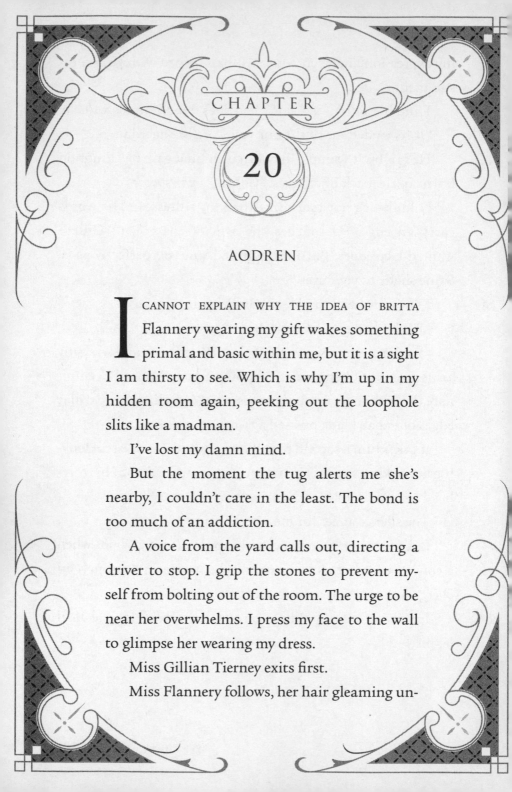

CHAPTER

20

AODREN

I CANNOT EXPLAIN WHY THE IDEA OF BRITTA Flannery wearing my gift wakes something primal and basic within me, but it is a sight I am thirsty to see. Which is why I'm up in my hidden room again, peeking out the loophole slits like a madman.

I've lost my damn mind.

But the moment the tug alerts me she's nearby, I couldn't care in the least. The bond is too much of an addiction.

A voice from the yard calls out, directing a driver to stop. I grip the stones to prevent myself from bolting out of the room. The urge to be near her overwhelms. I press my face to the wall to glimpse her wearing my dress.

Miss Gillian Tierney exits first.

Miss Flannery follows, her hair gleaming under the lantern light like gold coils on top of her head. Though not a classic beauty with generous curves and dark lashes, Britta Flannery is captivating in her own way. It's her strength, her press-forward attitude, her resilience.

Gods, I'm starting to sound like a drunken, besotted fool.

Britta lifts the front of her pale blue dress as she approaches the gate. The gown isn't one I gave her. The realization sinks to the bottom of my stomach. Serves me right for sitting up here, waiting for her arrival. Foolishness.

And yet, even though I know I'm acting a bit touched, I cannot help the disappointment that comes as I move away from the narrow window. Regret is a companion I know well. It is absurd for a king to say, and yet that's my life. Privileged to the point of solitude. If I were a different man, I could snap my fingers and change that aspect of my life, but it would be a falsehood. I don't want that. I don't want to surround myself with people who like me because I'm the king. I want them to like me because I'm Aodren.

I've spent too much time lingering here. I want to smack myself for losing my mind to Britta Flannery once again.

I sneak out of the room, dust off my suit, and stride toward the Great Hall. A smile attempts to crack my kingly composure, because despite my disappointment, I realize I should've expected as much from Saul Flannery's stubborn daughter.

When I walk beneath the arcading, I do not scan the courtyard for her. Nor do I wonder if she's meeting Cohen Mackay.

Omar and Leif approach me outside the Great Hall, where

the lanterns aren't as numerous. Shadows slide across the captain's face, giving the angular edges around his eyes a more severe look than usual, which is severe, indeed. For a moment, I think Omar might chastise me for losing my guards like he used to when I was younger. But then I notice that Leif's face mirrors the captain's grim expression.

Omar cuts a glance to the right and left. "Your Grace, Lord Jamis has escaped."

I stare at him, shocked. My legs turn to stone as the reality of what he's just said sinks in. On the night of the Winter Feast, this is the worst thing that could happen. "Jamis is gone? How?"

"I don't know, sir."

"What do you know?" Exasperation bleeds into my tone. It masks my rising panic. The man manipulated me my entire life. He sought to control the kingdom. He used a Spiriter to turn me into a royal puppet. I have a hard time swallowing. "Did the dungeon master see anything? Does he have a clue who might've helped? I want to speak with him right away."

"I'm sorry, sir. He'll be no help."

"Why is that?"

"The dungeon master is dead."

My eyes are frozen wide, unable to blink. First the attack in the woods, then the Channeler girl, and now this. "Get me the bounty hunter."

CHAPTER

21

COHEN

IN BRENTYN, THE GIRLS TAKE NOTICE OF THE bounty hunter's apprentice.

I roll my shoulders back. Stand as tall as I can at fifteen. Hitch a grin at a red-headed maid, hoping to get a rise out of Britta.

A snort comes from beside me. Sounds like it could be jealousy. I hope so. "Should I buy you a mirror at market?" Britta asks. "Then you can admire yourself whenever you like."

I throw back my head and laugh. "You cannot afford that. You spent all your coins on that new quiver."

Her pallid skin reddens. I didn't mean to hurt her feelings. I only meant to poke fun of how excited she was about her new quiver. Bludger.

"Don't be so loud." She tries to duck away, but I swing an arm around her neck, not caring that market-goers have stopped to watch.

"I'm sorry, Dove."

She wiggles out of my grip and scrunches up her nose till her freckles touch.

Her voice drops low. "If you spent half as much time on tracking, archery, or knife throwing as you do flirting, you might pass for a decent bounty hunter."

I stop on the cobblestones, chafed by her comment. "I'm a fine hunter."

"Tell that to me when your apprenticeship is over. See if you compare to my father."

I scoff as she walks away, as if her words haven't scraped a scab off my insecurities. "I'll be better," I start to say, and then stop because that doesn't really matter to me. What I want to prove ten times over to Britta is that I'm just as dependable as her father. That I can be someone she trusts as well.

In the past, I could never coerce Britta into venturing away from her father's side at the Winter Feast celebrations in Brentyn. I wait for her in the Great Hall, hardly believing she's here.

Servants bustle around, pouring wine into goblets that line the pine bough– and ivy-littered tables. Noblemen and ladies gather round the entrance, talking in murmurs as a herald calls out names of guests as they arrive.

"Mackay."

Leif rushes across the room, dodging the gathered nobility and long rows of tables to reach me. "Captain Omar wants to see you in the dungeon."

"I've known that for years." I cross my arms. "Settle down, Leif."

Leif blows out a breath, his demeanor not changing. "This isn't a jest. He needs to meet with you."

"What for?"

His voice drops and he leans close to my ear. "Lord Jamis is gone."

My head snaps back, nearly giving him a bloody nose. "Gone?" Without a glance back at the ballroom and its finery, I stride for the dungeon, Leif scurrying after.

The dungeon master's throat is slit.

His body blocks the base of the stairs in the lowest remote part of the dungeon where no other prisoners are held.

While Leif looks through the other celled caverns for clues as to how Lord Jamis escaped, I study the dead man's body. No bruises on his limbs or knuckles, no scratches or skin under his nails. No part of Lord Jamis's cell has been upset.

Must've been a surprise attack.

Leif reports back. He hasn't found anything that might point to who has taken Jamis or how they got out. I give the dungeon one more thorough search and find nothing.

We return to the dungeon master's body, where Captain Omar and King Aodren wait. When the captain asks for my input, I lay out the measly findings. I don't know how Lord Jamis escaped. Don't know who helped him. Don't know where he went. But I'll figure it out.

Omar stalks away from the cell and kicks the dungeon master's spit bucket. It flies across the torture chamber and bangs the wall.

Not the news he wanted.

King Aodren's gaze flicks to the can and then to where black juices run down the wall like blood. The night Britta saved the king, he looked like a corpse. Today he's stiffer than the statue of his grandfather that takes up the center of the Great Hall.

It's impressive that the king doesn't react to Omar's mess or the dungeon master's body. Just turns back to Omar, expectant, like the captain will be able make Jamis reappear.

"I'll take a group of men and head out right away." Omar straightens, his shoulders roll back.

King Aodren nods. "Jamis and Phelia have got to be working together. Perhaps he'll lead you to her."

Phelia. Britta's mother. I notice how the king's arms go rigid as he mentions her, almost like he wants to squeeze them in closer, but fights it.

I'm like Siron, chomping at the bit when all I want to do is go, but the king takes a moment for thought. "Take a larger group with you. Exercise caution. Jamis won't be alone."

Obviously.

"We'll take Ulrich, Geoffrey, and Wallace." Captain Omar turns to Leif. "Order them to be packed, fully armed, and ready with their mounts in twenty minutes."

Leif bows to the king and heads for the stairs. Before he's out of earshot, King Aodren says, "The escape remains quiet. No one can know. I do not want rumors spreading through tonight's feast."

It makes sense that King Aodren doesn't want nobility to know. With Lord Conklin's betrayal on the heels of Jamis's near-takeover of the kingdom, the king must be wondering how many more traitors are hiding in the fold. When my friend Kendrick sold me out to the soldiers, it leveled me. Made me rethink whom I should trust.

I don't envy King Aodren.

Casting one more glace at the deceased dungeon master, I wipe my hands on my slacks and nod at Captain Omar. "I'll prepare my gear and be ready shortly."

"What about Britta? She'll want to go." Leif's voice stops me in my tracks.

I want to tell him to keep his mouth shut. But I catch the jerk of King Aodren's chin, a reaction that has me fisting my hands. Why should he care whether my Britta goes or stays?

"A group of six will get the job done." The corner of my eye stays on Leif as I watch the king for any reaction. "With Ulrich, Geoffrey, Wallace, Leif, the captain, and myself, we'll have a full team. I cannot see how Britta would be any more help." Every word I've spoken is true, yet even as I say this, I know she's going to be spitting mad. She won't want to be left out now that Jamis is on the loose with Phelia.

Leif's mouth skews. "Don't you think two trackers will find Lord Jamis's trail faster?"

It's an unnecessary risk. Putting Britta near Phelia might expose Britta as a Spiriter. Frankly, I've no clue what all Phelia is capable of. But neither do I want to find out.

The king's reaction is minuscule, a twitch of the mouth; it's enough to suspect he doesn't like the idea of Britta leaving any more than I do.

Captain Omar steps away from the spittle mess and straightens his coat. "Cohen's right. She's not needed."

Good. Whether the captain's decision is based on logic or dislike of Britta, I don't care. All that matters is that she won't be in any unnecessary danger.

"No." King Aodren's crisp voice breaks into our conversation. All eyes turn toward him.

The man lifts his chin, gaining height. "Miss Flannery deserves the choice to go. The decision should be hers to make."

Shock the seeds right out of me.

It's obvious he doesn't want her to go any more than I do. So why give her the option?

I scoff, an interruption that raises the king's brow. "My apologies, Your Highness. Considering Britta's recent interaction with Phelia in the woods, and the likely possibility that Jamis is working with Phelia, it might be best to leave Britta out of this tracking party." The rest goes unsaid, though he knows exactly what I'm referring to. Britta told me that the king heard Phelia admit she's Britta's mother.

I may not like the attention King Aodren's paid Britta, but I appreciate that he seems to consider my comment. After a moment of deliberation, he says, "Agreed."

The last thing I want is for Britta to face danger again. This is for the better.

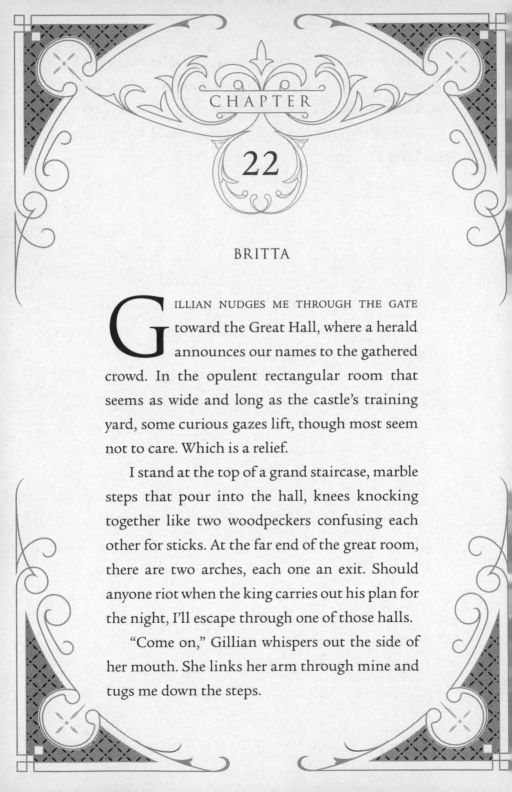

CHAPTER

22

BRITTA

GILLIAN NUDGES ME THROUGH THE GATE toward the Great Hall, where a herald announces our names to the gathered crowd. In the opulent rectangular room that seems as wide and long as the castle's training yard, some curious gazes lift, though most seem not to care. Which is a relief.

I stand at the top of a grand staircase, marble steps that pour into the hall, knees knocking together like two woodpeckers confusing each other for sticks. At the far end of the great room, there are two arches, each one an exit. Should anyone riot when the king carries out his plan for the night, I'll escape through one of those halls.

"Come on," Gillian whispers out the side of her mouth. She links her arm through mine and tugs me down the steps.

A pull toward the back of the room has me cringing internally. It's so much stronger here than it was in the stable yard. As always, knowing he's nearby infuriates. I feel drawn toward him. Tonight the struggle frustrates me more than usual because all I want to do is seek out Cohen.

My hands ball at my sides. I try to study the crowd. It's smaller than I imagined. I never feel comfortable in a small crowd. Too many people who can see you. Too few people to hide.

After a moment of searching for Cohen, I give in to the king's draw and allow myself to scan the nobility for the man I'm yoked to. I haven't seen him since the day he was attacked. I hope his shoulder has healed.

Ladies with giant coiffures resembling snail shells talk in whispery voices. Beside them, the men wear awful embroidered and silk ensembles with puffy trousers and pointed shoes. For a moment, I'm distracted by their ridiculous extravagance. Surely, the cost of one of their outfits could feed a family for a month. For some reason, I think of Lirra's comment about everyone being liars. Makes me wonder what is hidden beyond their baubles and accessories.

Voices mingle in hushed conversations that I care little to be a part of. Gillian mutters something about how odd it is no one has welcomed us. I snort, and then try to cover it with a cough. She doesn't understand that people who ignore me are the people I feel the most comfortable around.

I stick to Gillian like she's my anchor, keeping me from

drifting in the king's direction, even though I haven't yet spotted the man. He isn't seated at the head table. Or at the carved wood monstrosity of a throne parked at the end of the room opposite the entry stairs.

"Not so confident out of the woods, are you?"

I whip my head to the side to see who's talking. A guard stands nearby beside one of the wood columns.

Gillian's arm cinches tighter. "Jealous of her hunting skill, Niall? Figures, since you're stuck here, tending nobles like a nanny."

"Scrants." He hisses.

I straighten. Lift my skirt and march up to him. For a guard I've only just met, he needs an antidote for the venom he's spewing. "Glorified nursemaid."

His glare is so fiery, it could burn down the entire castle.

Gillian flips her fan open with a snap and turns on her heel. "What a fool."

But the guard is right. Eyes slide our way and feet scurry out of our path like we're wolves in a herd of sheep. Walking through the nobility is torturous. Their glares put Niall's to shame, weighing me down. By the time we reach the center of the room, I might well be dragging a millstone for how much I have to fight to keep moving.

I remain on a course to Aodren. Or where the invisible lead pulls me. I make an effort to search once more for Cohen, but, hang it, the king has commandeered my attention, directing me like one of the castle's homing pigeons.

Two men walk out of the east corridor, carrying long trumpets. Royal banners drop from the polished metal. Raising the instruments to their lips, they blow out resonant notes that fill the Great Hall, demanding silence. When the song ends, both men lower their trumpets and drop their chins to their chests.

"Honor the bearer of the crown, King Aodren the III, ruler and leader of Malam." The herald's voice booms.

Men's heads lower. Women dip into fabric puddles across the shining granite floor.

I follow suit, remaining that way until the herald announces we may all rise. I'm not expecting Aodren's eyes to lock with mine amidst the sea of faces. His skin is unusually waxen, and there's a tight pinch to his features that makes me wonder where he's just come from. I fight the rope connecting us, frustratingly aware that the bond is stronger than what I shared with Cohen.

Whispers sweep through the hall. I turn away from Aodren to find that the men and women around me have noticed the king's attention. Prickles dance along the back of my neck. This dress suddenly feels ten times smaller than before. I tug at the material where the skirt blossoms out from the waist, hoping to give myself breathing room.

No use.

The herald announces that King Aodren will move through the room to greet everyone. Thankfully, the interruption pops the moment of awkwardness.

Out of the corner of my eye, I catch Aodren's movement. Starting at the side of the room where lords and ladies stand shoulder to shoulder just inside the pillars, Aodren shakes hands, speaks a word or two, and moves on. Each interaction is no more than twenty seconds. That means I have five minutes or less before he arrives.

"Stop twitching." Gillian waves her fan over her mouth. If I wasn't already rubbing shoulders with her, I wouldn't have noticed she spoke. She's so stealthy about it. Until she smacks her fan closed and swats my hand. "Stand taller. Smile. Pretend you're happy."

I open my mouth to argue, but the words turn to vapor the moment Aodren stops in front of me. Gillian provided too much of a distraction for me to keep track of the man. I must look like a guppy fish, opening and closing my mouth, hoping words will land on my tongue.

A hundred eyes are on us as Gillian tugs me down into a curtsy. Somewhere in the background, there are titters about traitors and whores. The king must be realizing his mistake now. The idea that I could be noble is farcical.

"Rise, Miss Flannery, Miss Tierney."

His command grates on me. Forcing myself to straighten, shoulders back and nose up, I show the onlookers that I don't care a whit about their insults.

Aodren's hand snags mine. He brings it to his lips. The feather-light kiss on my skin could be a cattle brand for how it sends a whoosh of heat through me.

I try to tug away because everyone is watching. *Everyone.* Gods, how I wish the granite floor would ingest me whole. I wiggle my fingers, but the devil king's grip constricts. I mutter *bludger* under my breath.

His brows raise and, I swear, his eyes glint like polished emeralds.

"I'm pleased you're in attendance tonight." His voice echoes off the columns, the ceiling, the floor, the walls. *Seeds and stars.* I yank my hand away. Could he have spoken any louder?

"We're so honored to be here, Your Majesty." Gillian holds her hand out for him to shake. He doesn't place a kiss on hers. "How kind of you to invite us to the feast. You are a truly magnanimous leader."

Has she drunk tainted ale?

Gillian loops her arm through mine, ignoring the look I'm throwing in her direction. "Britta was just saying how thankful she was for the dresses."

My head whips to face hers.

Aodren's mouth twitches. "Is that so?"

I'm going to suffocate Gillian with a pillow tonight. "Actually—"

Her arm snakes tighter around mine, cutting off the blood flow. "Of course." Her little laugh sounds as frilly as her fan. "Britta would be wearing one this evening. However, the fit wasn't quite right."

"Regardless. You look lovely, Miss Flannery. Your father was beloved in this kingdom, and so your presence honors us all." His smile sweeps around the room and returns to me. It's a smile I've not seen from him before. It's strong and sure, arrogant and assertive. It's baffling, almost, for he seemed so shaken when he entered the room, and yet now he's the image of confidence. That's when I realize—the castle, the nobility, the subjects and servants—all of that is his Ever Woods. He's the hunter here, with manners and words as his weapons.

He pivots toward Gillian. "And you look equally fetching, Miss Tierney."

A few words from him and she's a flittering, blinking ball of blushes. "Your Majesty, you flatter me."

It's a relief when Aodren moves on. The next woman he greets has enough feathers on her headdress that she could pose as a peacock.

I wiggle away from Gillian and shoot her a glare. "Do not talk for me ever again."

"Calm yourself. I was only helping."

"Your help is not needed."

Her fan opens with a *fwack* and flaps in front of her furrowed brow. She inclines her head, nearly gouging me each time the fan comes close to my cheek. "You may think my help unnecessary. But you're unpolished, Britta. Here, addressing the king the way you've done at the cottage will get you sent to the dungeon. Or worse."

For all Gillian's fluff and fancy words, she has a point. Regardless of our connection, one word from Aodren could end my life.

"You're right."

She tilts her head, lifting her ear. "What was that? I'm not sure I heard you."

I snort, then chuckle.

"Britta."

I jolt, Cohen's voice catching me unaware. He stands in the west corridor. Shadows mix with the yellow lantern light like hornet-striped jigsaw pieces on his face.

Unlike the king, who arrived tenser than a deer downwind of a mountain cat, Cohen's face shows nothing.

A fleeting worry that he's displeased with my appearance niggles. Then I frown, irritated with myself. When did I start acting like a twittering town girl?

Gillian lowers the fan. Her lips part as if she's about to say something.

Ignoring her, I back away from the reception line. I don't want to hear her disapproval. I don't want to discuss propriety. I don't want a lecture on how I should smile, talk, stand, or walk.

The conversations from the Great Hall make a low, echoing drone in the corridor. I follow Cohen to a corner where the darkness is deepest.

The fancy clothes he had on earlier have been replaced by a faded gray cloak, scuffed boots, and patched trousers. The waist belt hanging on his hips holds Papa's dagger beside Cohen's sword. I cross my arms, studying him in meticulous measure. I'd bet my bow if he turned around, there'd be one more knife hooked through the back of the belt. And all would be newly sharpened.

"You're dressed to hunt." Accusation sharpens my tone.

He clears his throat. "I have to."

A moment ago I was worried he might not like my dress, when really he's been focused on hunting. It's doubtful he even noticed that I wore his gown. Cohen's leaving. Again. "Why now?"

"Lord Jamis escaped."

A chill pebbles over my exposed skin. "W-what? How?"

He scrubs a hand over his face. When it drops, I notice tight tiny lines around his eyes have replaced his usual confidence.

"Don't know," he says. "The dungeon master was murdered, and the guard who discovered him had just returned from checking another level of the dungeon. No one saw anything."

"But the trail's fresh. Your best chance at catching Lord Jamis depends on leaving immediately." I say this more to remind myself that his abrupt departure is standard for tracking. A trade I know well, having spent years saying goodbye to Papa at a moment's notice. Still, my words don't salve the sting that this night is going awry.

"Aye."

I peer past his shoulder to where music and chatter filter from the Great Hall. Gillian won't be pleased that I'm leaving. "What will I tell Gillian?" I muse aloud.

Cohen shakes his head. "Britta—"

"Cohen." Captain Omar's austere tenor identifies the man before either of us look down the hall. There, Leif and three other guards wait with the captain.

Cohen holds up a finger to them. "I—I have to go, Britt. The team has already been chosen."

"I'm coming with you. Finding Lord Jamis is as important to me as it is to you."

He doesn't speak. The resolution in the set of his shoulders leaves no room for misunderstanding.

My eyes lower into furious slits. "You said when you returned from Shaerdan, we would hunt together."

"Two minutes," Captain Omar interrupts. Judgment wafts off the abhorrent man like stink from a skunk.

I turn my glare on the captain. But Cohen winds his fingers into mine, centering my attention. He mutters an agreement to the captain and then waits while the man stalks away. Two of the guards follow, like pack mates flanking an alpha wolf.

Leif stays behind, an entreating smile on his freckled face. I don't return the look.

"Go on, Leif. I'll follow in a minute," Cohen says.

"What about Finn and Lirra?"

Cohen's jaw tics. "Finn knows. Already talked to him. Lirra will have to wait."

"You aren't going to tell her?" My irascible tone notches up a peg. I blink at him.

"There's no time to ride out to the cottage," Cohen says after Leif slips out of sight. "I was hoping you or Gillian could talk to her for me. It's not that I want to leave her in the middle of her plight to find Orli, but Jamis has escaped."

The same urgency came from Papa each time he had to leave Malam to hunt. It felt different though. It didn't hollow out my chest.

Suddenly, I'm angry with Cohen. He makes decisions for others based on what he thinks is right or best, without taking into consideration what the person wants. But because I'm all too familiar with the bite of being left behind, I promise that I'll find a way to deliver the news to Lirra.

"I'm a better tracker than any man on that team. And you know it," I argue. If Cohen wants me to go, he could convince the captain to add me to the hunting party.

His mouth dips at the corners. Lately all I've caught are frowns from him. "The men going are already assigned. You're not needed."

I flinch.

"Gods, that came out wrong." His fingers graze my neck, curling around my shoulder. The heavy warmth of his touch usually sends sparks through my core. I jerk away.

"Britt, it's safer here. There's no telling what we're facing out there. This isn't about whether or not you can take care of yourself. It's not even about Jamis. Phelia's still out there. I've a hunch that she's a part of Jamis's escape. At the very least, she could hurt you and expose you" — he lowers his voice — "as a Spiriter."

Deep down, I know that what he says makes sense. Papa taught me to be cautious, not reckless. I rub my eyes, trying to erase the image of Phelia. I stare at the charcoal veins running through the granite floor, no order in the markings, much like Phelia's skin. I feel like those same veins are winding through my innards, twisting my gut, and staining my thoughts with their black ink.

Voices echo from the Great Hall like muted bird warbles, reminding that the royal celebration is happening not far from us.

I lift my chin. "Those risks are mine to consider. Not yours."

"Seeds, Britt." His gaze flickers, the gold in his hazel eyes dimming, before a stony expression slides down, shutting off all emotions. "Please stay with Gillian. Enjoy the night."

I gape at him, unsure which bit exasperates me the most — the part where he thinks I cannot protect myself, or that he thinks I'll be able to remain at the feast and enjoy the night.

I put space between us, moving until my shoulders press to the icy castle wall. "Tell me this, Cohen, did Captain Omar make the choice not to include me on this hunt? Or you?"

A long silent beat passes. "Dove . . . please be safe," he says, his low voice sounding almost pained. A silent apology is written between the crinkles around the edges of his eyes.

The space beneath my breastbone throbs.

Cohen cuts the distance between us in a blink and drops his lips to my cheek. He lingers for a moment, drawing in a deep breath before he leaves and strides down the hall without looking back.

Bludger.

"You too," I whisper, ignoring the sting in the corners of my eyes. Not that it means I'm content to stay back and wait for him to find her.

CHAPTER

23

COHEN

WHAT HAPPENED TO HER?" SAUL'S VOICE *was no louder than a whisper, but the ferocity gave it the strength of a bear's roar.*

I laid Britta's comatose body on the bed. "There was a mountain cat ... it attacked. I—I didn't have my bow ..." The story, with all its sickening twists, poured out.

Saul reached for his daughter's hand. Never having seen a shred of weakness in the man, I felt kicked in the gut watching his fingers tremble over her ghostly pale skin.

My hands hovered over her, useless to help. I watched the subtle lift of her chest, and it cut my own breath in half. Bleeding gods, I hated myself. I'm the reason she came into the cave.

"She saved you," he said, voice broken in understanding as well as alarm.

I ripped at my hair as I sat down beside her. Then touched the new scar on my cheek. I knew nothing of Channeler magic, but I knew the girl I loved somehow paid a terrible price to save my life. It was a debt I'd never be able to repay, but I'd live my life trying.

The memory eases my conscience, even if the angry hurt in her voice is stuck in my head. The quick strike of my boots smacks the ground, punctuating each step from where I left Britta to the training yard. A fellow guard sees me, starts to tip his chin up in greeting, and then freezes. He moves out of my way.

How can Britta expect me not to consider the risk that Phelia poses? It's all I've thought about since Britta nearly died when she saved the king.

I shove open the door to my quarters. It slams into the wall, and Finn jerks into an upright position on the bed. He clenches a small ball in his hand.

He stares at me. I tamp down my anger.

Finn relaxes against the mattress and tosses the ball into the air. "That's quite an entrance." He catches the ball.

When he throws it up again, my hand snakes out and seizes it. "You going to be all right?"

"I'll be well." His expression sinks back into the same glum frown he had on earlier when I changed my clothes and told him I was leaving. "I take it you talked to Britta."

I wrap my fingers around the ball tighter and sit down on

the edge of the bed. "Aye. Tomorrow, have one of the guards ride out with you to see her. Her woodpile was looking low. Can you tend to it?"

Finn scoots beside me. "If she'll let me," he says. He holds out his hand for the ball. After I give it to him, he adds, "Seems like your talk went well."

A joyless chuckle slips out.

"I just met Britta, but you've talked about her for years, so I feel like I know her."

"Your point?"

He shrugs. "Maybe she wants to chop her own wood."

I give him a look. "Didn't think you'd be one to gripe about chores. All I'm asking you to do is talk to her. See what she wants."

"I'm not griping." He tosses the ball. "I'm saying that I'll ask, but if Britta wants to do it herself, it's her choice." He leans toward me, one brow lifted, eyes owlish—it's the same knowing look Pa used to wear when he was making a point. "I might not like it because, seeds, do I love chopping wood. But I like Britta a lot."

I smack his ball away. "You love chores, huh?"

He jabs my arm with his pointy elbow. The kid needs some cushioning on those bones.

"You know what I'm saying, Cohen?"

I mess up his hair and pull him in for a hug, even though he shoves me away. "Aye. I do. Take care, kid. All right?"

"Yeah, yeah. You too, Cohen."

My conversation with Britta sits at the front of my mind as I ride alongside Captain Omar. I dismount Siron and, taking the torch from Geoffrey, scan the woods. Even though there's a full moon climbing higher, the woods are good at keeping the light out. I want to be sure we're on the right path. Leif follows behind me while Wallace and Ulrich keep watch from their horses. Ulrich is a narrow fellow, whose sharp eyes and exactness with a bow make him a formidable travel mate. Wallace, however, is average in height and strength. But he's clever with a mace. His hand-to-hand combat skill will come in handy should we come under attack.

Our team of six has enough varying talent to take on a much larger group if needed.

So far, the tracks have led us here. The number of them indicates that Lord Jamis was traveling with haste, and he wasn't traveling alone. We don't know where they're headed or whom they're meeting with. So keeping our weapons ready, we follow the newly bent branches and boot prints through the Evers.

When we stop again, I cross through the brush to Wallace's side and study some broken branches. I run my fingers along the bends. The limbs are turned west, indicating the group is headed for the border. Makes sense.

Captain Omar approaches. "Find something?"

I lower the torch to the trail. "Fresh prints."

He stares west into the night. "They're heading for the pass."

The men exchange silent looks. No one speaks, but we all understand we need to move faster. There's no telling what Jamis has planned, only that he seems to have a plan in place. If anything, the former high lord is one of the cleverest and most vindictive men I've ever met. I feel like we're heading into a brewing storm. The kind that requires bringing extra buckets of water inside, stocking the firewood, and nailing the windows shut. Instincts tell me that if we cannot stop Jamis soon, his destruction will blizzard over Malam with a vengeance.

I think of Finn's roundabout advice and shake my head. There are no woodpiles out here. I'd rather face Britta's anger than let her charge into the squall.

We drive the horses hard up the mountain, stopping now and then to ensure we're on the right path. In the past, Siron's led the pack. Tonight, however, Captain Omar and Ulrich take the head position.

The farther we ride, though, the more the captain's horse slows. Siron cannot help but edge up beside the lead horses. Gut instinct tells me something is off.

When we're side by side, I notice Captain Omar patting the animal's withers.

"You all right?" I ask.

The man's frown is fierce. "He's been fed, watered, and rested." He strokes his beard. "He's lagging. It makes no sense."

The trees open up and we cut through a clearing. The moonlight glistens on Captain Omar's horse where sweat has slicked over its coat.

"He's laboring pretty hard." I point out the foam around his haunches. "We should stop."

The captain curses and stares off in the distance, want evident on his features. Any break we take will give Jamis more of a lead, but it cannot be helped. His horse is in a bad way.

Omar takes my advice and dismounts.

The horse huffs out a shaky breath as the captain examines his bit and reins. Hooves stomp the ground. The animal jerks, shaking his head side to side like he's trying to break out of his skin.

"You better move back," Leif cautions.

I agree. This behavior isn't normal.

"Settle," Captain Omar commands. He reaches for the horse's bit. I think he's going to remove it. Only the animal paws the ground, blows out a hard breath, and rears.

"Omar!" I shout in warning, but the captain doesn't have time to react. His horse's hooves rake the air and then come down hard, knocking the man in the head and chest. Omar crumbles to the ground.

One of the other men gasps. In that millisecond, I wait expectantly for Omar to roll to his side and stand.

He doesn't move.

We're all off our horses and rushing to the captain's side. Omar's horse darts into the woods before any of us have a chance to subdue the beast.

Shock chokes me. *Did this just happen?*

I drop to a knee, all thoughts gone aside from the fear that

Captain Omar might possibly be dead, or very close to death. Could he survive the horse's blow? No matter how many times I see death, it always surprises me. A person is there, and then they're gone. So fast. I was just talking to him, and now he's so still. A mark the shape of a horse's hoof is purpling on his forehead. Blood leaks from the edge of the wound.

I pray there's life still left in his body.

"Omar?" I touch his shoulder.

He doesn't move. I stare at his chest where the other hoof left it concaved.

Watch for the rise and fall.

Breathe, Omar.

I find myself waiting until my own lungs burn.

BRITTA

AFTER THREE ATTEMPTS TO COAX GILLIAN away from the center of the Great Hall, I forgo niceties and yank her arm toward the columns lining the room. Her glare could burn my skin off. Who knew it'd be easier to get Gillian's fat heifer to lay an egg than get Gillian to leave the throng of lords?

Once we're tucked behind a column, I explain my urgency, telling her what Cohen told me about Lord Jamis. Her anger seems to fade as I sum up my purpose for dragging her away. "I need the carriage driver to take me home so I can grab Snowfire, a change of clothing, some food for travel, and my bow. But I'm not good at talking. I need you to secure a driver for my departure. And excuse my absence to the king."

She sputters at me.

I put on my best hopeful smile.

"You want a royal driver to see you to the cottage so you can grab a change of clothes and your bow?" A squeak marks her question. She purses her lips.

"Yes." I lift my skirt and wiggle my boot, indicating where my dagger is. Always.

"Boots, Britta?" She huffs and growls all at once. "Where are the slippers I gave you?"

"Focus, Gillian. Boots are not the issue."

She folds her arms. "The answer is no."

"No? Why not?"

"Britta, you cannot leave. He hasn't granted you noble status yet."

"That doesn't matter. Lord Jamis is—"

Her eyes flare. Her lips go between her teeth. I glance over my shoulder, noticing the awful guard has taken up post near the column.

Motioning for her to follow, I walk to a private spot near the west corridor. Gillian has a way with words that I've never managed. I'm awkward at best. I plead with her once more.

"Why are you so determined?" she asks.

"I have to do this," I tell Gillian. "I have to go after him."

She gets a far-off look in her eyes. Servants move in and out of the room, bringing food to the tables, pouring goblets of wine, and placing name cards in front of plates. "If you leave now, you might anger the king. You could lose your chance." She turns to me, determined. "I cannot let you do that."

"Dammit, Gillian—"

"But—but I'll go for you." Her hand fists around the fan. Her mouth puckers like she's swallowed a bushel of lemons. "I'd rather you didn't go at all. If you must, let me gather your supplies while you stay here."

"That makes no sense."

"You'll have time for the king to elevate you to the nobility. And I'm a maid. No one will notice if I leave."

My first instinct is to say no. It'll put me that much farther behind Cohen.

I start to shake my head when she grips my arm and tugs me closer. "How do you expect me to get a message to the king? Imagine how he'll react if he announces your change in status and you're not here."

I chew my lip. She's brought up an issue I hadn't considered.

"The last thing you can afford to do is embarrass or anger him."

Gillian's logic is frustrating.

"All right," I say. "You go. I'll stay."

"Really?"

"Don't look so shocked. I'm not that big a fool."

The pleased smile that spreads across her face. She makes me promise I'll mingle. Which won't happen. And then agree to thank the king. I'll consider it.

She starts to walk away and then makes an abrupt turn back. "What about Lirra?"

Though I prefer to travel alone, it's safer to go together. "Have her pack up her horse. She'll go with me."

The smile on Gillian's face grows. "Good. She's going stir-crazy and could use a little out-of-the-cottage adventure."

This time I smile. I think it's Gillian who is going a little crazy with Lirra around.

After she leaves, I partially do as promised and move to the other side of the column so I'm closer to the gathered crowd.

Servants bustle past the lords and ladies with trays of breads and meats. The long tables look a tray away from collapsing because there is so much food. It is a bigger feast than I've ever seen. My stomach grumbles in appreciation. Four castle workers balance a roasted pig on a platter, carrying it to the head table. Saliva pools in my mouth. Eventually, the herald calls for everyone in attendance to find their assigned seat.

The crowd breaks apart, sliding around the tables, reading name cards, and chatting merrily when they discover their seat is surrounded by friends. They move as naturally and quickly as a herd of elk in the Evers.

I force my feet toward the tables.

Questioning eyes land on me as I pass chair after chair. It would be easier to march to the guillotine than walk the length of the tables in search of my name.

I pray silently that my chair will be farthest from the king.

The prayer goes unheard. My name card rests on the table closest to the king. It's at the head of the room for all to see.

The heat from the cavernous fireplace stifles. My throat is the Akaria Desert.

I lower myself into the chair, conscious of the hundred sets of eyes tracking my movement. Their whispers roll through the room. Their chins turn my way. I fidget with the name card, suddenly grateful that Papa taught me to read. This night would be one thousand times worse if I were illiterate like many of Brentyn's impoverished.

Aodren stands and the room goes silent.

"Lords and ladies of Malam, welcome to the Royal Winter Feast Ball." King Aodren shows none of the uncertainty he displayed in my cottage or in the woods. His commanding presence steals my attention.

I drop the card to the table and forget about the nobility sitting around me. Even the aroma lifting off the savory meats and cheeses littered across the table is no comparison to the golden-haired ruler of Malam. A crown of gold and emeralds sits on his head, matching a fine green coat with gold lining. It isn't like the gaudy outfit I once saw him wearing the day I was arrested and brought to the castle. His sleek, formal attire fit better with his personality.

He is the picture of poise and power. Perhaps he seems that way because I've seen him at his weakest. But I think the confidence he exudes has more to do with his upbringing. Here he is a lion leading his pride.

Since no one knows he was under the Spiriter's bind for much of his rule, Aodren has to change the country's perception of him. Considering I've struggled to change people's minds about me, I should've realized the difficult challenge the king faces.

Surely, many of these people ridiculed him once.

I certainly did.

"I commend you on the united front," he says, going on to address the recent war with Shaerdan. He names specific lords and praises them. I haven't spent any time trying to understand Aodren or the world he lives in. "Tonight, let us celebrate your brave support and unyielding loyalty to Malam. May our land always be prosperous and at peace." Kind words for this group of people.

My first impression is to wonder if anyone here is truly worthy of the king's praise. Then I realize that in just the last half-hour, the king has managed to shift my perception of him. Perhaps my judgments are not always right.

"Our hearts, our blood, our lives for Malam!" Aodren shouts.

The hall roars as all echo the same credo.

When everyone quiets down, King Aodren's gaze cuts to me. "On this special evening, I would also like to honor a man who once was a confidant of mine, a steadfast supporter, a man of strength and valor. Saul Flannery."

A beat, and then thundering applause bounces off the ceiling. Pride fills me, clogs my chest, and burns at my eyes.

"To honor Saul, I've invited his daughter here tonight, to extend my gratitude."

Every speck of me wants to flee from the humiliation of being singled out this way.

He gestures for me to stand. The lantern light gleams off his gold crown. "May I present Lady Flannery."

A guard appears behind me and pulls out my chair. It snaps my focus away from the discomfort of the situation. On wobbly legs I manage a quick rise, a small wave, and a grimace before sinking back into the chair like it's a lifeboat. The rushing sound in my ears drowns out some of Aodren's speech. But I catch him declaring my nobility status based on my father's service to the crown.

A tornado should appear for how loud a collective gasp sucks through the crowd.

Aodren goes on, like he hasn't heard a thing, but his eyes darken, a thundercloud moving over grassy plains. I want to strangle him for insisting I be here. At the same time, I want to thank him for quickly diverting the crowd's attention back to himself.

King Aodren holds up his cup, signaling the conclusion of his speech.

Everyone in the room follows. Goblets are raised toward the ceiling.

"To peace in Malam." Aodren's voice booms through the Great Hall, loud with conviction. "To Winter Feast, may next year be as bounteous as years before; and to Saul Flannery, for his unyielding service to the crown." Once more the room joins in as he repeats, "Our hearts, our blood, our lives for Malam."

He swings his drink in an arc, motioning to the entire room and then brings the goblet to his lips. Before he tips it back, his eyes catch mine, and an entreating smile peeks out from the side of his cup.

A spark of something different and shy cuts through my embarrassment. It's the type of curiosity I've only ever felt for Cohen. The awareness of his gaze on me slows my movements. While others are already taking a sip, I'm only just grasping my goblet. I lift it to toast.

Then, out of the corner of my eye, I see the shimmer of a sword.

A guard stands in the east hall, focus pinned on Aodren. He wears a hungry look that's predatory and cold.

My flesh rises in bumps regardless of the heat. My eyes snap back to the king, *warning* pulsing through every speck of me. He is still watching me, a line forming between his brows.

The man beside me sputters, spitting his drink on my dress.

I lurch back. I reach for a napkin to dab at the mess, and then realize another lord seated across the table is coughing violently. Half the room has suddenly developed a hacking cough.

I shove back from my seat, taking in the Great Hall at once, panicked.

The guard in the east hall who had drawn his sword has disappeared. The lady across the table slumps into her plate. Her husband coughs. His face whitens. Foam drips from his lips.

People begin to cry out. In fear. In pain.

"Don't drink!" I scream at Aodren, realizing that the goblets must be poisoned. I curse for not having my bow. I yank my dagger out of my boot.

Aodren's goblet tumbles from his hand, splashing red wine like blood across the tablecloth and his coat. Terror turns his face slack. "Do not drink," he cries out to the crowd. "It's poison. Stop drinking."

But his warning is too late.

The pound of boots, people running, others screaming. Men and women tumble forward, collapsing on the table. It's chaos, as if the castle is crumbling all around us.

Protective instinct has me launching myself around the table on a path straight for the king. Guards draw swords against guards. Even some lords and ladies have weapons drawn, attacking other nobility. At first I cannot make sense of what's happening. Then I realize—the poison, men turning on one another, the fighting—this is a coup.

Oh gods, the castle is under attack. Lords and ladies fall to their knees, hacking up foamy saliva and blood. I cannot wrap my head around how many people, out of the two hundred that are here, have fallen in this room. Half, perhaps more.

My insides turn watery like the time I accidentally ate spoiled meat. Grief and shock and fear churn beneath my skin.

Niall, the guard from earlier, lunges out from behind a column, nearly taking off my head with the sweep of his sword. I jump back and fall into a stumbling, frothing man. The man tumbles to the ground. Niall swings, nicking my arm with his sword. I yelp and clamber away. The dress catches on my boots.

Niall holds his sword over me, then swings it down.

His eyes roll back and go empty. The point of a sword appears in his chest. He tips toward me, but I manage to scramble out of the path. His body hits the ground hard. Aodren stands above me. His sword is stained with blood. Widened green eyes bounce from the blade to my face to the slain guard. His skin turns ashen.

I see it in his face. Shock. Nausea. This guard is the first person the king has killed.

He's a heave away from losing the contents of his stomach. I quickly scramble to my feet and tug the king behind a column. From where we're hidden, we can see the extent of the pandemonium. Vomit and blood and death.

A quiver rests on the ground beside the slain guard, Niall. I tell the king to wait as I dash forward. It disgusts me to think I'm stealing from a dead man, but he did just try to kill me. I grasp the quiver though it has only two arrows left in it, and shove the man over so I can steal the bow off his shoulder.

His blood is wet and sticky on my hands. I wipe them on

my dress, my stomach knotting. I'm almost back to the king's side. He's fighting off another guard. I grab an arrow from the quiver and test it to the bow, which is a tad heavier than I'm used to. When I get a clear shot, I release the arrow. It doesn't fly quite as true because of the different feel of the bow. It nearly clips Aodren's ear before it impales the guard's neck.

The king spins around, gaze wild. His lips move, I think in a curse.

I reach his side, and the two of us move behind another column. I gesture toward the closest hall. "You have to get out of here."

Beyond the pillar, I can see that just under half the room didn't get sick. Some wield weapons and fight the loyal guards alongside the traitors. Men cut through other men with shocking ferocity, quickly creating a path of gore. I turn away, unable to watch. I cannot catch a breath. If I don't get the king out of here now, it'll be too late.

"Which way?" I dig my fingers into the king's arm. "You know this castle better than me."

He points toward the west hall. I follow, weapon at ready position as we run behind the columns. We reach the west hall and take it through the inner keep.

When the draperies and glossed doors start to look famil-iar, I turn on Aodren. "We need to get out of the castle. What's the fastest way to the stable yard?"

He points back the way we came, his hand shaking.

"They'll be anticipating that we would go there. It would be safer to take the tunnels out."

I've heard stories about the hidden tunnels under Castle Neart. Cohen even mentioned using them when we'd planned on sneaking in to stop the Spiriter, but that would add time and put us out of the castle far from our horses. How will we reach Cohen and Captain Omar to alert them of the rebellion if we're on foot?

"Time is on our side right now. We got out of the Great Hall. Hopefully no one noticed. We need to get on horses and get you to the captain immediately."

He looks torn. "It's a risk."

"One you have no choice but to take. You must find the captain. Get somewhere safe."

I can tell by the clench of his jaw he isn't fully on board with my plan. Still, he turns around and guides me down halls I've never walked before. Some old and barren from the usual plush adornments. Some pocked with doors. Without him, I'd be lost in the maze of Castle Neart.

We are almost to the yard when shouting echoes off the arcading above us. We must be thinking alike because we slip into a curtained alcove. As footsteps bang the floor, moving past us, I realize Finn is in the guards' quarters.

Finn. "You have to go without me."

Aodren spins around to face me. The darkness hides his expression. The hall is quiet again.

"Finn, Cohen's brother, is in the castle," I explain. "I cannot leave him."

He steps closer; though I cannot see him, it feels as if his shadow is moving over me. He leans down, whispering, "We'll go together."

Since he cannot see me, I reach out and grasp his arm, squeezing so he understands the urgency in my words. "You have to get out while you can. It would be foolish for us both to stay behind."

"We're safer together," he argues, echoing a lesson Papa taught me long ago. *Two people often survive where one cannot.*

But he's king of Malam. His life is worth much more than mine. The longer we're in the castle, the greater the risk because it gives time for our enemies to flush us out. It's strange how I feel like I've been in this situation before. When Cohen was faced with leaving me and Enat in order to save his brother, I urged him to go. I knew then he would never be able to live with the knowledge that he'd let his brother be sent to his death. Now, if I let Finn die, Cohen will never be able to forgive me.

"Please," I beg him. "Ride out. I'll meet you in the Evers."

He doesn't need to ask how I'll find him.

"I promised Cohen I'd look out for Finn. But you, you need to leave and find Captain Omar. It's your duty to help the people caught here, before . . ."

An argument tightens his features, but it's softened by acceptance. His dislike of leaving me behind is obvious, but it doesn't matter because he knows I'm right. "Be safe," he urges, and before I can respond, his lips are on mine.

His. Lips.

I gasp the second he shifts back. Surprisingly, he blinks at me like he's just as shocked. His mouth opens and closes and opens. He mutters for me to be safe once more, and then he rushes out of the alcove and down the hallway.

It takes me a beat to shake off his kiss. I don't have time to even wonder what just happened. Instead, I rush toward the guards' quarters, hoping Finn is all right. That he's not heard the commotion and he's remained safe in his room. Keeping close to the wall, I scurry down the stairs that lead to the training yard.

At the bottom of the staircase, the grass is stained the deepest, darkest maroon despite the moonlight stealing the rest of the world's color. Slain guards scatter the field.

Shock has me frozen on the bottom step. Nothing makes sense. I stare and stare at the blades protruding from stomachs, hands flopped to the side. Halos of blood pool under lifeless bodies. I blink, needing the scene to be gone. How could all this have happened?

The magnitude of the many deaths boulders into me. Vomit rushes up my throat. My ears ring. I hold my hand to my mouth, keeping myself together as best I can, and stumble away, rushing into the quarters.

Doors fly open, banging walls. I call for Finn. I search every room, look under cots, shift through every wardrobe.

He's not here.

Where is he?

Air rushes in and out of my lungs too fast for me to catch my breath. Fear they've already caught or killed him turns me frantic. I rush out of the yard, leaving obsidian footprints on the stairs.

When I reach the main level of the castle, a face that's haunted my dreams stares back at me.

Lord Jamis stands under the arcading.

I skid to a stop. He's lost weight, and he looks more vulturine than ever. It's impossible to stop the shiver that racks through me.

His lips hitch open, displaying large teeth. "Hello, Britta. Have you lost something?"

I pant for a stubborn breath as I try to see a way to escape.

Even though I'm outnumbered, I lift the stolen bow and my last arrow, arms shaking. Hatred courses through my limbs. "Where is he?"

Phelia comes out of the shadows, flanked by traitor guards. Different than when I saw her in the woods, she has a brittle coldness about her. I shudder with revulsion. My mind seems to overcome the shock, replaced by the wry understanding that Cohen was right about Jamis and Phelia working together.

The guards force a frightened figure to his knees in front of her. The boy buckles, his knees folding and hitting the granite floor with a thud. Finn.

No!

My arrow is slicing through the air in a heartbeat, aimed at Lord Jamis's chest. Wind gusts around Jamis and Phelia, whipping at my dress. The arrow spins out of its trajectory, flying into the wall and clattering to the ground.

I stare, confused. What just happened?

Phelia's chin jerks. My gaze hones in on the movement and the girls to her rear right. Four girls, different heights, body sizes, and skin color, with one trait in common: blue eyes. *Channelers.* A guard thrusts one toward Phelia.

She takes the girl and presses their wrists together. The girl cries out and, to my horror, crumbles to the ground.

Momentarily unarmed, I toss the useless bow to the ground and slide out Papa's dagger. I hold it up, trying to figure out how I'll take on the entire group.

Phelia's palms lift to face me. The wind picks up again. It knocks me to the floor. I struggle to crawl forward, but the wind is a cyclone that pins me down.

There's no air to breathe. I suck at nothing, just as I did on the roof with Lirra.

My vision wavers. Blackness crowds in.

AODREN

I ALMOST MAKE IT ALL THE WAY ACROSS THE bridge when the link to Britta changes in a way I didn't know was possible. It bows and bucks. My palms turn clammy.

For a moment I wonder if that's my own internal reaction to having killed a man. The sight of the guard on the ground, eyes open and glossed, will be in my head forever. He would've killed Britta.

Each step from the castle causes my heart to pound, a war drum resounding in my chest. Leaving Miss Flannery is wrong. I don't know why or how I know, but I cannot shake the feeling that I need to turn back. *Now.*

Gods, this night is one bad decision after another.

I dismount and give my horse a hard smack

on the rump. She takes off for the woods, the moonlight catching on the gold and silver royal equine adornments. If anyone is looking for tracks, perhaps they'll find hers and think I've escaped.

Keeping an eye on the gate, I run the length of the bridge, back toward the castle. Men have gathered in the outer yard. They weren't there before, and there's no telling if I can trust them. Staying out of eyeshot, I sneak around the side of the guard tower and over the wall. I hold myself with my fingers and boots wedged in the lip of the stone bricks.

"They caught the girl."

The guards talk and I pause, body clinging to the wall.

The man laughs. "And ta think she was fixin' on bein' called a lady."

No. Britta has been captured.

"I'll make 'er my lady."

"You gonna do that in the dungeon?"

My knuckles whiten against the stone, the only thing preventing me from plummeting a quarter league to my death. Jamis has never been a merciful man. The thought of what he might do to Britta has me moving along the external wall, slowly, ensuring each foot placement and handhold is secure.

Each arm span takes me closer to Britta as I make my way toward the waste chute. Years have passed since I snuck out of the castle this way. I never imagined I'd use the waste hole to sneak back in. The smell wafts to me on a breeze. I try not to heave.

Commotion echoes from the castle. Every now and then someone yells. The slow going gives me too much room to think. The knowledge that I've let my people down weakens me to my core.

But I will fix this.

Whoever's taken my castle will pay.

Jaw clenched, breath held, I hoist myself into the tight square opening that leads into the castle. The waste hole has been used frequently lately, no doubt in preparation for the Winter Feast. Crawling through the grime and sliminess has to be the worst kind of torture. Surely, every chamber pot in the castle must've been emptied today.

Pausing in the chute beside the servants' stairwell, I listen for others. Hearing nothing, I push myself out of the hole and land on the stones of the narrow staircase.

The staircase leads to a number of suites. I pick the one I think has the best chance of being empty. Since I can remember, the doors have been locked to the queen's suite. I move from her privy to her study. Cobwebs stretch across shelves like someone has thrown gossamer drapes over the books to keep them from dust. Though they are not effective. Dust lies everywhere. No one has been in this room in over twenty years. Not since my mother passed giving birth to me.

I take advantage of the quiet, needing a moment. Each time I blink, a mesh of gore, screams, and nobles I've known since childhood fill my head. Lord Tadmier, Lord Crenlin,

Lord Greggor . . . ashen faces, blood dripping from lips, wives fallen beside them.

I grasp the edge of a chair, needing the brace. My fingers leave smudges behind. I am filth-covered and I smell like offal. I grapple with the horror, the memories, struggling to lock the evening into a manageable cell and push it behind what I must do. I cannot just stand here and break down. I need to locate Britta.

Though barely any light cracks through the drawn curtains, I squint to make out my mother's quarters. Out of respect, I never broke in here. Now, I scan for something useful. A weapon. A change of clothes.

All there are to be found are women's gowns and underthings, books, a hairbrush, and old powders that reek of rotten roses. I consider rubbing some over me to get rid of the fecal odor. Instead, I shed my coat, leaving it on my mother's chair, and use one of her gowns to wipe the muck off my pants. She'd forgive me for this . . . so I tell myself.

I take my sword and dagger off my belt and start rubbing the cloth all over, wiping off the grime. It doesn't do much for the stench, so I'll have to deal with that later.

I grab my sword and dagger and move to leave when my knee bangs a table. A pewter goblet falls over and clangs on the wood. Before it rolls to the ground, I grab it, noticing how the inside is ringed with crust. When my mother passed — when they closed her rooms — there must have been liquid inside.

I bring the cup to my nose and inhale dust. It holds no clue as to what type of woman my mother was. I put the goblet back down and head for the door.

When I'm certain the hall is clear, I undo the old lock on my mother's room and exit. The hall outside her suite leads to a spiral staircase. No sounds echo from above or below. Everyone must be down on the main floor, fighting. That is, I hope they're still fighting. How many men were loyal to me? How many have died?

Pushing the anxious thoughts to the back of my mind, I keep moving, heading for the dungeon.

Halfway down the spiral stairs, two guards emerge from one of the connecting hallways. They see me, and for a brief slice of time, we all freeze. My sword bobs in my shaky hand. What are the chances these men truly serve the crown?

Any hope for fealty is crushed the moment they draw their swords. One of the guards mutters a command to the other, and then they rush me.

Captain Omar and Saul Flannery were expert swordsmen and they trained me well. Even if I haven't experienced much true combat, I'm a better swordsman on the training field than any of my guards.

I draw my sword and shift my weight to the balls of my feet.

One man charges ahead of the other. I sidestep his movement and slam the pommel against the base of his head. He stumbles forward, hands crashing into the wall.

I turn to find the second guard and almost lose an eye. An arc of my sword parries an oncoming blow. He recovers and his blade slices up. I dodge it only to catch the tip as it comes back down. The sword slices clean through my shirt, but doesn't hit skin.

My pulse gallops through my veins. I block another hit and cut through his jacket with an upward swing. Swords clang. We scoot up and down the stairs.

The guard falters against my speed, and I manage to get the upper hand. My blood recoils in my arms, as if begging me not to deliver a killing blow, but the urgency in the link to Britta takes away my hesitation. A thrust to the chest and I've effectively killed a second man. He drops on my sword, falling into me.

Before I yank it out, I spin us around to use the man's body as a barrier. The remaining guard's sword slams into the man's body, giving me a chance to pull out my blade. Once it's free, I shove the dead guard off me. He crashes into the second guard and they both tumble down the staircase. A sickening crunch tells me I've likely added a third death to tonight's toll.

My innards go slick. A heave works through my chest.

I grit my teeth and force myself to hold it together. My steps are slow and cautious down the winding staircase, my movement almost silent as I head to the main level of the castle. The stairs wind to lower levels where the kitchens are located, but there's no passage through the mountain base on which the castle was built from the kitchens to the dungeon. The only way to reach Britta is by exiting the stairs here, sneaking past the Great Hall, and taking the arcaded hallway to the dungeon.

I can sense Britta now faintly somewhere in the depths of the castle below. If I can get to her, I can get us both out. And the Mackay boy, if he lives. I do not allow myself to consider that one or both of them might be too injured to run.

"Bet he's killed them by now."

A voice from the hallway stops me from making my move. It belongs to a man — probably a traitorous guard.

"He's gotten rid of them somehow. Plan was to get 'em to the cliffs."

The other guard says something I cannot hear.

"He could do it."

"Not all five."

"What do you know? I'd wager the hunter and the captain."

My stomach drops to my knees. One of the guards who went with Omar is a traitor. I rack my brain to think of whom Omar mentioned while we were in the dungeon — Cohen, Leif, Wallace, Ulrich, and one more man, Geoffrey.

"Naw, captain's got ears like a mountain cat."

"Whose side are you on?"

A snort. "Jamis's, course."

His name settles in my stomach like a millstone. I'd already figured he was part of the rebellion, but now I know for certain.

I peer out of the stairwell.

The dress shirt I'm wearing is whiter than a full moon compared to the muck on my pants. In the darkness of the courtyard, it'll draw attention faster than a waving white flag. I put my hands on the floor of the stairwell, hoping to gather dirt. I rub what I can on my chest, though it doesn't help much.

When the men leave, I dart out of the stairwell and continue along the ground floor. The quiet in the corridor amplifies each step. Each breath. Each beat of my heart as it tries to box its way up my throat.

I reach the west entrance to the Great Hall. Everything in me cries to stop and see the damage that was done, to see if I can help others trying to flee. But I force myself to move toward the dungeon. There's too much risk of getting captured near the Great Hall.

Time is critical. There's no telling what torture Jamis will inflict on Britta.

Two steps into the arcaded hallway, and voices echo from the direction of the dungeon. I duck into the draperies, hiding in the thick brocade fabric that puddles on the granite floor, grateful, for once, for my father's extravagance.

The pounding of their steps vibrates underfoot as they near my location. I flatten myself against the window.

From their conversation, I can distinguish at least four separate men, but the clatter of their steps sounds more like two dozen people. As they pass, I peek through the curtain, surprised to see four guards surrounding at least thirty teenage girls. *Jamis's weapons.* Their skin is splotchy. Some have gaunt eyes, while others are nearly swollen shut presumably from crying. All of them have bound wrists.

What can I do?

I wrap my fingers around the hilt of my sword. I stare hopelessly at a young girl in the back of the group. She's wearing no shoes. Cuts mar her feet, and blood stains her skin. I sink against the window, letting the curtain swallow me. How can I possibly save them all?

Not a second after they leave, a snap sounds against the stone wall at my back.

I spin around.

Outside the castle walls, three guards have spotted me through the window. At the bottom of the hill, one has his longbow nocked. *Bludger.*

I leap out of the way. The window shatters as I scramble from behind the curtains. No doubt the guards just heard the noise.

I lurch into the nearest tower. *Keep moving.* I have to keep moving. The shouts get louder and soon the small group sounds like a herd of men. But I'm already taking the stairs two at a time, jumping through the doorway to the second level. There, I slip into a study, praying that no one has taken occupancy in this old room.

No one has, and in seconds I'm behind the tapestry beside the fireplace, shimmying down the narrow passageway that once was my playground.

Nobody knows this castle better than me. They can hunt, but they will not find me. Not before I free Britta and Finn.

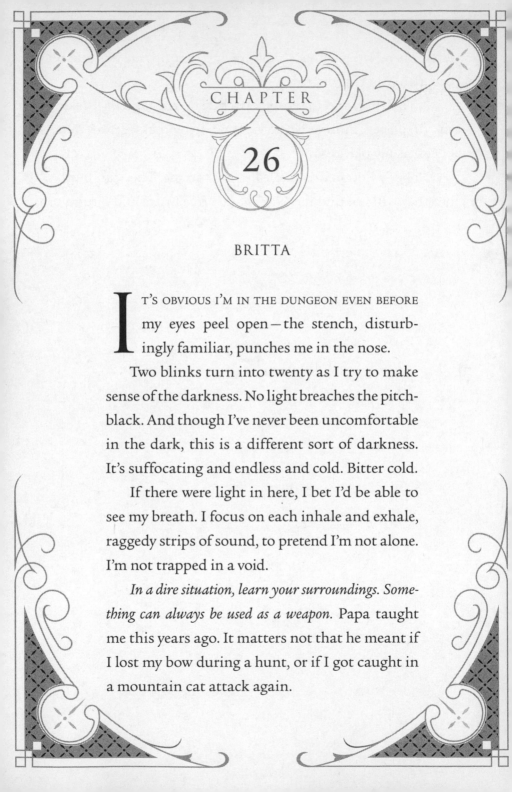

CHAPTER

26

BRITTA

I T'S OBVIOUS I'M IN THE DUNGEON EVEN BEFORE
my eyes peel open — the stench, disturb-
ingly familiar, punches me in the nose.

Two blinks turn into twenty as I try to make
sense of the darkness. No light breaches the pitch-
black. And though I've never been uncomfortable
in the dark, this is a different sort of darkness.
It's suffocating and endless and cold. Bitter cold.

If there were light in here, I bet I'd be able to
see my breath. I focus on each inhale and exhale,
raggedy strips of sound, to pretend I'm not alone.
I'm not trapped in a void.

*In a dire situation, learn your surroundings. Some-
thing can always be used as a weapon.* Papa taught
me this years ago. It matters not that he meant if
I lost my bow during a hunt, or if I got caught in
a mountain cat attack again.

I grope my way along the damp ground, scuffing and scraping my dress on the uneven stones. When my fingers meet with chilly iron bars, I want to cry in relief because I'm grateful for a spatial understanding of my surroundings.

This cell isn't where they kept me last time I was thrown in the dungeon. Unlike the smooth metal that imprisoned me before, this metal is raised and pocked in some areas, crumbling in others.

I move along the bars, searching for a door. My hand flattens into slick malodorous liquid.

I squeak, surprised. The metallic scent of blood taints the dank air.

A cold sweat breaks out above my lip. The Great Hall bloodshed fills my thoughts. I shake my head, trying to erase the gore. My throat swells and I gag. I scrub my hand on my skirt, telling myself it wasn't blood that I touched. It was old water. Perhaps piss. Though — *seeds and stars* — I hope not.

I rub my palm, rub till it's raw. It's definitely the smell of rust, not blood. It's rust from the corroding cell bars.

I rattle the rough, flaking rods. Rattle them harder. My teeth click. "Hello? Hello?"

Nearby, shuffling sounds, a pained moan, but the black obscurity is too disorienting to pinpoint where it came from. If only there was a hint of light, anything with the pretense of warmth that could keep my thoughts in check.

"Who's out there? Finn, is that you?" Please let Finn be alive.

Another shuffle, and then a cough. "Brit-t-tta? Th-th-that

you?" The easy smile and carefreeness has been stripped from Finn's voice.

"Finn, yeah, I'm here." Relief blankets me, smothers my wayward thoughts.

He lets out a sound that could be a sob or a scoff. "I'm c-c-cold, Brit-ta."

The tick of his teeth tapping together has me standing and reaching through the bars toward him. "I know it's cold. You're doing well though. Can you tell me what happened?"

"I—I heard yelling. I ran out in my nightclothes." His voice breaks. "The guards were killing themselves. I—I didn't know what t-to do."

"It was a coup," I say.

Scuffling and scraping come from his direction. "I didn't mean they fought each other. I—I meant they threw themselves on their swords."

Any response turns to acid on my tongue. They were killing themselves? Possible explanations run through my head, all of which point to Phelia, mind control, and siphoning energy from Channelers.

Finn sniffs. I think he's crying. He sniffles again and chokes on a small sob. I wish we were in the same cell so I could put my arms around him to share some warmth and comfort. He was captured in a nightshirt, he doesn't have the layers this gown does, and the horror he just shared is too much of a nightmare to believe.

"Shhh," I whisper to him. "We will be fine. Be brave, Finn."

His bars creak like he's leaning against them. "I'm n-n-not ever the brave one. That's Cohen."

"He's not here. It has to be you. No one else can face this battle for you." I don't mean to sound callous. But I know better than anyone that the darkness has a way of stealing hope. If Finn's going to make it through the frigid night, he needs some fight in him.

Down here there's more opposition than just our jailers. The dungeon is notorious for killing men with winter sickness before they can be sent to the guillotine.

"I'll be brave, Britta. H-h-how are we going to get out?"

I don't know what Jamis and Phelia have in store for us. "We'll find a way," I say, determined to make it so.

"Promise?"

"I promise."

Light sputters through the pitch-dark, yellow flashes providing a sense of the cavernous room, edged with cells. This level of the dungeon has one exit, a stairwell where the flickering light emanates. I was right—this isn't the part of the dungeon where I was previously held. I remember hearing the moans and cries of prisoners then. Now, I hear nothing. They've either cleared out the dungeon, or Finn and I are far from everyone else. It's only been a few hours since I woke in the dungeon. Could it be Lord Jamis coming back to tell us why we're still alive? I grimace at the thought of what he might want from Finn and me.

"Finn?" I whisper, alarmed that we're soon to have visitors. He doesn't answer.

I stare at him, but my damn sight is spoiled like drops of golden oil in black vinegar. I rub my eyes against the crook of my elbow since I'm still not sure what I put my hands in. Then I look around again. The light's coming closer.

Across the room, a huddle of limbs under a thin piece of material must be Finn. He doesn't move. For the first time since being thrown in the dungeon, I focus on his energy, desperate to sense that he's still alive. The low buzz of his life hums in the darkness. After a moment, his energy is joined by the accompaniment of soft, airy snores. Finn is sleeping. Only sleeping.

I rest my head against the bars, relieved.

Lantern glow fills the cavern.

The moment she enters, I recognize Phelia. The neckline of her dress and long sleeves cover her odd skin markings. I slink away from the bars, disgusted and frightened. And disgusted with myself for being so frightened.

Phelia's shoes clack against the stones until she stops outside my cell. I push aside my fear, but what remains is shame. For the things she's done. For sharing her blood. For wanting to know more.

I shield my eyes from her bright torch, but not before seeing the man-size onyx stain on the middle of the dungeon floor. Blood. These dungeons are filthy with old stains, but this one has a slight sheen. It's not very old. It's definitely blood.

It takes all my self-control not to examine my hand.

"Hello, Britta." A rake over soft soil, that's the texture of her voice. "Are you faring well?"

I screw up my face. In the dungeon? "Naturally," I grind out.

"Ah, you have your grandmother's pluck."

Her comment kicks me in the chest with a combination of grief alongside truthful warmth. I wasn't expecting to feel the verity of her words. She lowered the guard around her energy the day I met her in the woods. But I expected she would've put it back in place.

"Please don't speak of her," I say.

Phelia closes in until her face is nearly pressed between two bars. Her head quirks to the side in a hummingbird flick. She doesn't take her eyes off me. "Enat was my mother. Doesn't that give me the right?" The cadence of her question is more like a schoolteacher's or a minister's, as if she's about to make a point.

"What do you want, Phelia?"

Her mouth pinches. Her near colorless pale blue eyes appear eerily golden in the torchlight. She looks like a starved cat. "That's not my name."

"It's the only one I'll call you by." My anger turns me brazen.

Phelia looks at my hands where they've clutched the bars once again. "You're hiding behind boldness, Britta. But you're frightened. I can feel it in your energy. Frantic like a rabbit."

I scuttle away.

"I saved you once. Did Enat tell you?" Her eyes dig into me as she runs her fingers along the cell bars. "The Purge hunters were going to discover that you were a Channeler. They would've killed us both. So I took you to meet your grandmother at the border to have your power stripped so you could live in Malam without fear. The old crow wouldn't do it, though."

Her fingernails hit metal. *Tink, tink.*

I keep quiet.

Tink. "You have no clue what I've done for you."

My breath is fire in my lungs. I don't want to ask, and yet I want to know, even though I feel like a trapped mouse to a calculating mountain cat.

"A border guard found us," she continues. "I never saw his arrow coming until it hit us both." Her hand moves to her chest, resting just over her heart. Her eyes don't leave mine. "Through you and into me."

My shallow intake of air rakes through the icy darkness. This doesn't line up with the stories I heard. Papa said she left me when I was a few months old. The touch of her truth, though, tells me he lied. Only, that makes no sense. I would've felt the chill of his dishonesty.

She watches me shake my head. "We would've both died that day," she says. "But the guard was a fool, and he came close enough for me to grab him and take back what he tried to steal."

She grips the bars, coming as close as she can to me. "I saved you, Britta." It's a snarl of a whisper. Like the aftertaste of bitter ale, an unspoken threat lingers behind. *You owe me.*

I cross my arms, holding them tight to my body. "Why are you telling me this? I haven't asked for this."

A cruel smile stretches over her face. "This is what you want to know. I can see the questions in your eyes. You want to know more about me."

"I — I don't."

"Liar." She taps her forehead. Her cloak shifts around her like bat wings. "I saved you that day, Britta."

Every bit of me recoils from hearing the scratched way she says my name. I fight to keep my face expressionless. "Why have you come here?"

Finn coughs. She made me forget he was across the dungeon.

"Don't you desire freedom from the dungeon?" Phelia asks in a casual way as if she's offering bread and ale.

"Freedom in exchange for what?"

"The guards will release you if you agree to stay at the castle."

"Until when?"

She paces the width of my cell. "You will work alongside me until you've learned to master your Spiriter gift."

No time frame? That's ludicrous. Not that I'm tempted. I'd be insane to make a deal with someone like her, a murderer and manipulator. And yet, I cannot help but wonder if she would keep her word. I'm a quick learner. I could master my ability.

Which is madness. It must be a trap.

"You need time to think about it," she says, reading more into my silence than I wish her to.

I don't respond.

She props the lantern on a wall holder and departs, climbing the stairs and disappearing into the dark. Once she's out of sight, I glance around. It feels like a miracle that I can see my hand in front of my face. Leaving the lantern is such a small act, one Phelia likely gave little thought to, but the light she left in the room makes all the difference.

I can see the reprieve on Finn's face as he rests his temple against a bar.

His knees look knobby and cold under his nightshirt.

"She's your mother?" he asks.

"Yes." I clench my fist over my belly, holding pressure there until my insides settle. My fingers find the old scar on my chest, the one I always thought was from the woods.

"I'm not like her," I say, reassuring him. The words are swallowed by the frigid darkness.

I am not like her.

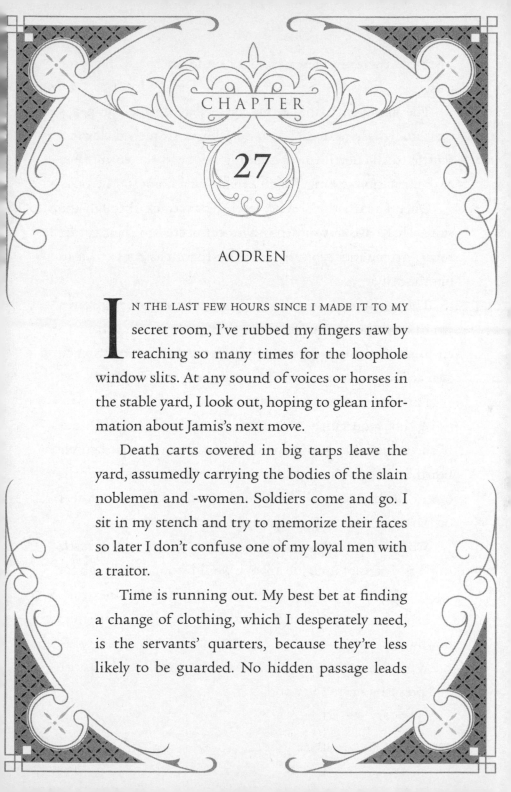

CHAPTER

27

AODREN

IN THE LAST FEW HOURS SINCE I MADE IT TO MY secret room, I've rubbed my fingers raw by reaching so many times for the loophole window slits. At any sound of voices or horses in the stable yard, I look out, hoping to glean information about Jamis's next move.

Death carts covered in big tarps leave the yard, assumedly carrying the bodies of the slain noblemen and -women. Soldiers come and go. I sit in my stench and try to memorize their faces so later I don't confuse one of my loyal men with a traitor.

Time is running out. My best bet at finding a change of clothing, which I desperately need, is the servants' quarters, because they're less likely to be guarded. No hidden passage leads there, but there are a few passages I could use that will get me close.

The moon isn't full, so my journey along the parapet is marginally less noticeable. Or so I hope. Crouched down, I scuttle to the north tower, shaking my head the entire time at the situation. A king, fugitive in his own home. Ludicrous.

Once I reach the second level, I backtrack through the suites that have servants' passages connected to their garde-robes. Attendants typically travel in these passages to clean out the privy.

The north tower is quiet as a tomb. Only the steps from a guard near the bottom floor can be heard now and then. To ensure he's not alerted to my presence, my descent is slow, each step achingly measured until I reach the second level.

I press open the door and it squeaks.

A thousand curses run through my head as I rush out of the stairwell and into the hall, knowing the guard surely heard. I reach a suite. Back the direction I came, someone calls out in the hall. I sneak through the door and open the next one that leads to the passageway behind the privy.

Seeds and stars, the stench. My sympathies go to the castle workers. I cannot imagine anyone would stomach this job for long, and yet I've heard men value this position. Madness.

I squeeze along the servants' walk and take the steep stairs downward.

When I reach the door that leads to a small yard, I pause and press my ear to the wood.

I hear nothing. The servants' quarters, protected by the exterior walls of the castle, are similar to the guards' training yard in that they're bordered on one side by a cliff. It wouldn't be feasible for enemies to attack the castle from the servants' quarters so this area of the castle is typically unguarded.

I'm counting on it.

I push through the entry. It's a relief to find no one waiting or watching. A small stretch of grass spans from the cliff to the castle wall where thatched roofs sit atop stone quarters. There, all the windows are dark.

I'm not sure how many servants made it through the attack. I'm not sure if those who did are loyal. But though it seems as if no one is around, all the unknowing fuels my caution.

Though I've spent years sneaking around my own castle when I don't want to be seen, it still requires effort. It's a balance of weight and movement. It makes me more fully appreciate the grace Britta engages to hunt stealthily in the woods.

I pass the first few doors, thinking that if someone was still loyal to me, though hiding in these quarters, they would most likely pick the door farthest from the castle to stay low. It may be faulty reasoning, but it makes me feel marginally smarter about my choices.

The window beside the last door shows no signs of movement inside. Never having actually broken into someone's living space, I cannot help but feel invasive as I twist the latch and open the door.

Thankfully, it glides without a creak. Some of the pressure in my chest dissipates. A few embers burn in the fireplace against the wall adjacent to the door. Across the room, old quilts cover three modest beds. Two of which have bodies occupying them.

My pulse kicks harder under my skin. I'd hoped no one would be here. At least they're sleeping. I step in, rolling my feet heel to toe, slow and quiet, as I cross to the small wood closet with doors cracked open and a peek of clothing showing through.

There, I slide out a pair of trousers. Though they look a tad large, they have a drawstring so they can be tightened. Keeping one eye on the sleeping forms, I back into the darkest corner and change quickly. I'd go in the yard, but if a guard was to look over the wall at the servants' yard below, that would be my death. With the trousers in place, I slip on a servant's tunic and then put on my belt under the garment to hide my weapons.

"Who are you?" A squeaky whisper catches me unaware.

I freeze, and then slowly twist around.

A small child with braids lining her face peers at me from one of the beds.

Gods, I pull in a breath so sudden and sharp, my lungs burn from the stretch. I press my fist to my forehead until I can breathe normally again.

The little girl twists her fists into her eyes. Many of the

men and women who serve in the castle raise their small families here, but I hadn't given children at the castle any thought until this very moment.

"Why are you wearing Pa's shirt?" She winds her hands into her blanket. "Yours is better."

I crack an uneasy smile. *Shhh,* I mouth, finger at my lips.

The streak of moonlight coming through the window paints her curious face in blue-gray hues. Fury fires through me. She can be no more than six or seven years. I'm tempted to wish, for her sake, that her parents are sympathizers with Lord Jamis. Then could this little girl be safe. But it would only be for a time. After my forces take back Castle Neart, the traitors will be gathered and punished. The law calls for it. Which means children like this one will be caught in the melee. It makes me ill considering she might be left an orphan either way.

Peace will not be found on either side, even when it's over. Not for a long time.

Mouth dry, I step back, moving to the door, not sure what else to say. I glance at the bed beside this girl and see the long dark braids of a woman. Perhaps the child's mother. I don't want her to wake, so I sneak back the way I came, steps careful.

The girl's raven eyes follow me to the door. She quirks her head to the side and I wave, a gesture to let her know I'm leaving. She waves in return and yawns before lying back down.

Hopefully, she'll think my visit was a dream. Etched into

my brain, her innocent features follow me down the stairs to the ground floor, along the main hall, and to the arcading passage that leads to the dungeon.

I'm ashamed to say I don't know all about what happens in the depths of the castle, though I've heard horrible stories. My anger flares brighter at myself for being so remiss as a king. I vow it won't happen again. If we make it through this, I'll be the king Malam needs.

I will return in force.

I will take back my castle.

I will free the innocents caught in the rebellion.

COHEN

WE'RE TOO DEEP IN THE WOODS TO FIND a healer. We've traveled at least forty leagues from Brentyn. I'm not even sure anything can be done for Omar. It seemed like ages before he finally took a breath. Now, his slow, measured breaths barely lift his chest. He hasn't regained consciousness. One look at the flow of blood coming from the back of his head and his caved ribs, and I know there's too much damage to move him.

"We need to send someone back. Someone has to find a healer." I stand and pace away from the captain. We have to keep moving. We also have to help Omar. No way to do both.

Ulrich kneels beside our leader. He's got worry in every line of his face.

"We have to do something." Leif leaves his horse's side and approaches me.

Ulrich nods. "Maybe some of us can go on and some can stay."

"We need a healer," I tell them.

"I'll go." Geoffrey's hands tremble as he grabs his satchel and a waterskin. Takes a swig. Gapes at the injured captain. Geoffrey has been in the king's guard a dozen years longer than me. Never seen him this rattled till now. "I can go on my own. One of you can stay, and the rest of you should continue the hunt."

We've been traveling for hours. The closest town is an hour away. Considering Omar's injuries, it's possible Geoffrey might not make it back in time before Omar passes. Our terse expressions tell me everyone has come to the same conclusion.

Still, none of us are any good to the captain if we stand around and wait. Omar would want us to continue on the hunt. Agreeing with Geoffrey, I ask, "Who will stay behind?"

Leif takes a step closer to Omar. "I will."

Both Ulrich and Wallace joined the guard a little under a year and a half ago. Don't know them much, but Captain Omar felt their skill was the best for this mission. I trust his judgment. They seem seasoned enough to be strong travel companions.

"Sounds like a good-enough plan." Geoffrey nods at me and then stalks to his horse. He's in the saddle and kneeing the horse into action, tearing into the woods before anyone else moves. We're all wooden in the sight of our fallen leader.

"Go on. Get Jamis." Leif points to the woods before placing a hand on the captain's shoulder. The older man's chest shudders.

I say a silent prayer for Omar. We move through the night, slowing our travel to ensure we're following the right tracks. Wallace isn't nearly as helpful as Ulrich at tracking. Ulrich finds as many tracks as I do, and thanks to him we make good time crossing through the Evers.

The rocky ledges of the mountain are littered with shale chips. The horses slow as we climb. It seems odd that Lord Jamis would've come straight into this part of the mountains. This area is nothing but cliffs and ledges that are hazardous to cross.

We break from the trees and move along the cliff, the scant moonlight turning the rocky path grayish blue.

The tracks we were following fade to nothing. We move ahead, and then backtrack, finding nothing again. This sort of thing happens often with hunts, but it's especially aggravating tonight, when all I want to do is find that bludger Jamis and put an end to this rebellion.

I search out over the cliff, trying to make sense of where Jamis might've gone. There's nowhere but down. And that's a sheer drop.

So where did he go?

Hands hit my back, slamming hard. I stumble one step forward. Shock hits me just as I realize it's too far.

Over the cliff. I'm falling, arms and legs flailing—

—scrambling at nothing but air.

The ground far below speeds up to meet me.

My shout rends the night.

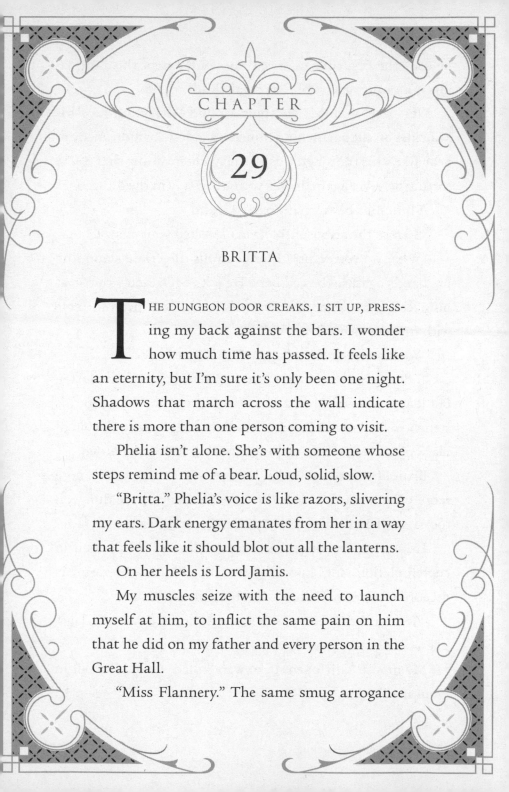

CHAPTER

29

BRITTA

THE DUNGEON DOOR CREAKS. I SIT UP, PRESSing my back against the bars. I wonder how much time has passed. It feels like an eternity, but I'm sure it's only been one night. Shadows that march across the wall indicate there is more than one person coming to visit.

Phelia isn't alone. She's with someone whose steps remind me of a bear. Loud, solid, slow.

"Britta." Phelia's voice is like razors, slivering my ears. Dark energy emanates from her in a way that feels like it should blot out all the lanterns.

On her heels is Lord Jamis.

My muscles seize with the need to launch myself at him, to inflict the same pain on him that he did on my father and every person in the Great Hall.

"Miss Flannery." The same smug arrogance

he used the first time we met comes out, except this Lord Jamis is a gaunt version of that regal, deadly man.

"It's been a while." He steps around Phelia and raps his knuckles on the bar. Behind him, the shadows of more men appear, likely his traitor guards. "I find it entertaining that you're rotting here, yet again. Is this your third stay in the dungeon?"

A hiss slips between my barred teeth.

"So nice the atmosphere hasn't affected your charm."

"What do you want?" I lunge in his direction, slamming my hands against the cell bars. He jolts back, and I cackle at him, feeling a rush of sick pleasure that he's as uncomfortable with my presence as I am with his.

"You think to intimidate me?" His lip twitches.

"I don't think to do it. I just do." My words are all bluster, but it aggravates the man, which is all the power I have in this stench-soaked cave. I push off the bars and slip into the pitch-black of my cell, watching his expression sour and harden.

Bruised crescents under his eyes make his beaky nose more prominent. It's clear the time he spent in the dungeon took its toll on his body. He is a scarecrow with a raven's face.

He steeples his fingers and taps them to his lips, as if in contemplation. But I know this man and I know how deep his deception can run. He has something planned.

"Aodren didn't escape." His words come out with claws, like a cat pouncing on its prey.

My mouth falls open. If he were killed, I would've felt it. Wouldn't I?

My instant reaction is to seek out Aodren's energy. It only takes a few seconds to recognize the pull that I always feel when Aodren's near. It's still there, still holding tight.

Ah, Jamis is a clever, sallow snake. He didn't necessarily lie. Aodren must still be in the castle. But why? Did the king come back for me?

Unexpected emotion itches my eyes. I blink hard, forcing it away. For the first time since I woke in my cottage and realized Aodren was on the other end of the invisible rope tied to me, I'm grateful, so very grateful, for our connection.

Phelia watches me with an expression like she's puzzling out a question. "I think she's still connected to him. Her expression says as much."

Seeds. Did I just walk into a trap?

A gleam refines Lord Jamis's carrion eyes; he's found himself meat to tear apart. "Miss Flannery, it seems you are useful to me, once again. You are going to tell me where Aodren is."

"I don't know what you're talking about."

Lord Jamis turns to Phelia.

Perhaps it's my imagination — she seems to hesitate. Phelia doesn't look at me when she speaks. "She lies."

I clench my hands so tight, blood vessels might burst. My revulsion for her escalates. The fact that she can dutifully work alongside Lord Jamis sickens me. How can this woman be my flesh and blood?

"Tell us where Aodren is." Still not touching the metal, Lord Jamis steps closer to the cell.

"No."

He quirks an eyebrow, raises his hand, and beckons the guards.

They walk out of the shadows, steps unhurried as they drag something between the two of them. I cannot see past the bright spot of the lantern to make out—

Oh, mercy. No.

Gillian—covered in so many mottled marks I know it's not a trick of the light—is nearly unrecognizable.

My breath heaves through my chest, shredding my throat. I rush to the bars, pressing myself against them to get closer. "W-what have you done?"

"You are confused." Lord Jamis moves, eclipsing my view of my handmaid. My friend. "This is what *you* have done by not cooperating."

My eyes bulge out.

"Cooperate and she lives. If not, she dies."

His terrifying truth burns like a thousand bee stings to my chest.

"Tell us where Aodren is hiding like a little mouse." His mouth twists and turns around the words. My hands choke the bars.

"I don't know where he is," I say, choosing my words carefully, just as Lord Jamis did. My gaze flicks to Phelia as if in challenge. It's the truth. I don't exactly know where Aodren is at this precise moment.

"No?" The lantern makes Lord Jamis's teeth look yellowed and decayed.

"Gillian hasn't done anything. Let her go."

His hand flicks in the smallest of motions. The guards drop her to the ground without care. Her body flumps on the soiled stone dungeon floor. I press a fist to my mouth. After all Gillian's done for me, the care and friendship . . .

"Please don't—don't hurt her." I take in all her bruises, and rage rises, a tornado under my skin.

"What about her?" I point at Phelia. "Have her tell you where the king is. Surely, she can sense people's energy better than I can."

Lord Jamis ignores me.

Changing tactics, I narrow my eyes on Phelia. "You say you're my mother. Then don't let him hurt her." Spit dots my chin from the force of my speech. "Please."

She takes a step closer to my cell. But she says nothing and does nothing, despite how I'm watching her, pleading with her.

I feel like the time I slipped through the ice on the lake beside Papa's training grounds—cold, numb, and full of useless frantic fight. My blood is slush in my veins. My energy throbs in my hands, wanting to push it into Gillian. To heal her. Save her. But she's not close enough for me to touch.

I shake the cell bars as hard as I can. "If you have the same power as me, then you find the king."

The challenge, thrown on the muck and stone separating

us, goes unanswered. Her gaze switches to something like awe focused on my hands, which are wrapped around the metal bars. Bars that are now bowed slightly outward. Not enough to escape. Just enough that it's noticeable.

Bloody seeds. How did I do that? I'm not strong enough to have muscled them into that position. Papa taught me to be capable. Not to bend iron bars.

Phelia blinks in a slow, centering way. Her lids gliding down and up before her pupils settle on me. "So much potential, Britta."

I want to stare at my hands and see if they look different than before, but I won't give Phelia the satisfaction of knowing how inexperienced I truly am.

"Don't you want to learn what more you can do?" Phelia's eyes gleam as she examines the bars.

"Enough." Jamis breaks the spell. "Make her talk. I want Aodren tonight."

"Have your Spiriter tell you." I tug at the cell again, but the bars don't bend farther. Perhaps because my energy isn't focused and my head is spinning too much to control it.

Phelia tsks. "You broke the bind, Britta. Your new bond masks his energy. Only you can tell us where he is."

I'm shocked she's admitting so much. This information seems crucial. It almost seems as if she's helping me. But that cannot be. Can it?

Lord Jamis walks to Gillian, and I freeze, watching his slow steps clacking on the ground. He lifts the toe of his boot.

At a snail's pace, he lowers it over her hand, the one part of her not battered.

"No" comes out of me in a tortured whisper.

Gillian stirs, an agonized moan slipping from her lips.

Every part of me cringes. "Stop. P-please, stop."

The challenge on Lord Jamis's expression doesn't falter. I want to kill him.

"Gilly." I try to get her attention. "Gillian, I—I . . ." I hate myself for having no words. Nothing to comfort her. No promise to give. Because what can I say? Can I turn over the king of Malam to save my friend?

My gaze volleys to Phelia. She scoots back out of the light's yellow spill, evident she's not going to stop him.

Lord Jamis said he'll spare Gillian if I turn over Aodren. It would be foolish of me to believe him, though. He could change his mind later. He just sanctioned the death of half the noblemen and noblewomen. He won't let us live.

There is no good choice in this situation. One life for another. The option is the most despicable form of motivation. I cannot send Aodren to his death.

Even so, I say, "I don't know exactly where he is. But I can figure it out."

Jamis's attention cuts to Phelia.

"Truth," she says, and she's right because I'm determined to find out exactly where Aodren is hiding.

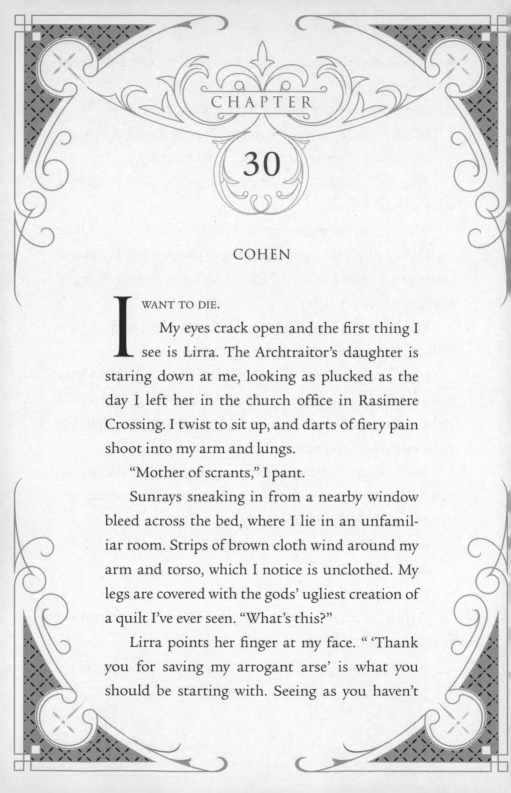

CHAPTER

30

COHEN

I WANT TO DIE.

My eyes crack open and the first thing I see is Lirra. The Archtraitor's daughter is staring down at me, looking as plucked as the day I left her in the church office in Rasimere Crossing. I twist to sit up, and darts of fiery pain shoot into my arm and lungs.

"Mother of scrants," I pant.

Sunrays sneaking in from a nearby window bleed across the bed, where I lie in an unfamiliar room. Strips of brown cloth wind around my arm and torso, which I notice is unclothed. My legs are covered with the gods' ugliest creation of a quilt I've ever seen. "What's this?"

Lirra points her finger at my face. " 'Thank you for saving my arrogant arse' is what you should be starting with. Seeing as you haven't learned manners in your twenty years, I'll excuse you. Once. That's all you get." She drops down on the edge of the bed, causing the mattress to shift.

"Bloody seeds." I bite my tongue against the fresh dose of agony.

"My father used to say a man curses because he doesn't have the wit to come up with anything original."

"You saying I'm an idiot?"

She smirks, her expression answering for her. Her finger shifts to point at my arm. "That's a brace. It'll keep your bones in place while you heal."

"I know what a brace is, Lirra. I meant the thing on my legs." The maker of the quilt used every color known to man.

Lirra's snarl is a bite away from rabid. "My gran made that quilt, so you shut your mouth."

I go to move my hands and remember . . . pain. *Bludger.* "No offense to your gran."

"You just offended her. You cannot erase it by saying 'no offense.'"

"Fine. Be offended," I huff, which earns me an eye roll. Lirra's got about as much charm as Omar.

Seeds, Omar.

"What happened? How'd I get here?" I ask.

Lirra purses her lips. I think she's going to answer, but instead she goes about poking at my arms and ribs, unwrapping cloth, and lathering my skin with the foulest-smelling poultice known to man.

Her fingers are torture devices. After the third *accidental* jab, I grab her wrist with my good hand, bite back the pain, and say, "Thank you for saving me." Even though I don't have any clue what she saved me from. Last I remember I was with Ulrich and Wallace, following Jamis's trail. "Where am I, and how'd I get here?"

"Do you remember being pushed?"

I stare at the plaster, willing memories to return. After a bit, I shake my head.

"It's probably for the better. Nobody wants to remember falling off a cliff."

I sputter. "Say that again?"

"You followed Jamis's trail to a dead end."

"The cliff?"

She nods, and a gauzy memory returns. "You got off Siron, walked to the edge, and looked over. As if Jamis would be there." She rolls her eyes like that was the stupidest thing I could've ever done. Like she's never checked out the edge of a cliff before.

"What happened after that?"

She stands, and the bed morphs back to how it was before she sat. Again, pain lances through me. I glare at her.

"Settle your feathers. I won't bump the bed again." She takes her poultice and puts it on the dresser before turning back. "Ulrich shoved you."

"What?"

She shrugs. Like I've just asked her something as silly as

whom she's courting. Ulrich is a man I've served with for the last year and a half. I'm boggled.

"Wallace tried to grab you, but Ulrich put a knife in his gut before he could get to you."

Lirra doesn't pretty up any of the truth. I lie on the bed, overwhelmed and shocked as the day I found out Saul had been murdered. This sort of mutiny in the king's guard is unprecedented. Men must pass vigorous mental and physical tests to be considered for the elite force. It's an honor and a status of lower nobility to be on the king's guard. I cannot fathom why Ulrich would turn on us.

"Wallace is dead." I let out a slow breath. It's my duty to inform his young wife once I'm on my feet again. Didn't know the man well, but I knew his wife had a babe months ago. I lost my father last year. At least I had him till I was grown. But Wallace's little one is still in swaddling.

"You're lucky I got there in time to help." Her chin jerks at my arm. "Else you would've been . . ."

Like Wallace is what it seems like she's going to say. But she goes quiet as she crosses the room to a small table and picks up a satchel. She withdraws a pinch of herbs, which she drops into a bowl and starts to grind with an iron pestle.

I study the crack in the plaster overhead, puzzling out the parts of Lirra's story that make no sense. Every speck of me aches like I've been squashed, but I'm here and I'm alive. That cliff was at least a hundred arm spans high. I should be dead. Nobody falls that far and breaks an arm and a few ribs. My memory may be foggier than a winter night, but I remember the drop. The cliff had a sheer face. Nothing on the side of that cliff would've been large enough to break my fall or provide a soft landing spot.

"How exactly did you help?" It comes out sounding more suspicious than I want.

She pauses, and her gaze turns up from the pestle as she pushes her dirt-colored hair off her forehead. Lirra's eyes are a shock of gray-blue. Where Britta's are a summer sky, this girl looks like pieces of winter were stolen to make her eyes.

Alarming is what it is. Doesn't seem natural. Not with her tawny skin and fan of black lashes.

"I used the wind," she says, and goes back to grinding herbs.

It hits me right before she says it. Blue eyes. Using the wind. Channeler. How did I not pick up on this before?

She mashes the pestle into the bowl, her hand movements choppier than before. "I'm an air Channeler. Before you turn your nose up, remember my ability saved your life."

I try to sit up, but damn my ribs, so I lower back down and gape at her. That gaping goes on for a good minute. "Why would you think I'd do that? And don't tell me it's because I'm from Malam."

Her hand stills. "I traveled with you for nearly two weeks, and every time you mentioned Channeling, you got a foul look on your face." She lifts a shoulder. "I figured you weren't a supporter."

"That's not true. I don't mind. I just worry for Britta—"

Her bark of a scoff cuts me off. "Oh, you don't *mind*? Stars. In all of creation, has there ever been a man as noble as you?"

I glare at her. "You're twisting my words."

"I'm twisting nothing. Shove your ego aside and think." Her pestle scrapes and bangs into the bowl.

My anger is right beneath the surface. "All right, please tell me, how'd you find me?"

Another one-shoulder shrug. "After Gillian and Britta left for the feast, I followed you." She lowers the bowl and scowls at me. "When I reached the castle, you were heading out with a group of men. Of course, my goal was to catch up and knock a reminder into you about finding Orli, but when I saw the captain get hurt, I suspected foul play."

I have the sense to look contrite. Her no-nonsense tone makes me think if Ulrich hadn't pushed me off the cliff, she might've.

"How did you stop me from splatting to my death?"

"Such a way with words." She points the pestle at me. "I coaxed the wind to push you up. But you're so heavy, probably that head of yours, you fell to the bottom of the cliff anyway."

I laugh and wince because of the pain. That's the most modest way to explain how she used the wind to soften my fall. Her derision has bite to it, but the image of my big head dragging me down is the funniest thing I've heard in a long time.

Lirra places the pestle on the table and grabs a waterskin

to pour water into the bowl. Her ability saved me. Twice now Channelers have saved my life. Makes me think Malam truly is the weaker country, considering we weren't smart enough to see the benefits of having Channelers in our midst.

She crosses the room with the bowl in hand and gestures that I should drink the liquid.

I scrunch up my nose and sniff at the bowl when she brings it close to my face.

"I'm not going to kill you after all the work I did to save you. I had to load you up on my horse and travel a half day to get here. I nearly collapsed myself from all the energy it cost to float your heavy arse back up the cliff."

Another laugh and a wince. "Where is here?"

"My aunt's secret meeting location, a home in Tahr. There were towns closer, but this place is safe. I won't get lynched if anyone suspects I'm a Channeler."

Makes me cringe, hearing her say that. Change needs to happen in Malam, sooner than later. "What about my horse?"

She gestures for me to drink first. I comply, gagging down the gravelly, mud-tasting drink. She puts the bowl on the edge of the bed and bites her lip. "In the stable, where he's been fed and watered and brushed. Good seeds, that horse loves to be brushed."

"Well, thank you for what you did."

"You're welcome."

"Have you heard any word on Omar?"

"He's in the next room over. Leif brought him here." She

picks up the bowl and stares down at the mix. "He's not looking good."

"What of Geoffrey, the guard who went to find the healer?"

"Geoffrey's horse lost footing coming down the mountain." She shakes her head. "Almost all the horses, except for Siron and Ulrich's steed, had been poisoned."

Another blow. I'm starting to go numb with everything that's happened. "Relax. Rest so your injuries heal. My aunt is one of the best healers in all of Shaerdan and Malam. It's time to realize I'm running this expedition now."

Yep. She certainly is.

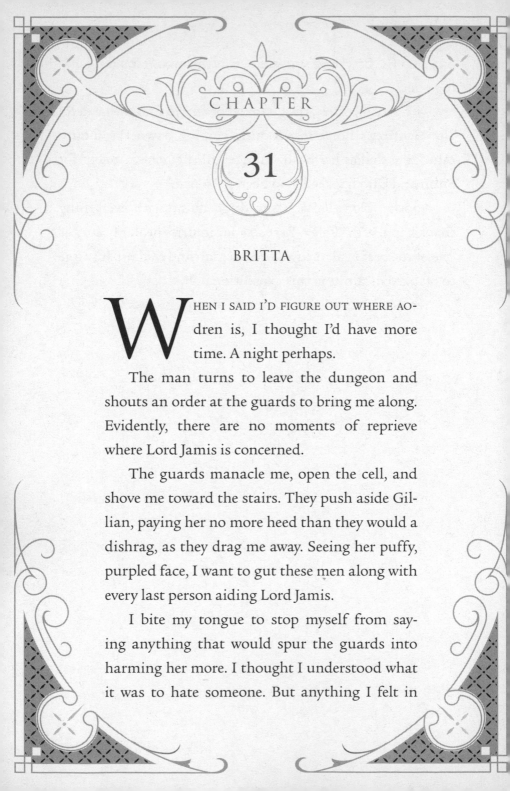

CHAPTER

31

BRITTA

WHEN I SAID I'D FIGURE OUT WHERE AOdren is, I thought I'd have more time. A night perhaps.

The man turns to leave the dungeon and shouts an order at the guards to bring me along. Evidently, there are no moments of reprieve where Lord Jamis is concerned.

The guards manacle me, open the cell, and shove me toward the stairs. They push aside Gillian, paying her no more heed than they would a dishrag, as they drag me away. Seeing her puffy, purpled face, I want to gut these men along with every last person aiding Lord Jamis.

I bite my tongue to stop myself from saying anything that would spur the guards into harming her more. I thought I understood what it was to hate someone. But anything I felt in the past is nothing compared to the wrath I now harbor inside.

The guard to my right yanks my arm so hard that pain zips through my shoulder. I yelp, and the man chuckles darkly, telling me to move faster. In that fleeting moment, I remember I'm not entirely powerless. The skin-to-skin contact reminds me of the energy flowing under the man's rough, leathery paws.

I could force him to his knees.

It would be in defense. Would Enat have considered that dark magic? At this point, do I care? My thoughts flicker, seeing the slaughtered nobility, the field of slain guards, the battered Finn, and the bruised Gillian. The idea of inflicting the same brutality on any of Lord Jamis's men brings more pleasure than it should.

"Y-y-you're not really gonna do it, are you?" Finn's teeth chatter, snapping me out of the daydream.

I blink, taking in Finn's shadowed cell, glad I cannot make out his expression. He knows I'm on my way to find the king. There isn't anything I can say to appease his worry. Instead, I look from the blot of black behind the cell bars that is Finn and then to Gillian. "Watch out for her."

He doesn't respond.

As we ascend the stairs, I know I've let him down.

The guards take me to where Phelia waits alone under the arcading.

Once my eyes get used to the early evening light in the corridor, I study her, this woman who is supposed to be my mother—the similar shape of eyes and the straight sloped nose. Her hair is a few shades darker than mine, but it's not hard to imagine that in twenty years I'll look a lot like her.

Honestly, the similarities bother me the most. They whisper that we're more alike than I'd ever want to admit. Since meeting Phelia in the woods, I've wondered if I have the same capacity for darkness and evil. I've pushed aside thoughts of her over and over again.

Now, as the guards remove the manacles, Phelia's gaze bears down on me, like she's puzzling out a problem. My fingers itch to tug at the tight seams of this dress. Her scrutiny holds me in place. I try to swallow, though my throat feels coated in dust. I glance at the guards out of the corner of my eye. I wanted to use my Spiriter ability to end them mere moments ago. Can she see that in my face?

When the men leave, Phelia's eyes drop to my wrists, where the manacles have left my skin red.

"If I need to subdue you, I can do it with a twitch of my finger," she says.

Can she really?

Her lip curls. "You wear your thoughts too easily." She gestures for me to go ahead of her. "Lord Jamis does not make idle threats. Remember that."

Her words tie knots inside me. But I do what she says,

moving toward the king's link. To an observer, I might appear more like her guide than her prisoner. We walk through long halls, some narrow and others wide.

I take note of where my connection to Aodren is telling me to go and I ignore it, like when it pulls me toward the stairwell to the servants' quarters.

We pass the Great Hall, though we don't enter. I steal a glance through the open doors. I stumble when I find the room empty. Only smears of crimson remain from the recent deaths. In the hours that have passed since the feast massacre, the remaining servants must've worked hard to move the bodies. The slushy frozen feeling returns to my veins. When I look at the Great Hall, I want to believe that it was a nightmare. But the evidence is immortalized in stains. Even if the servants scrub the blood away, the devastation and loss will always be imprinted on this castle.

I shudder, despite the numbness spreading into my limbs. I turn and continue down the hall in search of the king.

"You think me a monster." Phelia's voice scratches at the back of my neck.

"Should I think anything else?"

"I wasn't always one. I told you I saved you."

At the cost of another man's life. Yes, he was trying to kill us, so in comparison her act seems justified.

"You left my father and me behind," I say, and then point toward the north tower.

She stops under one of the castle's arches. "The border guard wanted to kill us. He mortally wounded us both."

Truth. She's already said as much, though.

I turn to fully face her and wait for her to continue. My eyes are drawn to the onyx markings that spiral down her arm, wrap around her wrist, and spread over the flat of her palm.

"You want to know why I left, don't you?" she asks. She's different today than the other times we met. Her jagged edges are softer.

I find myself nodding.

"When he walked close enough for me to touch him, his intent was to end our lives. That strong of a singular focus colors a person's energy. And in turn, stains the taker."

"What are you saying?"

Her fingers twitch toward me, though she stops shy of touching my skin. "I stole his energy to heal you. But it came at a great cost. After I did, I wanted to kill you."

The heat in her truth hits me, her words like hooks, luring me in to ask more. Not that I want to. I don't want to learn anything more about Phelia.

"It was madness," she continues unprompted. "His intent warred with my own motherly instincts. Instead of killing you, I stopped drawing his energy. I should've died. Except I passed out and woke days later, healed by Enat. Your father and you were gone, convinced by Enat that I was dead. But she saved me." Phelia's bitter scoff rings off the arched ceiling. "*Saved me* by lying to my husband and sending my child away."

"Why didn't you return till now?" My words have barely any voice, slipping out.

"It's taken this long to muddy the intent."

I press my palm against my belly. "And h-how do you do that?"

She steps away from the arch, a small sad twist on her mouth. A mouth that's so similar to my own. Her hand dangles by her hip like a spider dancing up a sooty web. "How do you muddy water, Britta?"

I shake my head.

Her tone shifts, morphing back into something hard: "By adding more and more dirt."

Heat invades my veins. I rub and rub my arms, needing to rid myself of the effect her words have on me.

Stepping closer, she lifts her sleeves, her not-quite smile gleaming in the lamplight. "Each swirl represents a life."

Oh gods. I might vomit.

Her eyes shine. "They were weak, useless wastes of people. Not like us. We're strong, you and I. Though I can sense the newness in your feelings for Aodren. Your energy sparks around him. But you'll have to keep that under control. Feelings only get in the way for people like us. We're survivors. Together we could be unstoppable."

The woman's moods shift in a blink.

I step back, recoiling from her madness. "I'm nothing like you."

Her pale brows twitch up. "If you don't want me to know

when you're lying, you'll have to put the wall back up between us."

Only, she knows I cannot do what she's saying. Is she trying to entice me or taunt me?

"I will teach you. You want to learn. I can see the hunger in your eyes." Her left hand lifts, reaching toward my cheek.

I jerk back.

"Your hope of escape is written across your defiant face." She taps her chin. "Stay, Britta. Stay here at the castle, agree to work with me, and I'll look the other way while Finn takes Gillian away."

Her offer should feel more repulsive than it actually does. "And the king?" I ask.

"You'll deliver him to me."

I repress a shudder. "Why let Finn and Gillian go and not King Aodren?"

Her palm drops to rest on her hip. "My dear, you must cut off the head of the snake to kill it."

"The king isn't the beast that needs to be slain," I argue.

She blinks, and the edges of her mouth soften, transforming her face. I stare at her, seeing for the first time a resemblance to Enat.

"Eighteen years ago, the Purge was set into action," Phelia says. "As a boulder set loose to roll down a mountain, it will destroy all of Malam. It's already caused so much destruction. So much pain. The high lord only wants to stop the damage.

Do you understand? Lord Jamis is our champion. Aodren has allowed the Purge. Lord Jamis wants to end it. He wants to welcome Channelers back with open arms."

My fingernails imprint on my palms, the pain stopping me from lunging at her and shaking her out of her madness. "What about the Channelers you've taken? You're using them to make you stronger."

Her lips shift into a sad smile. "We are at war, Britta. On one side, a king who has supported genocide. On the other, a mother who is only trying to win the right for women like us to live. To be free and unafraid. My gift is the greatest weapon we have. No matter how it grieves me, I'll do what I must. If I have to sacrifice a few to save all Channelers – to save my own precious daughter — then it is a burden I willingly bear."

I stare, blinking stupidly. She confessed to killing a guard in order to save me. Now she wants to take on all of Malam, in order to save the Channelers. Her actions are extreme. They're vile. But in an unsettling way, they make sense. After all, in the dungeon, I considered draining the energy from the guards to save Gillian, Finn, and myself. I killed a man to avenge Enat's death. It's alarming, the similarity of our motives when loved ones are involved.

The idea of Channelers being free to practice their abilities in Malam is an enticing picture. Since learning of my ability, all I've wanted to do is submerse myself in understanding more about Spiriter magic.

"Britta? Will you choose to save your friends?"

There are no good options. Papa used to say, *Make your own path when it seems there isn't one before you.*

Without answering, I turn and start once more up the stairs.

I'm loath to admit her manipulations have almost ensnared me. Perhaps that's what keeps me from opening my mouth and saying anything more to her.

Precious daughter. She's absurd. Not once in my eighteen years has she reached out to me to seek a relationship. I cannot bargain for Finn's and Gillian's freedom. Not with her.

Somehow, I'll figure out another way for us all to escape. I'll cut a new path.

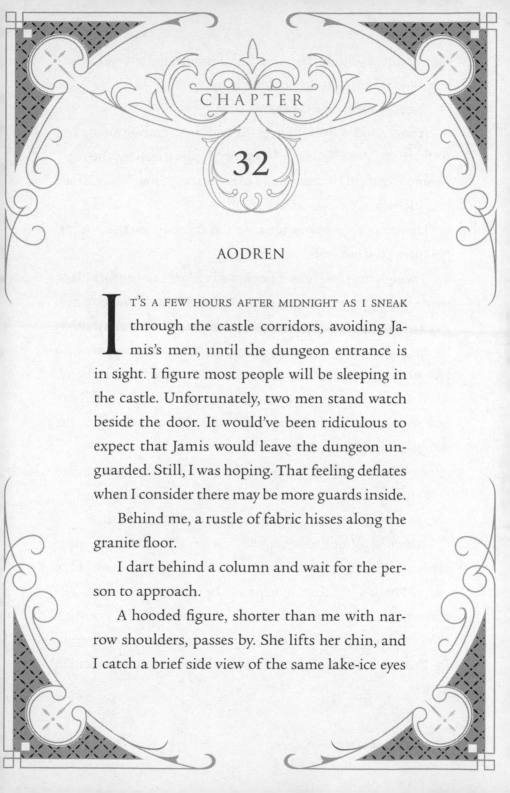

CHAPTER

32

AODREN

IT'S A FEW HOURS AFTER MIDNIGHT AS I SNEAK through the castle corridors, avoiding Jamis's men, until the dungeon entrance is in sight. I figure most people will be sleeping in the castle. Unfortunately, two men stand watch beside the door. It would've been ridiculous to expect that Jamis would leave the dungeon unguarded. Still, I was hoping. That feeling deflates when I consider there may be more guards inside.

Behind me, a rustle of fabric hisses along the granite floor.

I dart behind a column and wait for the person to approach.

A hooded figure, shorter than me with narrow shoulders, passes by. She lifts her chin, and I catch a brief side view of the same lake-ice eyes that haunt my sleep. The scant hall light reflected in Phelia's pale blue irises makes them look dead.

What is she doing up at this time?

A sneer slides over my mouth and, instinctively, my hand shifts to the sword at my side, palm grinding against the steel. Desire to end this woman's life roars through me. Never have I had such a visceral reaction to someone.

Her cloak flaps behind her. As she approaches, the guards' postures go stone-still.

Though my time under her bind is hazy, I remember black swirls like plumes of smoke covering her arms. There were moments that Phelia's bind had somehow weakened. She'd reach for me to increase the strength of the bind and send me into another stretch where I had no control over my mind or body.

If I had the courage Saul Flannery possessed, I'd kill her now, regardless of the two guards. Except the men open the dungeon, and Phelia disappears down the stairs.

My chance is lost. I unclench my fingers from the sword and shake out my hand, ashamed at the contradicting feelings coursing through me — disappointment and relief.

It's difficult not to see my hesitation as weaknesses, especially when the woman I'm intent on saving likely would've ended Phelia's life the moment the Spiriter was in sight. The thought sobers. I cannot hesitate when fighting for my kingdom. As king of Malam, there already is blood on my hands. It's been that way every day I've ruled while the Purge is still in action.

Chest pressed to the pillar, I peek at the two guards. Knowing what I have to do, a cringe starts at the back of my neck. The shadows provide the best camouflage, allowing me to sneak within dagger-throwing distance.

I'm a better swordsman than a marksman with the dagger, but I've no other choice. Gripping the handle, I take aim at the center of the larger guard's chest, whip my arm back, then thrust forward, releasing. The knife sails through the air, nailing the man in the hollow of the neck. No sound escapes his lips when he falls to the ground. I charge with my sword drawn before the other guard fully realizes they're under attack.

He reaches for his blade and manages to get it up in time to block my swing. But swordsmanship is where I excel. I parry his next thrust, swing and slide my sword between his ribs before he's even given a thought to alerting anyone else.

My breath powers through my chest as I step back. Blood seeps around the men like spilled wine, which seems to shine redder in the lantern light. I recognize the larger fellow. Though we haven't exchanged words, the familiarity churns low in my gut. I take my dagger from the first guard. Luck or the gods were with me tonight. I had missed my intended target—I'd meant to take him in the heart. Aim is something I'll have to work on.

I wipe my blades off on the traitors' royal coats and open the dungeon door to descend into the pit. Moans and snores of prisoners echo from the depths. Having been down here just days ago to seek out evidence surrounding the dungeon master's murder, I am familiar enough with the space to not entirely lose my sense of direction.

At a dead end, I pause, close my eyes, and allow the tug to guide me toward Britta. The connection was a shock, at first. When I'd visited her after waking up, my intention was to express gratitude. Only, upon drawing nearer to her cottage, I could feel the twist of something around my chest, leading me toward her small home on the outskirts of Brentyn. The strange sensation didn't make sense until she opened the door. I was certain a magical bond had formed between us because I recognized the similarity to Phelia's bind. Although hers had been more akin to a ghost that haunted me day and night.

Britta's face mirrored my surprise, so I was certain she hadn't intended to link us magically. Part of me was enraged at first, wanting nothing to do with Channeler magic, but it didn't take long to recognize the difference in Britta's connection. Hers is a comforting hand, warm and gentle, compared to Phelia's cold one.

Though we've never discussed the technicalities, it's clear we are both aware of the bond. Without the tie to Britta, I'd be lost. Literally. The dungeon walkways are black as pitch.

I take a rickety stairwell that is more ladder-like than stable stairs to the lowest part of the dungeon. The farther I descend, the more despair gathers. It's unimaginable that anyone would survive a week in this hell, let alone longer. If anything, Jamis's survival proves he's as tenacious as the roaches that infest the seedier taverns in Brentyn.

I'm nearly to the bottom of the steps when *that* voice, tree bark and scraped metal, echoes across the cavern. A harsh shock of light bobs ahead. I watch the movement of the lantern through the void, my feet freezing to the dungeon stones when it illuminates a woman's silhouette. *Phelia.*

My lungs refuse to fill with a decent breath. My body's immediate reaction whenever the woman is near is paralysis. I cannot allow fear to hold me back. Not when I'm this close to Britta. I slam down the anxiety creeping up inside me and force my feet forward. It's time to act.

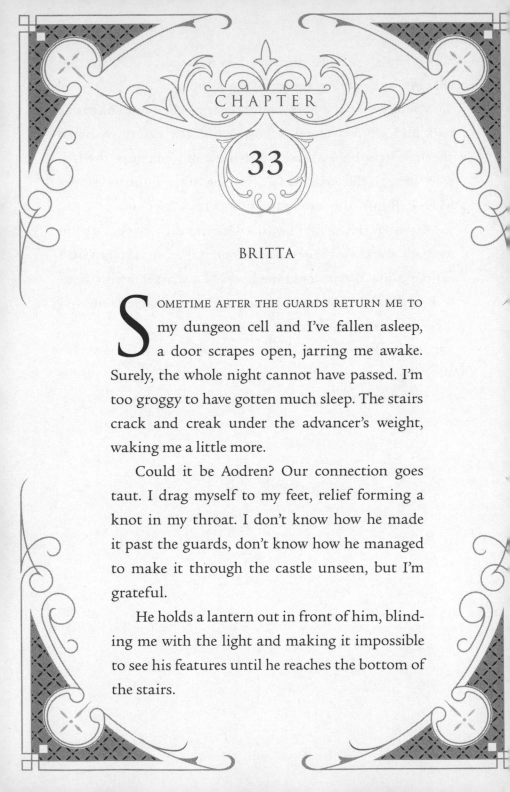

CHAPTER

33

BRITTA

SOMETIME AFTER THE GUARDS RETURN ME TO my dungeon cell and I've fallen asleep, a door scrapes open, jarring me awake. Surely, the whole night cannot have passed. I'm too groggy to have gotten much sleep. The stairs crack and creak under the advancer's weight, waking me a little more.

Could it be Aodren? Our connection goes taut. I drag myself to my feet, relief forming a knot in my throat. I don't know how he made it past the guards, don't know how he managed to make it through the castle unseen, but I'm grateful.

He holds a lantern out in front of him, blinding me with the light and making it impossible to see his features until he reaches the bottom of the stairs.

Only, it's not Aodren.

The relief I felt is eclipsed by confusion. Where is he? Has she captured him as well? Phelia sets the lantern onto a holder and withdraws a blanket from under her cloak. Her fingers spider over the material as she turns her focus to Finn's sleeping, huddled form. She pauses. Then shifts her attention to Gillian, who lies unconscious in the cell beside me.

Phelia glides forward like a dark angel of death, her cloak flapping out around her as she approaches Gillian's cell. She takes out keys and opens the cell door.

"What are you doing? Leave her alone." I rush to the bars separating us.

Her icy eyes flick to me. In a deceptively maternal move, Phelia lays the woolen blanket over Gillian. Then, reaching out with fingers that uncurl from her palm like spider legs, Phelia touches the swollen lump on my friend's cheek.

I'm frozen, confused, and tired from the endless passage of time in this death hole. I think we've been here two nights. What does Phelia want?

I want to scream. There's nothing I could do from this cell should Phelia harm Gillian. I don't know how I bent the bars earlier. Last time I ate was the morning of Winter Feast. Was that a day ago? Perhaps two? The lack of food and sleep has weakened me. Even if I knew how I'd done it, I don't have the energy to do it again. I've never felt so useless in my entire life.

"This wasn't my decision." Phelia's gravelly voice is soft. Imploring. "No one is all good or all bad. I didn't allow the guards to harm you when I returned you to your cell last night."

Is she saying that they would have? I wonder what the guards would've deemed an appropriate punishment for not having located the king.

"I want you to see that you can trust me, Britta. No matter how many years pass, I am your mother."

I was once a little girl who dreamt of nighttime kisses and bedtime stories. In those dreams, Mama held me tight before she tucked me in to bed. In those dreams, I was never alone. Stepping away from the bars, I scrub my fists against my eye sockets to erase the image.

Don't trust her. Don't even consider it.

The blanket, the soft-spoken words — it's all a part of her act to reel me in. She is the master of manipulation, evident by the way she controlled the king for nearly a year with no one the wiser. She doesn't care about me. She doesn't want a relationship.

Phelia exits the cell and locks it, dropping the bulging ring of keys into her cape pocket. "She doesn't have to stay here. If you were to help Lord Jamis . . ."

If. I recoil from the hook of her words while guilt and anger thrash beneath my frozen surface.

"He won't be patient much longer." Phelia tucks her arms into her raven cloak. "I've given you time to come to me of your own free will. But time is running out. It's a simple trade. Aodren for Finn and Gillian." Her eyes rest on Gillian. "Given rest and medicine, she'll recover. I cannot promise the same if she remains here."

Truth.

She withdraws my dagger from another pocket in her cloak.

"The guards took this off you." Her pointer finger caresses the handle, her movement reverent, if not a bit distracted, like she's lost in a memory. "Do you know the name of this blade?"

Papa's dagger in her hands is all wrong. I have to bite my lip to stop myself from snapping at her and demanding it back. For as much as I try to keep Papa's blade on me at all times, it's alarming how often the weapon's been taken away in the last three months.

Her finger moves to the tip, where she adds a little pressure to the edge until a bright spot of crimson bubbles to the surface.

"This is an Akin Blade, one of a pair. Where is its counterpart, Britta?"

I shrug. No way I'll tell her Cohen has it.

Her expression turns sly, like a happily fed cat. "Very well. Did you know Akin Blades are made in pairs, to be used together?"

She must see my uncertain expression, because she adds, "When two Spiriters of the same blood and similar energy are in battle side by side, the Akin Blades react to one another, becoming more powerful."

Is this why she wants me to join her? To fight by her side? My eyes linger too long on the blade.

She slips the dagger into her pocket. "You want to know more. I can see it. There's so much I can teach you, Britta."

She's right. There's so much I want to learn. But not at her hand. Not with the cost being the king's life.

A shadow leaps behind her.

I stop myself from screaming, realizing it's Aodren. Phelia spins around, her hand rising, wrist cocked. Aodren swings an unlit torch. But Phelia dodges it and grasps his arm. There's a split second where his face shifts into a question. And then his back bows in an unnatural arc. A cry of pain bursts from his lips.

Dread thunders through me. I fight to wrench the bars apart, but my energy's too frantic to use.

Desperate to distract Phelia, I yell, "Rozen! Mother!"

She whirls to me, ice-blue eyes clear with surprise. It is an age-old manipulation, one that I am shocked she fell for. She smiles, unaware of the bitterness filling my mouth.

Aodren recovers and slams the torch against the back of her head. Phelia's expression collapses. Her body plummets to the dungeon floor.

I shake off the odd wave of guilt, shifting my attention to Aodren, who looks greenish in the dim light. Relief and shock hiccup through me until I manage to find my voice. "You— you're here?"

He cants his head to the side and gives me a strange look. "Why wouldn't I be?"

"I just didn't think you had the . . ." I stop talking and shrug. Whatever I'd been about to say, I'd been wrong.

He reaches for the lock. "Where did she put the keys?"

"In her pocket."

Aodren scavenges through Phelia's cloak and reveals my dagger, tossing it to me, and the ring of keys. "There have to be at least fifty here."

He kneels at my cell and inserts a key, trying to twist the lock open, only to frown and move to the next one.

"Britta, Britt." Finn's calling my name.

I maneuver to see him. He thrusts his hand between the bars, pointing at Phelia. "I think she's waking up."

Phelia's eyes are still closed but her knee jerks. *No, no, no.* "Faster, Aodren."

He flips from key to key. Tries one. Mutters. Tries another. I keep my eyes on her, hearing the metal clank and him curse.

Phelia moves again, a small twitch in her chin, and I'm so full of anxiety that it takes me a moment to realize that Aodren's opened my cell and moved onto Gillian's.

Once he pops her door open, he tosses me the keys. "Work on Finn's, and I'll pick up Miss Tierney."

I shove key after key in Finn's cell lock, moving my fingers as fast as I can. Aodren is at my side a moment later, Gillian in his arms. If only she was awake now, she'd be a twittering, fidgeting, happy mess. It's not every day a lady gets carried about by the king of Malam.

Aodren's face is whiter than mine as he takes in her many bruises. "Her pulse is strong."

"She'll make it," I say, my voice shrill with false bravery as I keep working on opening the cell.

Finally, Finn's lock clicks open. He scurries out to huddle beside me, his poor twiggy frame awkward with sluggish movement. Shivers take over his body. I use the blanket that Phelia put on Gillian to wrap around him.

"W-w-what about you?" he chatters. I wave his concern away; we have other worries. Besides, this dress has so many layers, I could be in a blizzard and still not be cold.

Phelia moans.

"K-kill her," Finn says.

I fist my dagger, knowing it's what should be done. And yet, my arms lock. She needs to be stopped, but I cannot. It's not in me to end her life.

"Or lock her up," Aodren says, his face full of understanding. "That will hold her long enough for us to escape."

I crack a hint of a smile at his oddly positive attitude, all things considered.

Finn helps me drag her into my cell. The curved bars are what give me pause. I look at them and then squat beside Phelia, knowing she'll find a way out of the dungeon the moment she wakes.

I don't know what I'm capable of, but I know I have to

do something. My hand goes to her wrist and nearly flies off again at the heat emanating from her scarred skin. I wrap my fingers around her arm again, imagining it's an exercise with Enat in the woods.

The dungeon fades as Phelia's whooshing energy steals my sole focus. Her life force is a gale wind, raging loud beneath her skin. I figure if I can push my life force into another to revitalize and heal them, then I should be able to encourage my energy to do other things.

I concentrate on my pulse and wade through our connection, sending just enough energy to mix with hers.

Then I coax the entwined energies to settle. *Sleep.*

My arm tingles and drowsiness drags through my muscles. Her face goes slack. Her breath moves softly through her lips. I break contact, exit her cell, and lock it behind me. Phelia doesn't move, and I hope that means she's fallen deeply asleep.

"Ready?"

Finn and Aodren stare at me.

It takes a second for Aodren to snap out of his trance. "That was bloody amazing." He smiles. "I can lead us out through the hidden passageways. But we still might come across Jamis's men. If I'm holding Gillian, I won't be able to help fight."

"I'll do it." Finn clutches the blanket and puts on a brave face. "Do you have another blade for me?"

"Take the sword from my belt." Aodren inclines his head.

Once Finn is armed, we go ahead of Aodren and Gillian,

ensuring the path is clear. We make it out of the dungeon, where two slain guards lay in the hall. I glance at the king, and he ducks, as if in shame. In this aspect, perhaps we're more similar than I thought. Inflicting death has never been a light choice for me.

"One action does not define a man, but rather the sum of all his actions," I whisper, finding myself repeating something Papa once said. It sounds a little inane coming from my mouth.

"Wise words." Aodren gathers Gillian tighter to his chest. "Let's hope the sum of my actions proves I'm more than a man who's only brought death to his people."

CHAPTER

34

AODREN

HOISTING GILLIAN IN MY ARMS, I GESTURE for Britta and Finn to take the lead. On my direction, they cross to a connecting narrow hallway. This passage, not commonly used, is so tight that I have to turn sideways to carry Gillian. It's difficult to keep pace with the others and to make little noise, but I manage as we hurry to the exit that lets out by the stables and guard tower.

The gate that blocks the path to the bridge is closed. In order to leave the castle, we have to pass two guards on watch, enter the tower, and crank the pulley to lift the gate.

Britta motions me toward the stables. The moon is still out, lighting the yard. We use the shadows to slip into the stables. There, I place

Gillian on a bed of hay and turn to face the others. "If we want any chance at escaping, we have to be ready to go the moment the gate rises."

"How are we going to get it up?" Britta asks. I can tell by the way she sags against a raised trough that she's tired. I'm not sure if it's from what she did to Phelia or the night she spent in the dungeon.

Thinking of how to maximize our efforts, I turn to Finn and point out my horse, Gale, and Britta's Snowfire. Then I grab a saddle from the tack shelf. "Can you ready the horses?"

His brow wrinkles, making him look quite a bit like his older brother.

"If you and Britta cause a distraction," I explain, "I can enter the tower and subdue the guards."

"I'll ride out with Finn—that should be distraction enough." Britta pushes away from the trough. She steps to Gillian's side and rests her hand on the handmaid's shoulder. "They'll come after me and you can get in."

The idea is good, but she doesn't seem to have the stamina to fight anyone off. "What if they attack?" I ask.

She takes a quick glance around the dark stable. It's hours till dawn and difficult to see much. "Any bows around here? Arrows?"

"The closest weapons closet is back through the castle."

Unfazed, she pats the sword at her waist. "Guess this'll have to do."

I consider arguing her obvious exhaustion, but drop it. If she says she can fight, then she can fight.

The stables' windows for airing out the stalls give me access to the outer court. I get into position with my sword ready, though the thought of killing anyone else picks at my sanity. On my count, Finn and Britta ride out.

As planned, the horse's whinny grabs the guards' attention as Britta and Finn charge out of the stable. I hear a shout and then the guards rush from the tower with their swords drawn.

I grip my sword, eyes tuned to Britta's movements for a beat longer than I should waste. She'll be fine. She can take care of herself. I remind myself of this as I rush to the now-empty tower.

More shouts echo from the yard. Thankfully the night adds to our element of surprise. Though the guards are calling for backup, they sound confused.

Keeping low, I scramble inside the tower and to the pulley. I tug on the lever, but it's stiff and the metal chains won't give. Cursing, I drop my sword and put both hands on the pulley's lever to shove and pull. Shove and pull. The veins in my arms feel like they might pop. I hold my breath, exerting more effort than I ever thought possible, until the gate starts to rise and the chain slips into place, lifting the metal blockade out of Britta's way.

Once it's up, I sprint back to the stable, sword in hand.

Gillian lets out an agonized cry as I hoist her onto Gale and into a seated position. If there were time, something could be done to comfort her. There's no time, however. We're dead if we're caught.

I swipe sweat from my eyes. Adrenaline charging through me, I ride us out of the stable, Gale's hooves clattering against the flagstones.

One of the guards is in the tower. Britta is on the bridge, Finn seated behind her on Snowfire. I squint and notice the moonlight illuminating a second guard lying face-down on the planks at the horses' feet. I'm not sure how she subdued him, nor am I entirely certain he's alive.

But I hear the whine of metal. The gate is closing.

Britta yells my name, a clear arrow of sound in the night. The terror in her voice as I dig my heels into Gale, riding under the gate with my head ducked, tells me we missed the metal teeth by hairs.

Britta's horse runs alongside us, thundering over the bridge. The middle of the night chill pricks over my face as I race along beside her, my heart thundering along to the horses' rapid rhythm.

We make it into the hills above Brentyn, and Gillian coughs. I realize I'm clenching her too hard, so I loosen my grip and mutter an apology, though it's doubtful she hears me since she's unconscious.

"I—I didn't think you'd make it," Britta shouts over the scatter of gravel and rock under hoof.

Behind her, Finn rests his forehead against her back. His eyes are closed and his skin is ashen. It's clear we've all experienced untold horrors these last two nights.

Now that we're away from the castle, the moonlight curves around Britta's face.

Though we're running for our lives, the obvious worry in her eyes unlocks something in my chest. It settles some of the chaos inside. Up till now I'm certain she hasn't cared a whit for me. But when she looks at me like that, it makes me wonder if perhaps when this is all over, there might be something more for us.

"I worried about that too," I admit, and she smiles. It's small, not much to lift her cheeks, but it's a gift. One that makes it easier to breathe despite the intensity of our escape.

As we ride along the outskirts of the city, a change comes over Britta. Even though we're gaining distance from the threat at the castle, and no guards have popped up behind us, her shoulders creep up toward her ears, showing her discomfort.

The moment the horses reach the castle healer Hagan's cottage, Finn and Britta dismount. They both come to my side to assist with Gillian, but Britta holds her arms out expectantly to take the girl.

"Are you all right?" I ask them once I'm on the ground. "We got away. We can breathe for a moment."

Finn gives the slightest of shrugs.

"Let's get the horses in the barn," Britta says, not answering my question. "I don't want anyone seeing them when the sun comes up."

I take Gillian from Britta as she leads both our animals into hiding. Once they're hidden behind closed barn doors, she returns to my side where I wait with Finn outside Hagan's rear door.

Britta reaches out gingerly to touch Gillian's forehead. Some of the tension from escaping the castle has left her shoulders, but I can still see the tightness in the way she holds herself.

"I can heal her." Spoken so lightly, it takes me a moment to register Britta's whisper. I almost miss the questioning cadence.

"Is that what you want?"

Her fingers brush the crust of blood at Gillian's hairline. It's nearly the same color as the handmaid's deep brown hair.

"Are you worried she won't make it? Or are you afraid Hagan isn't trustworthy?"

"Neither." Britta lowers her hand. "I—I just want to make everything right. She's this way because I . . ." Her voice cracks, and she stops talking.

Her vulnerability nearly undoes me. I want to take this strong girl into my arms and comfort her. After everything she's done for me, I want to be the support she needs.

"Britta, this isn't your fault." *If anything, it's mine.*

"It's kind of you to say so." She glances up through the fan of her pale lashes. That same something I felt before snags beneath my breastbone. The urge to press my lips to her forehead comes like when I kissed her in the castle.

Only this time I don't act on it. First, because Finn's standing nearby, his face vacant where it isn't bruised. He needs food and rest. Second, because a glance at the surrounding farmland deters me. It's still dark, but dawn will be coming up on the horizon soon. Though we have these precious moments to breathe and regroup, we're still running for our lives. We will be until we find Omar. The smartest thing for us to do would be to spend as little time as possible dropping Gillian off, and then getting on our way.

"Come on." I clear my throat. "Come meet Hagan."

A frown tightens Britta's mouth and stays in place even after the healer has opened the door.

Hagan the healer casts a fearful look at the road. "Hurry. Hurry inside."

He twists the lock behind us. "Men have sieged the city and have locked it down. If they catch up to you, they'll kill you."

Of course Jamis's men have taken Brentyn. I shake my head. I should've already anticipated his move on the city. If Hagan lived in town, rather than on the outskirts, we might've ridden right into Jamis's hands.

Finn goes to sit by the fireplace while I follow Hagan to a room with an empty bed. I lower Gillian onto the mattress, making sure her head rests on the pillow. "No one saw us come this way. And when we go, we'll leave through the woods behind your property." The non-direct route out of the valley is for his benefit as much as it is for ours. If I can, I would keep Hagan from danger.

I tell him the harrowing details of what happened at the castle. While I talk, he touches Gillian's neck, checking for a pulse, and then moves on to her arms and legs to check for broken bones. His examination is thorough, despite how his countenance turns ashen as my story progresses.

"She'll be sore and tired for a few days, but I've a salve for her wounds and a tincture for the pain." Hagan lifts a couple of small jars from a wooden chest of drawers. "I also have Beannach water if you're all right with me using Channeler magic to heal her."

"Of course I am."

He nods his approval.

"I need to leave Gillian in your care," I explain, telling Hagan that Britta, Finn, and I are going to go after Captain Omar. While I'm discussing the details, I notice Britta's fists are white balls of tension. Her eyes cut to Hagan and back to me in a way that tells me she wants privacy.

When Hagan steps out of the room to grab the Beannach water, Britta eliminates the distance between us and rises on her toes, bringing her lips near my cheek. "I could just heal her. I could fix her and we could be on our way."

She grips my arms. It's such a surprising maneuver, aligning our bodies in this way that I don't think to lower myself and make it easier for her to whisper in my ear. I'm frozen by the proximity of her body.

I give myself a mental slap. Now's certainly not the time. "D-do you think that's best?"

"I don't know."

I tip my face down. Now we're eye to eye. "I don't know much about your ability. I do know, however, you took weeks to recover from healing me. You've been in the dungeon for almost two days, and you just did something to Phelia, right? That had to be taxing."

Her gaze drops to the scar on my neck. I ignore the rush it sends through me because it's ridiculous to feel this way given the danger we're in.

"If you heal Gillian, will you be strong enough to leave?"

She groans, obviously accepting what must be done. "No."

We'll need allies. Men. "We have to go."

She nods, an unconvincing tip of her chin.

"Britt." Finn stands in the doorway, leaning against the frame. He eyes us, and I step away from her, reminding myself that Britta and this boy's brother are . . . something. What, exactly? Does she love Cohen Mackay?

"I'll stay with her," Finn continues. "I'll only slow you down. Gillian's going to need someone here. Worst case, I'll have to hide her should Jamis's men come."

Fear sets his voice wobbling, but he's putting forth a strong front, and that should be commended. "Brave choice, Finn."

He blinks, apparently stunned by the compliment.

Britta walks over to Finn and clutches his hand. "Now who is the brave one?" She glances over her shoulder at Gillian. "Keep her safe."

Finn grows a smidge taller. "I will."

There's no more time for goodbyes so I pat Finn on the shoulder. I don't have any coins for Hagan, but I promise him repayment when we retake the castle—I will not let myself think failure is a possibility.

Hagan offers us bedrolls, a tent tarp, and some food for our travels. He even provides a better-fitting change of clothes to me, since mine are filthy. After hurriedly scrubbing myself with soap and water, I change into Hagan's trousers and winter tunic. When he offers his coat, however, I turn it down. It's his only one and should he flee, he'll need it. Though it's sure to be near freezing in the mountains, the winter tunic and trousers are thicker than what I was wearing. They'll have to do.

Britta accepts his bow and quiver of arrows. I can tell by the way her hands stroke the curved wood that her confidence in our ability to find Omar has grown.

After a quick meal, Britta loads up Gale while I keep watch. Snowfire will stay behind should Finn need a horse.

The sun is rising when Britta and I reach the woods, but it brings no warmth, only gray light that turns the frost on the horizon into colorless haze.

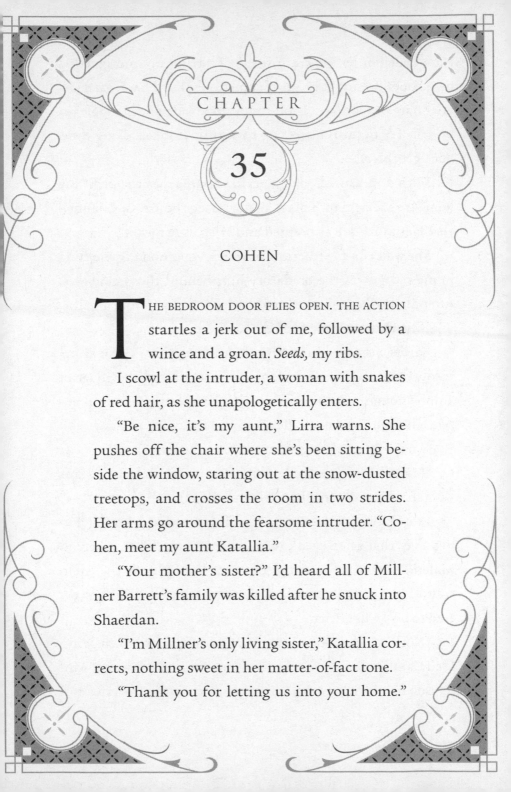

CHAPTER

35

COHEN

THE BEDROOM DOOR FLIES OPEN. THE ACTION
startles a jerk out of me, followed by a
wince and a groan. *Seeds,* my ribs.

I scowl at the intruder, a woman with snakes
of red hair, as she unapologetically enters.

"Be nice, it's my aunt," Lirra warns. She
pushes off the chair where she's been sitting beside the window, staring out at the snow-dusted
treetops, and crosses the room in two strides.
Her arms go around the fearsome intruder. "Cohen, meet my aunt Katallia."

"Your mother's sister?" I'd heard all of Millner Barrett's family was killed after he snuck into
Shaerdan.

"I'm Millner's only living sister," Katallia cor-
rects, nothing sweet in her matter-of-fact tone.

"Thank you for letting us into your home."

Hate that I'm lying here instead of sitting up and greeting her properly. I might be gruff sometimes, but I have learned a fair share of manners. I roll to my good side and struggle for breath. Try to push myself up to sitting. It takes a long time, but I get there.

With a measured gaze, Katallia approaches the bed. "My home is in Shaerdan. This is a safe passage house for Channelers." Her words are as pointed and crisp as her walk.

She waits for my reaction, of which I give none. Something in me recognizes the predatory hint behind those gray eyes. After all, I've been on the king's payroll for a year and a half.

"My niece said you needed a carrier pigeon."

Earlier, Lirra told me that this home, where I'm laid up, is south of Lord Freil's fiefdom in the small logging village of Tahr. Though we're at least one hundred leagues from Brentyn, a homing bird could fly a letter to the castle in a day.

"I need to get an urgent message to the king."

"And what will you tell them of my niece?" Like Lirra, this woman wastes no time in getting to the grit.

I wouldn't put Lirra in danger if that's what she's suggesting. I get that Lirra's walking a hazardous path being here in Malam. Should anyone find out that her father is the Archtraitor, Lirra would be killed. Same result if she was discovered to be a Channeler.

"Nothing. I wouldn't jeopardize a friend for my own gain," I tell Katallia, but my focus is on Lirra. I want her to see the intention behind my words. I want her to know she can trust me.

Katallia doesn't say more. She stands beside the bed, watching me. I figure she's going to allow me to stay here because she clips out, "Very well," and then pivots and leaves.

Her absence makes the air in the room easier to breathe. Not going to deny that.

"She can be frightening." Lirra coughs out a small laugh.

"Her? No way."

Lirra rolls her eyes.

"All right, she's intense, but I appreciate that."

"She's a member of the Guild." Lirra drums her fingers on her thigh.

"The Channeler teachers?"

Lirra latches the door and rests her back on the wood planks. "They're not just teachers. They're the leaders of the Channelers in Shaerdan. And they're working to overthrow the Purge."

That last bit is news. I get the impression that Lirra, like her aunt Katallia, is testing me. That she's got a limited range of acceptance for appropriate responses.

"So this home is owned by the Guild, not your aunt?"

"Correct."

She pushes off the door and comes to stand at the foot of the bed. "The entire Guild will be here tomorrow. Like me, they're trying to figure out where all the missing Shaerdanian Channeler girls are."

This catches me by surprise.

"Why would they meet here, and not in Shaerdan?"

"Well, all the missing girls are being brought to Malam, so who better to ask for help than the Channelers in hiding? The Guild will meet here to plan."

I always thought there were less than a few handfuls of Channelers still risking their lives in Malam. Perhaps there are more. Just to be sure: "You're talking about women *here?* The Guild is going to organize help from Channelers in Malam?"

Lirra nods slowly. "Yeah."

Right. I get that. "How many Channelers are we talking about?"

"Hundreds."

Not the answer I was expecting.

"That's why my aunt demands your silence. Can you imagine if she was accused? Anyone who starts turning over rocks would be able to connect the women Aunt Kat spends the most time with. The entire Channeler network in Malam would collapse."

Though I've been living with the gravity of what it means for loved ones to be accused of being Channelers, this information stuns me. The Guild, along with the hundreds of Channelers Lirra mentioned, could change the future of Malam. Is it possible they could overturn the Purge? Hope rises inside at the thought. The fear I carry daily for Britta would be eliminated if the Purge Proclamation is overturned.

I grin at her. "I'm a supporter."

Always skeptical, she chews her lip and goes back to sitting in the chair by the window. I debate whether I should try to lie back down or check in on Omar.

Knowing I'm rubbish at sitting still, I take a moment to mentally steel myself for the pain of standing. Once I'm on my feet though —

Mother of bloody stars. I huff out a horse of a breath.

Lirra sneaks under my good arm, supporting my weight with her shoulders. Her little hands are wrapped around me. I chuckle to myself, because when she was smacking salve on me earlier, they sure didn't feel so small. Reminds me so much of my sister, Imogen. Someone needs to teach Lirra to be a better nursemaid.

We hobble out of the room and along the hall of the two-story home.

"Gods' stars, you need a bath," Lirra mutters as she pushes open the next door and helps me inside.

I let her comment go because one, she's probably right, and two, Leif pushes out of his chair where he's sitting beside Omar. "You're up."

"I'm trying. Good to see you, Leif."

He eyes me from head to toe and responds with a relieved smile. "You too."

Taking my weight off Lirra, Leif helps me into the chair beside Omar. I start to ask how Omar's doing today and stop. Bruising crawls out of the captain's tunic, purple and blue.

Other than the mottled color, his skin is paler than Britta's, and that's never a good sign.

"He going to make it?" I rest my palm on the bed beside Omar.

Leif shrugs, weary and somber.

A fist of anger and frustration hits me in the good ribs. Omar might not be my favorite person, but he's stalwart and loyal. He's been the man I've reported to since I started bounty hunting. Our travel party has already lost Wallace and Geoffrey. I don't want to return to Castle Neart having lost Omar as well.

The Archtraitor's daughter moves to Omar's side and peers over the broken man. "Aunt Kat's done all she can. But he needs a true healer." The usual spark in her tone is extinguished. She turns and gives Leif a threatening look. "By now, I'm sure you've figured out that my aunt is a Channeler, and I'm one as well. This home belongs to the Channelers Guild."

Leif straightens, his shoulders stiff. "I wasn't going to—"

Lirra lifts her hand, silencing the guard. She rotates, her fierce glare absorbing me and Leif. "Should anyone in this room bring condemnation on me or my aunt, or anyone connected to our family, because of the gifts we were born with—" She walks her fingers over Omar's bruising and stalls over his heart. "I'll kill you. All of you."

Silence.

While I could try to muster up a laugh to diffuse the tension, her ferocity has dried my mouth. Gooseflesh raises the hair on my arms. Her promise could frighten the fur off a black bear.

Being the smart men that we are, no one dares move as Lirra stalks out of the room.

When the door opens, it's Katallia, not Lirra, who appears. Her gaze flicks to us before she says, "Lirra's assured me you can be trusted. Is that so?"

I glance at Leif. He's been quiet since the Archtraitor's daughter left. No doubt he must have a hundred questions. Thankfully he nods, understanding that we're dead men if we don't agree to secrecy about this location. I do the same.

Katallia's hands steeple together before she touches her fingertips to her lips. "There's no easy way to tell you this, but word has come from Brentyn that Castle Neart was attacked."

What? No. She must be mistaken. The place is a fortified stronghold.

Leif shoves his chair back and approaches the woman. "What have you heard?"

"Two nights ago at the Winter Feast, the king's own men turned on him. Townspeople are saying they had to cart bodies out by the dozen."

Oh gods. Britta. Finn.

Please don't let it be so. The rumors must be exaggerated, if not entirely false. I twist the edge of Omar's blanket in my hands, wanting to rip it apart. "Why would the guards start a rebellion? It makes no sense."

"She's only reporting what she's heard," Lirra says from the doorway. "Don't raise your voice. Besides, you'll injure something more."

I couldn't care less about myself right now. If what Katallia's said is true, it means a world of worse things than my own bloody injuries.

I hate that my body isn't in good working order and I cannot rush back to Malam. I know Britta can take care of herself. But knowing doesn't ease the pain that pierces through me at the thought of her or Finn injured.

Katallia explains that the members of the Guild will be convening in this home tomorrow. She says something about them using their combined powers to heal Omar. She asks for our assistance in return. But I'm still caught on the attack on Castle Neart.

"What kind of help?" Leif cuts in.

"The kind that returns our daughters," she says. "We want you to swear an oath that you'll hunt down the men of Malam who have kidnapped over thirty girls from Shaerdan."

That captures my attention. For Omar we have no other choice. Also, considering what's happening in Brentyn, swearing an oath to these women might have dual benefits.

CHAPTER

36

BRITTA

As we ride away from Hagan's home, I think of Gillian and Finn and wonder if Papa felt this fearful when he left me alone for weeks at a time. My guts twist around my stomach with worry. I press my fist to my navel. Having never experienced this sort of wrenching apprehension for another, I have to wonder if life isn't better alone. On my own, there's only myself to fend for.

Then again, there's only myself to pass the hours. I shiver and scoot closer to Aodren. That sort of solitude taunts me with the same menace as the pillory in Brentyn's market square.

We'll find Cohen, I tell myself. *He's alive and well.*

All this worry is turning the insides of my mouth raw. I sit up taller and relax my hands so they rest loosely on Aodren's waist as we ride his horse north-ward. In the woods, we'll be safer. It'll be easier to stay out of sight.

Once we're in the forest, Aodren puts Gale on a course westward. Our plan is to swing around Brentyn, cut across the road, and turn south to where Cohen and Omar were last headed.

Soon the rising sun will give us more visibility. For now, though, we make use of the slow dawn and how it cloaks the forest in shades of gray. Shapeless shadows blend, hiding us. As we travel, I listen to Gale's steps crunching the ground cover. Then it occurs to me that his movement is all I hear. My hair stands on end.

Gale's ears flick back.

Aodren twists in the saddle, looking around at the same time I do.

Three guards on horses peel out of the darkness, riding toward us from the east. *No.* Aodren takes in a cut of air. He digs his heels into Gale, pushing the horse to sprint. While the king focuses on what's ahead, I watch the rear, but I don't see the hounds until I hear them howl.

Four dogs bolt past the riders, coming for us like shot ar-rows.

"Go, go, go!" I shout.

Gale leaps over a fallen tree. The dogs bark.

I know the Evers as good as or better than anyone. We can lose them. But doubt screams over Gale's jarring run, telling me it'll be much harder to lose the riders with bloodhounds on our tail. How are we going to lose the dogs? They've got our scent.

It's good that they're following us because that means they're not pounding down Hagan's door. Gillian and Finn will be safe. Better us than them, right?

Keeping one hand on Aodren, I take Hagan's bow from the holder and count the arrows in his quiver. There are only six. I cannot waste a single shot.

I'm a good shot, but on horseback, sprinting through the woods . . . perhaps not so much. *Focus.* Papa's words come back to me: *Focus is a weapon as much as your bow.*

My pulse rockets in my veins as I draw my first arrow and set it to the bowstring. When a hound surpasses the others, I take aim and shoot. The pup yelps and rolls in the dirt while the others fly past.

I wince, wishing there was another option. But the men are all single riders, and Gale is laboring under the weight of two. They're gaining on us.

Clenching the back of the saddle with my inner thighs, I grab two more arrows, shooting them one after another, taking down two horses with arrows to the neck. The animals stumble and their riders fall to the ground.

I aim for another hound —

An arrow impales my upper arm. A scream, mixed shock and pain, bursts out of me. The bow tumbles out of my grasp, hitting the forest floor.

"Britta? Britta, what happened?" Aodren is pure panic.

"Got hit. Arrow to my arm," I manage, despite the fire radiating through my right arm. My shooting arm.

The hardened dirt trail winds to the left, climbing the mountain, but Aodren yanks the reins in the opposite direction, sending us on a sudden course downhill. Gale runs and stumbles, crashing through a small riverbed.

I fight to hang on to Aodren with my left arm, my face pressed against his back as we jolt and bounce in the saddle. Stabs of pain come from each movement. For a moment, hounds and riders disappear from sight.

"To throw off their scent," Aodren yells over his shoulder at me. "Stay with me."

Shards of icy water flick our feet and ankles.

In the distance, the bark of the dogs and shouts of men sound again.

The arrow has gone through my dress sleeve and the fleshy part of my arm, sticking out the other side. Though it hasn't hit bone, the jostling of the horse is killing me. It's causing more damage every time my arm bangs against my body or Aodren's.

Regardless of where Cohen and Omar may have gone, our goal at this point is survival. I need to get the arrow out while Gale's gait is relatively smooth.

Clenching my jaw and holding my breath, I bite one side of the arrow, then wrap my fingers around the other side of the shaft. On the count of three, I bear down and snap the wood in half.

Seeds!

I throw the fletching half on the ground and feel under my arm for the point side. My fingers are shaky. Breath saws through my lungs. I pluck the tip out, and my ears go fuzzy from the burst of agony. I hold tight to the edge of the saddle with my good arm, trying to fight the haziness filling my head. Blood oozes from the wound, seeping down the sleeve of my blue gown.

The stream curves, cutting farther south. Gale's front legs dip deep. He founders, and we're jolted forward. I manage to hang on to the back of the saddle, but Aodren flips over Gale's head and falls into the water with a great splash. He rises, short breaths punctuating his body's tremors from the icy plunge. I guide Gale to the side of the stream, looking back over my shoulder to make sure the remaining guard and dogs haven't caught up.

My brain races as I look over Aodren, sopping wet and shivering. He needs to get out of the wet clothes, but he doesn't have another change of clothes. All we have is a tarp and two bedrolls.

I reach back along Gale's flank, to where we secured our supplies. One of the blue rolls is gone, lost in our flight or in the stream.

I try not to show my panic as I tell Aodren to climb up

behind me. He can lean into my back for warmth while I get us farther away from the pursuers. Maybe the clouds will clear and the sun will dry his clothes.

"But your arm," he protests, pointing to the streaks of red coming down both sides of my sleeve.

I hold up my good hand. "I can manage."

Knowing we have little to no time, he scrambles up behind me and we set off.

I stay alert, putting as much distance between the remaining guard and us as I can. We cut across the main road to the southern woods and wind our way through the Evers to the most likely path Cohen might've taken.

Aodren said he heard the guards talking about a traitor in Cohen's midst and mention of the southeast cliffs. I keep all my thoughts at bay until we've gone two hours without any sign of our pursuers. We're near the path that leads to the cliffs.

Aodren hasn't stopped shivering. His cold has seeped into my ribs, where there is less fabric to my dress. While I'd hoped for sun, the clouds haven't cleared. I doubt his clothes will dry without a fire. I cannot stop thinking of all the warnings that Papa gave about keeping dry and warm during winter travel. It's been hours and I'm certain he's still wet. We need to find somewhere safe to set up camp. At the very least, I need to get him moving to keep his body temperature up.

"We should get down, look for tracks, perhaps find somewhere we can camp." I dismount and gesture for him to do the same. The adrenaline of the chase has worn off. The exhaustion from two nights spent in the dungeon without food is edging back in.

Aodren slides off Gale. "We cannot do anything until your arm is wrapped. You've lost so much blood." Aodren points to my dress's hem. "I could cut some off and use it for your wound."

Knowing it must be done, I hold my dress out for him, watching the way his hands shiver as he wraps one around his dagger and slices off part of my dress. He cuts the fabric in two pieces, one longer than the other. One piece wraps around my arm, and the other is constructed into a sling.

"Thank you." I cradle my arm even though it's held by the fabric. "But I'm worried about you. We need to find somewhere to make a fire."

Aodren pushes hair from my face. His fingers are ice. "Don't worry about me. I'll let you know if I get too cold. Anyway, you scared me today. I thought I might lose you."

I go to tell him that's not the case, but my words are stolen from me when he leans in and presses his chilled lips to my forehead. I understand why he kissed me in the castle. He wasn't thinking straight and it was reactionary. But this kiss? I don't know what to think. It settles in me, another layer of guilt.

I shift farther away. My head is hazy and my body tired and sore, but I press my point once more about needing to find camp so we can build a fire.

"It's barely past noon."

"You're freezing."

He lifts the shirt away from his body. "It's nearly d-d-dry."

The warmth of his words rings with truth. His clothes might be drying, but they're still damp and icy. His fingers are angry red, and his lips have a bluish tint. Physically, he's showing signs of being cold. Too cold.

I start to shake my head, to disagree, but he turns and strides away. "Finding Omar is our priority," he calls over his shoulder.

I roll my eyes. Who am I to argue with the king of Malam? If he's all right braving out the chill in damp clothing, there's not much I can do to stop the fool. And I thought Cohen was the only stubborn man in my life.

Tracking is easier in the frozen months because barren scrub oaks show damage from travel at a quick glance, instead of the scrutiny needed in the warm months. I move quickly, mindful of my injured arm in its sling, until I come across hoofprints and a bunch of broken branches.

Aodren approaches, his feet scraping along the frozen ground. He lacks the finesse of moving with any semblance of stealth. I wonder if he's always this way, or if his movements are jerky from the frozen river bath.

I gesture to the cluster of prints and damaged bushes. "Could belong to Omar and his men. I count about six sets."

He holds his arms crossed; his entire body shivers every few seconds, and his teeth chatter. "That's odd. B-b-because I'm certain there's another s-set over there."

My look of worry is silenced when he makes a show of pointing again. With a sigh, I follow the direction of his finger to the dense brush.

I don't tell him that he's probably mistaken. Maybe the cold's gotten to him. Or if he has found something, it's likely old, having been immortalized in the frosted ground until spring.

The brittle bush's thorns hook on my dress as I push between the leafless mounds to verify Aodren's find. He catches up to me, crunching the ground cover with every step.

"Perhaps you should stay there," I tell him.

"Yeah, perhaps." With a sheepish smile on his face, he wraps his arms around his body and stops moving. Which hits me with a touch of guilt for being so hard on the man. After all, it was because of him that we escaped.

The ground is dented with horseshoe prints. I squat down and run my good hand along them. Aodren was right. The ground is cold and hard, but there's still give to the dirt. The soil flakes in my fingers. This print could be recent.

"Do you think someone followed them?" Aodren asks, giving voice to the fear whispering in the back of my mind.

I hope not.

But I know these trails aren't traveled often. In the winter, they're mostly forgotten. The treacherous mountain passes and steep cliffs become impassable from the winter storms. The few logging towns that can be reached from this trail close down after autumn, ceasing trade until the summer months. If these are Cohen's tracks, not only do they have a traitor — they also have someone tailing them.

We mount Gale and continue onward.

The intensity of the day catches up to me. Along with Gale's monotonous walk, my body relaxes, to the point that I'm leaning against the king. It doesn't register in my mind until Gale starts downward, and then when our weight shifts, I realize how comfortable I've been in his presence.

I straighten. "I'm sorry."

"Don't apologize," he says over a yawn. "There's not much room to move. I don't expect you to sit with a rod in your back. Unless my damp clothes are making you uncomfortable." Which reminds me he stopped shivering a while ago.

"Are you dry now?"

"Almost."

Those words ring untrue. Even if I can't feel the chill of his clothes, I can sense the ice in his words. "You're still wet and cold?" I ask, knowing he must be suffering.

"If you lean closer, it'll warm me up."

True.

"Besides, the last time we were on a horse together, I'm certain you were the one holding me up," he adds. "I don't mind if you lean on me. Might as well make it even."

The idea of ever being even with the king of Malam is laughable. Though I've known him for only a month and a half, I have to wonder if sometimes he doesn't realize the importance of who he is.

"You rule a kingdom," I say. "You could take my land, my home, even my life. And somehow, I'd still owe you. That's how things work."

He doesn't talk for a while. "That was my father." His tone is pensive. I've not heard this from him before. "He treated the kingdom like a plaything. But that's not me. I'd hoped you would have seen that."

I wish I could turn back time and stop myself from making such a callous comment.

"I'm sorry. I have seen that." When he doesn't say anything more, I switch topics. "You came back for me."

"You sound surprised. You shouldn't be. I care about you. I wouldn't have left you to rot in the dungeon."

He cares about me? I don't need to ask because the truth of his statement warms me through. I try to keep my body relaxed so he doesn't notice how the sensation puts me on edge. Still, I cannot leave it alone. "Because we're bound together. That's why you care?"

"No, Britta. Not simply because of our connection."

Again, his truth burns through me, confusing everything I believed about the man. Not sure what to say in response, I return to asking him a dozen times over the next couple of hours if he's all right, if we should stop, if we should set up camp and start a fire. His response is "Keep going."

Gale maintains a quick pace until the light starts to fade. The temperature dips. Dark clouds move across the sky. The first few snowflakes start to fall.

It's then that Aodren wobbles in the saddle. His head falls back, resting in the crook of my neck. His skin is ice.

"Aodren? You doing all right? We should stop and set up camp now that it's starting to snow."

"Sotiredandcold" — his words slur together.

Seeds. I go on instant alert, knowing — even before Aodren's teeth stop chattering and his body slumps farther back so I'm balancing his weight — that we need to move rapidly. I made a terrible judgment in allowing us to continue this far. This is my fault.

"Aodren, hold on to my waist," I command, cinching tighter around him and talking into his chilled ear. "We're going to find somewhere to camp right now. Can you do that?"

I shouldn't have listened to his protests when I suggested we stop. I push Gale to pick up the pace as I scan the rocky face of the mountains for shelter. An empty shallow cave would do. Even if the idea of spending a night in one brings back dark memories, I bite back my fear. The man in front of me desperately needs warmth.

Gale comes up on a cave. Aodren rouses enough to hold himself up, so I dismount and lead the horse inside with the king still in the saddle. Aodren's head bobs side to side as I peruse the shelter. The cave goes back only a hundred paces, and there appear to be no animals using it as a residence. The ceiling is tall enough that we can safely build a fire.

Once I help Aodren dismount, he hobbles to the side of the cave and sits down, curling his limbs into himself. Worry is my constant companion as I leave him alone to gather wood and make a fire ring on the sandy floor of the cave. In our rush to leave Hagan's home, we didn't grab flint and steel.

I swallow back a cry of frustration. How foolish of me.

The branches have been exposed to frost for a month now. Most are too green to burn. It doesn't help that I'm limited to my non-dominant left hand and minimal use of my right hand. My head is hazy from exhaustion, but I cannot sit down, not until we have fire.

I find a few sticks that'll work and awkwardly grind them together, twisting and twisting as snow flurries start to float through the cave opening. My arm burns. My fingers go numb. I want to scream. The wind sings, promising a rough night if I cannot make any embers. My right arm throbs, pleading to stop, but I keep going.

A small spark and smoke plumes from the pile of wood-carvings I've circled around the spinning stick. Relieved, I push the carvings closer and blow into the pile, encouraging the flame to take. Once it sparks big enough to set in the dry kindling, I add bigger pieces of wood chips and shavings until the flame can support a log. For the first time since we left Hagan's home, I feel like I can take a steady breath.

It's not a big fire yet, but if Aodren slides close enough, he could start to warm at least his toes.

I glance up to tell him to come sit beside the fire ring.

He's slumped on his side.

"Aodren," I call out. He doesn't stir.

"Aodren?" I rush to him. He is colorless. *No, no, no.* "Please wake up. Aodren, please."

Nothing. Panic flares through me. I try to feel for his energy, but my hands are too stiff and numb. I cannot focus my hazy brain enough to try any sort of healing. Nor do I know if I have enough energy to spare.

I go into the survival mode I know best. I use my good hand to rip off his boots. Why didn't I have him take those off when we first got into the cave? I run my hand over his feet and realize how wet and frozen his toes still are. A sob breaks out of me.

"Wake up." I try again, squeezing his glacial flesh. Seeds, what a foolish mistake.

I lay the bedroll near the fire. Tear at my clothes. Bite my lip against the pain of each movement. Right now, pain is my punishment. I've been trained to keep dry and warm while traveling in the winter. I know the dangers involved. I should've demanded we stop earlier. I shrug out of the beast of a dress, crying out as the sleeve peels down my injured arm. The material can be another layer of added insulation. I toss it on the bedding and crouch over Aodren in only my chemise.

Using my teeth, I re-tie the bandage around my arm and set to work on his clothes. I push him on his side to yank off his tunic.

The man needs body warmth. He's slipped into dangerous sleep. The only way to get his body back to a safe temperature is skin-to-skin contact.

I reach for his trousers. But shock at the sight of his well-muscled chest stills my hands. The modest fire's flicker gives shape to his flat, toned stomach and strong arms. I push my new awareness of Aodren to the back of my mind and remember that this means his survival.

I don't look. I don't look anywhere lower than his chest as I tug his trousers down his legs. My arm smarts from the awkward chaotic maneuvering required to push his chilled body into the bedroll. Once he's under the layers, I climb inside and lie on top of the man, drawing the bedroll snug over us.

I don't think about what he's not wearing. All my focus is on warming his skin. Creating friction. I run my hands up and down his arms and over his chest. I wrap my body around his, hoping my warmth will seep through my thin chemise.

But he's so cold. Winter-lake cold.

I rub more vigorously, scrubbing his body with my own, ignoring the burn of my wound.

He groans. The sound nearly inspires tears.

Eyes closed, he turns his nose toward the fire. I take the small movement as a good sign and continue to run my hands along the strong lines of his face and plunge my fingers into his hair.

"Wake up, Aodren," I plead, full of hope. "Please, wake up."

I massage his torso, arms, shoulders, neck, and head, noticing tiny details I hadn't seen before. Like a small scar dissecting his right eyebrow. The stubble on his chin is a shade darker than his golden locks. The space between his shoulder and neck is . . . I slam my eyes closed. Stick to the task of warming him up.

Frigid hands find my waist and I yelp. Aodren's green eyes slide slowly open, piercing me with their intensity.

"Hello, Britta," he drawls.

It sounds wrong. It doesn't have Cohen's gravelly tenor. It makes me question what the hell I'm doing.

CHAPTER

37

AODREN

I'M NAKED.

"Hello, Britta," comes out a little slower and a lot more raspy than usual.

Britta's little feet find mine and start sliding vigorously over and under them. I think she's trying to warm my soles, but the movement only brings bouts of pinpricks.

"You have to get warm," I hear her say, but it's coming through a tunnel. And I'm so tired.

I yawn and fall deeper into this lovely, insane dream.

When I wake sometime later, it feels like the entire fire has been moved into the bedroll beside me. It's so wonderfully cozy. I blink, seeing Britta's face close to mine and wondering if I'm still asleep.

Why is Britta sleeping beside me?

Only, she's not sleeping. She keeps moving around, the lace of her dress scratching my stomach. Except, it's not a dress she's wearing. It's her underthings. And I'm . . . I'm naked. A vague recollection of already knowing this comes to mind.

Bewildered, I stare at her creamy shoulders, where freckles cascade over her curves like constellations. Gods, I could live beneath these stars forever.

She squirms on top of me. Her body heat scorches my skin, a sensation that would turn any man into an addict. I want to remind her of the fact that I'm currently without clothes. At the very least, I should have her stop moving. That's what a gentleman would do. But then I remember she must already know I'm naked since she must've been the one who stripped me down.

We're in a cave. I remember now coming inside with her, the chills turning my body heavy and sluggish, but I must've dozed off shortly after. Near the entrance of the cave, Gale stands with his head down. His saddle is propped against the curved wall. A small fire crackles an arm span from us.

Instead of thinking about how we're in a bedroll together and that Britta's lying on top of me, I focus on the fact that she took care of everything. Gratitude helps warm my core.

"Are you getting warm?" she whispers, her breath on my collarbone.

My head is stuffed with cotton. I don't trust myself to say anything so I nod.

She slides more to my side so her chest isn't resting on mine. Our legs are crossed, her feet still sliding lazily against mine. Despite the pricks of pain waking up my limbs, this is the best kind of agony.

She yawns, but I'm fully awake now.

"Can I ask you something?" She turns her hand into a fist where it rests on my chest. "Have you thought of me differently since you found out my mother is Phelia?"

I peel open her fingers. "No."

She looks down at me with wide, hopeful eyes.

"We are what we make of ourselves. You aren't your mother. Nor am I my father."

The interest on her face encourages me to continue. At the very least, it helps me forget the state of undress I'm in. "We don't have to live their sins or walk the terrible paths they carved before us. Every choice I make, every action, is mine. Whether I succeed or fail, it will be because I chose that path. I'll never judge you for anything other than your choices. And I hope you'll do the same for me."

Her lips slacken into soft curves.

"You know, you're not the man I thought you were. I—I'm ashamed to say I misjudged you. Can we start again?"

I grin at her. And when her gaze catches on my mouth, I nearly shove her away before I do something that will ruin this moment. She's not ready to know I'm falling for her. The way she reacted when I kissed her forehead tells me as much. Even if I wish that weren't the case.

"Name's Aodren." I lift my hand for her to shake. "I live just outside Brentyn."

She chuckles, her warm body vibrating torturously against my chest. "Britta." She moves so she can lift her good arm, sliding her palm into mine. At the touch, when she realizes my hand is still so cold that it lacks mobility, a small frown forms on her face. "What a coincidence, I live just outside Brentyn too. Seems we have much in common."

I hold her hand a tad too long before I let it slide from my grasp.

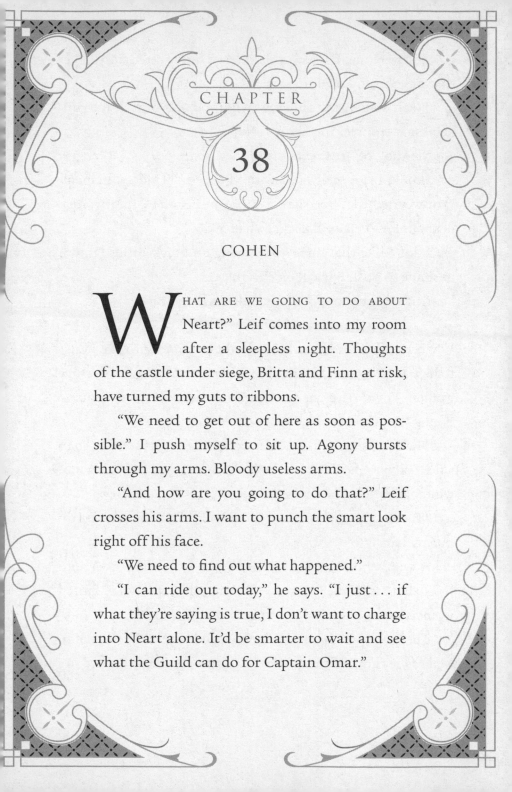

CHAPTER

38

COHEN

WHAT ARE WE GOING TO DO ABOUT
Neart?" Leif comes into my room
after a sleepless night. Thoughts
of the castle under siege, Britta and Finn at risk,
have turned my guts to ribbons.

"We need to get out of here as soon as possible." I push myself to sit up. Agony bursts
through my arms. Bloody useless arms.

"And how are you going to do that?" Leif
crosses his arms. I want to punch the smart look
right off his face.

"We need to find out what happened."

"I can ride out today," he says. "I just . . . if
what they're saying is true, I don't want to charge
into Neart alone. It'd be smarter to wait and see
what the Guild can do for Captain Omar."

If it were me, I'd leave this instant, no matter the danger that lies ahead. I tell him this.

"Yeah, well, Britta's always saying you get yourself into unnecessary trouble. You're too reckless."

Mention of Britta hits me in the chest.

"Look, I can see you're worried for her." Understatement. "I'm worried too. But she's a survivor. Let the Guild women heal Omar. Then we'll decide what to do."

I don't like that we're not moving on quicker. But I'm not in shape to push my will on this matter.

Leif's right about one thing. Britta is a survivor.

When Katallia said the Guild would be coming to the house to help Captain Omar, I imagined she meant more than three women. They arrive one at a time, their arrivals spaced out, no doubt, for precaution.

The first is a petite slip of a woman, less threatening than a field rabbit. She flits into the room, bringing in a big blast of winter air before she shuts the door.

"Torima, an expert water Channeler," Katallia says, introducing her.

A wide smile pushes Torima's sun-weathered skin into lines that frame her mouth. Like Katallia, the sandy-haired woman seems a few years younger than my mother.

The second is Yasmin. Wise eyes and skin like terra cotta. Makes me think of the great cedars that hunker in Shaerdan's dry lands, refuges from the blazing heat. "A gifted earth Channeler," Katallia says of the older woman.

An hour after the first two show up, a third enters the home. No knock beforehand. Her skin is as dark as night. Her eyes shrewd and cold as flint. Snow drifts inside on her heels, but melts before it touches her skin.

"Seeva, welcome." Katallia rushes to greet her, nearly turning over the table where I've been biding the time by playing cards with Leif and Lirra. Lirra is on her feet in a heartbeat, straightening her tunic.

"Seeva Soliel, the fire Channeler," Katallia says, with a touch of reverence.

This must be the mother of Rhea, the girl we saved from Lord Conklin and delivered to Jacinda.

The other women, who've gone off into other parts of the home, return. Yasmin first. She greets the women nonverbally and takes a seat beside me. Torima follows, flitting to embrace the newcomer.

"Thank you for coming," Lirra says. "I fear the captain will not make it another night."

Seeva's mouth pinches. "Then perhaps its best that he dies."

I sit up, on the defense. "What's this about?" My gaze kicks from the fire Channeler to Katallia. "I thought you said they'd help." Why are we still waiting at this home if they're not going to assist? We should be on our way to Brentyn.

"Cohen," Leif warns.

Seeva's gaze hones in on me. "Ah, you must be the honored bounty hunter." Her assessment drips with disdain, turning my usually respected title into an insult. "Perhaps you think we'll cower to you because you know what we are? That we'll jump to your aid?"

"Not what I said," I argue.

"Perhaps you shouldn't talk," Leif says out of the corner of his mouth, always acting the part of the tamed bear.

Lirra's fingers dig into my arm. "Don't be a fool."

I scoot away from her. Jacinda must not have told this woman who saved her daughter. I doubt she'd be talking to us like this if she knew. "Look, I agreed to keep all of your secrets—"

"The girl's right—you are a fool," Seeva sneers at me, her hand rising in front of her. A ball of fire hovers above her palm. "You're not helping us, hunter. We could destroy you and your broken captain," she snaps, and the flame zips out, "like that. You've no leg to stand on. Not when Malam's castle has been taken and your king is probably dead."

Her words give me pause. What does she know of King Aodren? I stand, frustration rolling off me like steam. "I've helped you plenty."

Before I can finish, Katallia steps between us, arms raised. "We've agreed to not make rash judgments. Let us help the captain, and then we'll discuss what you can do for us."

Despite last night's temperature drop, the room grows

warm from all the bodies and the fire. I fan myself while the ladies chat.

"Let me remind you that, last we met, we discussed an alliance." Katallia turns to Seeva. "There is no one better to have supporting our plight than the captain of the guard and the king's bounty hunter. Especially if the country is in turmoil."

The fire Channeler's eyes flick to me. Sweat beads at my temples.

"They've been our enemy for eighteen years," Seeva says. "I don't trust a single man from Malam."

"The hunter is a sympathizer. I can see he respects our magic. Perhaps an alliance with him would be beneficial." This comes from Yasmin. Finally a voice of reason.

I move my tunic away from my body and start to fan myself harder. My ribs twinge, complaining at the movement, but it's too hot to stop. Lirra shoots me a look that says, *Sit still, idiot.*

"Why haven't you told her we saved her daughter?" I whisper.

"I haven't had the time. Be patient. Stop squirming."

Easy for her to say. Perspiration pools on my upper lip.

". . . we will heal him. It is our way. Do good, never harm," Yasmin is saying, only the heat is too much. I wipe the sweat off my brow and neck. Consider running outside into the snow that piled up from last night's storm.

"Cohen, what are you—" Lirra jumps up to stand in front

of me. Her arms lift and a breeze swirls around me, taking the edge off the heat.

"Seeva." Katallia's tone scolds. "Cease. You won't have enough energy for the healing."

Instantly, the heat disappears. I turn to Seeva, anger brimming as my body cools. She just did something to my body temperature.

"Oh, Seev." Torima's singsong voice sounds more like she's talking to a small child instead of a woman who just tried to boil my insides. "We're here to assist. Come, let's find the captain before you use up all your energy on the hunter."

"We can help you, or we can hurt you. Remember that" is all the fire Channeler says before exiting the room. No apology for trying to turn me into a loaf of bread. Nothing.

"Look, I don't appreciate you trying to bake me," I yell after her, furious. "I saved your daughter. A little gratitude would be nice."

Seeva appears in the doorway. "You saved Rhea?" Her voice is a sliver of what it was before.

I nod.

I don't need to speak because Lirra launches into a rapid explanation of what happened in Shaerdan, and how Rhea was dropped off at Jacinda's home. While Lirra talks, the muscles in Seeva's face shift to something softer. Kinder.

"For that, I am grateful," Seeva says, once the story is concluded, her tone void of ire. "I will help your captain. And, as you've so nicely put it, stop trying to bake you."

Seeva turns and disappears. She doesn't offer an apology, but I don't expect one. I'm no stranger to pride, having buckets of my own.

Lirra gets up, and when she returns, she has a waterskin. "Drink this; you'll need to replenish yourself."

Leif stands. "Guess you learned your lesson." He chuckles, shakes his head, and follows the women to Omar's room.

If my body wasn't broken, I'd punch him.

But Leif's right. Lesson learned. I won't underestimate Seeva's power or that of any of the women in the Guild again. I reach Omar's room and squeeze in alongside Leif, Lirra, and the Channelers.

The women gather around the bed, and each one touches Omar in a different place. Katallia's palm covers the man's mouth, Yasmin's fingers touch Omar's collarbone, Torima's hand rests below his navel, and Seeva's holds his head.

Their heads dip, except for Seeva, whose mouth opens as she looks toward the ceiling. "Gods of old, grant us the energy to give this man, that he might walk again in this world."

Then her head bows and the women begin a collective chant.

Never having witnessed anything like this, I stand there, mesmerized.

A cough breaks their words. The women step back, and Omar hacks again. His eyes crack open. He looks as hazed as a tavern rat, but it's one of the best looks I've seen on him in a while.

Relief has me rushing forward, reaching for the man's arm with my good one, verifying he's alive even though his skin burns under my touch. "Thought we were going to lose you."

Leif is slack-jawed. "Praise the gods, you're going to live."

Omar takes a labored breath. "Not . . . so . . . sure . . . yet."

"He'll need a couple more days." Katallia sounds drained. "We each used our gifts. Pushed air in and out of his lungs and into his blood. Moved his blood faster through his body. Encouraged the bone to re-knit, and raised his body temperature to fight the infection."

"We don't have a couple more days," I say. "We have to get to Brentyn."

She taps Omar's shoulder. "I'm sorry, but he needs time. While we can encourage his body to make those changes, we don't have the energy to replenish what he's lost."

"Like a Spiriter would?" When Britta healed me, it was instant. Figured their healing would be the same for Omar.

"You know about Spiriters?"

Behind Katallia, all eyes of the others shift to me.

"Well, yeah. Been tracking one for the last six weeks before this mess."

"You've been hunting Channelers?" Seeva steps forward.

I move back. No shame in that. "Hold on, we're after the same person. You want the people who are kidnapping your girls. I'm pretty sure one of those people is a woman who goes by the name Phelia. She's a Spiriter who was working for the high lord of Malam to control the king."

Seeva's eyes narrow to slits. "You lie."

"It's true. Ask the captain. There was an attack on King Aodren a couple of weeks back by the very same Spiriter. The king saw girls with her at the time of the attack. And before that, Phelia bound the king's energy to her own so she could control him."

"How do you know these things, hunter? Did she tell you?"

While I might tell Aodren's secret, I won't tell Britta's. And I know the captain won't either, because he promised. "A woman named Enat told me about the Spiriter who put the king under a Channeler bind. I later discovered it was Phelia."

Murmurs move through the women. They've heard of Enat.

"If she is indeed part of the group taking our young, then she'll be dealt with by the Guild," Seeva says, dismissing the conversation. "For now, you must swear an oath to us. As agreed, we've saved your captain and spared your lives. But when we move forward to overturn the Purge Proclamation, we want your support.

"Do you swear an oath?" Seeva takes in each of us. The wind cries through the home's cracks. A flurry of snow batters the window.

Omar is the first to speak. "We do."

"We do," I repeat. I think of Britta in that moment, and what this may mean for her. The last thing I want is to draw more negative attention in her direction. But I hope like hell she can see I'm doing this to bridge the gap between our two worlds.

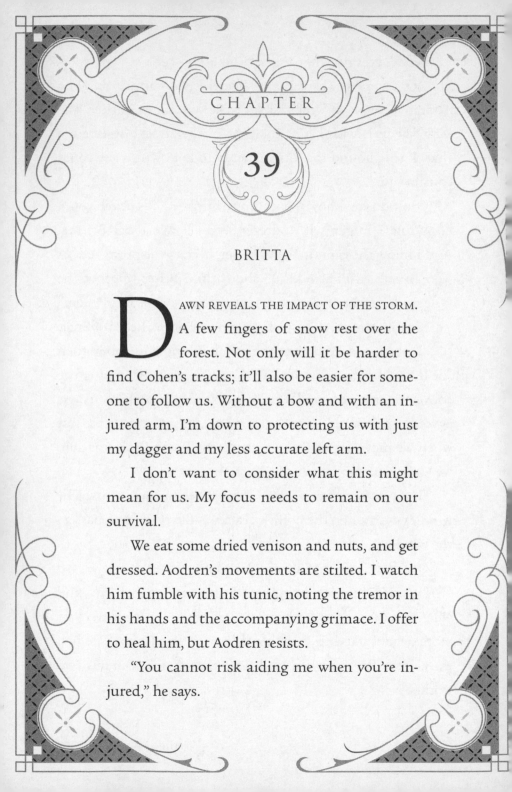

CHAPTER

39

BRITTA

D AWN REVEALS THE IMPACT OF THE STORM.
A few fingers of snow rest over the
forest. Not only will it be harder to
find Cohen's tracks; it'll also be easier for someone to follow us. Without a bow and with an injured arm, I'm down to protecting us with just
my dagger and my less accurate left arm.

I don't want to consider what this might
mean for us. My focus needs to remain on our
survival.

We eat some dried venison and nuts, and get
dressed. Aodren's movements are stilted. I watch
him fumble with his tunic, noting the tremor in
his hands and the accompanying grimace. I offer
to heal him, but Aodren resists.

"You cannot risk aiding me when you're injured," he says.

I let my suggestion drop because there's no time for me to rest and recoup my energy, and there's no telling what dangers we may face today. However, guilt pricks at my resolution when Aodren stands, walks stiffly toward Gale, and fails at lifting his foot into the stirrup. He tries to stifle a groan.

I need to find him somewhere warm to sleep tonight so he can heal from the winter exposure.

We ride Gale south as more clouds roll in overhead. Aodren sits behind me, holding on to my waist as best he can with numb hands.

For the first part of our journey, neither of us talks. It's so much harder to converse with him this morning. I don't know if it's our connection stealing all my words, or the fact that we're alone, or that I've seen him unclothed. Seeds, memories of last night burn my cheeks. The only man I thought I'd ever see unclothed was Cohen. But I cannot unsee Aodren, and every time I twist around to say something to him, my foolish blush is our constant companion.

Survival, I tell myself. Aodren wouldn't have made it through the night.

When Aodren asks me about my childhood, I latch on to the distraction. I talk about Papa, Cohen, training to hunt, and growing up in Brentyn. I tell him about the time Cohen and I got into a scuffle with some boys over a bag of apples. "There's a tree half on Papa's property and half on royal lands. As we picked Papa's apples, I got it in my head that the ones on the other side of the tree were better. So I picked some, but a couple of boys from town saw me. They told me if I didn't give them all the apples, they'd turn me into the guard."

"And did you?"

I move my head side to side. "No, but I gave one a black eye. Cohen told the other kid that if they said a word about the fruit or me, we'd come after them that night."

He laughs. "Ah, so you were brazen and friends with a bully."

"Cohen isn't a bully—he's just . . . protective." A warm smile spreads across my face. He was definitely an intimidator when needed. Which is why he makes such a great bounty hunter. It's also why he made such a good friend. I always felt safe. Cherished.

Aodren seems to mull over what I've said, pausing long enough that it almost tips into awkward silence. "You've been friends a long time."

"I cannot imagine what my life would've been like without him." All the guilt I've been holding at bay comes back full force. If I could do things over, I would. I'd be honest with Cohen about my bond to Aodren. I hate that I kept it a secret at all. It's such a silly thing to keep hidden from the man I love. I'd have more faith in our relationship instead of allowing my insecurities to guide my decisions.

"I'm glad he's there for you." His words register with conflicting temperatures. Truth and lie. "True friends are the one commodity unavailable to royalty."

"What do you mean?" I twist to look at him.

"I had Jamis as my regent—but as you can see, the man's a cunning snake. And I had Omar, who is as warm and kind as he is now."

"What about the nobles? Weren't you friends with any of them?"

Gale steps over a fallen log, jostling us. My arm twinges, but it's not as awful as it was yesterday. Enat told me that Spiriters heal faster than other people because we naturally absorb energy from the world around us. I hope that's the case. I need my shooting arm to heal.

Aodren's sigh hits my neck. "The castle is full of people. Nobles constantly in pursuit of gaining my favor. Or others who are unwilling to approach me because they believe if they glance the wrong way at me they'll be sent to the dungeon."

I shiver at the thought of going there ever again.

Aodren mistakes my body language for a temperature drop. His arms wrap tighter around my waist, eliminating any remaining space between us. My skin soaks in the heat of his touch like a sponge. Survival mode and all.

"I'm cold, and I cannot keep myself on the back edge of this saddle much longer," he says. "Nor do I think it's necessary since we've, well, shared a bed."

I laugh at the awkwardness of his comment. "Yes, we did."

Sometime between escaping the castle and now, I've stopped thinking of him as the king of Malam. He's surprisingly easy to be around. I imagine, had we grown up in different situations, we would've been friends.

"So, you picked royal apples?" Aodren jabs me in the ribs. I jerk out of my thoughts and throw a scowl at him. "That means you stole from me, Miss Flannery."

I burst out laughing. "Yes, well, add that to the list of things I owe you to make us even."

"As far as I'm concerned, I'll always be in your debt. So consider the apple tree yours."

"Aodren." I clear my throat. "You said you don't have any friends, but that's not true. I—I consider you a friend."

"Because of the bond?" Uncertainty laces his tone.

I've not wanted to cross any lines in our relationship, but last night trampled that idea. I sigh. "Even without the bond, I can see that you're a good man."

"Do you think you'll ever want more than friendship?"

He doesn't have to say *with me*. Despite my inexperience with men, I can see the way he watches me and feel the tension between us. And he kissed me. Only one other man has touched his lips to mine. I glance down at Aodren's arm, locked around me. He has strong arms, like Cohen. Cohen, the one man who's ever shown romantic interest in me. While Aodren's unprompted kindness and mention of something more is flattering, it pushes my heart onto an offbeat and sends me into a confusing spin. So lamely, I say, "I don't know."

Seeming to accept my answer, he falls silent.

Neither one of us talks again until we reach the cliffs and dismount. With the recent snowfall, it's difficult to see any tracks. We split up to hasten our effort, both prowling around the edge of the cliff searching for any recent sign of passage.

"Britta . . ." Aodren's voice quakes in a way that causes me to still. At first, I think it's the cold freezing his hands again. He's been holding them close to his body or mine all day. But I watch as he stiffly shuffles toward me and points at the ground where my boots have kicked through the snow. Beneath my print, a deep red crust is hiding on the cliff. "I think that's blood."

I inspect the mark closer, the faintest metallic scent grating my nostrils. My fingernails dig into my palms. *Please don't let it be Cohen.*

If the blood is from someone in his group, they would've needed to see a healer right away. Right now we're equally far from a town we've already passed and one of the mountain villages. Both are perhaps seven leagues away. Knowing Cohen, he would've chosen to move onward. I suggest we continue to the logging town of Tahr. If we hurry, we might make it there by nightfall. The idea of a warm inn for Aodren and possibly finding information on Cohen puts some more push in my movements.

However, when sunset comes, we're still a few leagues from the town, and thick gray clouds linger overhead, blocking the moonlight. A crisp, earthy scent fills the air. It's the promise of another snowstorm.

With no cave in sight, we have no choice but to set up

camp. For coverage, we throw Hagan's woven tarp over a low-hanging branch and then secure the ends out to scrub brush. Since there's only the one bedroll, Aodren lays it in the middle of the sheltered ground. That done, we take a seat on a large rock outside the tent and make supper of the remaining dried venison.

"I saw Cohen's scars once," Aodren says, staring up at the clouds.

I finish chewing my last bit of meat and remain silent, confused by his seemingly random confession.

His gaze turns to meet mine. He brushes his hand over the stubble around his mouth, dusting off invisible crumbs. "Did you save him as well?"

I chew my lip. I've never talked about what happened with the mountain cat to anyone other than Cohen and Enat. But I want to be honest with him, so I tell Aodren about the past.

When I finish the story, Aodren turns to face me. "I'm sorry if, in asking you about Cohen, I've overstepped the bounds of our friendship. When I saw his scars, I noticed their similarity to mine."

"No, it's fine. I—I just haven't talked about it much. There aren't many people I trust."

"Am I one of those people now?"

"Yes, you are."

His shoulders rise and fall in a deep breath. "Did healing Cohen change your relationship? Were you closer after?"

I'm not sure where his questions are leading. "We're not together because of that."

"No, of course not." His leg slides closer to mine.

"I love Cohen," I say, needing him to know.

Something flickers across his face. "Yes, I imagined you did. I only meant that what you did could bring friends together in a unique way. And I've noticed how he always watches out for you."

A sour taste coats my palate. "Yeah, well, he wants to keep me safe."

He pushes off the rock and turns to face me. "Is that what you want? Do you want to be kept?"

I don't answer.

Aodren's comment burrows into my thoughts. Cohen has proven that he'll go to great, frustrating lengths for me. And in return, I've reacted with anger that has always felt justified.

But if I flip the statement around, putting myself in Cohen's place, I know undoubtedly that I'd do whatever was necessary to protect Cohen. And I have.

The first snowflake lands on my nose. I touch it and then hold out my hand, palm flat, to catch a few more. When I was fourteen, Cohen stayed out all night with me to enjoy the season's first snowstorm. The night earned him a cold that lasted weeks. He wouldn't let me feel bad about his illness. Instead he said, *I would've stayed out two nights, if you'd asked.* I told him he was mad. He said, *Only for you.*

But I never allowed us to linger in the snow after that. I worried that he would catch the same illness.

Now as I follow the teeny white flakes falling slowly from the sky, I'm sad that this is the first time I've just sat and watched them since that night with Cohen. And though Aodren is here with me, it isn't the same. Some things cannot be replaced.

CHAPTER

40

AODREN

"A NOTHER STORM IS COMING THIS WAY. MAYBE A bigger one." Britta's hair, having fallen on her shoulders earlier, now flies around her face.

A gust of wind smacks against the tent. One side of the tarp flips up, and the securing band snaps in half.

We both rush to opposite sides of the tent. Britta reaches for the corner and winces. Her arm is still giving her trouble, which is likely because she never stops moving it around. Though it's not nearly as bad as I figured it would be. For having only sustained the injury yesterday, I'm impressed how fast she's healing. Especially since my hands are still numb and cold, and my feet feel as though they've been pricked with a hundred needles.

"You're going to injure yourself further. Allow me to do this." I move to her side. I fumble with the tent edge and grimace when my fingers won't properly obey.

Britta rolls her eyes and then draws a dagger from her boot. She starts cutting pieces of a nearby bush. Despite the pain, which is made obvious only by the flicker in her facial expression, she moves quickly. "These firebushes keep their green core all winter. That makes them difficult to cut. Also they're hard for the wind to break."

Using her boots to hold the branch in place, she whittles off the shoots until it looks like a thin whip. She tosses it to me, tells me to fortify the rope to tie the tarp down, and starts on a second branch.

It's times like this that she reminds me most of her father.

I take the stick and wind it through the hole of the tarp. It takes a few tries to get my fingers to do what I want, but I manage to tie it to the protruding woody root of a bush. It seems like it's been growing for quite some time and would be harder to uproot. After giving it a sturdy yank, I look up to find that Britta has shaped the remaining branches and has secured the other sides of the tent. I shoot her a sheepish grin. She frowns at my hands and mutters something that sounds like "one more night."

With Britta's help, I take the saddle off Gale. I brush him down and have him follow me to a place beside the tent where he can lie down. He won't be able to fit under the tarp with us, so I cover him with the saddle blanket.

Storms like this, with all the energy kicking through the air, have always made me feel more alive. I used to sit in my secret room and watch the storms rage around the tower. Of course, I made sure to wear warmer clothes and enjoy the comforts afforded to royalty. But the zing in the air feels the same now as it did back then. I don't think I could fall asleep anytime soon.

Britta hasn't said much since the snow started falling. The flakes are beautiful, in a world-slowing way, but also very cold. I fold my arms and tuck my hands close to my ribs to keep them protected.

We climb into the tent and sit across from each other, neither one of us moving to climb in the bedroll. I curl my knees to my chest and wrap my arms around them. The trousers are dry now, though I cannot seem to stay warm. The only time I've felt like the cold wasn't going to rattle me apart was when Britta and I were pressed together.

Outside the tent, winter is a lone wolf. The wind kicks up and howls around us.

It's a warning song of the brutal night that lies ahead.

Britta shifts her attention from the opening of the tent to me. "You're shivering."

"Y-yes, well, the cold and all."

She frowns. "It's too dangerous to build a fire out in the

open. Plus it's too windy now." Her eyes carry to the slits in the tent opening where the wind's icy fingers slide in. Then she looks back at me and chews her lip. "I can handle sharing a bedroll. Can you?"

I nod, trying to go for subtle, as if I haven't been praying for her to ask that question.

Her eyes flash to the bottom of her dress, which is damp from the snow and up to me. Another tremor racks through me.

"You'll be warmer if we share body heat . . . like last night," she says, though it comes out more as a question than a statement. She stares hard at the bedroll.

It's all I need as motivation to shrug off my tunic. I'm not ashamed to admit that I'm bitter cold and right now her body heat is as essential as food and water.

Her eyes flare, but she turns and starts to undo the ties of her dress.

"That would be good. The storm is getting worse," I say, to reassure her. She's as skittish as a new lord coming to his first day of court. It's one more night. We don't want to freeze to death tonight.

Not when we could possibly find Omar and Cohen tomorrow. Once I meet with Omar, we can plan how to take back Brentyn and Castle Neart. I'll decide which troops to gather. I'm not sure word has reached the fiefdoms about the lords who have died. Britta's comment about me being able to take whatever I wanted since I'm the king has stuck with me. The thought of seizing soldiers from a fallen noble's fiefdom and forcing them to fight for me without their fealty doesn't sit right. Even if it's the way of kings, the last thing I want to do is become the tyrant my father was. I won't be like him.

Britta tosses her dress on top of the bedroll. I follow it with my trousers and tunic. Then I quickly climb into the bedroll so I don't embarrass her further with my lack of dress. She's left standing in a body-hugging chemise that traces her hips and the rounds of her breasts and—

Gods, I have to stop staring.

"This connection between us," I forge ahead as she crawls into the bedroll and lies down beside me. Her eyes are turned upward while mine follow the lines of her face. "I know what you did for me was an extraordinary gift. One I'll never take for granted. It's not my intention to edge out Cohen."

She twists to face me. "You want to discuss that *now?*" A startled laugh puffs from her pale rose lips. "Right, then. You say my honesty is brazen. I'm not going to lie. The bond to you has been an adjustment. It came at a price I didn't realize I was going to have to pay."

I know Britta would never jeopardize her relationship with Cohen. It's clear by the way she talks about him that she loves him. However, I wonder if she'll ever see me past the bond. Will she recognize that I appreciate her rugged resilience? She may be slight, may appear breakable, but if there was ever a woman who could weather any storm, it'd be her.

Shivers make my body convulse while she's still leaning away from me, considering our conversation. Without asking,

I snake my arm around her and tug her over to me so our bodies are lined up. She lets out a surprised *oof*. I need the warmth right now. My hands itch to run over her back and along the curve of her hip, but I keep them fisted.

"I used to have a similar connection with Cohen," she admits after a beat. I feel her ribs expand and contract against mine. Her hands move, sliding over my chest and shoulders, then back down my arms. She mutters something about my icicle body before continuing with our conversation. "But when I saved you, it was broken. I don't know if it was because he gave me some of his energy to save you. Or if I can only be connected to one person at a time. That's the hardest thing for me. I don't know how this happened between us. Or how to end it. I spent the first while being angry at you for taking away what I had with Cohen."

"And now?"

"Now, I'm getting used to it," Britta says, hands pausing.

"So what will happen to us?"

She rests her forehead against my shoulder and turns her chin down so I cannot see her face. "I don't know. I wish I knew more about my ability. But the only Spiriter offering to teach me is bent on killing you." Her left hand ventures across my torso and then back to her side as if she cannot decide where to place it.

"Your mother?"

"Please don't call her that."

I flatten her fluttering hand to my chest, like pinning a

butterfly. "My father was a monster, remember? There's no shame in wanting even the smallest understanding of her."

"Thanks for saying that." Her voice drops to a whisper. "I think you're the only one who understands."

I wish I could erase the furrow in her brow. I imagine she's thinking of Cohen. That makes me come to my senses and release her hand.

"Good night, Britta." I roll to my side, facing away.

41

COHEN

IN KATALLIA'S MAIN ROOM, WE'RE ALL GATHERED around the fire, aside from Omar, who sleeps upstairs. Leif returned from town minutes ago. When he entered the home, snow clung to his hair. Now, as he addresses our group, it melts into drops that stain the shoulders of his tunic.

"Lord Jamis gathered his followers and planned a rebellion, starting with the castle," he begins. He launches into the story, sharing what he gathered in town. There's no way to lessen the gravity of Castle Neart being taken. We all sit around, stunned into silence at the lengths that Jamis, the power-hungry, blood-spilling madman, has been willing to go for control. The country would be in better hands if the Akarians from the south were to take over.

We need to fortify our group and lead a counterattack. We need to get inside Neart and see if there are any survivors. And see if we can find King Aodren, who's apparently missing. We need to put him back on the throne.

After experiencing Seeva's ability to manipulate temperature, I have no doubt these women would be a boon in the fight to take back Brentyn and Castle Neart.

I say this, and the women share a disdainful snort.

"What you're telling us may be the best news this country's had in eighteen years." Seeva stands in front of the fire, eclipsing the light.

"What?" The fire Channeler has lost her damn seeds. *Best news?* Horse dung.

"Lord Jamis has been a quiet supporter of Channelers," Yasmin cuts in, in her low, straightforward way. She pushes back in a rocking chair. Forward and back. "How do we know you're telling the truth about him being involved in the kidnappings? Lord Conklin was arrested for those, and the man hasn't named Jamis. Perhaps his intentions in taking the castle were for the benefit of the people."

Snow continues to fall outside the window, the piles now calf deep. Torima, who is curled beside the fireplace on an overstuffed cushion *ahem*s. "It's a horrific way to force new leadership, but—"

"But nothing." A growl tears out of my throat. "The man murdered half the nobility. At least one hundred people."

If I were in any condition to travel to Brentyn, I'd have left the second Katallia mentioned the rebellion. Britta knows how to stay safe. Despite my tendency to worry for her and go to ridiculous lengths to protect her, there isn't anyone I'd trust more with my life and my brother's life than Britta. Our last conversation comes to mind, and a hit of guilt gets me because I doubt she knows this. Doubt she realizes that when my life's full of upheaval, knowing she's a survivor is the one thing that keeps me sane.

"What kind of man can disconnect himself from humanity enough to massacre an entire group of people?" I scoot to the edge of a wood chair, elbows resting on my knees.

"You speak of the nobles' deaths as if we do not know brutality." Seeva stares down at me, eyes sparking like flint on steel. "In this kingdom, soldiers from every fiefdom have hunted our kind for sport for eighteen years. They've stolen daughters. Tortured mothers. The deaths of Channelers outnumber the hundred you speak of by more than a thousand. You tell me, hunter. What kind of men can disconnect themselves from humanity to murder thousands of women and girls?"

The validity of her point strikes firm — a hammer shaping a blade after it's been pulled from a forge's fire. The grief in her words pounds into me and profoundly shapes my perspective of the women who have suffered from the Purge.

I take a moment before answering. "I see how the Channelers have suffered, and I am so very sorry. I agree, change needs to happen. We cannot go on like this. All I ask is that you listen to me when I say Jamis is not the change you want."

Yasmin's chair creaks. She rocks back, rocks forward. "That may be. But until we know the truth of what happened, it wouldn't be sound to choose sides."

I push off my chair and pace away from the fire, having had enough heat today.

"What of our oath?" Leif asks the women.

"Your oath to us doesn't require us to vow ourselves to your cause. We've already helped you." That comes from Katallia.

"Aunt Kat!" Lirra stares at the woman like she's just admitted to aiding Lord Jamis. "We have to help."

"I'm sorry, Lirra. So far I've given you all the help you've asked for. Without question. I let you into this safe house with royal guards, knowing it could mean my death. What you're asking now is too much." Katallia's eyes flick to the other women in the room. "The Guild may discuss this matter further, but your input"—she looks pointedly at me and Leif—"is no longer wanted. You're welcome to stay while your captain is recovering. But once he's on the mend, I expect you to go."

We sit, shocked silent, as the women file out of the room. Their footsteps echo down the hall to another room. The door latches closed. Voices begin. I can pick out Seeva's cold tone and Yasmin's measured cadence, but no words.

"You all should rest." Lirra stands and rubs her hands on her skirt. She gives me a pointed look. "And you won't heal if you don't lie down and put salve on your wounds."

I move my arm to demonstrate how quickly I'm healing. "What's in that salve? It's taken the edge off the pain."

She nods to the closed door. "You should ask Yasmin. It's from her collection of herbs. But yes, it speeds up the healing."

It's nothing compared to what Britta did, but I'm grateful nonetheless.

When I don't move, she says, "Standing there isn't going to convince the Guild."

"Yeah, yeah." I turn away from the door. "Any idea what could?"

She shakes her head and leads me to the room we've been sharing. Although, now that I think about it, I've been sleeping on the bed. Don't know where Lirra's been resting.

"Do you really need them?" she asks. "Couldn't you reach out to the nearest fiefs, build an army, and fight your way back into Brentyn and the castle?"

"You make that sound so simple." I sit down on the bed and try to hide my wince. "What you're proposing takes time. Takes organization." I blow out a breath. I think of Finn and his freely given smile that's all gums and teeth. I don't want to wonder about where he is right now, because all I will do is spend the rest of the night worrying. "That's time I don't have."

Lirra points at the bed as if to say, *Lie down*.

I do as requested.

"I'm going to talk to my aunt. See if I can change the Guild's mind into helping us."

I like how she uses the term *us*. It says something about

Lirra, that she's willing to fight for this cause even if her aunt isn't.

"Hey, Lirra, I'm sorry I still haven't found Orli. I didn't plan for things to go this way."

She shrugs. "Does life ever go as planned? Besides, I figure we know exactly where Orli is now. She must be at the castle since that's where Jamis and Phelia are."

Lirra gently lowers herself onto the mattress, so as to make it move less. I wonder if she's doing this to spare me some pain, or if she's suddenly feeling shy about our proximity.

The thing is, Lirra's a beautiful girl. Her big eyes and pretty face could lure any man looking to be lured.

I'm not.

Someone shoves my shoulder, and ache runs through my torso. Nothing as bad as a few days ago, but it gets me to crack my eyes open.

The room's dark. Moonlight's pouring in through the window. Lirra's on my bed, kind of hovering over me.

I rub my eyes. "What's going on?" A yawn stretches out my words.

"Word just came. A man and a woman matching Britta's and Aodren's descriptions were sighted earlier today by one of the Guild's confidants not far from here, just off the road through the woods. Maybe a few leagues away." Her voice is a quick roll of words, one tumbling out after the other.

I sit up with a jolt and, *damn,* pain cracks me under the armpit. I shake it off and stand, searching for my boots. "Let's go."

I knew Britta would make it out. "Get Leif," I tell Lirra.

Leif comes striding in, looking sleepy but ready to go a couple of minutes later. Five more after that, the three of us are out the door, saddled up, and riding east.

Following the directional tip Katallia received from her confidant, Leif and I keep our eyes peeled to the woods. Snow has dropped as deep as my knees. Knowing most of it fell overnight, I doubt Britta would've risked traveling. Since there are no caves in these hills, Britta most likely looked for a tall tree that has some branch coverage against the storm. We press on, keeping our eyes open for a camp setup.

We don't risk calling out for them in case they've been followed. Wouldn't want to alert Jamis's men.

The horses cut through the fresh snowpack easily enough, but the dense white seems endless. Siron tips his head up, ears flicking forward.

"What's there, boy?" I rub his neck.

He runs straight at the trees and then slows. I lean on my good hand to slide off the saddle so I can take a look around. As soon as my boots hit the ground, I see the flap of a tarp by the base of a tree, where the snowfall is lightest. She was always the smarter one of us when it came to survival.

Emotion burns my throat. Must be the overwhelming relief at finding her after all we've both been through. I take the ten strides to the tent in five steps. I crouch, peel back the tarp, and —

"What the hell's going on here?" I gawk, not understanding what I'm seeing. Tucked up to the king's back, Britta's got her arms around his body and her nose against his neck. Her eyes crack open, and she looks at me blearily as Leif moves behind me.

"Cohen?" Britta sits up, and as she does, the bedroll splits open, giving a view of her fancy underthings to me, Leif, and King Aodren, who's slowly waking up beside her. The royal bastard. *Royal Naked Bastard.* The dress that I bought her, tattered and covered in muck, is piled on top of them, along with a man's tunic and trousers.

I shake my head, confusion rolling into disbelief spinning into anger.

The king sits up without a speck of clothing on and puts his arm in front of Britta as if he's shielding her from us. From *me.*

Something snaps.

The dagger's in my hand and I'm pointing it at the bloody king of Malam. "Get. Out. I'm going to kill you."

CHAPTER

42

BRITTA

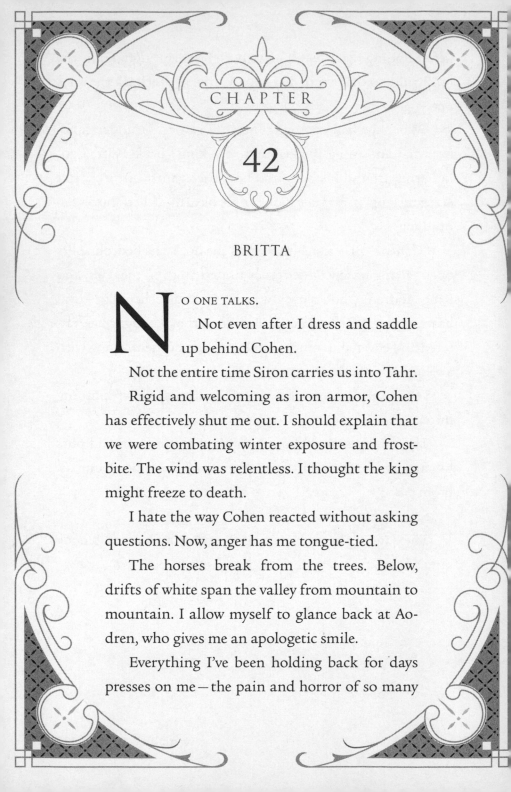

No one talks.

Not even after I dress and saddle up behind Cohen.

Not the entire time Siron carries us into Tahr.

Rigid and welcoming as iron armor, Cohen has effectively shut me out. I should explain that we were combating winter exposure and frostbite. The wind was relentless. I thought the king might freeze to death.

I hate the way Cohen reacted without asking questions. Now, anger has me tongue-tied.

The horses break from the trees. Below, drifts of white span the valley from mountain to mountain. I allow myself to glance back at Aodren, who gives me an apologetic smile.

Everything I've been holding back for days presses on me — the pain and horror of so many deaths, the struggle to escape, and now this. The exhaustion whispers at me to drop my head against Cohen's back, to wrap my arms around him and find comfort. But I'm not that girl. I don't need an arm around the shoulders, or a *We'll get through this.*

We ride up to a country cottage that is easily three times the size of mine. Icicles hang under the lantern-lit windows, giving this home a cozy, welcoming touch.

I dismount and remain beside Siron. I cannot walk away from Cohen without explaining. Even though I'm upset, it would be foolish to let him continue to misunderstand what he saw this morning. "Two days ago Aodren fell into the river," I explain, words so hushed I only know he heard them because he looks at me. Finally. "He would've died from the chill. And last night, he still hadn't regained full warmth. The wind was brutal. We had to fight the cold."

The hardness in Cohen's hazel eyes breaks with concern.

Even I can recognize the bit in my explanation that might be concerning. The first night is justified. The second? Should we have tried harder to get to town? Should we have braved the cold without sharing body heat?

I wait for Cohen's word. Anything to let me know where we go from here.

There's a glimpse of pain, and then nothing. Nothing to stave off the shock that's invaded my bones.

"If you head inside, Lirra will get you something warm to wear," he says, and then leaves, guiding Siron to the stable.

I stand there, a little defiant, a lot numb, and steeped in anger. Despite the part in my explanation that could be argued unnecessary, anger floods the empty spaces inside. Anger has me calling out his name. "Cohen. You left me. You made your choice."

He whips around. Breath puffs like steam from his nostrils. "I had to go."

My cutting look stops him.

"Of course I didn't want you to come with me. I was worried for you. I always am. If you're found out to be a Spiriter, you'll be killed." He rubs his fists against his eyes. "I live in constant fear that you'll be accused. I live in fear that being near me will draw attention to you."

"You can't protect me from everything."

He hangs his head. "I know that."

"I cannot change that I'm a Channeler."

"I don't want you to change. I love who you are. It's just that with me, the king's bounty hunter, you'll always be in the public's eye. Can't you see that I'm a threat to you?"

"Why didn't you tell me this before? Instead you left me behind at the castle. And I—I watched a hundred men and women die . . ." This comes out strangled, my thoughts fishtailing.

His hands reach for my shoulders, and I wince. Cohen's expression shifts to instant concern as he takes in the stain on my sleeve. "You're hurt. What happened?"

"We were chased through the woods after we left Hagan's home. One landed an arrow."

He scrubs his colorless face with his hands. "I cannot believe I didn't notice earlier. Gods, I'm sorry, Britt."

I want to curl into his chest, let the warmth of his words bathe me, but there are still things to share.

"Where's Finn?" The worry in his voice strips away the rest of his hardened exterior.

"He's hiding at a healer's home in Brentyn with Gillian. Gillian couldn't travel in her condition. Your brother stayed with her."

His touch, when it returns to my injured arm, is gentle. Calming. "Dove, I'm sorry. I had no idea about all that you went through. I want to be here for you, however you need. This morning wasn't . . . I was . . ." He rubs his cheek, his finger pausing over the scar. "Seeing you two together was . . ." He lets out a joyless laugh. "Seeds, I cannot get a word out. I'm trying to say that after the last few days, it wasn't how I envisioned our reunion. I'm a jealous bludger."

I duck my chin to hide my flattered smile.

Cohen's arms gingerly wrap around me, his soft lips press to my forehead, and his signature scent, pine trees and cotton, fills my nostrils. He murmurs a quiet apology against my temple, and then the space beside my ear, and then into the crook of my neck. I burrow into his heat, wishing this moment could last. His embrace has such calming power.

"Cohen, there's something I have to tell you."

He leans back to see my face. One side of his grin hitches up. "That you forgive me? I do trust you, Britta. I trust you more than anyone in this world. I know you're strong and capable. I just hate that I could be a danger to you. I fear losing you—that's why I try so hard to keep you safe."

I wilt a little. His talk of trust bathes me in remorse. Why didn't I talk to him about the king after I woke? Or when Cohen returned from hunting Phelia? There have been so many opportunities, and I ignored them all. What I have to tell him really isn't that big. It doesn't affect him. It's silly that I kept it a secret.

"Tell me, Dove." He slides a wayward hair around my ear.

"After the mountain cat attack, when I healed you, something happened." I lean back, giving him space. "At the time, I didn't know. It wasn't until you came back that I realized we had this"—my hands fumble awkwardly between us, a nervous gesture I haven't used when speaking to Cohen in years—"connection."

His sable brows arc up. "What do you mean by *connection?*"

"I started to notice strange things on our way to Enat's home. Like when you were in danger, I could tell. And when you were nearby, even before I could see you, I knew you were there. It felt like an invisible rope tied us together. It would tug on me when you came near."

His lips part and he gives a slow nod of understanding. "I thought we were in tune to one another. Didn't realize it was something else." He frowns. "So when you healed me, you left some of your Channeler magic behind? But you didn't realize what happened until this fall, when you hunted me down?" He smirks at the memory.

I nod. "I don't know how it works. Something about having my energy made it so."

"You say that like it's in the past."

I fist my hands, stopping them from moving. "It is. We aren't connected anymore."

A frown. "Oh. I don't feel differently."

"I know. It was something only I felt. The thing is, when I healed the king, I somehow broke our connection . . ." My mouth is drier than year-old jerky. I clear my throat. ". . . and created a new one with him."

"With the king?"

"Yes."

He rubs his forehead, hiding his eyes. "Huh, interesting."

"That's not all. The new bond with Aodren is different than ours was."

"In what way?" He glances up and cants his head slightly to the side.

"It's stronger." I look at the space between us. "He can feel the connection. He notices when I'm near. Or when I'm in a heightened emotional state."

Cohen's fresh-punched expression makes my chest ache. "He can feel your emotions?"

"Not all, just peak emotions. Like when I was captured at

the castle with Finn. I was panicked and afraid for our lives. He sensed that."

His boot pushes through the snow. "You're saying he felt you were in danger and came back for you?" The blow of his words breaks me. I don't want to keep hurting him.

"He risked his life to save ours."

"I—I . . ." He coughs out a broken laugh. Hands go to his hips. He paces away, kicking up snow as he goes.

"Cohen, say something."

He stares up at the sky, letting out a breath like a dragon blowing steam. His shoulders sink. "I don't know what to say, Britt."

CHAPTER

43

COHEN

A LINE WRINKLES BETWEEN HER PALE BROWS. Her lips tug down. Her hand pumps in and out of a fist. I recognize all her telling signs of frustration. They're pieces of her that I know so well.

"He's a good man," I eventually say, grinding the words between my teeth, a reminder to myself more than a confirmation of Britta's opinion. "I'm grateful for what he did to save you both."

I've served King Aodren for a year and a half. While I wasn't pleased with the way he led the country, I now know it wasn't his fault. Phelia had taken over his mind. Since the king recovered from the Spiriter's bind, he's proved many times over that he's a worthy leader. Saving my brother and Britta is one of those times.

I remind myself of this twice. Even then, I

want to break his royal face. It chafes me, knowing he's had a connection to Britta all this time. Bastard never said a word.

"Talk to me." Britta's fingers touch my back, and a tremor of need rolls through me. She'll never realize how much she affects me.

"I don't know what to say." I turn around.

"Something, anything. Are you angry?"

Of course. But not with her. My fury is solely pointed at King Aodren. Behind Britta, the wind catches the snow on the barn's roof and kicks some off. It's a white veil picking up the morning light.

Because I'm a fool, I ask, "You care about him?"

Her chest rises and falls in a measured breath. "Cohen, I don't want to hurt you. But I—I do. I care about him."

Bloody stars. I spent the last couple of years fighting so hard for her, to keep her safe. Never imagined I'd lose her anyway.

I didn't think she even liked the man.

Could her connection to King Aodren be the reason she's been distant lately? How much does it affect her feelings for a person? Was the connection we once shared what swayed her feelings toward me? I scrub my eyes, hating the turn in my thoughts.

Concern parts her sea of freckles. Britta's face has been in my dreams so often, it's a fight not to wrap her in my arms and try to kiss our connection back to life. If only Channeler magic worked that way.

"What does this mean for us?" I dare to ask.

A snowflake catches on the pale fan of her lashes. I move to brush it away, but she does it first. "I—I don't know. Can we not just be the same as we were before?"

But that's just it. We aren't how we were before.

"I don't know, Dove. Last thing I want is to hurt you." I fight the urge to mold my palm around her cheek. "I keep thinking that I've spent the last year and a half hunting for the king. While you—"

"While I what?" Her eyes narrow.

"You haven't had the same opportunity to figure out what you really want. I'm not trying to tell you what to do. I just . . . all I'm saying is I've had my chance to figure this out." I gesture between us.

Britta scoots back, her feet digging trails in the snow. "What does that mean?"

I swallow, somehow feeling older than the trees around us, older than the valley under our feet, older than the moon slipping out of the sky. "I'm not a perfect man. You know I've got buckets of flaws. I'm stubborn, reckless, and sometimes thoughtless . . . and I've hurt you deeper than any other man." Her expression turns questioning, so I press on. "Thing is, I know exactly who and what I want. And that's you. I know it when I wake in the morning. Know it when I fall asleep. You're the first and last thing on my mind. Your name plays on every beat of my heart."

Her frown softens.

"But I also know that I'm not necessarily what you might

want anymore. Or need." I shift my hand over my belt, feeling for the dove feather beneath. I hate every bit about what I'm going to say next, but it needs to be done. After all, my weakness is doing what's best for Britta. Even if it pains me. Britta is loyal. Last thing I want is for that loyalty to lead her to misery. "I want you to figure out what you want, Britt."

"Are you making me choose between you and my friendship with Aodren?" Her voice squeaks as she says this.

I tighten my fist over my belt pocket and draw a breath through my nose. "No, course not. I'm giving you space, to decide what you really want . . . who you really want. We always had the bond between us. Now that it's gone, you should decide if you really want a life with me."

"You think the bond is the reason I want to be with you?" She scoffs, blinking rapidly before dabbing her eye. She stomps away toward the barn, where Siron's head pokes out of the door. Britta rubs his nose. "This entire conversation is ridiculous."

"Maybe." I shrug. "I hope I'm being a complete bludger, and one day when we're old and hobbling around, we'll laugh about this. But tell me this, Britt, have you ever considered the possibility that our connection influenced your feelings for me? Or that the years we spent together influenced you?" I cough, forcing myself to say this last bit. "There are other men out there. I need you to be certain that I'm the one you want. Faults and all."

She opens her mouth. And for a second I'm praying a

protest comes out. But it's the hesitation, the space between heartbeats, that speaks the truth. "Consider it."

She stalks away and my heart cracks.

The door slams behind her.

Cold and wet, I reach into my secret pocket and slide out the piece of parchment. I withdraw the gray-tinged feather. Wind kicks past the barn, scooting it right out of my hand. I suck in a short breath, gaze ricocheting around the yard in a desperate search.

But it's gone.

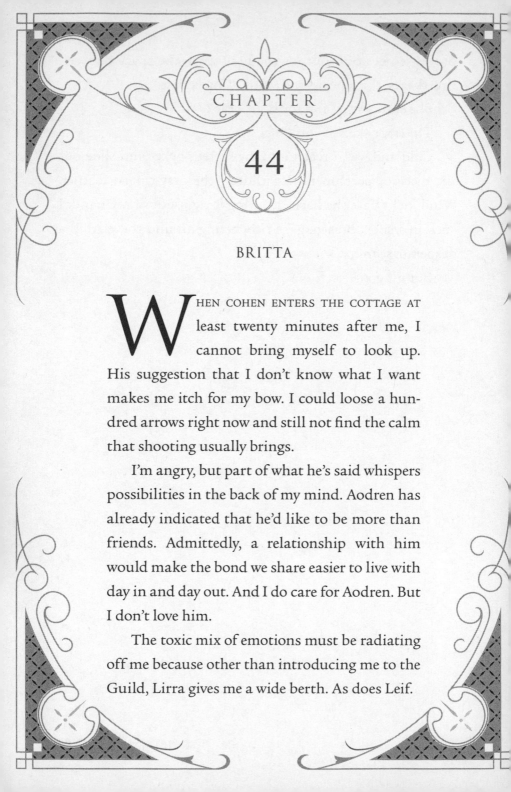

CHAPTER

44

BRITTA

WHEN COHEN ENTERS THE COTTAGE AT least twenty minutes after me, I cannot bring myself to look up. His suggestion that I don't know what I want makes me itch for my bow. I could loose a hundred arrows right now and still not find the calm that shooting usually brings.

I'm angry, but part of what he's said whispers possibilities in the back of my mind. Aodren has already indicated that he'd like to be more than friends. Admittedly, a relationship with him would make the bond we share easier to live with day in and day out. And I do care for Aodren. But I don't love him.

The toxic mix of emotions must be radiating off me because other than introducing me to the Guild, Lirra gives me a wide berth. As does Leif.

The Guild provides me and Aodren with Beannach water and some Channeler paste for my arm. At first it stings the arrow wound but then leaves the area numb.

A couple of hours later, we're a broken, ragtag group gathered around Katallia's table. Omar sits upright in a dining chair, but judging by the pallor of his skin, I'd guess he's missing his bed. Leif stands by the captain while Lirra and I sit on the opposite sides of the wooden slab, facing the men. Aodren takes the head of the table.

Cohen doesn't sit down at all. He stands in the doorway, arms folded, mouth in a grim twist. The tension between us is like invisible hands pushing us together and simultaneously pulling us apart. Makes me wonder if anyone else in the room has noticed.

"What do we do now?" Leif asks.

"We find allies." Aodren speaks first. "We build a competent army by drawing from the fiefs of lords who were killed in Jamis's coup because we know they were loyal." His shoulders settle and his expression hardens while he talks.

It must be difficult, knowing that he'll have to talk to families of men and women who were killed. Unease is written in every line around his eyes. I'm sure the fiefs will rally around him. Anyone who knows him must realize that he'll never be the kind of ruler his father was.

"Gathering that kind of army takes time," Cohen argues.

"It can, but that is why we'll split up." Aodren taps the table. "You and Leif will head to the northern border. Captain

Omar and I will head east after meeting with Lord Freil's family. The northern tip of Lord Freil's land is out of the mountains, but away from the main road. The flat land will give us a good place to set up camp and prepare to move on Brentyn."

We talk for hours, everyone chiming in. In the end, though, Aodren's plan demands we act quickly. Everyone will leave in the morning. Time is essential.

"What about Britta and myself?" Lirra moves to stand in the doorway.

Aodren pauses, and then turns to me. "Britta. I . . . had thought we would continue to travel together —"

Cohen's cough interrupts him, but I speak at the same time. "Sounds good to me."

"My apologies, Your Highness." Cohen stares out the window, jaw hard. "If you'll excuse me, I'd like to make preparations to leave."

Aodren flicks a dismissive wave in the air, and Cohen exits the room.

Omar grips the table to stand up. "One more thing. We made an agreement with the owners of this home. We've sworn an oath to help them."

I think Omar's waiting for the king to pass judgment for aligning with an underground ring of Channelers. I know he expects punishment because, if their roles were reversed, Omar would punish.

Aodren glances up at Katallia, who's popped her head

through the doorway. He nods gravely. "An alliance has been needed for quite some time. Thank you for taking the lead on that, Omar."

The captain stares at Aodren while the king concludes the meeting. Lirra is the first to exit the room. I assume she's going to speak with Cohen.

I pretend as though I'm not watching her retreat, wondering what she'll say to him.

In the morning, we dress and ready ourselves for travel. I could use a few more days of rest, but as Aodren pointed out last night, time is essential. Dagger in my boot and sword at my side, I still feel naked without a bow.

I follow Lirra to the main room, where we wait for the men to finish gearing up.

Seeva, the tall woman with skin the color of rich earth, stands just inside the door. Lirra introduced her last night. She seemed marginally pleasant then. Now she radiates tension that has me taking a step back, bumping into Cohen, who I didn't realize was behind me. His hands touch my shoulders and then leap off.

I fight to keep my expression neutral. Pretend I'm not saddened.

"You brought them here . . ." The woman's voice quakes. Her hands flick at her sides, and I swear flames leap between her fingertips. I glance around in confusion. The room fills with the rest of the men and Lirra's aunt.

The woman growls, "You brought the king's guard to our doorstep."

My confusion multiplies as Lirra curses and rushes for the window. She spins around so fast, her dark brown braid smacks her face. "Jamis and half a dozen men have spread out around the cottage. We're under attack."

I dart to the opposite side of the window, keeping cover to view the field beyond the cottage. Six guards, bows drawn, stand at the tree line one hundred paces away. Jamis holds position on a small rise of hill to the left of the men, his gaunt equine features ghoulish in the early morning haze. Beyond him, movement breaks the shadows.

"There's more than six." I lean against the plaster, dread weighing me down. "They have more men in the woods."

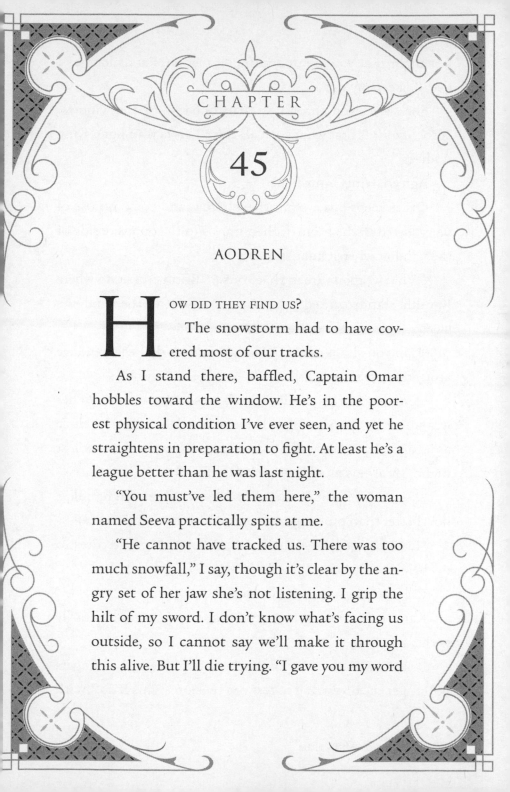

CHAPTER

45

AODREN

HOW DID THEY FIND US?

The snowstorm had to have covered most of our tracks.

As I stand there, baffled, Captain Omar hobbles toward the window. He's in the poorest physical condition I've ever seen, and yet he straightens in preparation to fight. At least he's a league better than he was last night.

"You must've led them here," the woman named Seeva practically spits at me.

"He cannot have tracked us. There was too much snowfall," I say, though it's clear by the angry set of her jaw she's not listening. I grip the hilt of my sword. I don't know what's facing us outside, so I cannot say we'll make it through this alive. But I'll die trying. "I gave you my word last night that you are under my protection. For as long as I live, I'll keep my word."

She scoffs and throws an arm out toward the window. "Protection? Is that what you call this? This is your fight, King Aodren."

Agreed. Jamis is my fight.

Omar keeps one eye out the window, and one on those of us gathered in the room. Cohen moves to the opposite side of the window where Omar stands.

"What weapons are in this house?" Britta crosses to where Katallia stands tucked against the wall out of the window's view.

"Can you shoot a bow?" The woman studies the bandage around Britta's arm.

Confidence brightens in Britta's eyes at the mention of her weapon of choice. She moves her arm in a demonstrative circle as if to say, *Look, I'm healed.* "I drank some Beannach water last night. My arm is much better than before."

"Injury or no, the bounty hunter's daughter can handle a bow better than probably any man in this room," Cohen says.

"Even one that's nearly her same size?" Lirra gestures to my height.

Cohen shrugs. "Aye. Seen it before."

Katallia hurries from the room and returns momentarily with a longbow.

Britta takes the weapon without argument, her fingers pulling at the bowstring to test the tension. "This'll do." With the window in her focus, she adds, "Maybe it'll give me some more distance."

"Jamis won't hesitate to bring the fight to us," I tell Britta, knowing the man's ruthless rules of war. *Strike first. Destroy your opponent before they have a chance to weaken you,* he once told me. "If you can take a clear shot, do it. Are you sure you're up to the challenge? Your arm—"

"My arm is fine." She turns to Cohen. "How many men have you spotted in the trees?"

"Six so far," he responds. "All appear to be archers."

"Six in the trees and six on the field?" She worries her lip.

Leif hurries into the room, with a smaller bow in hand. It's a closer-range weapon, but Britta takes it. "It may be more manageable, but I can try to use both. If I had my recurve bow—"

Glass breaks. I run toward the commotion with Britta on my heels. We stumble into the next room, finding a burning arrow on the ground. Flames have spread to the curtains.

I rush to them. Grabbing a blanket to cover my hands, I smack the flames away. But the blanket lights on fire. My palms pulse with pain.

"Stop, stop." Britta rips it off me.

The smoke is thicker now. It takes a beat before I realize a charcoal plume is crawling along the ceiling, coming from another room. The door of that room bursts open, and two women I briefly met—Yasmin and Torima—run out.

"Men are shooting arrows from the back woods!" Torima

yells in warning. She halts, her angry gaze seeking out Seeva. Torima drops her face into her elbow, her blond hair pooling over her arm as she coughs against the smoke.

Seeva pushes the woman toward the main room while Yasmin follows behind, appearing more focused than the rest of the group.

I hold my burned hands close to my body, cursing myself. In the main room, chaos from fiery arrows has erupted. Jamis's shooters land two more arrows inside. But based on the flames I can see outside the window, our bigger problem is that we're all going to be burned alive. Smoke and flame dance through the thatching.

"Seeva. Need help here." The drawn wrinkles in Lirra's brow shine with sweat. At first I think it's because of the intense heat, but then I notice the unusual wind moving through the house. When Lirra was introduced to me earlier, someone called her an air Channeler. I think she's trying to blow out the flames, but it's only making the fire worse.

I yell at her to suck the air out of the room, but she shakes her head and gestures to the open door and the window.

"Too much coming in," she says.

I point out the new batch of the crawling flames to Seeva. "Can you do something?"

"I already am," the woman snaps. Beads of moisture break out on her brow.

Smoke thickens the air and burns my eyes. I notice Seeva's

extended hands shaking. One at a time, the arrows extinguish, but the amount of smoke in the room makes it impossible to breathe.

We have to get out. Which has to be exactly what Jamis wants, and yet we'll die in here. I yell for everyone to evacuate and to take cover as they go. Other than the archers, we don't know what else is out there.

Leif and Britta exit first. Bows drawn and ready, they provide cover as the rest of us pour unceremoniously out behind them. Little fires rage all along the walls, leading from the home to the barn and stable. Before Lirra can make it to where I am tucked beside the stable's opening, an arrow lands at her feet. She yelps and jumps back.

Across the way, protected by a pine tree, Britta leans out from the trunk and returns shots. She continues loosing arrows one after another by holding a cluster in her release hand. As soon as one is gone, she has another one loaded. Jamis may have started with six archers and six men on the field, but Britta's arrows hit two. Leif knocks out a third.

"Take cover by the stable," Omar yells.

"Two left," Leif calls over his shoulder. He remains at the corner of the stable so he can pop his head out and shoot when necessary. We're safe here, for the moment, but the roof of the stable is thatched. If they light more arrows, it'll only take one well-placed fiery tip to burn the roof down.

"One left," Britta says. "And my quiver is empty."

"Got him!" Leif's cry sends a sigh of relief over the entire group. Against their arrows we were nothing but prey for the taking. Now they must come after us, fight on an even field.

"With half his men gone, he'll retreat. I know the man. We'll be able to get everyone out of here safely." Omar coughs and leans against the fence.

"Run from the fight?" Cohen stares at Omar.

"Look around, Cohen. We're in poor condition. What Leif and Britta have done is given us time. We would be fools not to take it."

Would we? I disagree with Omar. Jamis cannot be a threat if he isn't alive. "We should end this now. Jamis cannot make it back to Castle Neart." If we succeed, we can take Brentyn back without a pitched battle, without paying for it with the blood of hundreds of lives.

Cohen agrees.

Omar dips his chin in a terse nod. "All right. We'll split up and flank them, half of us going around one side of the stable and the other half going to the opposite side."

"Will you join us?" I ask the women.

"This is your battle." Yasmin, the shorter women, speaks for the group. Seeva and Torima glance at her, surprise writ across their faces.

Katallia spins around, her wild red curls flashing against the background of snowy trees. "This may be their fight, but I'll not let my niece die here today."

"I give you my word now," I cut in, speaking quickly while

keeping one eye on our attackers. "I will keep the same oath the other men have agreed to. Help us stop Jamis and I'll see the Purge Proclamation overthrown."

Despite what I've promised, Yasmin crosses her arms and stands her ground. "And what good is the king's promise if we end up dead on this field? I say we leave. The Guild sticks together."

"Lirra?" Katallia steps out of the shadow of the stable.

Lirra shakes her head. "I stay and fight with my friends."

Katallia gives one decisive nod. "I stay too."

"This is madness." Yasmin clenches her fists over her chest, pleading with the other women. She edges closer to the stable's doors. "If you stay here, you're risking your lives. Jamis is the champion of the Channelers. He wants to elevate us. How can you trust this man's word? He could be speaking lies out of desperation."

Seeva's lids lower over her ebony eyes. "Yaz. What have you done?"

She says nothing.

"Did you inform Lord Jamis of the king's whereabouts?"

Yasmin's head swings side to side. "I didn't!"

I notice Britta's posture go erect. "A lie."

The other ladies exchange shocked glances. "Spiriter?" Seeva tips her head to the side. One nod from Britta, and Seeva's eyes flare a touch in awe before she spins to face Yasmin. "You betrayed us."

Katallia jumps in front of the fire Channeler as Yasmin

creeps back, stricken. "Forgive me. Forgive me, my sisters. I wanted only what's best for—"

"Leave. Before I set you on fire." Though barely louder than a whisper, Seeva's threat tremors through me. I could only be so lucky to have this fearsome woman as an ally.

Yasmin claps her hands over her mouth, catching a sob, and scrambles away. I watch her dart into the woods. Her sudden flight comes as a shock. She betrayed them. Wouldn't they detain her? Punish her somehow later?

Katallia moves beside me. "Exile will be punishment enough."

Perhaps that's true. My experience in the mountains is enough for me to know it'll be difficult for her to get away, especially now that we're under attack. If she does make it, she'll be turned away from anyone associated with the Channelers Guild.

"It's an honor to work beside a Spiriter," Seeva says, giving a small bow to Britta. "Let's fight."

The two remaining Guild women flank her while the rest of us spread out to take on Jamis. Leif and Lirra follow Britta, while Cohen and Omar stay with me. Coming at them from opposing sides, we break from the stable's coverage and charge Jamis and his remaining six men.

Taking on a man I've sparred with many times before, we meet with a clash of swords. I thrust and parry. The metal clanks and rings. I grunt against the exertion and sweep my sword up again and again. He is sharp, swift, strong. But thanks to renewed energy from the Beannach water, my precision has returned. Seeing an opening, I force myself to follow through. To not lessen the impact. To kill because otherwise I'll be killed.

My blade slices through the stomach of the rebel guard. His body seizes around my sword. I open my mouth, intending to apologize, ridiculous as it sounds.

Across the field, Cohen makes a clean sweep with his blade, gutting a man. A slash of red stains the winter-white world.

Another man appears at my side, his arm raised. There's no time to react. His blade will hit before I can swing. *I'm dead.*

A burst of wind slams me to the ground. It's so sudden, it pushes the breath out of my lungs. I scramble back, expecting the guard's blow to land any second. But the man falls at my feet. Above me, Lirra holds an extended blade. Stains of the man's life splatter the fresh snow around him.

I shake the shock out of my head and scramble to my feet.

"You're welcome," the brazen girl shouts at me before running off. There's no time to wonder where the Channeler girl came from. Lirra yanks a knife from her skirt and throws it at a rebel just as Leif limps out of the way. He clutches his leg where blood soaks his trousers.

"I'll live." He pants and hobbles toward her side.

Beyond him, Britta and Omar fight two more of Jamis's soldiers. So where is the leader of the traitors?

"Aodren."

I twist to find the man sitting astride his horse, twenty

paces away from where Cohen cuts down the last of the rebel soldiers. Jamis eyes the carnage on the field, lifts his hands in the air, and claps. Slow, punctuated hits. "Well done, my king." He echoes the same sentiment he used when I was younger, when I thought of him as the closest thing to a father.

Another rider appears from beneath the trees. No, two riders, doubled up on the same horse. Their faces register. I might as well have taken an arrow to the chest.

A startled gasp comes from Britta.

Finn bobs on the horse in front of Phelia, his gaze wide-eyed and lost.

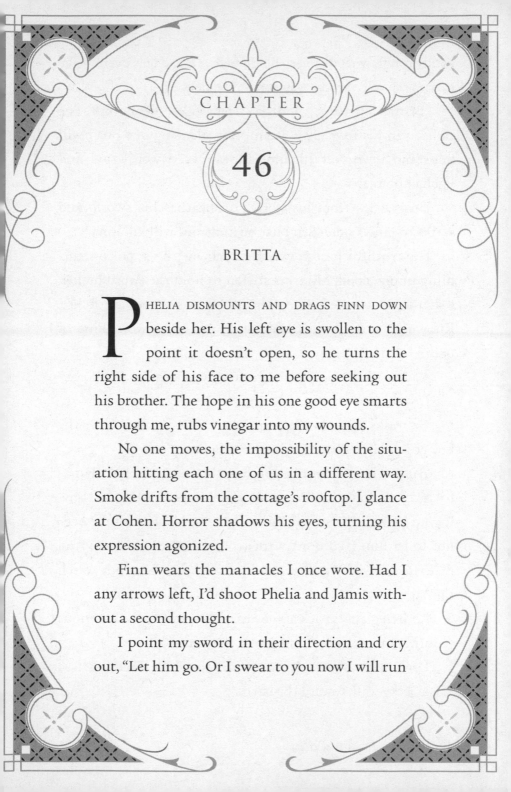

CHAPTER

46

BRITTA

PHELIA DISMOUNTS AND DRAGS FINN DOWN beside her. His left eye is swollen to the point it doesn't open, so he turns the right side of his face to me before seeking out his brother. The hope in his one good eye smarts through me, rubs vinegar into my wounds.

No one moves, the impossibility of the situation hitting each one of us in a different way. Smoke drifts from the cottage's rooftop. I glance at Cohen. Horror shadows his eyes, turning his expression agonized.

Finn wears the manacles I once wore. Had I any arrows left, I'd shoot Phelia and Jamis without a second thought.

I point my sword in their direction and cry out, "Let him go. Or I swear to you now I will run you through with this very blade before the day is over." Rage carries my voice all the way across the field.

"Britta, fall back." Aodren's steps falter beside me. The caution in his tone is an attempt at silencing me. But I will not stand down. Not this time. I meant every word I said, and Phelia knows it.

Jamis leaps from his horse, unsheathes his sword, and stalks to Finn's side. "Send us the king, or I will kill him."

His truthful heat crawls through me; it's a poison curdling in my blood. My arms stiffen to hold the sword higher. I should've never left Finn behind. He was my responsibility. Knowing I've let down Cohen and Finn is the worst kind of pain.

Aodren's knuckles brush against mine. "This is my choice."

His choice?

He walks away, headed straight for Lord Jamis. "Let the boy go," Aodren yells. "I will take his place."

Truth. The suddenness of his choice steals my chance to react. I don't have time to comprehend what he's giving up by walking straight into their hands. Part of me begs not to let him go. I don't want to lose Aodren this way. And neither can Malam afford to lose him. Yet I cannot watch Finn die.

Aodren glances back at me, unspoken words and emotions painting his eyes a brilliant green. "Be brave."

Lord Jamis shoves Finn toward the field. Finn starts a brisk, jerky walk toward the barn.

My eyes burn with unshed tears. Never before have I felt less courageous than I do now.

My throat locks over the words I want to say. I realize why Cohen always chose my safety first. It's too painful to watch fate play its cold games with the life of someone you care for. I did not realize how much I care for this man until now. Good, kind, intelligent, compassionate — Aodren's one of the truest friends I have ever had.

"Britta. Look."

Lirra points across the field, where a handful of crows flap out of the trees. Snow showers the ground near the birds' movement. I cannot see anyone. But something about Finn's body language catches the corner of my eye. His stride is all wrong. The closer he gets to Aodren, the choppier his movements become.

A peek of silver glints between Finn's fingers. What's he carrying? I glance across the field, trying to make sense of the scene.

Still as the snow around her, Phelia watches Finn.

"Stop!" I break into a sprint for Aodren.

Aodren twists around just as Finn thrusts a blade into his shoulder. A pained grunt comes out, and Aodren shoves the younger boy back. The two struggle, the king's one good arm fending off Finn's attack. Cohen shouts. Finn lunges for Aodren's throat.

Right before I reach them, Finn collapses, a puppet whose strings have been cut.

The suddenness of his fall has me skidding to a stop, focus whipping to Phelia. She's not alone. Four girls, bound wrist to wrist, form a semicircle behind Phelia. Off to the side of the girls, two more guards hold swords ready.

"Orli," Lirra cries out. A girl with ebony braids starts to thrash against the restraints.

Aodren holds his shoulder, applying pressure to the wound. "I don't know what happened. Finn was attacking me, and then he just fell . . . Is he alive?"

Urgency bleats *hurry, hurry, hurry* through my veins. I check Finn's pulse — sluggish.

Cohen appears at my side. "Let me get Finn out of here."

I nod, wishing there was more I could say right now. At the very least, wishing he knew how sorry I was.

Seeva and her remaining Guild women meet Cohen at the edge of the field and gather around Finn.

"Britta, you could end this now." Phelia's voice rings like claws scraping down a window. She has a way of ripping my attention from everything else happening. Phelia grasps the two girls at the ends, completing a circle. They buck and squirm, a futile effort against the leather straps securing them to one another and the guards posted at their sides.

"I will never join you!" I shout at her.

In challenge, Phelia raises the arms of the two girls connected to her. "Is that so?"

I'm frozen in place, unable to turn away from Phelia, anticipating what her next move will be. *How do you muddy water, Britta? By adding more and more dirt.*

Phelia's head twitches to the side. She stares me down as she lowers the girls' arms. Her chest rises and falls in great gaping breaths. Her eyes roll back, whites gleaming against the black swirls that crawl around her neck.

"No!" Lirra cries out. She points at her friend who's no longer fighting the restraints. "Phelia's using a rune to draw out their powers."

At the same time Cohen yells, "Britta!"

I spin around to find that Cohen has lowered Finn to the ground and is now kneeling beside Seeva. The Channeler lays on the snow, hand flattened over her chest. Her fingers dig into her shirt.

"The heat," Seeva cries. Sweat coats her face. Her lips twitch. The snow nearest her face melts.

"What's happening?" Terror creeping through my question, I look from Seeva to Phelia.

A shift in Cohen's expression shows his understanding. "Phelia's burning Seeva from the inside out."

I blink, unsure how he came to the conclusion and at the same time horrified.

Torima crouches beside Seeva and places her hands on the Channeler. "I'll do what I can to cool her with liquids from the inside out," she says, "but can I get some wind, ladies?" She looks from Lirra to Katallia.

Both women agree. Lirra lifts her hands, and wind swirls around Seeva. The woman's moans quiet.

"Keep it up," Katallia tells her niece. "I'll send a message to Phelia." She then extends her hands toward the opposite end of the field. A wintry gust bursts past me, straight for Phelia.

Phelia stumbles to the side, her cloak flapping in the Channeler's wind. But she doesn't release the girl's hands. The distraction allows Leif and Omar to sneak away from our group, in an effort to close in on Jamis and Phelia.

Seeva coughs and coughs until she can sit up. She grabs handfuls of snow, sucking the powder into her mouth.

A strange groan moves through the trees. It's an unfamiliar sound that makes everyone pause. Seeva holds the snow in her palm, where it melts into a small handful of water.

Torima leaps to her feet and points at the trees nearby. "Run," she shouts. "Run!"

The women rush toward the center of the field just in time. The first tree tips over, landing with a thud that scatters sticks and dirt and dust. Tree after tree falls. Our group frantically moves away from the falling forest, Cohen carrying Finn, Aodren clutching his shoulder and walking beside them, Katallia helping Seeva, while Lirra and I take up the rear.

Leif, who has snaked around the field to Jamis's side, finds a bow from one of the fallen archers. He pulls an arrow to the string and waits for an opening.

Omar takes cover behind one of the fallen pines, close to Phelia.

"What can I do?" I ask. "Seeva, can I help you regain your strength?"

The woman allows me to help her. Clasping her hand, I try not to gasp at the warmth of her skin as I seek out her energy and push some of mine into hers. To give us time, Katallia and Lirra send gust after gust of wind in Phelia's direction. When they take a break, Torima gathers the moisture in the air and pelts Phelia with jagged pieces of hail.

Phelia screams into the wind and hail, but somehow manages to keep hold of the girls' arms. Obsidian veins pulse against her white-as-snow skin, shifting like a nest of snakes in the storm. The girls around her start to drop, one at a time, to their knees until they're all wilted beside her legs.

Another groan sounds nearby. I release Seeva's hand so I can look at the woods and see where the tree is going to fall. The tree falls, but it's too far away to do damage to our group.

Seeva pushes to her feet, anger brightening her energy as she snaps fire into her palms. Seeva throws her balls of fire in the air, and in a move that makes me think these women have practiced Channeler combat many times before, Katallia adds a gust of wind that sends the fire straight at Phelia.

The distraction is what Leif needs to shoot off an arrow at Phelia.

Phelia's cloak flaps out, and moments before Seeva's fire and Leif's arrow hit, air blows out from Phelia's circle, redirecting the fireballs at our ragtag bunch and sending the arrow straight at Omar. It happens in an instant. The tip slams right into Omar's chest.

While Lirra blows the fireballs into two fallen trees, the rest of us stand in a shocked trance.

Only Leif moves. Surprise slackens his mouth and makes his arm hang from the weight of the bow. "Omar?"

Oh mercy.

The captain sputters for breath and tips forward, slamming into the frozen earth. Caught in a nightmarish pendulum between Phelia and my friends, I whip around just as Leif reaches Omar. Dread turns me wooden as I watch my sweet friend fall to his knees and wail. "I didn't mean to hurt him," he cries. The sound of his agony breaks me.

"Kill them all," Jamis yells at Phelia.

Phelia's veins throb.

The world groans and shakes underfoot. I sprint for her with my weapons drawn.

The guards move to intercept me. Before I can throw my blade, a dagger flies past my shoulder, hitting a guard below the collarbone. He crumbles to the ground.

I jerk to the side.

"I'll take the guards." Lirra's staccato steps catch me unaware. Her shoulders slump and her breathing is labored. She's exhausted from using so much energy to control the wind. "Get . . . her." Her sword is extended, though her sporadic movements spur little faith in her ability to fight right now.

She must see my indecision because she swings her blade

up, pointing it at my nose. "Stop her . . . I can manage. Get Phelia."

Without wasting a moment, I rush at Phelia. I'm expecting her to blast me with wind or an earth shake, but she allows me to come close. I swing my sword, wanting to end this with one blow. Faster than humanly possible, she releases the girls, dodges my weapon, and seizes my arms. It all happens so quickly, a heartbeat and I am caught in her grip, unable to move, sword on the ground.

I thrash, desperate to get away. Only, I'm no match for Phelia's power.

At the smell of smoke, I crane my neck around to find fire eating across the fallen trees, trees that I only now realize have penned in all the people I care about. They're going to burn to death or suffocate from all the smoke.

I realize how fragile they are. How easily Phelia could end their lives. How weak and foolish I was to think I could beat her. It's too much to take in.

I close my eyes, wanting the fight, the suffering, the violation of the young girls and my friends . . . all of it, to fade away. I'm stuck in Phelia's impossibly strong grip. Every time I try to jerk free, she tightens her hold. There's nothing I can do to help anyone, not even myself.

I hang my head, hopeless. Will they kill all of us?

The tug that I struggled with until this last week tightens a fraction. It's a nudge between my ribs, coming straight from Aodren. The sensation rattles my senses. I've grown so used to

Aodren's connection that I've stopped noticing it. But feeling it now, in this dark moment, brings a sudden clarity.

I just have to be close enough to the Spiriter to unravel her energy. Enat told me as much in the woods. When Aodren was under Phelia's mind control, all I needed to do was find her at the castle, touch her to access her energy and his, then unwind it.

But the scene at the castle with Aodren didn't go as planned because Phelia was already gone.

I stop resisting and twist my hands, wrapping them around Phelia's wrists. My palms cover the runes. My invisible touch brushes against the wild storm of energy inside her. But unlike the scene in the woods, her frenzied energy is complicated with other zips and zings. If they were colors, Phelia's would be black. The others would be strands of yellow, green, blue, and orange. I imagine a hand created from my own energy, attempting to separate the colors, plucking them off and throwing them into the wind. But Phelia fights me. Her black is resistant and full of tentacles that whip around, catching the escaping colors.

I focus on the black, drawing it through my palms. Raw power surges up my arm, hot and sweet as summer molasses. I am *alive*. Energy sings in my veins. Strength multiplies in my arms.

Suddenly, I'm not the one caught in another's grip. I'm the aggressor. Hands wrapped around Phelia's wrists, I force her down to her knees as easily as moving a small child. Her eyes, two round moons, wide and old, shift from my face to the hand that's wrapped around her wrist, drawing energy like I might empty a waterskin.

But along with the energy comes a surge of murky thoughts and emotions. At first they're terrorized whispers. A child's cry in the dark. And then they grow clearer, painting perfect pictures of nightmares and dark desires.

Her screech coils through my ears.

The darkness is divine. Delicious. I want it. I drink it in, my goal no longer to subdue Phelia, but to take everything she has. Everything.

No, a voice cries from the back of my head. *You're not like you're mother. You can stop this.* I resist tugging the thread of black power, despite how my body cries for more.

Pain explodes in my back and burns, burns, burns through my belly. The suddenness of it rattles my thoughts and causes me to release Phelia. I look down to where my hands have gone to my stomach. Only, my fingers stop, hovering in front of the crimson-soaked blade protruding above my navel. *A blade.*

A cry of anguish rends the air. It's not mine. I've no air to even gasp for the pain and numbing. Phelia's gaze meets mine one last time. Shock, sadness, and sorrow.

I try to talk, but nothing comes except a gurgle. A metallic tang coats my tongue.

And then I'm falling,

falling,

falling.

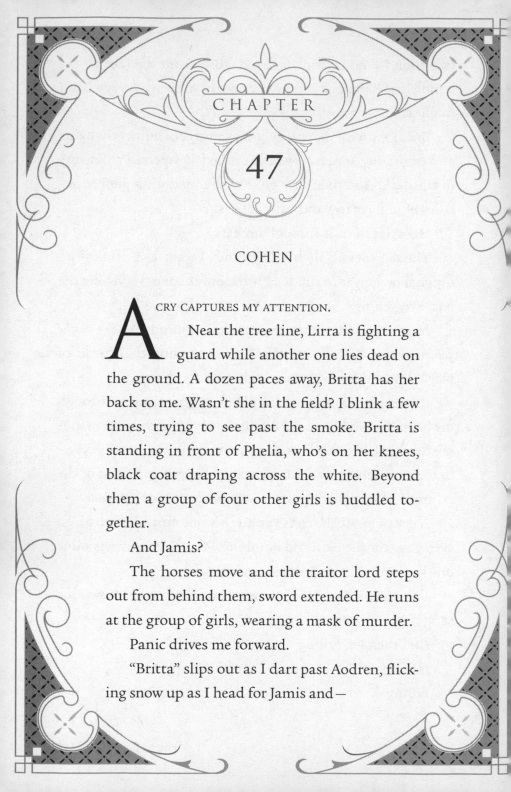

CHAPTER

47

COHEN

A CRY CAPTURES MY ATTENTION.

Near the tree line, Lirra is fighting a guard while another one lies dead on the ground. A dozen paces away, Britta has her back to me. Wasn't she in the field? I blink a few times, trying to see past the smoke. Britta is standing in front of Phelia, who's on her knees, black coat draping across the white. Beyond them a group of four other girls is huddled together.

And Jamis?

The horses move and the traitor lord steps out from behind them, sword extended. He runs at the group of girls, wearing a mask of murder.

Panic drives me forward.

"Britta" slips out as I dart past Aodren, flicking snow up as I head for Jamis and—

Jamis's sword slides into Britta's back. No warning at all. He just stabbed—a cry of anguish tears from my lips. *No!*

Jamis runs for the horses. He'll be my concern later. I race to Britta's side, arms pumping, legs carrying me as fast as they can. A shock shudders through Britta's body. I chuck my sword on the ground, reaching for her body before she can fall.

"No," I hear King Aodren choke out beside me.

I hold Britta to my chest, dragging in dry breaths that provide no air. *Dove. Please, please live.* If only I possessed the power Britta has, I'd give her all my energy. Everything I have.

Swords clatter. A ring of steel echoes around us. The king shouts something.

I glance up to see Aodren fighting Jamis. It doesn't take more than a few moments for the king's swordsmanship to overwhelm Jamis. King Aodren's blade thrusts through the traitor's heart. Jamis gags. His beady eyes bulge. But I don't have it in me to care.

I adjust Britta in my arms, careful not to inflict any more pain. I shield her face from the smoke. Her eyelids flutter. My chest cracks wide open.

"I—I love you," I whisper, dropping my lips to her forehead. "I was a fool. Please, Dove. Please don't leave."

Someone jostles my shoulder. "Let us take her."

The Guild women and Lirra gather round. Fury pours out of me. It wipes away my pains and has me passing Britta's shell of a body to the extended arms of the Guild. I pick up my sword and stalk to Phelia, who has scrambled toward the Channeler girls. Wrath pulsing along my arms, I raise my blade. I will run it straight through her chest where her heart would be. If she had one.

"You. Did. This." My words are fists, slamming the air.

The weakened woman stumbles, collapsing on the ground, and pulls her tattooed arms over her face.

"Stop." King Aodren's command makes me pause. My arms quake. The blade wobbles a knuckle of space above her sternum.

"She deserves to die," I tell him, spit flying from my mouth. I see Britta, broken, pale, and lifeless in the Guild women's arms. The image turns everything inside me to dust. Who am I without her?

"Yes," he says. "But not if there's something that can be done to save Britta."

Phelia's eyes, which are now blacker than they are blue, flicker with something that looks briefly like sadness before they grow hard and gleam at me. "Nothing can be done for her."

Her cold hate-filled rasp seals my decision.

I thrust my blade between Phelia's ribs, ending her life.

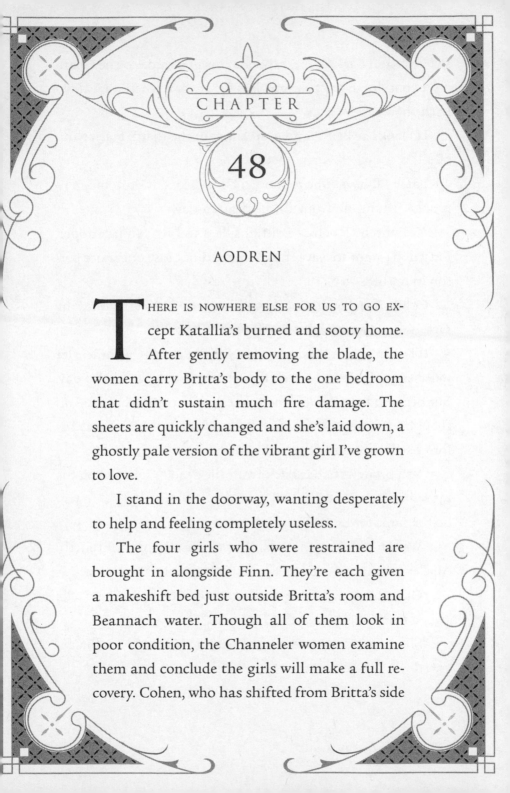

CHAPTER

48

AODREN

THERE IS NOWHERE ELSE FOR US TO GO EX-
cept Katallia's burned and sooty home.
After gently removing the blade, the
women carry Britta's body to the one bedroom
that didn't sustain much fire damage. The
sheets are quickly changed and she's laid down, a
ghostly pale version of the vibrant girl I've grown
to love.

I stand in the doorway, wanting desperately
to help and feeling completely useless.

The four girls who were restrained are
brought in alongside Finn. They're each given
a makeshift bed just outside Britta's room and
Beannach water. Though all of them look in
poor condition, the Channeler women examine
them and conclude the girls will make a full recovery. Cohen, who has shifted from Britta's side

to Finn's and back again, expresses his gratitude to the Channelers but doesn't appear any less upset than when we walked in the home.

He looks at Britta and everything in the man's face crumbles.

Later, I'll have time to mourn Omar's loss. It's too much to process. I'm numb from all the death today.

As I watch Cohen at Britta's side, I feel like an interloper. But I don't want to leave the room. I cannot lose one more person in my life.

Cohen touches her neck and her wrists. "She's gone," he says over and over again, ripping at his hair.

If I wasn't connected to Britta, I might think the same. Her muscles are slack and her skin is the color of a gray winter day. But beneath her exterior, there is a line that connects us. And though it's a single thread to the swath of material it was before, I still sense her. "She's alive. Barely."

"You brought Omar back from the dead." Cohen's voice is rattled with defeat as he looks to Seeva and Katallia. "Can you do the same for Britta?"

"We can try," Katallia says. "But we are missing our fourth. All elements are needed to start a body on its way to healing."

"Orli can do it," Lirra says from the doorway. She wicks away a tear. "She's an earth Channeler."

"She hasn't done this sort of healing before," Katallia argues.

"Please try." Cohen takes his eyes off Britta to look at each one of the Guild. He wears his anguish plainly.

Katallia gives a reluctant nod, and Lirra leaves the room to talk to Orli. She returns a moment later with a brunette girl in tow.

The women assemble around the bed, each placing her hands on Britta's body. After she's instructed, Orli follows along. Their eyes close and their heads bow. Seeva lifts her face to the ceiling and chants, "Gods of old, grant us the energy to give this girl, that she might walk again in this world."

Hope rises inside as the women begin a collective chant. Orli, who is newer to the group, stammers but catches on.

The good feeling plummets the moment the women's eyes snap open and they shake their heads. "She has lost too much life." Seeva's fingers run over Britta's forehead. "Only a Spiriter could heal her."

Cohen drops his forehead to Britta's hand, his shoulders silently shaking.

"I'm sorry. It shouldn't be long." Seeva bows her head.

I edge closer to the bed, wanting to say my own goodbye. I walk to the opposite side of the bed, to give Cohen space, though I doubt he knows I'm here. He must hate me. I would understand if he did. I shouldn't be here with her. I run my finger down the length of her arm to say goodbye. When I touch her wrist, her line of energy squirms. It takes me by surprise. I give in to our connection and reach for the exit wound on her belly. My stomach churns at the amount of blood coating her dress. Just before I withdraw, her energy stirs beneath my fingers.

"That's it," someone whispers. The dark-haired girl stands at my side. Her eyes are round.

"What's that, girl?" Seeva moves closer, looking over Orli's shoulder.

"I think they're connected." Orli points to me.

Seeva's eyes widen. "She has given you her life force?"

I nod. "A little more than six weeks ago, she saved my life."

Seeva's hand covers mine. "If her energy is connected to yours, you can use a rune to guide her energy toward her wounds."

I shake my head, not understanding.

"If she healed you, her energy is in you, reaching for home. Only a rune can release it. You must've felt it before, yes?"

I nod in shock, understanding for the first time why I could always sense Britta's nearness.

Cohen is suddenly at my side, his expression shifting from shock to awe.

"Give me your wrist." Seeva holds out her palm.

I rest my arm in her hand. She dips her finger in Britta's blood and draws a circular pattern on my arm. I resist the urge to wrestle from her grip. There's nothing natural about having someone's blood painted on you.

"Now let your connection guide her energy to where she needs it most." The Channeler moves my hands over Britta's wounds. Beneath my palm, it feels like a thousand tiny ants are marching to work. The rune blazes wherever it touches more blood. I stay still, doing what the Channeler says as the other three Channelers surround Britta.

Torima wraps her hand around Britta's wrist while Seeva holds Britta's head. Orli and Katallia place their hands in different spots on Britta's body. They chant words I've never heard before, continuing until all four have shortened breath, perspiration on their brows, and shaky hands. My body grows weaker by the minute. I slump into a chair and rest my head on the bed beside Britta, needing sleep, despite my brain's desperate attempts to stay awake. To heal her.

I may have fallen asleep, but after a while, Seeva lifts my arm off Britta.

One at a time, the women touch their chests, dip their heads, and say, "Go well with the spirit."

I watch them leave, panic creeping back into my numb arms and legs. Britta's eyes are still closed.

CHAPTER

49

COHEN

ODREN'S BEWILDERED GAZE BOUNCES FROM me to Britta to the door where the Channelers exited. I don't think he heard them explain that she received enough energy from him and now they both need to rest. His head drops back to the side of the bed, and his arm, marked in Britta's blood, flops to his side.

While it's a struggle not to be jealous of the man, I couldn't be more grateful.

His head bobs a few more times. He mumbles Britta's name. I try to tell him twice that Britta is alive, but he's too incoherent. I suggest he go with Lirra to find a bed to sleep in. She'll let him know the good news. Seeva mentioned that he would be giving up at least half of his energy.

Which would in turn mean the man would need to sleep for days.

When Lirra walks to his side of the bed, Aodren's arms flex, like he's struggling to hold himself together. She gently guides him to the door, and then nearly collapses as his head falls against her shoulder. Once they're gone, Britta and I are alone in the room.

The last time we were alone, I ended our relationship. What a fool I was.

I don't know if she'll ever forgive me. But when she wakes up, I'm determined to be the first person she sees.

As night draws closer, there are fewer scrapes and bangs of repair work on the cabin. The Guild members have put Leif to work to keep his mind off Omar's death. We are all affected by the captain's passing, but I don't blame Leif. No one holds Omar's death against him.

Leif doesn't see it the same, however. I hope someday he'll forgive himself.

Behind the closed bedroom door, I stay at Britta's side. A thousand promises to the gods have passed my lips as I beg them to spare her.

She hasn't moved a knuckle since the Channelers left. As when she risked her life to save mine and then the king's, she lies, motionless, almost colorless. This time, however, she's covered in her own blood.

When my head starts to bob and my lids dip, I allow myself

rest, hunched in the chair beside her bed. Though I've never been a churchgoer, I say a prayer — that I won't have another grave to dig in the morning.

I wake a dozen times in the night, full of aching muscles and creaky bones.

There is no change the next day.

Nor the day after.

The Guild women have come in to dress her wounds; wipe her face, arms, and legs; and drizzle Channeler concoctions over her lips. They've brought me bowls of pottage and water. On the third day, King Aodren comes to the room. I don't know the extent of the man's feeling for Britta, however, I took note of the many times he sought her out the morning before the attack. Like his eyes were homing pigeons and she was home.

His sallow skin takes a greenish-yellow tint under the lantern light. He moves like his bones are made of glass. The cost of returning Britta's energy is apparent. He could pass for someone afflicted with the ague.

"You don't look so good," I tell him.

"I was about to tell you the same."

I rake a hand through my unkempt beard and into my hair, which could use three solid washings. A quarter smile cracks my lips. "I've seen better weeks."

The king leans against the wall and gazes out the window at the gray morning. "I've come to ask you to leave for Brentyn."

My spine groans as I sit straight.

"I've received word back from Lord Freil. He has nearly one hundred men armed and ready to march."

I stare at Britta and wonder if I'll ever see her smile or smirk or glare at me again. I scrub my eyes and turn to face the king. "You need a commander."

"Yes. I need you and Leif to take this army with me, and together we'll march on Brentyn. I don't believe we'll meet with much resistance. Now that the rebels' leaders have been killed, I suspect most will accept a deal. If they lay down their arms and accept defeat, they may live out their lives beyond the borders of Malam."

"And if there's strong resistance?" I ask, though it's unlikely. The head's been cut off the beast.

"The sons of two lords from the northern borders who were killed during the castle attack have pledged their loyalty to me. Should more men be needed, we can call on another hundred and fifty from the northern fiefs."

At my hesitation, the king says, "The Guild said it might be weeks if not longer before Britta can travel."

Though the thought of leaving her drives me mad, restoring harmony in the land will give Britta a home to return to. And perhaps she'll have the freedom to live her life without fear of who she is.

"When do we leave?"

His eyes flick to her sleeping form and back to me, an apology written in the lines around them. "Immediately."

My fingers find Britta's, covering her hand as if I might secret away a prized possession. I nod, accepting my role to come in ending this dark time in our countries' histories. "My heart, my blood, my life for Malam."

Aodren exits, giving me a few moments alone. There's a huge part of me that wants to tell him no. I want to stay by her side until she wakes. But I've made peace with the fact that I have a tendency to make choices that suffocate Britta. That's something I'm not going to do anymore. My staying by her side might not make her feel like I'm trying to govern her. But it might. I have faith that whatever the king did for Britta will heal her. And once she's on the mend, I want her to have the space and freedom to finish deciding what she wants in this life.

I drop a kiss to Britta's forehead and then to the pale curves of her lips. "Come back to me, Dove." My whisper washes over her mouth.

I hold for a moment, praying a miracle will happen, hoping for some sort of change that'll confirm she'll make it. That this isn't our final goodbye. But nothing happens. Pain daggers through my heart as I turn and walk out the door.

Before leaving, I go to Finn's side. The kid's mottled face and weakened body threaten to break what's left of my weak heart. I softly chuck his shoulder and tell him I love him. Then after bidding goodbye to Lirra, the Guild, and the Channeler girls, we travel to the camp outside Brentyn. There, King Aodren meets with the commander of Lord Freil's soldiers. We spend two days organizing the men. On the third we march.

It takes four days for our army to seize control of Lord Jamis's men. Many of them stand down as soon as their leader's death is announced. Those who resist are subdued with little fighting.

Despite their betrayal, King Aodren offers a merciful punishment. The rebels are exiled from Malam. They may live out their lives in the Akaria Desert or north in the wastelands of Kolontia. But never again may they set foot in Malam.

In my opinion, King Aodren's mercy is more than most of the rebels deserved. In the few days Jamis occupied Brentyn, the havoc he caused led to hundreds of deaths. The royal city, once called the heart of Malam, isn't the same. Death stains the streets.

Time moves quickly over the next week as we see to the many grieving families.

With the rebels gone, we have the task of washing blood off the streets and wiping it from Castle Neart's Great Hall. Graves are dug and filled. Cobblestones are scrubbed clean.

The hardest part about returning to Castle Neart, however, is finding the young girls who have been imprisoned in the dungeon cells. Most are timid mice, shying away from our lanterns. It takes soft words and patience to coax them from the pit of the castle. The king orders the suites to be set up as additional healing rooms for the girls who have suffered from exposure and lack of food. Leif helps me gather blankets and clothing and hot meals. The work is humbling to me, but more so, it's good for him. Every girl he helps lifts his spirit a little more.

The work is endless. So much so that Finn and Lirra's arrival at Castle Neart three weeks after I left Britta comes as a shock.

"They've come to help return all the Channeler girls to their homes," King Aodren explains inside his private study. He stands beside his absurdly large desk. His father must've had a thing for flashy furniture. "You are more familiar with Shaerdan than any of my men. I am not asking that you personally escort all the girls safely home, but I do need you to organize their return."

I cross my arms, hiding the fists of my hands under my biceps, calculating how long I'll be gone.

"Split the girls into groups based on where they're from. Then assign a few men to each group of girls. I want to ensure their safety."

He goes on to talk about restitution. I consider his orders, willing back my frustration. Returning the girls means I'll be on the road another few weeks. However, if I'm in charge, I can decide which region to go to first. The Channelers heading to the southeast corner of Shaerdan sound like the perfect group to chaperone home.

"Questions?" The king drops into the seat on the other side of the desk.

I shake my head, a smile forming inside. "None at all."

Before leaving Brentyn, Finn takes me and Lirra to Hagan's home, where Gillian has been staying. Finn originally left her because she was too weak and broken to move. When rebel guards came to search Hagan's home, Finn covered Gillian with boxes and blankets in the attic space. Then he distracted the men by riding away on Britta's horse. Unfortunately, he didn't get very far. Finn was captured a quarter league from Hagan's home.

The door opens, and Gillian greets us through a mess of her tears. "Finn! Cohen! Lirra!" She wraps us in her arms, attempting an awkward jumbled group hug.

I untangle myself from the others and straighten my tunic.

"Let's not do that again." Lirra steps back.

Gillian waves a dismissing hand at her. "Get in here."

She demands we tell her everything. But as I cover all that transpired in the last couple of weeks, Gillian's hand lifts to her chest, clutching her dress until I finish. Moisture pools in the edges of her eyes.

"I want to go to Britta. See how she's doing." Gillian stares out the window.

Lirra crosses to the woman and cautiously lowers a hand to Gillian's shoulder. "She's in the best hands right now. Give her more time to recover."

Time. Time is torture when you're away from the one you love.

I haven't heard much from the Channelers Guild since the king and I returned to Malam. Any mention of her progress has been limited to a handful of promising words. *Healing slowly. A bit better today. Color returning.*

Gillian's pinched expression tells me she doesn't want to stay in Hagan's home any more than I want to prolong my time away from Britta. But she agrees when Lirra stresses the need for recovery time. With a grave nod, Gillian promises to visit Leif and keep an eye on Britta's cottage until she hears word that Britta is well enough to receive visitors.

Later that morning, Finn, Lirra, and I leave for the southeastern region of Shaerdan. Joined by a couple of royal guards, we escort two carriages of Channeler girls. The carriages squelch through the half-melted patches of snow and mud on the road that winds toward Brentyn. Signs of spring, shoots of new plants and buds on branches, peek through winter's crust.

The girls huddle in the confines of the carriage. But as we gain distance from Castle Neart, eyes exchange glances, small smiles sneak out, and sparks of hope crack through wary expressions.

As we roll over the town's cobblestones, people gather in the market like any other day, chattering the latest gossip. They gather around the signs posted throughout the royal city. It's a royal decree — the Purge has ended.

Lirra motions for the carriage to stop so we can read the parchment.

> *A kingdom ruled by fear is destined to fall. Channelers are an integral thread in the weave of our nation and our nation's history. The eradication of Channelers will forever be known as our country's greatest and gravest sin. I hereby wholeheartedly abolish the Purge Proclamation . . .*

"About time," Lirra mutters.

She steps out of the carriage and I follow behind, wanting to get a little closer to the posting to finish reading the decree.

All rights and privileges given to other citizens of Malam shall be returned to Channelers. King Aodren demands those affected by the Purge be treated with respect and equality, lands returned to those who were once stripped of their property, and restitution made for the lives lost. I don't know how a country could ever fully repay the depth of loss, but the decree is a strong start. King Aodren's apology is followed by an issue that any person caught harming a Channeler will be placed in the pillory.

"Wonder how that'll affect you." Lirra taps her chin.

"What do you mean?" Finn pops up beside her, Siron close behind him.

"Just that change doesn't come about so quick." She snaps her fingers. "Some people are going to resist."

True. Some will fight. Change often comes on the tail end of pain and tears. But this country has been bleeding for change for the last decade. Some will resist the decree, but my guess is most will embrace it.

"We better get going if we're planning to be back for this." Finn points to the bottom of the post.

The decree calls for a gathering of the lords. In three weeks' time, all nobility are called to a court meeting, in which King Aodren will introduce his newly formed inner council and discuss implementation of the new laws in Malam.

"Aye." I reach for Siron, giving my place in the carriage to Finn. "Let's get going."

The air might still carry a bitter bite, but I can see spring trying to edge its way in. Change is happening all around us.

I never imagined this day would come so soon, when rights and freedom would be returned to Channelers. Filled with hope for Britta and the future, I urge Siron into a gallop to lead the girls home.

COHEN

EACH SHAERDANIAN TOWN GREETS US A LITTLE differently. Some welcome us with open arms and demand we stay for a night, celebrating with spirits and meat. Other Shaerdanian towns want us to leave the second we've delivered their missing daughters.

The hardest part comes when we travel to the families of the girls who didn't make it through Jamis's rebellion. It's difficult to see their tears. To watch them fall to their knees in grief. Losing a loved one brands you. It carves space in your heart that will always stay a little empty.

A week after leaving Brentyn, I break away from the traveling party. Lirra, Finn, and the guards will go on to see the remaining girls safely returned home. But I cannot stay away from a specific Channeler any longer.

Lamplight glows from cottage windows in the town of Tahr, yellow spilling onto the gravel road. Siron breaks away from the village, headed for Katallia's home in the outskirts of the valley where shadows separate her land. But one single lantern shines against the wooded mountain backdrop. A beacon in the night.

It's dark and impossible to see inside the stable, so I dismount Siron right outside Katallia's door. His nose nuzzles my hand as I turn to leave. Maybe he can sense how hammered I am. Time apart from Britta has made me realize how many mistakes I've made. Instead of giving her my trust and support, my actions were often suffocating.

At Katallia's door, I slide off my cap. Run fingers through my hair. Smack the dust from my coat and trousers. Then knock.

The blaze in the hearth glows behind Katallia, her red curls taking on the look of smelted metal. She opens the door wider. Her brows lift in surprise. "Cohen, I wasn't expecting you tonight as well. Though I figured you'd come break down my door sooner than later."

"Didn't want to interrupt her healing till now," I admit with a shrug. Maybe I should've come earlier. "And King Aodren's had a lot for me to do."

"Has he?" She taps her chin. "Well, don't stand there, letting in all the cold." Katallia sweeps her arm to the side, gesturing for me to enter.

The room's been cleaned and painted and the furniture

fixed up since the last time I was here. No signs of the attack show anywhere. I tell her as much.

"Yes, well, it took almost a month to get this home in order. I can only imagine how busy you've been in Brentyn."

I give a polite nod. "Is Britta awake?"

Katallia flicks a glance at the hallway before facing me with her head tipped to one side. "She is. But I'm not sure if now is the best time."

Right. It's after supper. Still, she said Britta wasn't sleeping. "I traveled all day to get here."

She crosses her arms and drums her fingers against her sleeves. The woman's indecision could cause madness. "Cohen, I—"

"Please," I insist, crossing the room to her side. "I'll be quick. It's been too long. Too long. I'm half mad knowing she's in the house and I'm not already at her side."

Her sigh sounds like an approval. I don't wait to ask. I dart around her and down the hall to Britta's room. I knock once. When she doesn't say anything, I crack the door open. "Britta? It's me— Bludger."

Don't know what I was expecting, but it sure wasn't King Aodren, seated in the wooden chair at her bedside. Britta's blue eyes fly to mine. She's lying beneath a woolen blanket, only her face and arms visible. Still, it's enough to know she's worlds better. No more deathly pallor. Her cheeks are tinged the color of summer peaches.

For a swollen pause, no one speaks. My gaze cuts between

them, taking in the way he holds her hand between his. Cannot say the sight doesn't wound me.

"Perhaps I should've waited for your answer," I say. "I didn't mean to interrupt." Seeds, I've never felt so out of place.

"No." Britta speaks right as the king stands, his chair scraping against the wood.

"Excuse me. I didn't know you were planning a visit." King Aodren's formality makes me cringe even more. "I was returning from a meeting with the Guild. Since I was nearby, I thought I'd stop in and see how Britta was doing."

"I was . . ." I pause. But I wasn't in the area. Hadn't finished my assigned duties. I've no good excuse other than wanting to see her. "I wanted to see how you were doing." I look at Britta.

A smile cracks her lips.

Aodren gives Britta a long glance before he turns to me. "Good seeing you, Cohen. I'll let you two have some privacy."

He leaves and I sit in his chair. Keeping my face neutral, I fight down the jealousy. I hate that he saw her before I did. "How're you doing, Britt?"

"As Katallia would say, I'm 'on the mend.' Though it still feels as if I'm barely holding myself together."

"Bad as before?"

She shakes her head. It's been worse.

I lean forward, loathing the distance between us. "I'm sorry I haven't come before now. Katallia said she'd let me know when you were ready for visitors. Still waiting on her letter."

"And yet you're here?" Britta smiles, but it's tired, not reaching her eyes. To punctuate the image of exhaustion, she lets out a yawn. It makes me feel guilty for keeping her up so late.

"Tired?"

She shrugs. "A bit."

Bet if I had her ability, my innards would flash icy cold.

"Why'd you come all this way, Cohen?"

I prop my elbows on my knees and stare at the wood slats that make up the floor. There are a dozen things I want to say, but now I'm questioning myself. I wanted to return and annihilate the distance between us.

Yet I'm wondering if that's what she wants. Last Britta and I talked, I suggested she have time away from me to decide what she truly desires. Fact of the matter is, whatever I had with Britta ended when I chose to give her space. I cannot fault her for possibly entertaining the thought of a life without me, if that's what she wants most. Nor can I push her into remaining with me.

I'm not doing a great job of giving her space. I promised I wouldn't hover or try to govern her decisions.

I hold my breath, steeling myself to stay true to my word. "I'm here because I care about you. Wanted to see if you're doing good. That's all. Not staying long."

She frowns.

"Just wanted to let you know that if you need me, I'll be here," I add. I clear my throat and force myself to hold her gaze.

There's been something scratching at my conscience. The way I treated Britta after discovering her with the king was wrong, considering I'd kissed Lirra.

"When I was traveling with Lirra, we had to pretend to be newlyweds. A barkeep called for us to kiss to prove as much." Britta flinches and I feel it in my gut. "Didn't mean anything. I should've told you before now. I . . . I'm sorry."

"But you were so angry over Aodren . . ."

My head hangs. "I'm a bludger."

"Thank you for being honest with me."

Her response hits hard, reminding me how much I've hid from her in the past. If she chooses a future with me, I'll never hold anything back again. I issue another apology, and when her eyes droop, I say, "I'm going to give you the space you need to decide what you want. More than anything, I want you to be happy."

Bloody gods, the words nearly kill me. The jealous part of me demands to know what the king is doing here, but somehow I manage to hold the question back.

I wait for her reply, but all that comes is a small "Thank you, Cohen."

I catch up with Lirra and Finn two days later and finish out the assignment King Aodren gave me before returning to Brentyn. Once there, I ride straight to Britta's cottage. She's not one who would stay away from her cottage for long. Since she was alert when I last saw her, there's a good chance she's returned to Brentyn.

Only, her shutters are closed. No smoke rises from the chimney. The stables show no sign of use all winter.

The loneliness that's taken residency in my bones tightens its grip. I scratch my beard, letting my fingers graze my scar, the one piece of Britta I'll always have. Then I set to work. Don't know if she'll ever return, but I want her land to be kept up and her belongings safe.

Over the next few days when I've some free time away from castle duties, I ride out to Britta's cottage and tend the property. On a cold sunny morning, I find another horse there.

"Hello," I call out, hand reaching for my blade.

Gillian throws open the cottage door. Her face, now clear of bruises, greets me with a wide smile. "I was wondering who cleaned up the stable."

I hug her, laughing as she makes another comment about her fat heifer, and follow her inside.

"This where you snuck off to the other day?"

Leif's voice has me spinning around. He's sitting in Britta's favorite spot—her papa's wooden chair. A fire burns in the hearth. I make a mental note not to let myself get distracted by my thoughts in the future. Didn't even see the smoke coming out of the chimney.

I shrug. "Figured it needed looking after."

"I understand. Britta's cottage reminds me of better times."

Leif's voice is morose. Though leading the troops against Jamis's forces gave him purpose for a time, he hasn't returned to his jolly self. Makes me wonder if he ever will.

"What are you guys doing here?"

A blush crosses Gillian's cheeks. "I came to air out the rooms for Britta, should she ever return. Leif was kind enough to help me."

They share a small smile. It's the softest expression I've seen on his face since Omar's death. I'm glad for him. Aodren insisted he take Omar's position as captain of the guard—cannot be easy. We haven't talked much about Omar, though I've expressed my opinion a number of times. What happened on the Channeler's field wasn't Leif's fault.

"I noticed the roof needs patching." The sun has peeked out and melted the snow enough to show the thatch. "I'll work on that."

Gillian and Leif leave an hour or so later, but I work until the sky darkens. The best way to keep myself from drowning in *should've*s and *would've*s concerning Britta is to keep busy.

On another day, I mend a stall in the barn.

A time after that, I paint Britta's door.

Winter gives way to spring, and Britta's house remains empty and silent.

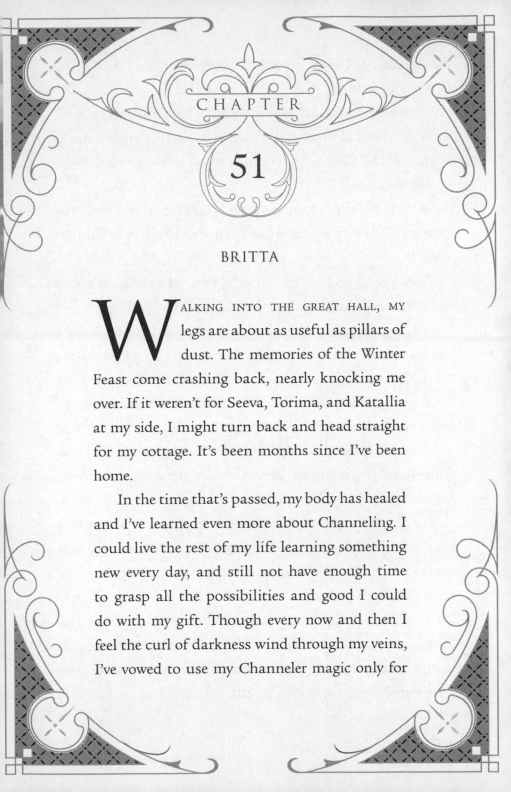

CHAPTER

51

BRITTA

WALKING INTO THE GREAT HALL, MY legs are about as useful as pillars of dust. The memories of the Winter Feast come crashing back, nearly knocking me over. If it weren't for Seeva, Torima, and Katallia at my side, I might turn back and head straight for my cottage. It's been months since I've been home.

In the time that's passed, my body has healed and I've learned even more about Channeling. I could live the rest of my life learning something new every day, and still not have enough time to grasp all the possibilities and good I could do with my gift. Though every now and then I feel the curl of darkness wind through my veins, I've vowed to use my Channeler magic only for good. I am not Phelia, nor will I ever be like her. I'll be stronger, kinder, better.

The herald announces our arrival. "Lady Britta Flannery, Miss Torima Lolear of the Channelers Guild, Miss Katallia Barrett of the Channelers Guild, and Miss Seeva Soliel of the Channelers Guild."

All eyes in the room land on us. A hush falls over the nobility—many new faces mixed in with a handful of familiar ones.

Seeva gently pushes my back. "Go on," she whispers out of the corner of her mouth. "Be brave."

As an official member of the Guild, I'm here today as a noblewoman, presenting these women to the kingdom. Across the room, just as on the night of the feast, Aodren sits at the head of the table in his father's atrocity of a throne. His smile quirks as we walk down the stairs into the Great Hall.

No longer am I bound to Aodren by my Channeler magic. Through the rune, he was able to return my energy that lived within him. There's nothing left to inform him of my presence. It's our friendship that connects us. But it's a struggle to look straight at Aodren when my eyes desperately want to seek out Cohen. I thought he'd be seated at the head of the room with the others in Aodren's inner circle. Only, he's not there.

It makes my steps into the room a little harder to take. But I continue on. When we reach the three stairs that lead up to Aodren's throne, we lower ourselves into curtsies, our dresses draping on the floor, mine a puddle of palest blue.

Katallia had this dress made to resemble Cohen's dress. It's the same color and cut the same way. I'd hoped when Cohen saw me he'd . . . actually, I don't know what I'd hoped. I've had a month since last seeing him to think about us. To ponder our connection and whether or not it influenced our relationship. It took over a month for my body to completely heal. In the time we've been apart, I've grown more certain that regardless of the connections I've had, and the current lack thereof, I love him. I love his desire to do what's right. I love his recklessness. I even love his protective nature.

I wanted to tell him these things face-to-face. That's why I waited.

I also hoped he'd be here to see me embrace who I am. It's taken all this time apart for me to accept that being a Channeler is integral to who I am. And it's not something I ever want to hide again.

My smile slumps, but I hitch it higher. Today I serve a great purpose. One that feels surreal and at the same time perfectly right. "Your Royal Highness, may I present my fellow Channelers, the women of the Guild."

A few murmurs echo through the room. Under the lantern glow that paints the surrounding columns in golden hues, a handful of lords and ladies sit stiffly in their seats, whispering behind gloved hands.

I notice them, and just as quickly dismiss their chilling reception. Many people now understand for the first time that I am a Channeler. Not everyone is bound to be open to the idea of Channelers in Malam. It'll take time. But thanks to the decree, we're not hiding and living in fear. Even so, every now and then the temptation to be afraid comes, but I tamp it down. I have as much right to be here as these people. After all, I am Saul Flannery's daughter.

Aodren asks us to rise. He then stands and bows in return to us. "Your presence here is always welcome. We are honored by your service to the kingdom."

Broken applause can be heard throughout the Great Hall. I jerk in surprise, shocked that anyone would be pleased. At least half the room isn't showing any form of approval, but I cannot ignore the half that is. Having been a pariah for so long, the support of anyone in the nobility is overwhelming.

Reading my confusion, Aodren gestures to me once more and a few more claps are added to the crowd's cheer. My heart expands. Tears of wonder blur my sight. I blink them away so as not to embarrass myself.

Aodren walks down the steps and extends his hand to Seeva. She takes it and follows him up the stairs, where he gestures for her to take a seat beside the other nobility at the head table. "May I present Miss Seeva Soliel, Channeler ambassador from Shaerdan, and newest member of my Inner Advisory Circle."

The nobles' focus shifts to Seeva, and I exhale in relief—a breath it seems like I've been holding all my life.

As we're ushered to our seats, I catch a glimpse of a decorated guard beyond one of the pillars. He's standing inside the castle's hallway, ribbons adorning his royal coat. The sight of his sable hair and golden skin set fire to my veins.

Cohen.

He's in the exact spot we said goodbye, last time we were in the castle.

Even though we no longer share a bond, every particle of me yearns to go to him. To touch him and breathe him in and put my arms around him. To tell him I know *exactly* who I want.

But Aodren begins talking, and now that I'm nobility, I have to show some decorum.

It's late in the afternoon when the nobles' lunch is over. The moment we finish, I'm on my feet and cutting across the hall to the passage where I last saw Cohen.

But when I get there, he's already left.

I take the road along the Evers that leads to my cottage.

Drained from a day spent with the nobility—a day in which I've conversed with more people than in the rest of my life altogether—I want nothing more than to curl up in Papa's chair beside a warm fire and listen to the silence of the woods from my cottage.

I sent word to Gillian that I've returned, so I've no doubt she'll come visit later. I considered sending Cohen a letter as well, but I didn't know where he's living. I assumed he was in the guards' quarters. Only, when I inquired about where Cohen is staying, Leif shook his head and shrugged.

On the way home, the sun peeks from the clouds. Now that I've come down from the high of the nobles' lukewarm reception, the gnawing ache of missing Cohen intensifies. I really hoped for a chance to talk with him. Despite the afternoon light, sadness has a way of burrowing under the skin and turning even the brightest day bleak.

When my cottage comes into view, I notice smoke wafting from the chimney. Gillian must've made it here before me.

Happy to see her, I force a smile over my frown. I ride Snowfire into the yard and dismount. After leading her into the stable, I remove my gear and take a few minutes to brush her down. Her water's already been topped off. Another Gillian surprise, perhaps?

I rush out of the stable to thank her for doing so much, when I notice that Papa's cottage has never looked so good. New paint, mended roof, pruned trees. When did she have the time or energy — or the know-how — to do all this?

Following the *whack, whack, whack* of an ax, I walk around the back of my cottage.

The sight of Cohen — coat off, tunic stained with sweat, arm muscles flexing with each strike — swipes my breath.

His swings are fluid and precise. Like chopping wood is a dance instead of a chore. I could watch him do this, watch the way his body moves, for days. The familiarity I've missed so much beats through me.

I don't speak, so it takes a half-dozen logs before Cohen glances up and notices my presence. He slams the ax into the wood and leaves it. Sliding his forearm across his brow, he clears the perspiration from his eyes and studies me.

Seeds, I want him to talk, to say my name, to say anything. The last time we were together was punctuated with awkwardness. I'd just told Aodren that I could never love him the way I love Cohen. This man before me is my best friend, my support, my champion. And while he might sometimes be stubborn and mulish, so am I.

"Hi," I say at the same time he talks. Thankfully it comes out clearly despite my club of a heart banging on my ribs.

"I didn't realize you were coming home so soon." He slides a handkerchief from his pocket and mops his brow. Lips sucked between teeth, he gazes at my cottage before refocusing on me. "I — I'm sorry you found me here. I was . . . I mean —" He sighs.

I've never seen Cohen this flustered in my life. It's endearing and adorable.

Finally he gets the words out. "I saw you were back, and I wanted to have the place ready for you."

The banging inside my chest stops. Inside it feels like my heart's suddenly about to burst.

"Cohen." I walk forward. "You didn't have to do any of this. But I'm grateful. Thank you so much."

He hangs his head and murmurs something that sounds like "It's all I can do." He lifts his chin. "You did well today. You . . . you looked stunning. You were confident. You commanded everyone's attention. I was so damn proud of you. And I know if Saul were here, he'd say 'well done.'"

His approval warms me from the top of my head to my toes.

"Thank you. Do you want to come inside?" I smooth my hands over the waistline of my dress. "You look like you could use a little rest."

He chuckles and follows me to the door, but stops before entering. He studies the wood grain and frowns.

"Actually, Britt, I'd probably better not."

My name on his lips shoots a tremor under my skin. I've missed the sound of him saying it. "Oh? Do you have to get back to the castle?" I toy with the door handle, pretending I'm not a little bit devastated.

He shifts his weight on the moss-covered stones just outside my cottage door. I notice that the snow has been shoveled to the sides of the walkway. "No, I just think I'm going to need some time to get used to being around you."

"Why is that?"

He tugs on the back of neck. Lets out a heavy exhalation. "Thing is, I love you. I love you so much that it hurts to be around you and not be yours. I know I said you should take some time and decide what you want. I want to punch myself for even suggesting it. But then . . ." He drops his head, and the words seem to tumble out end over end. "I can understand why you'd pick him. He's a better man than me. He's not a jealous fool. He's not made an arse of himself trying to protect you from things you're perfectly capable of handling. He hasn't wronged you like I have."

Cohen looks up at the sky. The sun paints the curves and valleys of his features, showing that he's lost weight in the weeks we've been apart. "I can be your friend. I can. I need time."

I feel the chill in his words. The liar.

I think of the faults he just listed about himself and smile inwardly. I spent so long putting Cohen on a pedestal that I didn't realize he had faults. However, at the same time, I wouldn't let myself believe I was a good match for Cohen because all I could focus on were my shortcomings.

Neither one of us is perfect. We make mistakes all the time. But we're changing. We're growing. We're learning to be better for each other. He's not the same Cohen who held secrets from me and went overboard in efforts to protect me. I'm not the same Britta who trusts no one and avoids going into town for fear of townspeople's ire.

I used to believe that a happy life with friends and family wasn't fated for me. That Cohen wasn't meant for me because he could have anyone else.

But I was wrong. I didn't believe in myself enough. I didn't see my worth.

Loving yourself, and believing you are good and capable, is a journey. One that I want to take with Cohen.

I close the distance between us and force his hand open so his fingers can wind into mine. "Thing is, Cohen, I love you too. I want you to come inside with me right now, and I don't ever want you to leave. I care for Aodren. As a friend. He's not the man I want. The man I love is sometimes jealous and sometimes a little overprotective. But we're working on that. And I have to disagree about Aodren being the better man."

I brazenly run my hand over his chest.

His eyes flash before softening. He grabs me to him. At the same time, he reaches back and opens my door. We stumble over the threshold, our boots clattering against the wood floor.

A laugh, and then his heartbeat kicks against mine. His nose runs along the column of my neck before he draws in a deep breath of me. "Is that so?" His voice takes a husky turn I feel down into my core.

This man. The way he spins my world.

"Yes." I grin. "The best for me is you."

He moves his head to align his lips above mine. They hover there, teasing me. "Then I expect we'll be getting married in the next few weeks."

Is that a proposal? I roll my eyes and at the same time chuckle.

"Seems about right to me." I run my fingers into his beard, grazing his scar.

Cohen's smile could rival the glory of the sun. I see it for all of two seconds before his lips are on mine and his kiss becomes my world.

Acknowledgments

First and foremost, my gratitude goes to you, my wonderful reader, for supporting my dream and allowing me to take you on this journey. I am ever grateful.

That being said, I could not have completed this novel without the guidance and help from my brilliant agent, Josh Adams. Thank you for being the calm voice when I'm an erratic storm of thoughts. Or the enthusiastic cheerleader when I'm the author equivalent of Eeyore. I couldn't have found a better literary agent.

To my editor, Sarah Landis: thank you for trekking through the Ever Woods with me. You took on my crazy ideas and helped mold them into something special. You have expertly guided me through the woods. It's been an honor to work with you and the amazing team at Houghton Mifflin Harcourt.

Special thanks go to the tenacious Erin DeWitt and the kind Lauren Cepero — thank you for entertaining my slew of emails and taking such good care of my cast of characters. To Alexandra Primiani, my tireless publicist, thank you for spreading the love of the Clash of Kingdoms books. Your enthusiasm means the world to me.

Caitlyn McFarland, plotting genius, you pulled me through the trenches of mapping out this novel. It was a hellacious month. But you never walked away. Thank you for pushing me on, devouring caramel apples with me, and helping me sift through the muck.

Rahul Kanakia, your wisdom and insight entertained me, brought new levels of understanding, and shaped me as a writer. You're my favorite phone call and my romance-reading partner in crime.

Madalyn and C.J. Nuccitelli, I would've been lost without you. Your hunting knowledge and skill gave Britta life. I might never hunt a buck, but I'll smile and pretend the one mounted on your wall is the coolest thing ever. I love you both.

Jessie Humphries, your wit and sass have kept me laughing and smiling along this publishing journey. I hope we'll be in this together for a long time to come. BFFs, always. You can't get rid of me.

My heartfelt gratitude to Kate Coursey for reading my work and writing alongside me. To Peggy Eddleman for starting this journey with me and sticking it out thus far. Like I said in the beginning, "If you're game, I'm game." Let's see this journey through. To Elana Johnson, Kathryn Purdie, Emily King, Taffy Lovell, Nicole Giles, Charlie Holmberg, Veeda Bybee, Lindsay Leavitt Brown, Sarah Larson, Julie Olsen, and Brekke Felt—you women are invaluable to me. Thank you for writing with me at Write Night when really all we did was stuff our faces with candy. Your friendship is a gift. I love you all.

To my amazing debut sisters, Laura Shovan, Erin Schneider, Nicole Castroman, Evelyn Skye, Shannon Parker, Rosalyn Eves, Traci Chee, Tara Sim, Jessica Cluess, Randi Pink, and Tricia Levenseller—thank you for staying with me through the end of the debut year, for sharing your stories with me, for every email, every text, every uplifting gift. One of the greatest gifts of publishing is finding such wonderful friends.

To Laurie McLean and all the agents at Fuse Literary for your friendship, advice, and support.

To all the lovely bloggers, librarians, YouTubers, and book enthusiasts, you've given my book and so many others a voice. I send my biggest hug your way. Never stop what you're doing.

To CJ Redwine for entertaining my emails and giving me some of the best writing advice I've ever received. Your tips helped me finish this book. I'm forever grateful.

To my dear friends—Tammy Merryweather, Shanelle and Erik Bayles, Alecia Bales, Emily Hammerstad, Ruby and Garth Fielding, Skipper and Evan Coates, and Tad and Tami Rabin —thank you for loving me and my kids. Despite my hermit-like ways, I'm grateful that you've not given up on our friendship.

And last, my most heartfelt gratitude and love go to Mom, Dad, my siblings, my husband, and my children. Thank you for believing in me, showing up to book signings, and talking about my books to all your friends. Thank you for allowing me to have late nights and lazy mornings to sleep off the writing binges. When I see your social media posts or hear you speak about me, you make me sound so much cooler than I really am. Thank you for that, and for proving over and over that family is what matters most.

TURN THE PAGE FOR A SNEAK PEEK!

As King Aodren attempts to end the bloody divide between Channelers and the giftless in Malam, he hears rumors of a deadly Channeler-made substance. When Lirra, a Channeler from a neighboring country, offers to help him discover the truth behind the rumors, Aodren begins to see a way forward for his people. But only if he can rewrite the mistakes of the past before it's too late.

AODREN

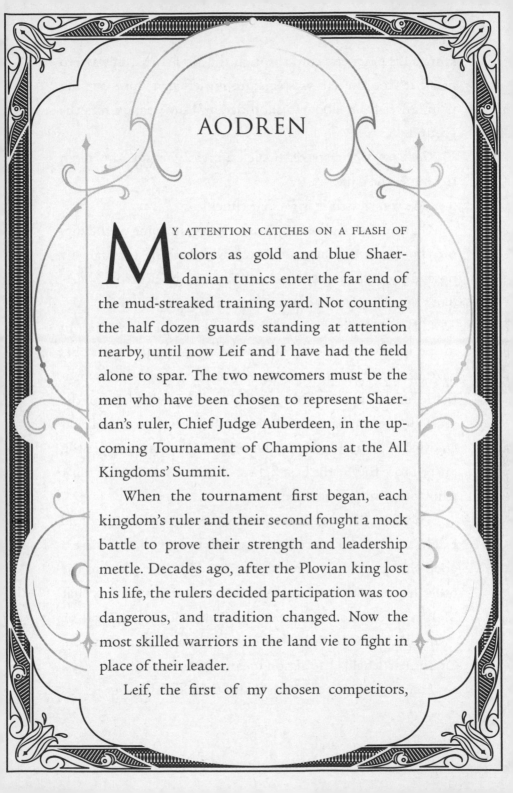

MY ATTENTION CATCHES ON A FLASH OF colors as gold and blue Shaerdanian tunics enter the far end of the mud-streaked training yard. Not counting the half dozen guards standing at attention nearby, until now Leif and I have had the field alone to spar. The two newcomers must be the men who have been chosen to represent Shaerdan's ruler, Chief Judge Auberdeen, in the upcoming Tournament of Champions at the All Kingdoms' Summit.

When the tournament first began, each kingdom's ruler and their second fought a mock battle to prove their strength and leadership mettle. Decades ago, after the Plovian king lost his life, the rulers decided participation was too dangerous, and tradition changed. Now the most skilled warriors in the land vie to fight in place of their leader.

Leif, the first of my chosen competitors,

swings his practice sword through the air. I thrust upward to block. It's too late. His waster slams my left arm. Bone-rattling pain lances from elbow to shoulder, and my weapon hits the ground.

Godstars! "Solid strike." I suck a breath between my teeth to temper the pain.

"Are you whistling, sir?" Leif chuckles.

Glaring, I straighten my posture, regain some of the dignity he knocked away, and switch to breathing through my nose, despite the moisture that clings to my nostrils. Shaerdan's humidity is also out to kill me today.

"I shouldn't have landed that," Leif says in a low voice. In my periphery, I notice one of the ever-present guards avert his gaze, and I wonder if he heard Leif's comment. It's too sympathetic for the captain of the royal guard—the elite force of the most skilled combatants in Malam. He needs to control that emotion if he and Baltroit, the other Malamian competitor, are to prove they're the best fighters in the five kingdoms. Grit wins tournaments, not sympathy.

The last All Kingdoms' Summit was five years ago, and I didn't attend. It's more important than ever that we have a good showing during the tournament. We must prove to the other leaders, my late father's peers, and to Malamians that Malam is worthy of being here. That I am worthy of being here.

I roll out my bruised shoulder. "I shouldn't have let you. On the battlefield, distraction means death."

Leif watches the Shaerdanians through the slits in his

helmet. "Lucky there's no risk here." He reaches for the fallen practice waster and swings it in an arc. "Not with this blunted sword."

I move into position. "Enough talk."

"Oh, you're recovered? Ready to get beat?" Exhaustion helps Leif forget himself, a benefit of our sparring sessions. Too often, he lapses into the formality he feels the captain of the royal guard should maintain around the king. He forgets I am just a man and he is my closest, if not only, friend.

Chuckling, I switch grips to take the sword in my dominant right hand. "Captain and court jester, let's see how you fare now."

He snorts and swings his waster. I've spent the last six months training with Leif. I've studied his movement. He is quick, but I'm faster. I block his blade and push my weight into his. He stumbles. A vulnerable space opens between his elbow and ribs, and I strike. Leif grunts against the pain.

The rhythm of our clanks and curses echoes across the yard. This rigorous sparring session keeps Leif competition-ready for the Tournament of Champions. And it tempers the uneasiness that came on earlier today when my traveling retinue exited the forest and first beheld Shaerdan's summer castle. The stone fortress is designated for all leaders and dignitaries during the summit and sits north of Celize like a solemn gray throne.

My absence from the last summit sparked rumors that spread like a scourge. *King Aodren's too young. Soon he'll be just like his hateful father and the blood-spilling regent. Malam's people are divided, and the kingdom is weak. Under King Aodren, only time re- mains until the kingdom falls.*

Malam's history has more shameful spots than the sky has stars.

My father was a prejudiced man, whose fear of Channel- ers spread to his advisers and led to the Purge—a kingdom- wide Channeler eradication spanning nearly two decades. The feverish hunt for magic users turned neighbor on neighbor. After my father died when I was a child, a regent ruled until I came of age. He closed the Malamian borders so no one could leave or enter Malam. Trade halted and our economy suffered. This dark time was further blackened when, a year ago, the regent didn't want to relinquish power. He led a coup, killing hundreds of citizens and half of Malam's nobility.

The rumors hold some truth—I am the youngest ruler at the summit, my people are divided between support and op- position for Channelers, and Malam has been weakened.

But I won't be my father.

I won't allow Malam to fall.

When Leif and I are both aching and bruised, we stop fighting. I lean on my sword, breath sawing through my lungs. Leif tugs off his helmet. He swipes sweat from his beard and shakes out his hair. The usual amber color is now a slick mud- brown. "I could sleep till the first night of the tournament."

My thoughts as well. However, "It wouldn't do well to miss dinner."

Leif mutters an unenthused agreement.

Once our gear is stored in the yard house, two guards follow me and Leif off the field.

"See how in sync they are?" Leif glances at the Shaerdanians before they're out of sight. "If Baltroit would practice here, we'd have a better chance of winning the cup."

I scratch the day's stubble on my jaw. The summit, the tournament, and the jubilee are key factors in turning Malam's tide. We must do well in all three. When Lord Segrande insisted his son be chosen as the second competitor, I complied. Segrande was integral in the negotiations to reopen trade with Shaerdan, and going forward, his support is necessary to boost Malam's economy. While Segrande and I form alliances and trade agreements during summit meetings, Baltroit and Leif will be fighting in the Tournament of Champions.

Thousands of Malamians have traveled to Shaerdan to attend the events. A tournament win will inspire pride. It'll give Malamians a reason to rally together. A reason to set aside their differences. And hopefully, later, a reason to spread unity back in Malam.

Baltroit is a fierce fighter, but he's arrogant and refuses to train with Leif. While I could order Baltroit to the practice yard, it may offend Segrande, who has spent as much time training his son as I have with Leif.

"He won't let us down," I say, determined. "The two of you will do well."

Leif shoots me a look that argues otherwise.

The castle's grand hall is a clamor of voices, thuds, and scrapes, all under the aroma of rosemary and bread. As we pass through, conversation dims and everyone in sight bows. Our boots clack loudly against the stone stairs leading to the third floor, where Malam's private rooms are assigned. The two guards who followed us from the practice field take up posts at our closed corridor, while Leif enters my chambers.

He points to the stack of letters on the desk. "The courier delivered these to the castle. Also, the welcome meal will begin in two hours."

Half of Malam's fiefs have new leadership, and the repeal of the Purge Proclamation has made it possible for Channelers to return to Malam. A difficult transition, to say the least. To stay abreast of brewing tension, each lord reports on his fiefdom. Even during the summit.

"Inform Lord Segrande and tell him to come to my chambers at a quarter till." I start toward the washroom.

Leif lingers. "Your Highness, one more thing."

Your Highness. Few dare meet my eye, let alone speak to me directly. Some decorum is expected, but Leif's slip back into formality is aggravating. And isolating. "I'm scarcely six months older than you, and not a quarter-hour ago, you were trying to hit me with a practice sword. Call me by my given name."

"You're the king." He coughs into his fist.

"I'm aware. Trust me, rigid formality isn't always requisite. Understood?"

"Aye." His gaze shifts to the door. "At tonight's dinner, though, it'll be formal. Yes?"

"Yes. But you may talk with the other dignitaries."

"I — I'm not sure I can." A maroon tint stains his neck. He yanks his beard. It's hard to reconcile the man before me with the bear from the practice field. "Thing is, talking is not my strength."

Leif has notable battle experience, good rapport with the royal guard, and is unfailingly loyal, but he is also new to nobility. Too busy trying to bring Malam out of the darkness, I've overlooked his greenness.

"Talk about the tournament," I suggest. "King Gorenza will no doubt have much to say, since his youngest son is competing."

"Could work." He focuses on the floor stones for a long minute. "I won't be skilled like Captain Omar was with conversation. But I'll try."

I laugh, loud and irreverent. The long day is bringing out Leif's wit and humor.

But he doesn't join in, his mouth is pressed into a grim line.

Oh gods. Is he serious? My previous captain spoke in monosyllabic sentences.

"Leif." I restrain my laughter. Composure has been drilled into me since birth. "Omar used to say it's the message that matters. Remember that. Treat this dinner like those at Castle Neart."

"I mostly talk to Britta at Castle Neart. She's not here."

The comment comes unexpectedly.

The words settle over me like a scratchy wool throw. Britta and her husband are on their wedding trip instead of attending the summit. It's odd to consider her married, since I once hoped she would share my life. But . . . Britta is on my council. We will continue to work together. She will still be a friend.

"You'll do fine," I say, tone clipped.

Silence, and then, "Certainly, sir." Leif bows and leaves my chambers.

So much for convincing him to use my name. I walk to the desk and study the letters, though it's a fight to focus on any one of them. Perhaps Leif is right to remind me that friendships should be the furthest thing from my mind right now.

My focus must be Malam.

Correspondence to Aodren Lothar Cross, King of Malam:

March 25

 To the King our Most Sovereign Lord,

 By dictate of your wise council, I begin my monthly report of the affairs concerning my humble fiefdom. The abolishment of the Purge Proclamation has been posted in the markets and common areas, and all countrymen have received notice of the new law sealed by your great hand. May the news be received well. Or perhaps I should write, may the news be received better than it has been thus far. I'm certain those displeased with the return of Channelers will soon welcome the newcomers.

 Last, Sir Chilton, who inherited the bordering fiefdom after Lord Chamberlain was killed in the tragic attack on the castle, has struggled to manage his lands. The poor lad. If he needs to be relieved of his land, I offer my guardianship.

Your servant,
Lord Wynne of Jonespur

April 19

To the King, Lord of Malam,

This past month, four Channeler families returned from Shaerdan to reclaim lost lands. Unfortunately, their return was met with opposition—one barn fire, three travel carts destroyed, and numerous fights in the market square. I wish I could report these numbers amounted to less than last month.

In addition, the ore mine can no longer keep men employed until trade demand increases. The line of needy outside the church has doubled. And yet traders continue to come from Shaerdan. Considering Malamians have no coin to buy Shaerdanian goods, the traders must be foolishly optimistic.

Regardless, I hope the bordering kingdoms will welcome our trade soon. They cannot turn us away forever.

Your loyal man,
Lord Xavier Variant

April 24

To King Aodren Lothar Cross of Malam,

Difficulties have arisen as returning Channelers have declared ownership and sought possession of land that has been in another's hand for nearly two decades. Last week, a disagreement led to the destruction of two alfalfa fields, a Channeler booth in the marketplace, and a clergyman's entire cart of bread for the needy. It's impossible to say if these actions were meant to harm. I believe they were intended to scare.

Scribe for the Lord of Tahr,
Sir Ian Casper

May 5

To the King our Most Sovereign Lord,

Though your wise changes in the law dictated that the market be open to all, the appearance of Channelers has caused disturbances. Truly, I do all I can to keep peace. Channelers have been so bold as to ask friends and family to boycott the merchants that have refused business to persons of magic.

However, not all merchants have excluded Channelers. A new trader in the market square has been selling Channeler-made healing balms. A portion of townspeople have shown interest in his goods. One remedy gaining popularity is called Sanguine. It is a healing oil, and quite effective from what I've heard. Perhaps it could be a boon to our economy.

As always, I am humbly dedicated to overseeing my fief's needs, just as I could be with any additional land you might wish to grant upon me.

Your servant,
Lord Wynne of Jonespur

May 22

To King Aodren,

Calvin Bariston of Fennit passed on from injuries sustained in a tavern fight. It's uncertain who stabbed him, since he first stabbed two other men and one woman. Calvin was acting erratic, and was, we believe, possessed by a devil.

Rumors started that the cause was the Channelers. Those rumors were quickly proved unfounded.

Scribe for the Lord of Tahr,
Sir Ian Casper

June 1

To the King of Malam,

Rumors about the Channeler oil have spread after an

occurrence last week. Onlookers reported that Mr. Erik Bayles met a passing trader in the market square to purchase Sanguine. For unknown reasons, Mr. Bayles became angry and struck the trader, who then hit back, punching Mr. Bayles once and killing him. The trader left town before he was questioned. I've sent men after him.

Without answers, many blame Channeler magic. Either Sanguine gave the trader unnatural strength, or it caused Mr. Bayles's death. Those who knew Mr. Bayles best have insisted he was a hard man to kill. I did not inquire how many times they tried.

The dispute has divided the town. Some businesses have refused service to anyone associated with Channelers. While I could force businesses to open their doors to all, I fear it will not end the division.

I must know, is Sanguine truly harmful? Please advise on how to restore order to my fief.

Your loyal man,
Lord Xavier Variant

After I dress for dinner and Leif returns with Lord Segrande, I scan the letters I received over the last few months and compare them to the newest batch.

"Anything promising, Your Highness?" Segrande surveys the letters. His salt-and-sandy hair has taken a severe combing, unlike his untamed beard that twists and curls over the starched collar of his dinner coat. The mismatch suits Segrande, who is known for earning as many calluses as the people working the fields of his fief.

"More reports of division and opposition. Poverty in the ore fiefs. Destroyed property, disturbances in the market.

More rumors that feed wariness of Channelers." The chair scrapes the floor as I push back from the desk and pace away.

Our retinue spent two weeks traveling through Malam. Two weeks of passing through towns and farmlands and seeing firsthand the chasm between countrymen that should've been mended by the Purge's abolishment.

Those two weeks confirmed that decrees don't assuage distrust.

We are a gray, threadbare tapestry in desperate need of new threads to strengthen us. But my people have spent two decades fearing the very color we need now. Regardless of the abolished Purge, our factionalism leaves us weak.

Ignoring the powerlessness dragging through my veins, I stalk across the room, drop down on a bench, and fasten the buckles of my boots tighter.

I remind myself that this is why I'm here. The summit, the tournament, the jubilee — they will be the start of change for Malam.

"What of this one? Sir Casper mentioned Sanguine, the Channeler oil. That's a pebble of good news." Segrande leans over the desk. His dinner coat bulges around his buttons. "More people buying the oil means more people are trusting Channelers."

"Look at Jonespur's letter. Or Variant's." I stand and scrutinize my shirt for lint, finding none. "Two men have died, and rumors link them to Channelers and the oil. People believe the oil is dangerous."

"Fools," Leif grouses from where he sits on the hearth's edge. "If they knew anything about Channelers, they'd know there's no danger. They're not going around killing anybody."

Segrande abandons the desk to wait at the door. "Some ideas are hard to bury. Those people have feared Channelers all their lives. That rock won't be turned over easily."

It's always rocks with Segrande. In this case, he's greatly underestimated the size of the problem. The prejudices dividing Malam are mountains. I look out the window at the city of tents stretching across the land to the southeast where thousands of foreigners have come for the Tournament of Champions and the jubilee.

"Has the Archtraitor reported anything?" Segrande asks.

"Millner." Leif mutters something more about unturned rocks.

"Slip of the tongue." Segrande chuckles. "We're the only three Malamians who refer to Millner by his given name. Most still consider him an enemy of Malam."

Irritation hardens Leif's face. I hadn't realized he had an opinion about Millner. He said nothing weeks ago when I mentioned my choice to hire the man. But perhaps Leif's insistence on respect is because he and Millner share a commonality. Millner was once captain of the royal guard. Years ago, he protested the Purge. Because he was nobility, his defiance was considered traitorous. Guards burned his home, killing his wife. In retaliation, Millner ended those men's lives and became a fugitive in Shaerdan. Over the years, rumors have twisted the story, marking him as Malam's enemy—the Archtraitor.

But I know better than to put much weight in rumors. I've always admired Millner for standing up for what was right.

"He's sent no word yet," I admit, albeit reluctantly. I hoped his information would shed light on Sanguine and give me something positive to report to the Channelers Guild. It would be remiss of me to put off informing them. I tug on my dinner coat and turn to Segrande. "Draft a letter to Seeva. Explain the situation."

A cough sputters out of him. "The entire situation? The men who died? The rumors?"

I understand his apprehension. As a member of both the Channelers Guild and my advisory circle, Seeva Soliel won't be pleased to hear the rumors. And even less pleased to discover I waited to tell her. The Guild was reluctant to pledge their support to Malam, and though Seeva serves me, her loyalties still lie with Channelers first.

"Tell her everything," I command as we exit the chambers.